THE DRAGON IN THE GARDEN

ERIKA GARDNER

Tirgearr Publishing

D1348055

Published by Tirgearr Publishing
Ireland
www.tirgearrpublishing.com

ISBN 978-1-910234-24-2

A CIP catalogue record for this book is
available from the British Library.

10 9 8 7 6 5 4 3 2 1

DEDICATION

To Eric: For not divorcing me in the process.

ACKNOWLEDGEMENTS

All stories are journeys. All my love and gratitude to the people who helped me and Siobhan on this one.

Thank you to my darling husband, Eric, who has backed me all the way.

To my kids, David, Katie, and Anna, who keep me on my toes at all times. I love you.

To Dad for Oz and Mom for Prydain.

The best critique group ever, my fellow authors- the fabulous Beer and Bacon Babes (BBB's): Wendy Spinale, Jennifer Fosberry, Cameron Sullivan, Amy Moellering, Georgia Choate, Jerie Jacobs, and M. Pepper Langlinais. We've laughed, we've cried, and we've eaten a lot of great bacon!

To my wonderful Beta Readers- Thanks for being my guinea pigs Fred, Miriam, Mitch, Sheila, Monica, Peter, Danielle, Robert, Jessica, and Carla. To dear friend and fellow author Kimberly Emerson.

To Ed & Seth at Eddie Papa's and Jerome & Austin at Specialty's, both places where much of this book was written.

To Kemberlee, Sharon, and Cora at Tirgearr Publishing for their expertise, editing, and cover design.

And most of all, thank you to all the readers out there for choosing to read this book, I hope you enjoy!!!

Chapter One

The memory has haunted me for years.

In the middle of a bright California summer, dark days came. My mother and grandparents spoke in hushed, serious voices, arguing about my absent father. Was it my fault he left?

A soft whimper escaped my throat and my eyes burned. I needed a hug, but no one paid any attention to me that day. So I ran away to the refuge of my grandparents' garden where I could hide among its statues and flowers.

My eyes lingered over the familiar garden ornaments. I passed the old birdbath, the statues of gnomes, and a cheerful squirrel. I ran one hand over the stone deer. Its brown paint had faded from years under the sun. Walking with quick steps down the gravel path, I made my way to the center of the garden, my special spot where my favorite statue waited.

A gnarled apricot tree grew there. Right now it was covered with tiny green apricots. Later in the summer the sweet fruit I loved would ripen. I would get to pick them with my parents, no, just with my mother. My lip trembled. My father wouldn't be here.

The bright-green dragon lay curled at the foot of the apricot tree, partially covered by vines. My mother called the color jade green—the same shade as my eyes. As a child she talked to all the statues, but I only spoke to the dragon. I named her Daisy. Sitting down next to her now, the tears welled up at last, spilling over my cheeks. I wrapped my arms around my legs, making myself into a little ball of five-year-old misery.

"Child, why are you sad?" said a woman's voice.

1

"Who said that?" I asked, wiping my cheek.

"I did."

"Where are you?" I stood and peered at the plants and statues around me.

"Right here."

"Are not," I retorted.

A soft laugh filled the air and the woman spoke again. "Perhaps you are right. Easy enough to fix, I suppose."

The breeze picked up. The space beneath the apricot tree shimmered. Ripples warped the air like the heat over the barbecue when my father cooked. The sweet notes of wind chimes filled the yard. Grandma and Grandpa didn't have any wind chimes. I whirled around to find the noise.

Under the branches appeared an enormous green dragon's head. My mouth opened in a silent O and I held my breath.

"Now child," said the woman. "I won't hurt you." Her voice came from the dragon's mouth.

I opened my lips to scream, but no noise came. Backing away, I bumped into the hammock and froze.

"I don't eat little girls." The dragon's huge golden eyes twinkled.

"How did you know what I was thinking?" I whispered.

"I am a good guesser. Besides, I know I must be very big to you." The voice sounded kind, like my teacher's.

"As big as Daddy's car," I said.

"Oh, I am *much* bigger than that," the dragon said, smiling. Her teeth shone white and enormous. "I'm only showing you a bit of me right now."

"Where is the rest of you?"

"All around us."

"Why aren't you smooshing everything?" I gestured around the garden.

The dragon chuckled. "You are a smart little thing." The jeweled head tilted to one side. "You would be Siobhan, yes?"

"You said it right. Sha-vauhn." Everyone messed up my name. I wished on every first star, each night, for a different name—a *normal* name.

"In the old country Siobhan means 'God is gracious.'"

"Yep, that's what Mommy says, too," I said glumly. "What's your name?"

"*Gwyrdd ferch Heulen ferch Caden ap Haydn.*"

"Gwyer-eth?" My mouth struggled with the unfamiliar name.

"Not bad," said the dragon. "I like the name you gave me—Daisy."

"It's easier to say," I said.

"I am not smooshing the garden because I am not quite here. Only part of me is here. What year is it?"

"It's 1993, Daisy."

The dragon stirred. "It's too early, child. The prophecy says I should not be here yet."

"What's a prophecy?" My tongue stumbled on the unfamiliar word.

"It's a prediction of what might happen in the future."

"You mean like the weather? My daddy says the guys on TV mess up all the time," I said.

Daisy chuckled, a low rumble deep in her throat. "Your father is not wrong."

"What does it say will happen?"

"I am supposed to meet someone, but our appointment is for later," said Daisy.

"Can't you stay here until the appointment? I won't let you be late," I said.

Daisy frowned. "It's a secret appointment. There are some people I don't want to know about the person I'm supposed to meet."

"Bad people?" I asked. "Is that why you hide and pretend to be a statue?"

"Have you ever had a friend," asked Daisy, "a friend who misbehaved and needed a break?"

I knew all about that. "Sure, Danny hit Carter. They're friends, but they both wanted the bike, and wouldn't take turns. Miss Sarah told them to go sit down and have a time out."

"Miss Sarah must be very smart," said the dragon. "As it

happens, friends and I have been fighting over something and we needed a time out."

"Are there more dragons?" I asked.

"Yes, many more."

"Are there dragons hiding in any other statues?"

The jeweled head moved slowly back and forth. "No, just me. The others cannot pass between worlds."

"Why just you?"

"I have a job to do," said Daisy. Her voice sounded sad.

"Are the dragons good guys?" I asked, scooting closer to Daisy and laying a hand on her warm nose. I didn't want her to be sad.

Daisy snorted, tickling my hand so I giggled. "Yes, dear one, I think we are good."

"But, if you come back now it would be bad?" My laughter faded.

"It would be very bad indeed, but later, when it is right, I can return." Daisy sighed.

"I always knew you were real." I straightened my shoulders. I had found a dragon in hiding.

"Really?" Daisy asked.

"You're the only statue I named," I answered. "Nobody fools me."

The breeze picked up again. Daisy sniffed the wind. "Siobhan, I'm afraid it's time for me to leave or the bad things will happen. Will you be all right?"

"My daddy's not coming back, is he?" My worries returned.

Her scales sparkled in the bright sunshine. "No, he is not coming back to your mother although he will visit you and your brother."

I sighed. "Daisy, will I ever see you again?"

The golden eyes twinkled. "Yes, I believe you will."

The air warped again. I tried to watch, but a bird warbled close by, and I turned my head. When I glanced back at the apricot tree, the air shimmered and the small, dragon statue lay where Daisy's head had been. "But, Daisy, who were you fighting with?"

A whisper floated on the breeze. I bent closer to the statue to listen. "That can't be right," I said to the empty garden.

On that day everything changed, especially me.

My name is Siobhan Isabella Orsini. It would be twenty years before I saw my dragon again.

Chapter Two

It wasn't my grandparents' home anymore. It wasn't quite mine either.

Hiding my disappointment, I listened to the contractor drone on in the hot summer morning. My younger brother, Alex, stood beside him in the front yard.

George Hunt continued, "I'm afraid I'll need a larger deposit up front than we discussed."

Alex nudged me and I shook my head almost imperceptibly. My brother had heard enough. "So, let me see if I've got this right," he said, ticking off points with his fingers. "You want additional money up front, the job will cost more overall, and it will take longer than you and Siobhan agreed upon?"

George blinked several times. "Err," he stammered. "Well, yes."

Alex laughed in his easy way and clapped a hand on the contractor's arm. "We both know that's not going to happen."

It crossed my mind that George probably had an inflated idea of my finances. I inherited the house, our mother received the cash, and Alex got the café. Such were the worldly goods of Lillian and Patrick Lydon. The inheritance helped, but my unemployment precluded sitting around eating bonbons. Renovating meant a huge financial stretch. Our daily work crew consisted of me and Alex. Still, as handy as we were, some things required a professional.

George straightened and said, "Now wait, I'm doing the best I can."

"So am I." Alex cut him off. "Of course you can understand a brother needs to watch out for his sister?" Alex used every bit of his six-foot-three-inch height and broad frame to emphasize his point.

George stepped back, saying, "Sometimes things don't work out the way we want them to and that's life."

Recognizing my cue, I pasted on a fake smile. "Oh, thank you for understanding, Mr. Hunt," I said, "That makes it so much easier on all of us."

"It does?"

"Certainly," I continued. "We signed the contract Wednesday and today is Friday. Under California Law any consumer has three business days to cancel a transaction, as I am doing now."

"It needs to be in writing."

"I appreciate your professionalism," I agreed reaching into the back pocket of my jeans and pulling out his paperwork. I signed the back of one receipt, handed it to him and signed the other for myself. "If you sign here in acknowledgment of said cancellation, we'll be all set. I'll stop my check."

He scowled, but initialed and handed me my receipt. "Well, if you change your mind, you've got my card."

"I do." I smiled. "And believe me, when I have that kind of money I'll call you." The likelihood of such an occurrence bordered the fantastical, given that a month ago I dropped out of law school when the bills became too much.

Alex and I waved as he drove away.

"He lied, I take it?" asked Alex.

"What do you think?" I let out a weary sigh.

More than the heat wore at me. I could always spot the truth, or its lack, but it didn't fill me with thoughts of rainbows and butterflies. I sat on the porch swing and folded my legs under me. My little brother took a chair next to me.

I used the word "little" in loose terms. At twenty-two, my younger brother stood tall and handsome. Not dark, I won that lottery with my jet black, unruly curls. Alessandro Padraig Orsini displayed an amazing combination of our parents' brief Italian-Irish marriage. In contrast to my dark hair and green eyes he sported deep-red hair and brown eyes. He tanned while I burned and freckled.

Neither Alex nor I were married. He said he hadn't found

the right woman. I had. Found the right guy, that is. At least I thought I had. It hadn't worked. The problem with being able to spot a lie was I did it even when the person told me the very things I wanted to hear. It broke my heart every time Chuck said he loved me. He parroted lines he truly believed, but I saw their emptiness. In the end, I walked away.

That seemed to be my method of operation: walking, even running away. Growing up I saw more than lies. I saw things other people couldn't. Doctors, shrinks, tried to tell me the people and creatures I saw were all in my head. Sometimes I believed them. Other times I railed against them, but it didn't matter. All that mattered was I didn't fit in. No place existed for me in Calistoga and I knew it. I left town, shut out my past, and tried to build a normal life. The girl who could see through lies played make-believe.

I've always known where illusions and falsehoods lay. At the birthday party, I was the kid who knew the magician wasn't doing *real* magic. At poker I spotted when someone bluffed. I'm not psychic or telepathic. I can't tell you how to do the magic trick. I'm not a good enough poker player to tell you which cards you're holding.

I'm never wrong about a lie. With a glance Alex asked me if George told the truth and my brother trusted my answer. He's good that way. He frowned now, his eyes faraway and unfocused.

"Yes?" I prompted.

"I have someone doing work on the café right now."

"Going well?"

"Great."

I waited for the other shoe to drop.

"Actually…" Alex cleared his throat. "It's Tim."

I hadn't expected that. "*Oh*," I murmured. "How is he?"

"He's fine."

Conflicting emotions assailed me as I thought of Tim and the history we shared.

Alex waited for me to process the idea. I swallowed. "So, are you suggesting I hire him?"

"He does good work, Siobhan. You won't have to worry about

him lying to you or cheating you. He knows better," he said.

Tim did know better. Memories of summers spent with my grandparents in Calistoga flashed through my head. We settled in the small town for my last two years of high school. Mom and Alex stayed after I left for college. Tim figured in a disproportionate number of my memories of this place.

I swung my legs off the porch swing and stood, punching Alex in the arm. "How about we grab some lunch and find him?" I suggested.

"I'll text him."

I drove. Moments later Alex put his cell away. "He's at Ace. We'll meet him there and then we can swing by the deli for sandwiches before we get back to work," he said in a satisfied tone.

"Sounds good."

The Mustang's air conditioning brought me back to life. My senses perked as we pulled up to the hardware store. "He's in the yard." Alex pointed.

"Over here, guys." I knew that voice. Tim directed a couple of men loading lumber on to a pickup truck and headed to us.

He bounded up in that infectious, happy way I remembered. My nervous stomach settled. "Siobhan." He hugged me, swinging me around in his enthusiasm. At five-ten I'm not swung around every day. "What's it been? Six? Seven years?" he continued, his light blue eyes glowing.

"About," I said, as he released me. "It's been too long."

"Definitely," he agreed. "'Sup, Alex?"

"Hey, Tim. Siobhan needs help with our grandparents' house."

"Excellent. More business for me. I'll be sure to overcharge." Tim grinned.

I rolled my eyes and explained what I needed. Tim asked the appropriate questions. Alex chimed in from time to time. An odd assortment of women ranging in age from late teens to middle-aged soccer moms chatted to one side of us. Their attention fixated across the parking lot where Tim's workmen loaded a truck with lumber.

"OMG," said a blonde, sighing. "His muscles are, like, ridonkulous."

"You know it, Tammy," said another, a cute Hispanic woman with a high ponytail. "Yum."

"He said good morning to me yesterday. I about died," said an attractive auburn-haired woman in her forties, her voice breathless. "Think what our children would look like."

"Duh. Like their father, but with my hair color and sense of style. Don't be such a cougar, Ally," said Tammy, tossing her hair back.

"Right, bottle blonde," muttered Ally, her face flushing to match her short, red hair.

"Um, Tim, what's up with them?" I asked.

Tim grimaced. "Oh, them? They all worship at the altar of Ian."

"Which one is Ian?" I asked then closed my mouth. One of Tim's men had taken his shirt off in the heat. His chest and sculpted stomach were hard to ignore, especially glistening with sweat. The man demanded attention with his dark hair and blazing blue eyes. With a face that flawless, he should be on romance novel covers or calendars. He would make a pretty calendar. Meet Mr. September. I swallowed.

Tim groaned at my reaction. "Aw, Christ, not you, too?"

"What?" I croaked. My voice cracked on the word.

"I can't have you obsessing over him, too," Tim pleaded. "That's bad enough." He thumbed at the giggling group.

"Sorry, Tim, I had a girl moment." I folded my arms. "I'm in control of myself again. I swear."

My eyes lingered on Ian. I gasped, "Oh, Tim, what happened to his back? Those scars. The poor guy."

Tim and a couple of the women frowned at me. "Girl," said one, "stop. His back is perfect. It's perfectly gorgeous, like the rest of him."

"Yeah, perfect," echoed the women.

Alex and Tim stared at me. "Tell me you see them, too?" I asked.

Alex pursed his lips. "See what?"

"The scars. Two jagged ones running the length of his back."

They both avoided my eyes, shaking their heads. Panic grew inside me. This couldn't be happening again. I closed my eyes against a wave of dizziness. The fleeting thought ran through my mind, should I leave? Sell the house?

Biting my lip, I studied Ian again. He had paused at my words, observing us. His cool gaze bored into mine. He gave me a nod, as though we had met before.

What I saw overcame me, yet I couldn't to tear myself away. As if in an overlay, Ian appeared to be more than one thing. A beautiful creature of pure light and fire hid within, but shrouded by darkness and hate. The physical perfection of the man masked an emotion beyond spite. Evil lurked beneath his chiseled features. It compelled me to run and hide.

Ian flicked his stare away and I swayed as though released from a tractor beam. My head swam. I blinked to clear my vision. Alex didn't miss a thing. "What did you see?" he asked.

I shrugged.

"Maybe we should think about some food now?" Alex asked, his light touch at my elbow buoying me. "Sure, great," I said, my voice faint. Tim still didn't meet my eyes, but said, "I'll swing by later to see the remodel. Okay?" As I left, I knew Ian watched me. It didn't take any special ability to identify the malevolence in his expression. Why did he hate me? My mind remained filled with the image of the two jagged, hideous scars side by side down his back. They stood out in horrible clarity, vivid red and purple against his smooth tan skin. Who did we have here? What could he be?

"Go on ahead," said Alex, "I wanna talk to Tim."

As I walked to my car, Tim and Alex spoke in soft voices behind me. I pretended not to hear.

"She still sees things?" asked Tim. He sounded worried. "Even after all this time? Is she okay?"

"Sure she's okay," said my brother, his tone sharp. "You know Siobhan. Just because we don't see what she sees, doesn't mean she's wrong."

"Yeah, but scars? C'mon, that's a little different than when she said I cheated at Monopoly."

"Was she wrong about you cheating?"

"No, she's always right."

"Then maybe you should trust her now."

"Right, right." Tim didn't sound convinced. "Still, scars?"

"Let it go, man." My brother's voice deepened with emotion.

I shut them out and got in my car. After years of peace, my vision had returned. Had I been a fool to think will power could make it disappear? Once again, I saw something no one else did.

Tim never showed. His voice mail said sorry and could we do it another day? Okay. Maybe I weirded him out. Wouldn't be the first time. A breather from the ghosts of my past—things could be worse.

Chapter Three

Monday morning, I faced the garden. I rarely came here. Long ago the stark isolation of life with my strange ability replaced the thrill of my childhood discovery of Daisy. For many years, through a dozen psychiatrists, the garden represented a symbol of my "condition." Now, little by little, I ventured back among the flowers and the statues, like a swimmer testing cold waters.

As an adult, I built a wall separating me from my past. I bricked myself off using college and next law school. I led a life of denial. It contained little thought of Daisy. If I left off questioning my sanity or the true nature of reality, life got a lot easier. I decided I needed to bury my nose in a book, to find a new home.

Avoiding my past proved easy until my grandparents passed away a few months apart from one another. My financial need combined with a yearning inside presented me with a choice. Fate handed me a reason to go back. When I decided to come live in the house they left me, I answered the garden's call. My demons waited for me there.

I hadn't banked on my demons finding me so soon. Two weeks in Calistoga and already my protective walls crumbled after years of painstaking rejection of any hint of a vision.

Involuntarily, a picture filled my mind, an ostrich with its head in the sand. Disaster would still befall the bird, whether it saw the danger coming or not. After meeting Ian yesterday and glimpsing what lay beneath his mask, my heart agreed. Denial wouldn't protect me from my sight or from him.

I took a deep breath, smelling the sheltering oaks, the dirt, the flowers, and the herbs. Putting my coffee aside, I walked the path and let it all soak in. I wanted to see everything around me. My eyes lingered on the jade statue my child-self named Daisy. For the first time in many years, I tried to See—on purpose.

On one plane of sight lay a figure of molded stone, but on another, deeper level I saw it shine. Energy surrounded her, like a light spilling from behind a closed door.

My knees went weak. With a thump I collapsed on the stone path, hard enough to wince. I couldn't ignore yesterday as a fluke. My ability had returned. This went beyond knowing a lie from the truth. I saw things. That might mean doctors, possibly hospitals, if anyone but Alex, and maybe Tim, suspected. I stifled a groan and rubbed my forehead. Unhappy memories hurtled through my mind, the heartbreak of my adolescence compressed into seconds.

Still, I allowed myself a small smile. Daisy was real. Color me not crazy. Of all the figures in the yard, this one was no statue. For a moment triumph washed over me, only to be quickly suppressed.

I gazed at the little figure curled in a tight ball amongst the roots of the old apricot tree. Vinca vines with their delicate periwinkle blossoms partially covered it. A person could easily overlook the little statue.

I sighed. My return to Calistoga heralded the reemergence of my unwanted vision. Would Daisy come back, too?

"Siobhan?" called a voice.

I froze. That could only be Tim. I drew a deep breath. "Back here, Tim," I called.

Watching Tim open the side gate and stride down my gravel path through my garden unsettled me. Tim I remembered: sandy, light-brown hair, the wide smile, deep laugh crinkles in his face, a twinkle in his blue eyes, and a bounce in his step mixed with the quieter man of today. His laugh came slower now, the jokes sprang fewer and farther between, but I had changed, too.

"Hey." He ducked his head. "Look, I'm sorry I didn't make it here on Friday. Things went haywire. Had a guy go MIA and it messed with the whole schedule. I ended way behind."

"It's okay," I said. "Not sure I was up to a consult anyhow."

"Oh, good. I mean, not good if you weren't feeling great. Just good..." he stammered and trailed off. "I mean..."

"No, I get it," I said. I thought for a second. "Which guy?"

"Huh?"

"Which guy went MIA?" I persisted.

"Oh, Ian." Tim frowned as soon as he said the words. "Huh, that's weird."

"Yeah, real weird." I kept my voice neutral.

Tim's eyes narrowed and he seemed to be assessing my mood. He shifted gears. "So, you've come home at last?"

I gazed at him, a hundred memories in my head, and yearned for simpler days. "I guess you could say that."

"Better late than never."

I shrugged.

"Of course, you always were late to everything."

I didn't know how to answer, so I contented myself with a smile.

"You want to talk about what happened with Ian yesterday?" he asked.

My smile faded and I shook my head. "Not even a little bit."

"Come on, embrace the weirdness. What do you think made you see those... scars?"

"I don't want to talk about it." I wanted to forget Ian. I craved normalcy. Let me plan my remodel. "Drop it."

"Right," he said, his words clipped. "I believe you need some work done?"

I showed Tim the bathroom, the master bathroom, and the torn-up kitchen. Clearly, they screamed works-in-progress. My mood lightened as our conversation stayed in safe channels, no Ian and no memories of us. We went back to the backyard, taking a seat on the deck overlooking the garden.

"I cleared some space in the schedule later this morning and into the afternoon," said Tim, drumming his fingers on the glass tabletop. "If you want it?"

"Really? What with MIA guy? Aren't you behind?" I asked.

"Seeing as you and Alex are my oldest friends and Alex already has me working on the café, you're a priority." He paused. "I'll write you a super-duper extravagant quote." He didn't mean it.

"Thanks," I said dryly. "Hey, wait."

"What?"

"Seeing as you are being so accommodating," I said, darting to the kitchen.

"Yeah?" he called after me.

"Got something for you," I called back. I returned with a mason jar and a bag of tortilla chips, placing them on the table with a flourish.

He squinted. "Wow, is that your grandma's special salsa recipe?"

"Yep, made it yesterday."

Tim didn't stand on ceremony. He ripped opened the bag and unscrewed the jar. "Hey," I said, "Don't you want to wait until you get home?"

He grimaced as if he thought I had uttered the ultimate in idiocies. "Uh, no." He hesitated, chip poised above the vibrant *pico de gallo*. Tim glanced at me and then at the salsa. "I'm scared to try it," he admitted. "What if it isn't as wonderful as I remember?"

Our eyes met for a minute. "Oh please, you never had it so good," I said quietly.

Tim gave me a mischievous grin and scooped a chip full of the dip. His eyebrows lifted in delight. "Better than I remembered. When will you let me have this recipe?"

I basked in his enjoyment, but didn't answer. As I walked him through kitchen to the front porch Tim said, "So I'll see you in a couple of hours."

"Sounds good," I said.

Tim's blue eyes searched my face. He sighed. "Well, Leia will be waiting for me."

"Your significant other?"

He grinned. "Yep. She's got the most beautiful brown eyes you've ever seen."

Conflicting emotions passed through me. I didn't see a ring and Alex hadn't mentioned a girlfriend. I blinked. "You're married?"

"Nope, but I've got the greatest girl in the world. She's crazy about me, too." He winked, adding, "And she's got legs that won't quit."

16

Darn him. I knew he told the truth. I wondered how much my face gave me away. Tim could always read me.

He shook his head. "She's my dog, Siobhan. I go home at lunch to walk her."

"No one else?" Could he hear my heart, pounding out of my chest?

"No. You?"

I shook my head. "Came close with one guy, but it didn't stick."

The silence grew awkward. Tim waited, but I didn't know what to say. I gazed toward the quiet street, listening to the birds. "I need to get to another glamourous day of sanding and spackling. I bet that poor puppy is dying for her walk."

Tim moved closer. For once, he didn't wear a smile. I bit my lip. Tim saw and the ghost of a grin crossed his face. "You still bite your lip when you get nervous?" he asked. "It's just me, Siobhan."

He pulled me to him. I thought he might kiss me, but instead he gave me a tender hug.

As I said good-bye and watched him go, relief and disappointment warred inside of me.

* * *

Tim's word proved to be gold. A couple of hours later he and his crew showed up. So did my brother. No more time to wonder about dragons. My day turned left at the corner of insanity and obsessive compulsion, with never a backward glance. Alex, Tim, the workmen, and me on one project meant too many cooks in the kitchen.

Later as I took a break, I listened to Tim and Alex wrangle over where to place the island. My brother, the young restaurant owner, possessed strong opinions regarding kitchens. I stifled a sigh as their volume increased.

To my surprise, they went quiet.

A moment later Alex and Tim joined me.

"Um, guys," I asked with a frown, "how did you wrap that up so fast?"

They exchanged glances and shrugged.

I groaned. "Tell me you didn't?"

"Didn't what?" answered Tim.

"Tell me you didn't just Rochambeau for my kitchen."

"Siobhan," said Tim.

"Sis."

I narrowed my eyes. "Straight to hell, the both of you. Start decorating your hand baskets now."

They grinned like a pair of monkeys.

"You are making good decisions, aren't you?" I asked. Their expressions did not comfort me.

Shaking my head, I headed back inside for a diet coke. When I got back the sight stopped me in my tracks. Ian stood with Tim and Alex. I watched from behind the screen door. He spoke to the two of them in a low, intense voice, but I couldn't make out the words. Ian strode the garden path toward the apricot tree.

The garden grew darker, as if clouds hid the sun. Despite the heat of the afternoon, I shivered. I made myself open the door and walk across the patio.

"Hello?" I called. Ignoring Tim and Alex, my eyes locked on Ian. He's too close to the apricot tree, and then wondered why that entered my mind.

His shoulders stiffened at my voice.

Ian approached the deck. He waved one hand toward Alex and Tim. He extended the gesture to include me in the motion. I frowned. What on earth?

In a quiet, commanding voice Ian said, "You never saw me, right, my friends? I was never here." He considered me and repeated, "I was never here. I am not who you saw."

My eyes widened as Alex and Tim headed back inside to join the workmen. It took everything I had to keep my voice from trembling as I said to Ian with empty bravado, "Okay, Obi-Wan, what's the joke?"

He came closer and frowned. "You should go inside. You have seen no one."

I waved one trembling hand. "Yeah, yeah, I get it, 'These aren't the droids you're looking for.' C'mon, everyone has seen

Star Wars. What's the deal?"

Ian's dark brows bent deeper and then his expression cleared. "Star Wars? Oh, of course, so humorous. Clever of you to see the gag."

He closed in on me. A shadow of yesterday's hatred crossed his sculpted features. I backed away and his expression smoothed to polite regard. "I do not believe we've been introduced? I am Ian." He took my hand in that limp fashion somewhere between a proper handshake and a kiss on the hand.

Through his introduction, I saw again the conflicting images cross his face, an even more intense experience close up. There burned a creature of pure light and fire, a dark being whose gaze made me want to crawl away in terror, and the perfection of his physical mask. I suppressed a cringe. One fact screamed in my mind; his name was not Ian.

When my eyes cleared, he waited, observing me with intense interest, as a child studies a dragonfly, curious to see what I would do next. A hush blanketed the garden. I heard the voices of the men inside, working on my kitchen, but the birds in the yard fell silent. In the kitchen, Tim and Alex wondered aloud where I had gone.

Ian stepped even closer to me. There was nothing overtly threatening in the movement, but I retreated, my heart pounding. A slight breeze kissed my cheeks. To my relief, I could breathe again. Wind chimes tinkled in the distance. Ian tilted his head in a gesture so perfect, it didn't seem human. "I did not realize you had wind chimes," he remarked.

"Yes, they were my grandmother's." Folding my arms across my chest.

"You lie," he said, wagging one finger at me. "You have been gone from this area, I think?"

Swallowing, I blustered. "I've been away for years. Why do you care?" My heart rate continued to gallop.

"And now, now you return?" He stroked his chin with one hand as he contemplated me.

"Not that it's any of your business."

Ian chuckled. "A little fire, eh? I like that."

His brilliant blue eyes held mine. Conflicting images swirled.

19

I struggled to concentrate. The world wobbled beneath my feet.

"No one told me," Ian mused, "what truly beautiful eyes you have. Why, it's been ages and another land since I've seen emerald eyes like yours. Could it be—?"

At that moment my brother and Tim burst out of the French doors. "Found you," said Tim.

I called to them in relief. When I looked back at Ian, he'd vanished. The air wavered, like the waves of heat over the road. I sank to my knees and hugged myself.

What could Ian be?

* * *

"So, let me see if I've got this straight," Tim said, back out on the patio. "There's a dragon hiding in your grandparents' garden, Siobhan can spot a lie at four hundred paces, Ian is some quasi-demon scary dude, Alex and I were Jedi mind-tricked, and I'm still stuck with the kitchen job?" He chuckled, like someone had told him a big joke.

I accepted the glass of whiskey Alex handed me. Such a traditionalist, my brother, he gave the perfect two-finger pour of scotch.

"Yep," I said. "I think that about covers it."

Tim poured himself a glass of scotch. "I've always known not to lie to Siobhan," he said with a smile. "Only an idiot lies to her. It never works out."

He drank deeply and continued, "As to the dragon, God, Siobhan, you told me about her when I was eight."

"And Ian?" I asked. He seemed awfully blasé about all this.

Tim set the drink aside. "He is pretty."

"Screw pretty," I muttered. "He's beautiful... and powerful. I can't explain it—he's cursed. And...he hates me." I shuddered, partly from the whiskey's burn and partly at the memory of what I saw in Ian.

"Not every guy can fall for you," said Tim.

Tim's attempt at humor fell flat. "Ian scares me. Besides, he was heading for Daisy's statue," I said.

"How do you know?" asked Alex.

"I don't," I admitted, "but what else could he want in my garden?"

"Hey," said Tim, his face serious, "you know I trust you, right?"

I nodded.

"And I care about you...very much," he continued, "but isn't it possible this is all in your head? What has Ian actually done? I mean, other than coming to work and introducing himself to the homeowner?"

"I am not making this up." My cheeks burned.

"I know, I know," he said soothingly. "But isn't it possible you could be wrong?"

"I wish," I said. I met Tim's eyes. "You have to fire him. He's not... a safe... person."

"Dude," said Alex sharply, "this is Siobhan. If she says he's not human, then that's it. He's not human. End of story. Finito."

Tim leaned forward. "What is he?"

Shrugging, I peered into my glass. I wasn't used to drinking in the middle of the day.

Tim set his glass on the table. "Okay, okay. I may not believe this exactly, but I do have faith in Siobhan, always have. If you are sure, the next time I talk to him—I'll give him his two weeks, okay? Besides, he never explained why he went MIA in the middle of work yesterday and now he's gone again without a word to me."

"Thanks." I ran my fingers over my hair. "Why did he leave like that?" I muttered. "He controlled you earlier, but when you came back, he left. It doesn't make sense." My head swam.

"What do we do next, Siobhan?" asked Alex.

I shrugged. "I need some information and maybe we can figure this out?" I meant it as a statement, but it came out as a question.

Alex frowned at me. "How do you get more information on this? Craig's List?"

Tim snorted and said, "Yeah, right. Can we go to the authorities about Ian?"

I chose my words with care. "A former child of therapy still clings to the notion of a dragon hiding in her backyard and now says the local heartthrob is a nasty, err… something, call it demonic. That would play well with the police, right, Tim? Besides, as you pointed out, he hasn't actually done anything to me. It's all feelings."

"Okay, conventional authorities are out. Where else can we go?" said Alex.

"Grandma told me she found the dragon statue here when she and Grandpa bought the house. Do we know anything about this place before our family moved in?" I grabbed my laptop. It didn't take long to ascertain that the online records did not include my house.

"Well?" asked Tim.

"I guess I need to go to the city offices," I said.

Alex checked his watch. "Damn. I'm supposed to be at the café."

"So, go," I said.

"I can't leave you," he protested.

"I'll stay." Tim volunteered.

Alex's face cleared. "You sure?"

Tim nodded. "I'm Ian's boss remember? At least until I see him again."

"And you'll back Siobhan up? Really?" Alex pressed.

Tim shifted in his seat and looked uncomfortable. "Hey, I may not be completely on board the crazy 'not human' train, but if Siobhan thinks there is something off about this guy, that's good enough for me."

Alex stood. "Awesome. Thanks." He clapped one hand on Tim's back. "Siobhan, you be careful. And call me if anything happens. *Anything.*"

He gave me a quick hug. "Gotcha'," I said.

After Alex left, I glanced at Tim. "You don't need to stay. I know you aren't copacetic with this. I mean, I'm just a client."

"You'll never be just a client." His voice dropped and he added, "Besides, for what it's worth, I've never seen you so rattled, Sh'belle."

"You don't get to call me that anymore," I said. It came out sharper than I meant. I pushed away the memories the pet name

conjured. "Especially when you basically said you don't believe me."
He flinched. "I know you're scared though. I want to help."

I winced as I packed my laptop into a backpack and grabbed my keys. "I don't know for sure what I'm scared of yet."

"But you have an idea."

I tried to contain the fear that passed through me, but I think he saw it. "Yeah, I do."

"So, to City Hall we go?"

"Okay, sure." Even if he didn't believe me, I was glad not to be alone.

Tim drove us the couple of blocks to Washington Street. The antiquated, but charming white building sat on a corner. It still looked more like the fire station it had once been than City Hall. An unnatural silence lay over the empty street.

We parked and walked to the city offices. Tim must have sensed my mood because he took my hand in his. His warm, familiar grip comforted me and I squeezed his hand in return.

"Thanks."

"My pleasure." We shared a good moment.

A deep voice said, "Excuse me, miss?"

I pivoted to find an Arab sheikh. At least, that's what he reminded me of despite his jeans and T-shirt. He was about six-feet tall and seemed to be in his early forties. He possessed that distinctive, noble hawk's profile I associated with a prince of the desert. The olive-skinned stranger's thick, black hair fell to his shoulders. He wore a mustache with a close-trimmed beard.

"I'm sorry to bother you. Can you help me find Fair Way? I'm a bit lost." He smiled. A touch of sunshine lightened the newcomer's expression, and the lines around his dark eyes were etched of laughter.

He shifted his backpack as he spoke. Something about his back, or at least the space above his back bothered me. It shifted in and out of focus.

Perhaps I should not have scotch at lunchtime.

He saw my puzzled gaze and his smile broadened. "I always pack too much," he said in a self-deprecating tone and shrugged.

23

"Well, you're close," I answered. "It's maybe a block from here, that way." I pointed down the street ahead of us.

"Thanks so much," the stranger said. His eyes met mine with an open, honest expression that made it easy to respond in kind. He adjusted his pack and walked up the street.

Tim and I continued toward the pristine white building with its cheerful flower boxes. As we approached the city offices I saw telltale, shimmering lines warp the air. Tim inhaled sharply and I realized in surprise he saw what I did.

Ian stepped *through* the rippling waves. Tim's grasp on my hand tightened. I did not respond. Gazing at Ian, I viewed again the layers of faces: fiery light, dark malevolence, and the beautiful human face. My stomach twisted at the sight of the darkness.

Ian flicked a glance at Tim and waved his hand as he had earlier. "Run away, forget, there is nothing here for you."

To my surprise, Tim did not back away. If anything, his fierce grip on my hand tightened, to the point of pain. His brows furrowed in concentration. Ian's perfect features twisted. He regarded Tim and our joined hands and his expression cleared. "So be it," he said. Ian made a stabbing motion at Tim.

With a strangled cry, Tim flew through the air. He slammed to the ground in the street with a dull thud and lay in a crumbled heap.

I screamed.

Before I could run to him, Ian caught one of my arms with a painful twist. Unlike earlier, his expression exuded neither neutral nor curious. It had turned predatory. The hatred in his eyes, no longer veiled, burned. Something had changed. I swallowed hard. My mind raced. The conflicting kaleidoscope of images filled my vision. I struggled to move, but stayed immobile in his impossibly strong grip. Terror built then exploded inside me.

Ian roughly grabbed my shoulders and spoke intently, "*Haroa. I see you, Watcher.*"

"*Lo, Innon!*"

I spun at the powerful shout, breaking Ian's grasp and the visions' hypnotic spell.

The man I had helped yelled at Ian in fury. "*No, Innon!*"

24

Ian stepped back. His face contorted with rage. "Turel, I found her. I *see* her. This is my right."

The dark-haired man folded his arms. He radiated authority. "No, for now I see her and there are laws that will not be broken. The human Haroa shall be present. She is in my Sight and in Our gaze. You will submit or pay forfeit, Innon."

The two men locked stares. I gasped as the man called Turel began to glow. The light, the sunshine in his eyes suffused his entire being. Shifting waves undulated above him. The area above his back and shoulders concealed a pocket in reality. As Daisy once hid her bulk from my five-year old self's eyes in the garden, Turel masked his wings.

Turel's light grew brighter, more dazzling than a morning sunrise. He barked a command. "*Hit'alem, Innon, I say begone.*" Ian shot one more covetous glance at me and disappeared.

"Holy shit." Tim sat up and stared at us, his face dazed.

I shielded my eyes with one hand as I stared at the glory of an angel revealed.

Turel cupped one hand under my chin, tilting my face to meet his gaze. He kissed one of my cheeks and then the other. His expression softened as he regarded me. "Siobhan Isabella Orsini, my blessing is on you," he intoned.

How did he know my name?

"My name is Turel. I am one of the Two Hundred Fallen. We are the Observers of this war. You have my blessing and my protection as foretold. May you always see true. Shalom." He pressed his lips to my forehead.

"I can offer my blessing and my protection over your home," he offered. "Do you wish me to include your garden, too?"

I opened my mouth, but for once, nothing came out of it. I tried again. "What?"

"I say unto you; do you want me to include the garden?"

Thinking of Ian in my yard earlier, I found my voice. "Yes, I need my garden protected."

Turel winked at me. "Good girl."

Chapter Four

I stared at the jar of mayonnaise in front of me. With a click and a hum, the refrigerator switched on. Blinking, I realized I'd left the door open too long. My eyes focused on my meager food options: mayonnaise, beer, an onion, raspberries, and soy sauce. None of it screamed appropriate for company, especially this company.

I tried to breathe at a normal rate. The light of an angel's glory warred with a twenty-year-old whisper.

The one thing I never shared with a single soul, because it would have made me sound really, truly crazy, was who Daisy told my five-year-old self were her enemies. Angels. Yet Turel radiated only goodness.

I went with the raspberries. Passing the counter I grabbed a loaf of sourdough, a knife, and a cutting board. Under one arm I stuck the balsamic vinegar and the olive oil, and used my knee to push open the door to the backyard. Luckily, I found wine, but then, we always had wine.

I wondered how much of recent events Daisy followed from the garden.

As I approached the patio, I glanced around the table. There sat my ex-lover, my brother, and an angel. Every instinct screamed he could not be the enemy.

Thankfully, Turel didn't glow. I missed Tim's usual smile. His eyes did not twinkle. Alex for once remained quiet while his leg fidgeted in a rapid bounce. My brother smiled in the dim porch light as he watched my frenzied preparations.

Our family has a thing about food. Food can make anything better. Well, almost.

On the table I laid out the hors d'oeuvres. A bottle of Calistoga's Clos Pegase cabernet waited, open.

I broke the ice. "Okay, what did I miss?"

Tim, Alex, and Turel sat like statues. I settled myself on the wrought iron chair, praying someone else would begin the conversation. No one did.

Clearing my throat, I tried again. "Okay, here's our opportunity for answers, right guys?" I glanced at Tim and Alex. No response.

Turel leaned forward and rested one hand on his chin. His eyes sparkled as he surveyed the awkward company. "There is no need to be nervous around me, friends."

After a moment Tim poured himself a glass of wine and grabbed a couple of slices of bread. I followed his example. "Can we ask you anything?" I said.

Turel nodded.

Alex asked, "So, are you really, a, you-know-what…"

Turel surprised us by pouring himself a glass of wine. He raised it in a toast. "Yes, Alex, I am a 'you-know-what.' However, you can say angel. It's allowed."

I swallowed at the word angel.

Alex frowned. "Prove it," he said.

"Hold on to your socks," Tim muttered to me.

Turel set his wine on the table and rose. He radiated amber light, becoming brighter and brighter. The blanket of darkness over my garden lifted as the shadows fled before the golden glow. His wings unfolded: huge and white. In spite of my worries, his beauty and radiance lifted me up.

Turel tucked his wings away and retook his seat. Sipping his wine, he waited. Even though the light faded, hope remained. Gazing around the table Tim and Alex both looked more at ease, too.

"Why is Daisy in my grandparents' garden?" I asked. "What is special about this house?"

Turel shook his head. "It isn't the house. It's who lives here, the Watcher."

"Who is the Watcher?" I asked. "What is the Watcher?"

Turel frowned. "Didn't Gwyrdd explain that?"

"Gwyer-eth?" I repeated. The sensation of déjà vu rippled over me. I knew that name.

"You called her Daisy," said Turel in a gentle voice. "She left her gateway here to wait for the prophesied Watcher."

"Yes, I named her that." Memories flooded my mind. I blinked. "Who is the Watcher?"

Turel set his glass down. "*You* are the Watcher, the Haroa, foretold by prophecy. You will make a choice that will save or doom humanity."

Even outside I felt trapped, boxed in. The night air stifled me. A choice? I shook my head. "I don't understand." My stomach lurched. Save or doom humanity? Me? Why me?

"The Watcher sees what is. No more, no less. You see the truth in all things. Your vision is beyond any magic or glamour. No illusions shall divert you from divining the essence of reality." Turel's voice rang with sincerity. "You shall choose mankind's path—their fate."

"How? When? What does the prophecy say about me?" I asked. "Daisy spoke of a prophecy. What does that mean?" Sweat trickled down my forehead and the back of my neck. The yard seemed to shrink, confining me.

"We're not entirely certain of all the details," admitted Turel. "Bits and pieces, hints, promises, have been dropped over the centuries, but we needed your arrival in order to hear the whole prophecy."

"Why?" asked Tim. "Why is Siobhan walking in blind?"

Alex elbowed him. "Hardly blind. You heard the man, er, angel."

"Touché," said Tim, fist bumping Alex.

How could they banter like this? Weren't they listening? Save or doom? I wiped my forehead with the back of my hand.

Turel smiled. "Correct, of all of us, the Watcher is never blind. As to the prophecy? The oracle tells each their own role—not someone else's. For instance, the prophecy for Gwyrdd told her where to wait."

Tim frowned. "So, Siobhan doesn't know yet because…"

"Because she has never been to an Oracle, of course," finished Turel.

I listened, but the conversation didn't feel real. Crazy. Turel must be insane. Yet, he exuded sanity from every aspect of his being. My sight told me he told the truth. I should go. Where could I go?

The old fear haunting me needed to be voiced. "Wait," I began. "You said you were fallen? Does that mean what I'm afraid it means?"

Turel raised one ebony eyebrow at me. "Yes," he said. "I am a fallen angel."

A fresh chill came over my heart and my childhood fears sprang to life. My throat tightened.

"You're a demon?" Alex burst out, leaping to his feet.

"No."

"But, you followed Lucifer?" asked Tim, his eyes wide as he also stood. Part of my brain wondered if he planned to fight or run for the hills.

Turel held out both hands. "Peace, my friends. I mean no harm to you. I did not follow the Deceiver, nor am I a demon."

I stared at him and my shoulders sagged as I exhaled and saw. "He's telling the truth."

"But," said Alex. He glanced at me and I patted his hand.

We waited through a tense silence, still staring at each other.

"Sit down, guys," I said in a firm voice. "I promise, he's not lying."

Turel inclined his head toward me. "Thank you," he murmured. He sat back and his obsidian-colored eyes shone as he examined the starry night sky.

Tim and Alex grimaced at one another, but sat. Their faces took on matching solemn expressions. "So, wait. This is real?" asked Alex.

"As far as I can tell," I said.

He blanched. Tim gave a low whistle. They each took a deep sip of wine. No more fist bumping.

Alex recovered first and asked, "Who is the Deceiver?"

Tim put his wine glass down. "He's talking about Lucifer, Alex." I had forgotten his deep, quiet faith. He attended church regularly, unlike Alex and me.

"Oh," my brother said, impressed. "Wowsa."

"Turel?" I prompted after a moment. "You said you would explain?"

The angel roused himself. "Yes, of course." His smile held a touch of sadness. "A Fallen Angel, my friends, is an angel who has fallen out of favor with God, one who has lost God's Grace. It is a terrible thing to have lost one's direct connection to our Father."

Turel shifted in his chair and spoke in a low tone. "There are two kinds of fallen angels." An accent shaded his rich voice, but I couldn't place where from. "The first kind is like me. I am one of two hundred angels God sent into the world to serve mankind. We were paired with the best, the purest souls of humanity. God instructed us to teach you, to help you forge a better life."

"What happened?" I leaned forward.

Turel smiled and the sunshine returned to his eyes. "They were the most beautiful souls of humanity. How could we not fall in love with them? Created as they were in our Lord's image?

"I wed a mortal woman. The Two Hundred married humans and we fell from grace."

Tim whistled and said, "You put another before God."

"It is even so, Tim. I allowed another love in my heart, a love I placed above God."

I shook my head. "This doesn't make sense. Setting aside the whole idea that loving someone would make God mad at you, which I don't get, I thought God embodied love? That being said, you still act like an angel. You have wings, you disappear into thin air, and you do the whole glowy thingie." Talking about someone else helped. My sweating stopped.

Alex spoke at last, "Yeah, you don't seem like someone outside of God's club. What's the deal?"

"The deal," repeated Turel, "is due to what came next. There is another kind of fallen angel. Lucifer, the Morning Star, the greatest of all the angels, rebelled against God."

"Why?" I asked.

Turel remained silent.

"The Bible doesn't tell us," said Tim.

"It's not something we talk about. Not only did Lucifer rebel, but one third of the angelic host followed him." Turel's voice lowered and the sparkle in his eyes extinguished.

"Um, how many angels are we talking?" asked Alex, his brows bent.

"Millions. Disgraced in Heaven and sent to hell, but they didn't stay there," said Turel, taking a sip of his wine. "Not for long anyway."

"They didn't?" I asked.

"No, they came here," said Turel, "to Earth to fight The Ones Who Came Before and take this world. It may not be Heaven, which is forever denied to the Fallen, but your world is much preferable to Hell and they want it. They will take it and enslave mankind. It will be a second hell on Earth. Unless we, unless the Watcher, can stop them."

And back to me. My stomach lurched again. For a moment I couldn't hear anything. The pulse of my own heartbeat drowned out any other sound.

My surroundings reasserted themselves with the sound of Alex's voice. "The Ones Who Came Before? Demons?" His frown deepened.

"What is this fascination with you and demons? No, they are The First Ones," explained Turel. "This was their world to begin with. The First Ones and their allies, the other children of Mother Earth and Father Sky, who walked this world before my Father remade it and created new plants and creatures, as well as the humans who are in His image."

"Wait." Tim's voice sounded strangled. "Are you saying we live on Earth 2.0? That the world already existed and God somehow used it as a rough draft for his final version?"

"Yes," Turel said.

"No wonder it only took Him six days," Alex said. "So, who are the First Ones?"

"Dragons," I answered, even as Turel opened his mouth.

He waved a graceful hand in my direction. "She is right. The First Ones have many names: The Old Ones, The Ones Who Came Before, and, the name you know best, dragons."

"So," I said, piecing remnants of memory together, "if Daisy said the dragons needed a time out, this is what she meant?"

"Yes, Siobhan," Turel said, nodding. "The dragons and the Fallen nearly tore this world apart with their battles. My Father stepped in and took matters into His Hand. This was supposed to be the humans' world and this The Age of Man. To protect you, He set certain limitations on both sides. Lines the Fallen are not allowed to cross. Also, He came to me and the other Two Hundred with a new path."

"What path?" I asked. A memory flickered through the back of my brain. I tried to pin it down. Something important. What had I missed?

"That we serve Him once more, this time as His referees. We are charged with keeping each side in check. We ensure this world and mankind are not destroyed in the process. In exchange we have His Grace again and perhaps, when this is over, a way home. For the moment the dragons are Elsewhere and the Fallen largely confined to Hell."

Alex shook his head and folded his arms. "I don't get it. If God has the power to set ground rules and make *you* all enforce them," he pointed to Turel, "then why can't He end the war and tell the demons to go back to Hell where they belong?"

"Angels," corrected Turel again, "not demons."

"Whatever. Why doesn't He end it?"

"Free will," said Tim.

Turel smiled and raised his glass to Tim. "You are correct. The angels are creatures of free will, as are man and dragon-kind. We must all make our choices as we see fit and those decisions will guide us to the end of this war, an end, I admit, I cannot see. That is why we need the Watcher to choose, not an angel or some other race. Only a human can represent mankind."

I smacked my hand on my knee, more frustrated with myself

than with the angel's words. The elusive memory refused to coalesce in my head and reveal itself. It nagged and teased on the edge of my thoughts. "Don't say that. What's next?" I exclaimed. Fear pushed the frustration aside.

Turel opened his mouth to answer, but then frowned and closed it. He held his finger to his lips. Every part of his body tensed, on edge as though poised for an attack. I gazed into the night, thinking I heard something in the garden by the apricot tree. Turel held a hand out to us in a staying gesture and got up, his movements slow and stealthy. "I'm sorry, friends. I'm afraid we'll all have to wait and see."

As he spoke, Turel prowled the shadows across the patio toward the garden, still holding his hand up. I listened so intently I felt like my head would burst. From the expressions on their faces, Tim and Alex were doing the same thing.

A crash exploded from the back of the garden. The unmistakable sounds of running feet filled the air. Someone climbed the back fence, followed by more footfalls. I blinked and Turel disappeared. The three of us jumped to our feet. "Someone's running toward the street," exclaimed Alex.

We raced through the house. Tim threw open the front door. We burst on to the porch. In the street stood Turel with his wings spread, Ian, seething with malice, a beautiful woman who looked as dangerous as she was gorgeous, and a middle-aged man who acted normal enough. The four of them stared at a large man in the center of the group.

Even from the porch my head ached at the sight of him. My vision alternated, showing me a burly man in a trucker's cap and a huge, menacing creature who spoke in a twisted, guttural voice, "Give it to me."

"What is that?" I asked.

Without turning his head, Turel answered me, saying in a grim voice, "That, my dear, is a demon."

Chapter Five

A chill fell over the summer night and I resisted the urge to cover my eyes.

"Siobhan," Alex said, "What is it? You're white."

"She's shaking, too," Tim whispered to Alex. "Wonder what she's seeing that we're not?"

"The man did say demon." My brother gaped around him with wild eyes. "That can't be good. Where do you suppose it is?"

"I don't know," said Tim. "I see a woman, Turel, a big guy, Ian, and a pale man. What do you see?"

"Hush, children," commanded Turel. His gaze never wavered from the man/creature. The blonde woman shifted her stance, like a warrior about to dive into the fray. She flickered and shone in my sight, revealing she, too, was more than human.

"Turiel," snarled the demon. I started at the name it gave Turel. The demon sounded like it chewed the words as it spoke. Shuddering, I couldn't tear my eyes away. In the overlay of my alternate vision it appeared immense, horned, and possessed leathery wings, like a huge, mutated black bat.

"Chernobog," Turel responded, barely moving his lips.

The demon rasped horrible sounds. They sounded like choking or eating. My skin prickled, goose bumps rising. I realized the thing laughed. It shook one fist at Turel. "Turiel, you're weak. You're always weak."

"Strong enough to bind you, though," said Turel, his expression bleak.

I couldn't stop shaking. Alex wrapped his arms around me and squeezed. "It's okay, everything's going to be fine," he said.

34

I didn't answer him. My brother couldn't see what I saw. Nothing would ever be fine again.

The demon beckoned to the middle-aged man. He seemed very ordinary with his white skin and regular features, in his forties, easy to miss in a crowd. "Come, it is mine." Responding to the demon's voice, the man shuffled forward. In the faint glow of the street light the trickle of blood from both ears shone against his pale skin. The man swayed on his feet and lifted his small burden to Chernobog with both hands. Out of the shadows the jade green caught the light.

With a cry I sprang forward, shaking off Alex's arms, but Turel cried, "Hold, Siobhan." I froze, held in place by an unseen force.

Turel and the woman converged on the demon in a blur of motion. Ian cursed and threw himself into the fight as Turel's companion sprouted silver wings and glowed brighter than the moon. Ian and the silver-winged angel grappled.

Chernobog held Daisy's statue over his head with both massive hands. "I deny you, Gwyrdd. Stay in your refuge Elsewhere at Knotlow and rot." The reverberation of his gruesome laugh penetrated my bones.

Turel lunged at Chernobog. The demon let loose a hoarse scream and smashed the figurine on the street. It shattered. With an exultant roar Chernobog disappeared. The nights wallowed him I felt, more than heard, his last guttural whisper, "Events converge upon us, Turiel, the last chain is about to break. I shall triumph, restored to my full strength."

I could move again and ran to the street. Dropping to my knees, I sobbed, clutching the pieces of Daisy's statue to my chest. They were just broken bits of stone now. Daisy did not hide there anymore.

Hands gripped my shoulders, trying to comfort me, but still I cried.

"Enough." Turel pulled up me gently. "That is enough, Siobhan. All will be well, I promise."

Anger coursed through me, chasing away my tears. "How could you let that—that thing do that?" I lashed out as I stepped back from Turel.

Ian, still grappling with the blonde angel, laughed. "The Watcher shows fire. How I shall enjoy breaking her."

He doubled over as his opponent directed a savage kick to his side. "Silence, cur," she hissed. With a spin she directed a roundhouse kick at his head. Ian leapt aside and wrapped her in a headlock.

I tore my eyes away from the embattled pair and faced Turel. "Can't you do something? Fix this." My voice broke as I focused again on the pieces of statue in the street. Fear for Daisy frayed the edges of my anger. "Isn't that your job?"

Turel's mouth tightened, but he did not answer. Instead, he bowed on one knee and brought his fist to his forehead. A pulse of light speed from him like a visible sonar wave.

With another startled curse Ian released the female angel. He bowed to me in a flamboyant manner. "Watcher." He saluted and vanished. The air shimmered for an instant at his passing.

"Well," I said to Turel, "answer me. What happened here?"

"Patience," he said, "this is not finished."

"Quite," drawled the other angel, glancing at her nails and buffing one on a feathered wing. She pointed to a figure lying in the now quiet street. "Bigger fish, frying," she said, her tone nonchalant.

I tried not to grind my teeth at her logic. Whoever the nondescript man might be, this stranger who had offered up Daisy's statue to a demon, he could not be allowed to die in the street. He needed help and, afterward, I had questions for him.

We gathered in the house. The man lay on my tarp-covered couch. As the two angels bent over him, a faint glow emanating from their hands on his chest and head, numbness spread through me. I noted the bleeding from his ears had stopped.

"Do you know him?" Alex leaned over to me and wrapped an arm around my shoulders and squeezed. I shook my head, grateful for his comforting presence. "Siobhan," he continued. "It's going to be okay. I mean, there are two angels in your house right now, for Pete's sake. That has to count for something."

"One would certainly hope so," the female angel agreed in cool tones, eyeing us before returning to her patient. "Turiel, I think we've got him stabilized. Let's see if he wakes up."

Turel nodded, his face concerned. He straightened. "It may be a few hours, but I agree, Nefta. We've done all we can without his help."

"Healing, angels, and demons," muttered Alex. "What a night." He headed out the back, saying, "I think we all need a drink."

Tim frowned at Turel. "I don't understand. Can't you heal him? I thought angels possessed that power."

Nefta grabbed one of my barstools from against the wall. Her actions were graceful and light. Taut muscles rippled down her arms as she brushed back her ice-blonde hair. "What do you think we've been doing?" she snapped.

"Nefta," Turel chided. "This is new to them, you know."

"I know, I know," she muttered, dropping her gaze. "You heard Chernobog. The last chain is about to break. We don't have time for them to be children."

"They don't understand everything that is upon them," said Turel. "The Watcher does not yet accept her role."

"I thought we'd be further along by this point," said Nefta, her classic features twisting.

"Peace, my friend."

"Sounds like we all better take a seat," broke in Tim. "I'd say you have more explaining to do since our new friend isn't waking up yet."

"Right," said Turel and dragged two more stools over. He sat on one and I took the other. Tim perched on the arm of my plastic covered armchair.

Alex joined us, bearing our food and wine. He distributed these around the room. My brother gave a polite nod to the irritated blonde angel, his eyes appraising her. "You are Nefta, I take it?"

She smiled for the first time, and the change in her lovely face startled me. If one called Turel handsome, then Nefta could only be termed breathtaking. She inclined her head. "I am sorry. I am unused to being anxious." She bowed at the waist. "Yes, my name is Nefta. Well met, my new friends."

"It's our pleasure, Nefta," said Alex, smiling in his most charming manner. "Shall I pour you a glass of wine, too?"

"No, thank you. I do not care for your food and drink." Nefta's manner remained stiff and distant, but at least she tried now.

As Alex sat on a step ladder near me, Tim asked Turel, "Why do people keep calling you 'Turiel'?"

Nefta scowled. "That's his name, of course."

Turel smiled at her and made a vague mollifying gesture at her with one hand. "Patience. Again, they know so little."

"Clearly," she said, under her breath. "Sorry, sorry. I should not have said that."

Turel sighed. "My angelic name, my given name, is Turiel. On earth, my wife called me Turel and I have kept that name over the years. I have… I have become accustomed to it, much like I have to your food and this lovely wine." He raised his glass to the light and for a moment seemed lost in thought, or perhaps memories, as he regarded it.

"Turiel does sound more angelic," Tim said. "Like Gabriel, Uriel, Michael, a lot of 'els'."

"'El' means of God," explained Turel. "Gabriel means strength of God, Uriel means fire of God, Michael means who is of God, and so on."

"And your name?" asked Alex.

"My name means rock of God." Turel's reply sounded clipped.

"What do you want us to call you?" asked my brother.

"I prefer Turel."

This conversation seemed pointless. My anger spent, I stared at the pieces of my grandmother's dragon statue on the table. I kept rearranging the fragments, trying to reassemble the figure. If I could fix it, would my Daisy be back? What had I forgotten? Something about Daisy coming back.

Turel's thoughtful gaze fell on me. "She's not been harmed, Siobhan," he said.

"She hasn't?"

"The statue provided her a doorway, nothing more." He waved his hand in the direction of the pieces. "Chernobog wanted to prevent Daisy's access to you."

"Why me?" I asked. The question reverberated through my mind. Oh, why me? Why did I have to be the Watcher?

"Who's Daisy?" asked Nefta.

"Gwyrdd," said Turel, answering Nefta. "Siobhan met her as a child and gave her the name 'Daisy'."

Nefta shot me a friendlier glance.

"Why me?" I repeated.

"Guess everyone has more than one name," said Tim before I got an answer. He glanced at Alex. "Except us mere mortals. Speaking of which, how come Ian gets two names, too?"

"Innon is *not* human." Turel's emphasis of the word not matched Nefta's earlier icy tones. "Innon is an angel."

"What?" I gasped. "He doesn't have wings though?"

Alex gave a low whistle.

"But," protested Tim, his brows furrowing, "what's he doing working for me?"

"The same as Gwyrdd, obviously," said Nefta. "He waited, searching for the Watcher."

The hairs on the back of my neck went up at her use of the term, Watcher. Me? My thoughts raced, trying to make sense of the past twenty-four hours.

"His scars," I exclaimed. "The scars I saw, that first time. Were those scars from his…?" I didn't finish.

"Yes, the imbecile is one of those fools who cut off their wings," said Nefta in her cool voice. "Idiots."

"Why would they do such a thing?" I asked, distracted.

"Remember how I explained there are two types of Fallen angels?" reminded Turel. "I am one of the Two Hundred. We sinned through love, but Innon is one of the other kind."

"Who followed Lucifer," finished Tim.

A chill settled in my bones as I remembered the evil behind the icy blue of Ian's eyes that afternoon. What had he planned to do with me?

"Exactly," Nefta said. "Half of those geniuses of Lucifer's decided to show their separation from Heaven, their rejection of God, by severing their connection to our Father. They thought cutting off their wings would free them entirely."

"Did it?" Tim and I said in unison.

Nefta's mouth twitched at one corner in an ironic half-smile. "No, it weakened them. Robbed them of much of their strength. Ha. I find a great deal of justice in their fate."

Alex chuckled. "I guess I don't have to ask which type of Fallen you are. What is it like being a referee?"

Nefta raised one exquisite blonde brow at my brother. "And what makes you think I've Fallen?" she asked. "I'll have you know I jumped."

I glanced around. Tim and Alex looked as confused as I felt.

"Nefta is a volunteer of sorts," clarified Turel. "She's not Fallen. She is still part of the Heavenly Host."

The three of us stared at her. There sat a real, live, active duty Angel of the Lord. Nefta rolled her eyes. "At your service, I'm sure," she replied.

My pulse pounded at my forehead. "Turel, what did Ian want with me this afternoon?"

Turel's eyes darkened. "He wanted to take you. If he can kill the Watcher, or turn you to their side, the dragons and mankind lose."

"How?" asked Alex.

"It goes back to the prophecy," said Turel. "The Watcher has a part to play, a choice only she can make for good or ill. Without her, events cannot proceed."

Nervous energy ran over my body. Like a key fitting a lock at last, Daisy's words came back to me. "Turel," I blurted. "You believe I'm the Watcher because you think Daisy waited for me? That's why you think I'm the person who's supposed to fix everything?"

"Yes, Siobhan." Turel leaned forward, resembling more than ever some desert sheik, his sculpted profile catching the light from the one standing lamp in the room.

"But, I, I can't…that can't be right." I stared sightlessly ahead. Nothing made sense.

"You *are* the Watcher," said Nefta.

"No, you don't understand," I said. "Daisy met me years ago and she left. So I can't be the right person to help. She would have stayed if it was me. She said she was waiting for someone. She had an appointment, but not with me. You've got the wrong person. I can't be the Watcher." Relief washed through me. The night smelled sweet once more.

"An appointment requires a time as well as a person," said Turel in a gentle voice. "You still needed to grow up."

I shook my head, remembering Daisy's voice when she said she could come back *when it was right*. I pushed the memory away. It couldn't be me, a law-school dropout, unemployed, scarcely two hundred dollars to my name, and a history of psychiatrists behind me. "No, you're wrong," I whispered.

Turel and Nefta exchanged glances. "You are the Watcher," said Turel. "You will fulfill the prophecy. This is what it means to be the Watcher."

Beads of sweat broke out on my forehead once more. My pulse raced, my blood pounded through me. "Not me, please, not me." I didn't know I said the words out loud until my brother's arm slid around my shoulders. I closed my eyes and leaned on him.

"In time, you'll adjust, you'll see," said Turel. "It is foretold."

I raised my head and gazed at the dark angel. Turel seemed in earnest, but his eyes kept darting toward the window, his expression expectant.

Who does he think is coming now? Numb, I blocked out the sight of the ruined statue, the result of the last visitors to my house. I tried not to panic. My fear increased when Turel vanished. Tim and Alex swore. My head whirled.

"What is that?" asked Alex craning his head. Rhythmic sounds came from every direction outside of the house.

"I don't know." Tim walked to one of the front windows. He turned and we stared at the motionless Nefta.

Her wide blue eyes were fixed far in the distance. The curve of her profile reminded me of a ship's figurehead. At last she smiled; a genuine smile this time. "I thought so. They all came," she murmured. "Turiel called a meeting."

"When did he do that?" I asked.

"After Chernobog disappeared, when Turiel went down on one knee. You told him to do something. You mean, you didn't *feel* it?" Nefta shook her platinum head. "I would have thought even you humans would have sensed that. It shook me to the core. Why do you think Innon left in such a hurry? We both knew Turiel called the others. We just didn't know what he said."

Alex said in a hushed voice from the window, "Wow. Hey, guys, you have got to see this."

Tim and I joined him as he continued, "We heard wings. *Really* big wings. Holy shit."

Outside my home, where a short while ago a demon exulted, now gathered eight angels, nine counting Turel. I'm not sure what I expected from angels. There were no harps, trumpets, or flowing robes. The male and female angels resembled soldiers, no, warriors, I corrected myself. All armed with a variety of weaponry, and leather appeared to be the clothing of choice. Their skin and wings radiated a rainbow of color, no two beings alike.

I gaped, lost in contemplation of the golds, viridian greens, indigos, and lavenders. I had never seen so much beauty gathered in one place. Yet with their formidable weapons and grim expressions, their magnificence inspired an awe bordering on terror. Their muted glow lit the street, but a mist or a veil surrounded them, obscuring the angels from clear view.

"Who are they?" I breathed.

"Leaders of the Two Hundred," said Nefta, her ice-blue eyes focused.

"How come you guys can see them, too?" I asked my brother and Tim.

They shrugged, staring at the group outside.

"They aren't hiding their true forms right now, Watcher," explained Nefta.

"Why don't you go out there?" asked Alex.

"Clearly, because I am not one of the Fallen Two Hundred," she said, her tone short. "It would not be appropriate."

The angels gathered around Turel, who, from his body language and gestures, endeavored to make a point. I strained to hear what they said and frowned. A sense of music filled the air, like a song I knew, but could not grasp the melody of it.

Nefta nodded at me. "Sorry, Watcher, but they speak in our language. It isn't something that translates to human senses."

I grimaced. "Figures. Can you tell us what they are saying?"

"Certainly," she said. Nefta closed her eyes and became still while I tried to make sense of the haunting strains emanating from my front yard. Just as I achieved the resultant inevitable headache, Nefta spoke, "Turiel is telling them about Innon's attempted abduction of the Watcher today."

"I'm gonna' kill that guy," Alex growled.

Nefta frowned and waved one slender, pale hand as though brushing him aside. "Shush."

She opened her crystalline blue eyes. "Now he's telling them about Chernobog' s creature's invasion of your home this evening despite Turel's protection of it and the destruction of Gwyrdd's doorway." Her eyelids flickered shut once more.

We waited as seconds ticked by. I wondered if Alex and Tim's heads hurt as much as mine.

After a few minutes Nefta chuckled. "Ah, clever Turiel. He's telling them these acts are an affront to their authority. Less about the humans, more about the rules. Very good, my friend."

"I don't get it," I started, but Tim cut me off.

"Siobhan, just a guess, but what referee ever liked cheating? I think Turel's trying to get them to throw some penalty flags."

"Indeed," said Nefta. She resembled an exquisite statue, too lovely to be real. Nefta cocked her head to one side. "Well, I certainly didn't think they'd say yes to that."

"What?" We chorused.

"Turiel has argued the signs point to a crisis." Nefta opened her eyes and surveyed me, one eyebrow arched. "It is time for Gwrydd to return, as foretold."

"Huh?" said Alex.

"Daisy is coming back." I exhaled, my heart skipping in a painful mix of anticipation and fear. "Daisy is coming *back*."

Chapter Six

The dream visited me again. Part of my brain thought, what dream? The other responded, you know, the bad one. The one with the woman. The woman who hated me.

My bleary, sleep-filled eyes blinked, adjusting to morning's light. I tried to recall details of my dream. The images faded like mist at the sun's touch. The harder I concentrated, the more elusive became my memories. I shook my head and gave up for now.

Something smelled good in the kitchen. Could that be bacon? My stomach rumbled. Sure enough, Alex flipped pancakes at my stove with an expert's touch. The plastic-covered table was laden with fresh berries, country potatoes, and a plate of bacon. He had found my paper plates and plastic ware. Everything else I owned resided in boxes. "You went shopping," I observed.

"Yep," he said, winking. "Used your onion though."

"I'm glad I contributed something to this feast." I smiled at my brother. "Thanks, Alex."

"No sweat."

The events of last night seemed more bizarre in the sunlit kitchen. Angels, a demon, a dragon returning, all ran through my mind. My thoughts centered around Daisy, or Gwyrdd. Perhaps I needed to talk to the gang regarding a moratorium on names. This could get confusing. I refused to think about the Watcher. Later.

"Where are Tim and Turel?" I continued as I munched on a piece of bacon and made myself a plate.

"Tim's outside playing nursemaid to your house guest and Turel sort of fluttered away," he answered as he served me two pancakes with a deft hand. He tossed me the maple syrup.

45

"What?" I asked with a moan as I caught the plastic bottle. "No warming it for me? And hey, Turel doesn't flutter. C'mon, Alex."

He grinned. "He's an angel. At some point, I shall expect him to flutter. Oh, and serenade us with a harp."

I rolled my eyes at him as I poured the not-warm syrup. "Nefta?"

Alex shrugged. "No idea. There's been a lot to keep track of."

Frowning and a little shell-shocked, I processed Alex's earlier statement. "Where'd my house guest go?"

By way of answer Alex indicated the back door with a nod. He had his hands full as he piled pans into my beautiful, newly installed sink and filled the basin with soap and water.

Through the sliding door to the garden I saw Tim's familiar profile. Next to him stood the man from last night. They headed back into the house. "At least he's walking around again." I wished I could talk to Turel. There were so many questions. My head started to ache again. Coffee, I needed coffee.

"Breakfast ready?" Tim called.

"Yep." I held up my plate as I slid a bar stool to the table.

"Siobhan, this is Gilbert," Tim said, introducing the man next to him. Gilbert's sandy hair was thinning and fading into gray, not a crew cut, but close. His watery, light-blue eyes met mine briefly. I noted his pale skin, even at the height of California summer. He shifted his rounded, thin shoulders, closer to fifty than to forty, but I liked his hesitant smile.

Gilbert cleared his throat a couple of times. "Morning. I'm not sure how I ended up on your couch. Everything seems to be a little blurry today." He coughed. "I'm awfully sorry. Thanks for giving me a place to stay."

"You're welcome," I said. My heart sank. No answers. Tim glanced at me in sympathy. He understood. Tim poured me a cup of coffee and handed it to me, giving my shoulder a squeeze.

"Thanks." I kept my tone bright, doctoring the coffee with milk and sugar. The first, deep sip tasted heavenly.

For a few moments, we ate in an awkward silence. Gilbert

coughed. "Err, miss, uh."

"Siobhan," I supplied.

"Siobhan, well, now." He shifted on his stool. "I hope I didn't, I mean, I hope I hadn't had too much to… That is, was I?" He trailed off and pushed pieces of potato around his plate.

It dawned on me. "Oh, you're worried you were drunk?"

He nodded and kept his eyes on his plate. Alex, Tim, and I considered one another. Alex gave a short laugh. "If only."

Gilbert inspected my brother with wide eyes. I hurried to reassure him. "Oh no, Gilbert, nothing like that to worry about. You were fine, I promise."

My uninvited house guest shifted in his seat and bowed his head back to his plate. "How'd I get here?" He sounded like a lost child.

A knock came from my screen door. To my delight, Turel appeared on my porch, smiling at us. "Good morning." I hurried to open the screen. "Look at you, using the door and everything."

He shrugged in a self-deprecating manner. "One does not always need to make a scene."

"Oh, really, one doesn't?" Nervous energy tinged my brittle laugh.

Turel carried his backpack again, but now that I expected it I saw his wings folded against his back. Did he have to cut his clothes to allow his wings to be free or did he use some sort of angel hocus pocus to get around the whole problem? My introspection ended when Gilbert said, "Who's the rag head?"

In the stunned silence Tim frowned at Gilbert. "What did you call him?"

Gilbert stuck his chin out. "You know, one of those Al Qaeda guys, A-rabs." He stretched the word Arabs into two words.

My face flamed. "Turel is not a terrorist."

Turel put one hand on my shoulder. "Peace, Siobhan, it's all right." His voice deepened with amusement. "Besides, the gentleman is mistaken. This body is Persian."

"Whatever." Gilbert's blue eyes blazed with a fanatical light. "They're all a bunch of Muslim freaks. Sickos."

I found this incongruous, coming from someone who the night before took orders from a demon. *Live in a glass house much?*

Turel walked into the kitchen, grabbed the step ladder, and pulled it to the table next to Gilbert, saying with great dignity, "I assure you, sir, I am not a Muslim." He sat, looking solemn, but I saw a mischievous twinkle in his dark eyes.

I bit my lip, trying to hold back a fit of nervous giggles. Tim and Alex exchanged glances and burst out laughing. "What's so damn funny?" demanded Gilbert.

Turel ignored him. "Well, friends, does he remember anything from last night?"

We all responded with negatives. Turel pursed his lips. The angel's thoughtful gaze rested on my jumpy guest.

Gilbert tensed. He flinched as Turel leaned toward him. "What the hell?" Gilbert yelped.

"I'm not surprised." Turel smiled, ignoring Gilbert's protest. "Listen to me—what is his name?" Turel broke off, glancing at me.

"Gilbert," I answered.

"Listen to me, Gilbert. We're going to see if we can't find out what's been going on with you, lately," Turel explained.

"The hell you are," said Gilbert, his face reddening. "Here, I'm real grateful for breakfast and you being kind enough to take me in last night. I'll… I'll send you a check for your trouble." He started to rise.

"Sit," said Turel and his voice reverberated with power. The air around him burned incandescent. His golden halo comforted me. In the bright, morning sunshine, the aura might be mistaken for a trick of the light.

Tim and Alex relaxed in their seats. Even Gilbert settled down, mechanically doing as Turel bid. His eyes glazed over as the angel went on, "Now, my friend, we shall retrace your steps. We must see where you have gone, and what you have done. What is the last thing you can remember?"

"Yesterday, after lunch. I ate a ham sandwich and some grapes. I went back to work. Then, I don't know. I woke up this morning here, on the couch." Gilbert murmured, his words low and dull. His eyes never left Turel's face.

"I see, friend Gilbert. That must be troubling. We can help you remember. It is important to know who you spoke with. I can help you recall. Will you allow me to assist you?"

The rich tones of Turel's voice filled the quiet room. The way he spoke to Gilbert compelled. It went beyond mere hypnotism. What other powers might angels command? Gilbert's face relaxed, becoming peaceful. The careworn lines eased. "Yes," he answered Turel.

"Thank you, Gilbert. This will be easy. Just relax and listen to my voice. Close your eyes. You don't need to do anything or think about anything in particular except to answer my questions. Can you do that?"

Gilbert nodded. His eyes fluttered shut. Turel leaned closer and placed his hands on Gilbert's head. The amber glow suffused both men.

After a moment Turel spoke, "He is hearing me in his head now. I am questioning him and guiding his mind to the places and things I need to see." Turel's eyes closed.

"How can you be doing that when you are talking to us?" I asked.

"I'm multi-tasking. Don't you humans do it all the time?"

"Well, yeah, the women," I said. "The men? Not so much."

"Hey," protested Tim.

Turel opened his eyes and quirked one eyebrow at me. "My dear Siobhan, I'll have you know, I am no ordinary man." The angel focused on Gilbert again and his lids shuttered closed.

Strained, silent moments passed. Gilbert and Turel went rigid, eyes wide open. They stared at one another, locked in a silent, frozen struggle. I tried to call them, to speak to them, but nothing would come out.

Gilbert screamed, an awful hoarse sound ripped from his throat. Through his mouth something vile streamed forth, something felt as well as seen. It flowed like a sick, oozing mist, existing between liquid and smoke. As it came, it stole the light and

49

joy from the morning. The warm air chilled before its advance. An anonymous evil churned and roiled in growing power, covering the floor and spreading throughout my kitchen.

Instinctively, I recognized its malignancy, its sickness as it reached for us. It wanted us. Its sick need dominated, its desire to take, to consume. Alex and Tim went white. With a groan first one and then the other fell to their knees. The bitter cold settled in my limbs, my breath squeezed from me, and my eyelids grew heavy. Cold, icy tendrils of black goo stretched toward me. I sank into hopelessness. I wanted to lie down and die, for what was the point to anything anyway?

But I held on to the joyful moments, the happy times, I refused to close my eyes. People had been telling me what to think, feel, and believe for as long as I could remember. I saw no difference here. I fought for consciousness. The evil wasn't real, just another lie.

Turel chanted Hebrew in low intense tones. He finished with a mighty yell, "*Hit'alem! Begone!*" Brilliant luminescence filled my home, more dazzling than anything I had ever seen. For an instant, the sun itself shone in my small house. The darkness fled. The evil howled in rage as it disappeared.

I swayed on my feet, weak, and half blind, but I fought on. Turel repeated to himself, "*Hit'alem, hit'alem,* begone, begone, oh demon, begone."

Reality crumbled, becoming unsteady and unsure. My knees gave way, and I dropped to the ground, heavy and graceless. I would have slammed onto the kitchen floor if Turel had not been there.

With quick strides he rushed to my side. "I am here, Watcher, I am here," he murmured, catching me. Haste roughened his urgent grasp. The amber aura colored everything in my sight, but not with the blinding painful blast the angel had fought the darkness off with. The soft glow emitted a gentle joy. Warmth cradled me as hope and life filled my body. The truth returned.

The cheerful morning filled my kitchen. Summer brightened the air again. As Turel released me, I managed to keep on my feet.

Strength restored my limbs. Tim and Alex stirred. I met Turel's gaze. His dark eyes gleamed with light and kindness. "Thank you," I said.

"Of course, Watcher." He bent to Tim and I to Alex. We helped them to their feet. Meanwhile, Gilbert lay motionless. The blast threw him from his stool. He lay sprawled on his back, limbs akimbo.

Alex spoke first. "What the hell was that?"

Tim croaked, "Hell being the operative word, I imagine."

"Chernobog. You experienced his soul or at least a small part of it," Turel said softly. He regarded Gilbert's crumpled form. "He placed a bit of his essence in that man. A trap set to attack if I pushed the right places, asked certain questions. When I did, well, you saw what it unleashed. We were lucky."

"You call that lucky?" said my brother, shaking his red head in disbelief. "I've never been so scared in my entire life."

"What did you see?" I asked him.

"Not much," he admitted. "Turel and Gilbert went from eyes-closed peacefulness to an angry staring contest. Then Gilbert yelled, and everything got cold and hopeless. I would have been happy to die. I think I almost did."

"Indeed, it was touch and go for you in that moment," said Turel.

"And you?" I scrutinized Tim. He held out his shaking hands. "Pretty much the same," he agreed. "I didn't see much, but I experienced everything Alex described. When I woke up everything was back to normal, or maybe even better, because I was so thankful the despair had gone." He shuddered and examined me. "You didn't pass out?"

I shook my head. "No."

"Why not, I wonder?" Tim asked.

Turel stroked his beard. "I think the Watcher is a stubborn woman. Strong."

Alex snorted. "Duh," he said.

"How strong remains to be seen, even by her," said Turel, his gaze fixed upon me.

"You freak." Gilbert struggled to stand, his features twisted with emotion. "You sick bastard. What did you do to me?" He raised his fists to his head, swaying.

Turel spread his hands. "Peace, friend, I tried to help you."

"Help me?" echoed Gilbert. "There are nightmares in my head. There are things I have never seen or done. These memories can't be real. You did this to me." His agitation grew with each shrill word. "What's wrong with me? What did you do?"

With jerky motions, he pushed past us, toward the front door. Alex put out an arm to stop him, but Gilbert shoved my tall brother with a strength I would never have imagined the stooped man possessed.

"Freaks," Gilbert yelled as he fled. "Sick, fucking freaks!" He slammed the door and sprinted through the yard.

Turel stared sadly at the swinging screen. The door bounced back and forth before settling in place, ajar. "I fear for that man. He is damaged. Without healing he will be a danger to himself and to others. I may need to call for someone to watch him." He shook his dark head and ran one tanned hand over his short beard. "One does not bear a demon's soul, even such a small piece, unscathed."

"What about Chernobog?" Tim wondered. "Can he still use Gilbert?"

"Oh, yes," said Turel. "The demon has a hold on him. Now that Gilbert is panicked, I am afraid I have made it even easier for Chernobog to use him. He possessed more strength before he remembered what had been done to him. Perhaps I should have left him alone." Turel rubbed his beard. He muttered to himself. "But I had no idea what would happen. I needed to try."

"We have to help him," I said, my heart twisted in pity, despite my relief at his departure. A mere few minutes of Chernobog terrified me. What had Gilbert endured?

"You are right. We have to try. I will alert the Two Hundred. They must find the poor creature. And soon," said Turel.

Alex frowned. "What do you mean you'll alert the Two Hundred? Aren't you going to help? Can't *you* do anything?"

Turel's face appeared shuttered, no emotion. "My place is with the Watcher. It is foretold."

"But..." said Alex.

"You heard the man," said Tim. "He's her guard. Do you want her defenseless?"

To my chagrin heat from my blush overwhelmed me. Who wants to be a delicate maiden needing a guard? Awkward. The tick of the hallway clock sounded abnormally loud.

"Turel," said Tim breaking the silence at last, his face white, "what did Chernobog mean when he said the last chain is about to break?"

"Chernobog is a prisoner, bound by four archangels in the beginning of days," said Turel, "but with the passing of the ages, his bonds failed. Only one chain still holds him."

"Wait," I said, "how could he be in my street, smashing Daisy's gateway and tormenting that wretched man?"

"You tasted a small slice of his power," said Turel, "a mere projection of a shadow of his full self."

"You mean," said Alex, appearing very young, "he's worse?"

Grim lines etched Turel's face as he answered, "Yes, much worse."

Chapter Seven

"I fear I've ruined what must have been a lovely breakfast." Turel gestured toward the table. His tone reminded me of my old babysitter once she decided to change an unpleasant subject.

"It didn't suck, if I do say so myself. Perhaps you'd like to clean up?" Alex asked, his face still pale, indicating the remains of the meal he'd prepared.

Turel glanced at the counter. "Griddlecakes," he exclaimed and grabbed a plate. "I adore griddlecakes."

We smiled at the angel's delight, though my expression felt forced. Alex served Turel. "Well, in this case, just pancakes, but I'm glad you're happy," my brother said. "I'm happy, too. I can't stand leftovers."

Turel dove into his breakfast and Alex, proud cook, cleaned up, humming as he did. I knew my brother well enough to know he had one eye on Turel's every mouthful. I couldn't blame Alex. Even if no one ever knew about it, having an angel as a satisfied customer had to be something of a coup for a chef.

With the last bites gone and the kitchen cleaned, we mere humans waited, all eyes on Turel. "Well?" I prompted.

"Well, what?" responded Turel.

"You know what," I said. "Where is she?"

"I assure you, I most certainly do not know what, as you put it."

I frowned at Tim and Alex, then at Turel. "But you said, last night you promised, and Nefta said, too." I folded my arms.

"Yes?" Turel folded his arms matching his posture to mirror my own. His face took on a grumpy expression. I realized he mimicked me. "I... said what?" His tone held only innocence.

I shook my finger at him. "You stop that. You said Daisy would come back. Now, when is she coming?" Turel grinned, but didn't reply. "Turel, stop teasing me." I rounded on Alex and Tim. "Can he do that?" I demanded.

Alex shrugged and Tim said, "I think he just did."

I stared at Turel. "But, you're an angel," I started. "This is all very grave and important, right?"

"So?"

"Aren't there rules, etiquette, or something?"

"Humans." He sighed, rolling his eyes. "You'll take the fun out of anything. Try to live in the moment."

"What?" I squawked.

"What's life without whimsy?" Turel asked.

I glared. Last night he spouting doom, fate, and prophecies. This wasn't the time for jokes, laughter. Was it?

"There is always time for laughter," said Turel as if reading my thoughts. "Laughter heals."

Knowing I gaped at him, I made a conscious effort to close my mouth. He smiled, saying, "Yes, Siobhan, I promised. Forgive me for enjoying your reaction. You better pack a bag."

"What for?" Tim asked.

"Daisy's doorway here is destroyed. We need to go somewhere where she can cross over. It's not like you can land a dragon anywhere in this world these days. And frankly, once she does come, I don't know what will happen. Siobhan should plan on the possibility of being gone for a bit," Turel explained.

I swallowed. Me? Leave with Turel? Granted he seemed to be one of the good guys, but events had developed so quickly these past hours. The words "the Watcher" filled my thoughts.

"What a sec," said Alex. "You think I'm letting my sister run off with some..." He frowned at Turel. "Some...guy, angel, we've just met, after her home's been invaded and some other guy tried to kidnap her?"

"Alex," I said, but he cut me off.

"No, no way. I'm going, too." He folded his arms, his expression set.

"Humph," grunted Tim. "Well, there's no way you're leaving me behind."

I shook my head, but relieved warmth spread through me. I wouldn't travel into the unknown alone. Watcher or not, I remained me, Siobhan, and I had people who cared.

"Right, pack three bags," said Turel. I raised my eyebrows at him. The angel didn't seem surprised or upset that he would have two extra charges chasing him. I wondered why.

"Where are we going?" asked Alex.

"To the sea, we must be there by sunset."

***

A couple hours later I glared at the boys. "Okay, not to sound sexist, but why am I the only one ready?" My packed bag sat in the car. Alex spoke on the phone, pacing back and forth, as he argued with Maddie, his right hand gal at the café. Tim came back from putting his four bags in the car.

"Four? Are you flipping kidding me?" I stared him. "What? Are you bringing an entourage, too?"

Tim blushed and said, "Well, one is for Leia."

"That's just like you, blaming the dog," I muttered.

To be fair, Tim had been unable to find someone to watch his German shepherd on such short notice. I understood not wanting to leave the animal alone. The resulting extra bag contained her water bowl, food, leashes and other canine accessories.

I bent to where Leia lay on my kitchen floor and stroked her soft head. "How about that, baby girl," I said to her, "the two girls each have only one bag. Check out those boys." She whined in what I chose to call canine agreement, her mouth open and tongue lolling in a doggie grin.

"Hey," Alex protested, putting away his phone. "I only have two bags."

"Yeah, and they're each big enough to hide a small person in, or a large dog," I noted, shaking my head at the two men. "Honestly, boys, come clean, how many pairs of shoes did you pack?"

Alex and Tim exchanged guilty glances, but didn't answer.

Leia exhaled in a, "Humph" sound and put her head on the ground, brown eyes gazing at the three of us.

"You said it, girl." I smiled. "How's Maddie?" I asked Alex.

"Mad." He shrugged. "Maddie's pissed she'll be covering for me. She had tickets to see Weird Al in concert. She and her friends wanted to dress up in fat suits as an homage to his Eat It period."

"That's what she gets paid the big bucks for," said Tim with a wide smile.

"Uh, yeah, huge, gy-nor-mous." Alex grimaced.

"Boys," I said, sighing. "Leaving? Today? While we're young?"

"Hey," Tim countered. "Just because you don't have a business to run, responsibilities, a life, don't get on those of us that do. We can't all be footloose and fancy free like you, Siobhan."

To my surprise, tears stung my eyes. His logic rang with truth. There I was, unemployed, no boyfriend, and no responsibilities. Heck, I didn't even have a fish, just this house, empty except for me. I ducked my head so the guys wouldn't see my face and headed for the door, calling, "Jealous much, Tim?"

Outside Turel waited, leaning on Alex's Jeep Wrangler. A hand grasped my shoulder. I turned and met Tim's bright gaze.

"I'm sorry, Siobhan. What a shitty thing to say."

I ducked my head to avoid his eyes. "True though."

"No, I was kidding, but I took it too far," he said. "We okay?"

"Always, Tim," I said.

"Oh, you two," said Alex. "When are you crazy kids going admit you're made for each other and give me the happy ending I always wanted?"

My face flushed, and I would have loved to kick my brother's shins. Instead, I stuck my tongue out at him. "Let's make like a baby and head out."

Tim and Alex groaned, but they went outside and I locked the house. Walking down the porch steps, I squirmed inside at Turel's indulgent grin. Did angels also possess extra keen hearing? It wouldn't surprise me. Nothing would at this point.

Leia wagged her tail enthusiastically and jumped into the car without any encouragement.

As we loaded up, Tim asked, "What about Nefta? Why isn't she with us today?"

Turel pursed his lips. "Nefta comes when Nefta pleases. Besides, it is not usually a good omen for her to appear."

"Why do you say that? She seems like she's good in a fight," Tim said.

"Naturally, she's a Valkyrie," said Turel.

Alex tilted his head to one side, perplexed. "I don't get it."

"The name Valkyrie means 'chooser of the slain' in Old Norse," the angel said. "Valkyries decide who lives and dies on the battlefield. They guide the souls of heroes."

"So, you're saying I shouldn't tell her I like the junk in her trunk," Alex said.

"I'm saying, if she shows up, get ready for some bloodshed."

Silence reigned as we processed those implications.

"Bummer," Alex said, starting the Jeep. "She's smoking hot."

"I am surprised, Turel, that an angel is driving to the coast," I remarked, ignoring Alex as we backed out of the driveway. "Can't you fly? Or do that disappearing thingie you do?"

Turel's voice from the back seat sounded amused. "Yes, I could fly or I could go in between dimensions, that thingie as you so eloquently call it, but I need to stay close to you, Watcher. Nor do I wish to draw undue attention to ourselves. Besides, I enjoy the company. You mortals are endlessly fascinating in your unpredictability."

"Yeah," Alex said. "Kids say the darnedest things."

* * *

We made good time. Alex, under Turel's direction, navigated the back roads and avoided the worst of Sonoma County's early afternoon traffic. As we got closer to the Pacific, I relaxed. We were early. In fact, we were so early Turel insisted we stop for dinner at Dinucchi's Italian Dinners, a restaurant outside of Bodega. Situated in Valley Ford, the restaurant lay only ten minutes out of the way, but I chaffed at the delay.

Turel took his time eating. I wanted to leap over the table and shake him. My relaxed mood shifted to intense impatience and frustration. It didn't help that Turel found my behavior hilarious. "Rushing me won't make sunset come any sooner, Siobhan," he remarked, his calm maddening.

"What's the big deal with sunset?" Alex asked. He ate his tiramisu with relish. I envied him. My stomach remained tied in knots. I hadn't enjoyed dinner.

"We're trying to be circumspect," answered Turel, taking another bite of his panna cotta.

"Come again?" Tim asked. I compulsively checked my watch for the eightieth time. Tim ate chocolate cake. The restaurant bustled with warm, casual air and a welcoming staff. Only I did not enjoy myself. Did this hit home for Tim and Alex? Much of what had been happening, they couldn't even see. As I always had, I saw more.

"The world you live in, friend Tim, the world of man," said Turel, "is an illusion. You are kept in the dark on many levels, by many different supernatural factions. It is simply easier to operate without mankind being aware of what is really going on. The panic that would ensue, the belligerence and willful misunderstanding, it is easier for everyone in my reality, good and evil, to put that eruption off."

"Why?" I asked. "Why bother? What could we even do?"

"Never under estimate the human spirit," said Turel through another bite of dessert. "I have seen humanity accomplish amazing feats. Why waking the sleeping giant? You are so numerous, and many of you are infernally clever."

I frowned. "But, you're talking about angels, Fallen angels, even demons. What on earth could we do to you?"

"Everything dies, Siobhan, even those called immortal." Turel paused, his dark gaze on me. "The demons would dearly love to come for you, Watcher, and for Daisy."

"Why me?" I eyed the surrounding tables, as though this attack might come at any second. "Why Daisy?"

"You have an important part to play in the fate of this world." Turel's tone grew serious. "Without you, the prophecy cannot come to fruition and chaos would reign. The agents of hell are fond of chaos. In effect, they would win by default through killing you. That is certainly what Innon wanted."

A chill washed over me. I felt small and vulnerable. Alex scooted his chair closer and wrapped one arm around my shoulders. "Not going to happen, sis."

"Indeed," agreed Turel. "Why do you think I have stepped into the fray? I am no longer an Observer. I am now a participant. As foretold, I protect the human Horoa, the Watcher."

"And Daisy?" prompted Tim. His tone sobered. "Are there other dragons?"

"Yes, but they are trapped, banished. Daisy is the last dragon in our world," explained Turel. "She alone can pass from Knotlow to Earth."

I tapped my fingers on the table in a restless rhythm. "That horrible thing, Chernobog, said Knotlow. What is it?"

"The dragons' refuge, or their place of banishment, depending on your point of view," said Turel.

"How did they end up trapped?" asked Tim.

Turel pursed his lips. "That," he said, shaking his head, "is a long story. A story for another day I think."

"Will they ever be able to return to this world?" I asked.

"One hopes," said Turel, "but I cannot say. For the sake of mankind, I pray it will be so. This world needs its champions back."

My emotions churned. It sounded like the dragons were on our side. It also sounded like their arrival meant war. My head throbbed, and I rubbed my temples.

"Okay, that makes sense, but how does sunset play into everything?" I asked.

"We're opening a door between realities." Turel ate his last bite of dessert and went on with his narrative. "Plus, we need a really big door for a dragon."

"So?" said Alex.

"So, there's a noise, actually, it's more of a feeling, when one transitions through realities." Turel shrugged. "Others can sense it. They'll know when someone or something journeys from one world to the next. Make a big enough hole and everyone will know a dragon is entering this place. Since there is only one dragon who can travel back, her enemies will have an excellent idea where she is to be found."

"Would it be the same if Daisy used her statue?" I asked, frowning.

"No, a spell lay over the statue. Call it cloaked, if you like. It acted as a portal and would have made little noise. It had been specifically keyed to Daisy. She could open it a crack and still slip through. Her enemies would need to be close to sense her entry. This is a different type of portal today. We're seeking convergences, a place where land meets sea, as day turns to night. She'll cross exactly as the sun sets. The fine point in space and time of these opposites colliding at once will help cover the sensation of reality splitting. It should buy us time."

"Buy us time?" Tim repeated.

Turel's face was set. "Time to get a head start in case someone from the other side catches on to what we're doing. Now pay the check. The sun's going down."

We drove north out of Bodega in silence. Turel guided Alex to Gerstle Cove at Salt Point. A crescent-shaped inlet waited for us. The dirt parking lot appeared empty except for some screeching gulls. The pounding of the surf soothed my jangled nerves. Dusk fell on a beautiful evening.

Alex and Tim took Leia to the edge. They threw rocks off the short cliff above the waves. Walking the path, I stared out over the water. Many years had passed, but the cove remained exactly the same as I remembered it. Alex and Tim laughed and made jokes behind me. They tested who threw rocks the farthest, like kids at play. I marveled again at the difference in our moods.

"Siobhan," Turel said. The intensity of his tone caught my ear, and I turned to him. He lingered a few feet away from me, his eyes fixed serenely on a point far away.

I joined him, my eyes on the horizon. The setting sun painted the sky a vivid seascape of blues, pinks, violets and oranges. As the sun lowered to the lowest point in the sky, in the instant before its rays spilled over the back of the world, there shone a beam of concentrated light, as precise as a laser. After a second, the light expanded, becoming a brilliant, white ray. It continued to grow, morphing into a tunnel in reverse, but instead of darkness, it blazed a corridor of light. The white light became prismatic, flickering with a rainbow of dancing diamond sparkles, splashing colors of all hues in front of my dazzled eyes.

Turel enclosed one of my hands in his warm grasp. "It is something to see, yes?" His tone reflected true awe.

"Is this your first time seeing this?" I asked in a whisper. The tunnel became larger, dwarfing us. With my free hand I shielded my eyes. Leia sat at my side, gazing in the distance.

"No, I have seen this many times." He held out his other hand and waved it at the mighty light show. "But a miracle is no less glorious for having previously happened."

To my left Tim and Alex continued their ridiculous rock throwing competition. Their stones sailed right through the expanding brilliance they could not see. "Guys, are you kidding me?" In the emotion of the moment, my voice growled, low and hoarse.

They stopped and gave me matching blank expressions. "What?" Alex said.

"Hey, what are you guys staring at?" Tim sounded defensive.

Before I could answer their questions, I heard it. A sweet sound, soft at first, barely a whisper, carried on the breeze. Turel's smile grew even brighter, matching the shining portal. "She comes." His eyes shone as they met mine.

Alex glanced this way and that. "Does anyone hear that sound?" he asked.

Tim craned his head. "I hear it. It sounds like bells."

"Wind chimes," I corrected, still staring straight ahead. "It's wind chimes." The air shimmered. Light danced in an intense aurora borealis. Patterns of colors streaked and swooped in a heavenly painting. One hue dominated the others. The deep shade of jade green spread. An enormous form took shape, dressing itself in swathes of color. The huge outline solidified: graceful wings, a serpentine neck, and a curving tail. Two amber lights appeared like jewels in the viridian air. Everything intensified, heightening each of my senses; the lights pulsed. A beautiful, green dragon hovered in the air. With two mighty beats of her massive wings, she crested then landed behind us. I ran forward with a cry. "Daisy."

"Damn it," growled Tim. "I can't see anything even a bit like a dragon."

"Unless it's a super little one," said Alex, his face downcast.

Turel laughed—a big, belly laugh full of joy. "Gwyrdd, you sly minx, show them. Drop the glamour and let our friends see you."

Daisy twisted her head to one side in a coquettish gesture and in that voice I had never forgotten said, "Certainly, Turiel, dear one." Suppressed mirth laced her tone. "How's this, children?"

When she spoke these last words the music of wind chimes came again, louder this time. As their bright notes sounded around us, I saw the precise instant when both my brother and my first love, the two who believed in me all these years, finally saw my dragon.

Chapter Eight

The music of wind chimes faded from the air, leaving behind the song of the breeze and the cry of the waves. None of us spoke. Tim and Alex's expressions fixed into dumbstruck masks. Daisy had dropped her glamour; Tim and Alex saw her now.

Though the painted sky faded and the glow of twilight dimmed, Daisy shone in verdant beauty. Her scales sparkled like gems, lit from within.

Leia barked incessantly at the wyvern form. Daisy laughed, and then she lowered her graceful neck, bringing her head to the dog's level. Her amber eyes twinkled as she scrutinized Leia's warm brown ones. Dog and dragon both sniffed. After a moment Leia wagged her tail with furious delight. The dog pranced and scampered then crouched, tail and hind haunches up and front paws on the ground in the universal doggie posture of let's play. The German shepherd woofed and whined. Daisy rose to her full height and murmured, "Maybe another time, girl."

Tim's eyes, wide and filled with awe, met mine. I wanted to sing. "Daisy," I exclaimed.

"My own dear Siobhan," she said. Her mellifluous voice filled the cove. I loved hearing it in the real world, instead of in my memories, locked inside my head.

"Daisy." I waved a hand toward Alex and Tim. "This is my brother, Alex, and our friend, Tim. You've already met Leia." I caressed the shepherd's soft ears as the dog regarded the dragon with canine adoration.

The reptilian head nodded at them both. "I very much like your dog," Daisy said to Tim.

"Well, she seems to love you," he replied, his eyes wide and unblinking.

Alex shook his head. "So, you appeared out of nowhere? Like Turel skipping through dimensions?" he asked. "Or were you beamed here?"

"Star Trek," I said. "How can you go to Star Trek at a time like this?"

"How can you not? This deserves a big story." said Tim. "It's that or Star Wars." He joined me and stroked Leia's head, but his eyes never left the shining dragon above us.

"I did skip through dimensions," she said, "but I came using an established portal rather than simply making a hole and coming through. A matter of discretion, you see."

"Right," Alex replied. "Turel explained that. I guess I got confused because it seemed like Siobhan and Turel saw you before we did. Why is that?"

Turel stroked his mustache, one hand covering his mouth as he asked Alex, "Are you sure you've known Siobhan *all* your life?"

. I bit my lip to keep from laughing. Turel hid a smile.

Alex's shoulders stiffened, but Turel continued, "How does she always see things you do not? Why do you think I've been calling her the Watcher?"

My brother flushed. "Yeah, right, silly question. Still, you saw her, too. Why couldn't Tim and I?"

"You do remember I'm an angel, right"

"Oh, right," said Alex.

"Do you know what a glamour is, young one?" Daisy asked.

"Um, sort of. Isn't that how vampires get their victims to come to them?"

Turel turned his head to one side, his mouth twitching again.

Daisy sighed then rolled her eyes. "In your movies, yes," she said.

"But not in real life?" Alex asked.

The jeweled head moved back and forth. "No, young Alex. Put simply, the best way to think of a glamour is as an illusion. Your mind is tricked into thinking something is there when nothing really is or that something appears completely different than it truly is."

"I take it that's why Siobhan isn't fooled?" asked Tim.

Alex frowned at his friend. "I give. Why isn't Siobhan fooled? Because she's super smart?"

Turel waited, his expression patient, as Alex and Tim sorted out the realities of my life.

"No." Tim's eyes narrowed. "I think Siobhan sees what we don't because a glamour is a kind of lie and she always sees through lies."

"Exactly so," approved Turel. "The Watcher sees true."

"How come she gets confused sometimes?" pressed Alex.

"Hello, I'm standing right here," I said.

Daisy ignored me and answered Alex. "Because she sees the true image with her Watcher's sight, but her mortal eyes give her the false vision, too. As she progresses, Siobhan will be able to see more and she'll be able to better distinguish between realities, or in this case, falsehoods."

Tim frowned again. "So, you glamoured us, Daisy?"

Daisy brought her head down to Tim. He started, but did not back away. "Yes, you clever thing," she said. "No one casts a better glamour than a dragon. No one."

"You're the best and Siobhan can even see through you?" Tim appeared impressed.

Daisy nodded. "Easily."

Alex punched me in the shoulder. "You badass, Siobhan."

"Now you're getting it," said Turel, his eyes focused on Daisy as the breeze blew his long, dark hair back.

In a gesture I remembered as though I'd seen it yesterday Daisy lifted her head, listening to the wind. Her golden eyes shone like citrines in the dying light. She shifted, restless. "Children, we must go."

"Did anyone hear you?" asked Turel.

Daisy's emerald head tilted to one side. "I'm not sure, but why take chances?"

"Demons?" Alex twisted his head around.

"Fallen angels?" Tim asked in the same instant.

"Yes and yes," said Daisy. "Now, quickly, my dears."

Turel cleared his throat. "Gwyrdd, aren't you forgetting something?"

Daisy's eyes flashed. "I'm sure I don't know what you mean." Her tone held studied innocence.

"Gwyrdd, come now, it will be much harder for them to find you," Turel went on.

Daisy's voice became sharper. "Oh, bother, Turiel. Must I? It's so uncomfortable, simply stifling." The dragon exhaled in a huff.

Turel shook a finger at the massive figure above him. "Yes, you must. And stop calling me Turiel. Turel will do nicely. Thank you."

Daisy snorted. Everyone except Turel jumped back as smoke and flames went up. "Fine, fine, as you wish, Turel," she grumbled. Her barbed tailed lashed back and forth like an angry cat's. Turel raised one eyebrow and folded his arms in an expectant manner.

"I don't understand," I said. "What do you want Daisy to do?"

"I'd like her disguised," Turel explained. "We can't go gallivanting around the county with a dragon in tow."

"Right," said Alex, his tone faint. "Whatever would the neighbors think?"

"Exactly." Turel did not smile. His dark eyes rested on Daisy.

"Oh, fine," she said. "Stand back, please."

All of us, including Turel, backed away from her emerald form.

Daisy exhaled a massive flame, lighting the parking lot, the low cliffs and the beach below. Even the waves glowed from her fire. The flames resembled nothing I had ever seen, brilliant golden-orange flares with a greenish tint to them. I gasped as she stepped into her own flame, even as she continued to breathe more fire around and over herself.

We shielded our faces against the intense heat of her flaming breath. The blaze danced around Daisy, faster and faster. A swirling maelstrom of pure fire appeared. In the increasing heat, I began to sweat. Straining my eyes, I tried to see the dragon's outline within the flames. For a few seconds the bonfire obscured the dragon in gold, orange, and green.

All at once the fire extinguished. Smoke swirled just as the flames had. For a moment it was impossible to see anything. I gasped. The dragon had disappeared.

In her place appeared a woman in a jade-green sundress while everything else about her exuded golden. Her smooth hair shone the color of ripe wheat. Her exposed skin glowed with a summer tan and her eyes sparked in a familiar amber. Although she lacked real height, she carried herself with a regal air.

The woman who was Daisy ran her fine-boned fingers through her hair in irritation. "You realize they're still going to recognize me," she complained to Turel.

"Some," he agreed. "Some of the smarter, more powerful ones will see you for what you are. However, their underlings, their human servants, and the less intelligent ones will pass right by you now. After all, most of their side is none too bright."

"Truly," Daisy said in fervent agreement.

"How? What?" I stammered.

She shrugged. "I'm magic." Her smile curved with an impish cast.

"Well," Turel said, "there is a bit more to it."

Daisy inclined her head at the angel in gracious acknowledgement. "Turel is right. While I am, in fact, able to wield magic, this is a bit more elemental. Dragon breath is the fire of creation, and I can use it to help me change my form. I can recreate myself, as you see here." She waved one hand toward her torso, indicating her altered state.

"Wow," whispered Tim.

"Damn straight," said Alex.

"Thank you, Lady Gwyrdd," Turel gave a small bow.

"Call me, Daisy, love." She waved a hand at him, dismissing his thanks, but her golden eyes twinkled. "Now, we *really* should get moving. We don't need to make it too easy for anyone who might have been paying attention."

We piled into Alex's Jeep. Leia, relegated to the back on top of the bags, seemed perfectly comfortable. She continued to regard the back of Daisy's head with single-minded adoration as we drove away from the cove.

"Where to?" inquired Alex.

Turel and Daisy exchanged a speculative look. He raised an inquiring eyebrow at her. "So be it," Daisy declared. "Take me home."

* * *

We progressed south, back toward Bodega Bay, but at Jenner we headed east and inland. The grassy bluffs of the coast gave way to the lush redwood forests of Cazadero. Following Daisy's directions, my brother drove off the main road on to a dirt path that barely passed for a track. Weeds and grass threatened to take the trail back, yet it remained just passable. In our shared silence, I tried to visualize what a dragon's house might be like.

The gravel road to Daisy's home led up a hill to a clearing in the redwoods. Above us a crescent moon and a million stars illuminated the shape of a cottage. We parked the Jeep alongside what in the dark might be a vegetable garden and everyone got out.

As we approached the house, a series of conflicting images assaulted my eyes. They struck my brain in rapid fire. My vision blurred and my ears rang. I stopped and reached out, blinded, searching for something to hold on to. Hands steadied either side of me, supporting me. I recognized my brother's strong grip on my left and Tim's familiar touch on my right. "Siobhan?" Alex's voice sounded worried. "What's wrong?"

"There's too much to see." Even to me, I sounded breathless. Closing my eyes, I swallowed hard. I had to shut out the dizzying images.

"I should have thought of this," Daisy tsk, tsked. "I'm sorry, dearest Siobhan; my home has been many things over the ages. Not to mention, it's been in different times and places. For someone with your sight it must be overwhelming."

"You could say that," I said.

"Hmm," mused Turel. "This is an excellent teaching opportunity."

"I agree," Daisy said. "She needs control. Now, my child, keep your eyes closed a moment longer."

"Not a problem, Daisy." My legs steadied with my eyes closed, but I still needed Tim and Alex on either side of me.

"You'll need to open yourself to the images," Turel said. "There will be a moment of discomfort. Do not allow the chaos to consume you. One image should seem more concrete than the others. Concentrate on it as hard as you can. The others should begin to fade."

"It's key that you relax," said Daisy. "Let the pictures wash over you."

"Ready, Siobhan?" asked Turel.

I took a deep breath and exhaled, as if doing yoga. "Yeah, I think so."

"Open your eyes," said Daisy.

Gingerly, I opened my eyes. Sure enough, a veritable kaleidoscope of impressions assailed my sight, like the highest speed slideshow imaginable. Multiple upon multiple versions of this house came and went. I received flashes of more cottages than I could count, in different places and times.

My eyes saw mountain tops, castles and manor houses. Images of caves and hollow trees, even the inside of a volcano swirled around the confines of my head. Places Daisy called home from all over the world, throughout the ages and yet somehow, they were one. Though this optical cavalcade differed wildly in its many aspects, the pictures showed this home. Within the chaos, there existed some thread of Daisy in each of them. The spectacle passed through my mind like the pages of a flipbook and then one image steadied. As though someone spun a prize wheel and the needle stopped here.

As I regained control, I saw again the summer night sky in northern California. Around me lay an open meadow surrounded by redwoods. A rose-lined walkway led to the front door and a welcoming porch with swing drifting in the light breeze, inviting me to sit among the potted plants. It reminded me a little of my house.

I turned to Daisy in wonder, brushing aside Alex and Tim's supporting hands. "How can this be here? You were in another world, another dimension. How can you have a house in our world, in this place? How can it be maintained and cared for?"

In the night, Daisy's teeth flashed as she smiled at me. "There are certain places where the world is still more ours than mankind's," she explained. "These are pockets of wild where dragon magic works best. They are vestiges of days passed." She indicated the meadow and the house it contained. "This is one of those spots. Welcome to my home."

"So, what?" asked Alex. "Are you saying you just whipped this up?"

"Yes." Daisy chuckled. "Now come, let me show you around. You can see your rooms."

* * *

Snug in my comfortable bed, I tossed and turned. Despite the lateness of the hour and my exhaustion, sleep evaded me. The off switch in my head eluded me. Too much had happened—my brain couldn't process everything. Abandoning hope of a visit from Mr. Sandman any time soon, I decided to go stare at the stars.

Alex and Tim's snores resonated through the doors to their rooms as I passed them in the hall. Leia's sounded almost as loud. I smiled at the memories the noise brought back. Every time we'd tried to camp in my grandparents' backyard as kids, I always ended up going back into the house in the wee hours of the morning, driven away by those same snores.

I stole to the porch, taking care as I closed the screen door behind me. The night proved to be balmy with a light breeze. Sighing, I sat on the swing. Beyond the roses, the stars twinkled benignly at me.

"Why up so late, dear one?" I started as Daisy spoke from the yard. She moved closer and sat next to me.

With my vision acclimated to the dark, I could see the dragon inside if I peered into her eyes and concentrated. "I can't seem to sleep yet even though I feel wiped out." I studied her. "You have dragons in your eyes.

"Windows to the soul," Daisy said matter-of-factly. "I can understand why you can't settle down. It's been a busy day."

"Tell that to Tim and Alex," I said, waving my hand back toward the house. "They don't seem to be having any troubles. They lived the same day."

"Well," Daisy said, "they missed seeing quite a bit of it, too. Don't you agree?"

I shrugged and nodded. "That has occurred to me, too."

Daisy surprised me by patting me on the knee. "My poor, young friend," she said. "They certainly put you through the wringer over me, didn't they? So many doctors."

I blinked at her. After a moment I said, "It wasn't so bad. Beats the past day and this whole Watcher deciding the fate of mankind extravaganza."

She chuckled. "You'll get used to it."

"I think not," I said. "Anyhow, by comparison, my childhood seemed like a picnic."

"Please, I watched from the garden. I saw most of it," the disguised dragon demurred. "They made you doubt yourself, your sanity, everything. If you had said you dreamed me up, they'd have let you be. Why didn't you deny me?"

I hesitated, remembering. "I thought I might hurt your feelings," I said. "You seemed so alone. I had people who cared about me, my mother, my father, four different stepmothers over the years, but I didn't know if you did."

She slipped an arm around me and squeezed. "Thank you, Siobhan."

For a moment we sat in a comfortable silence. "Daisy, there's something I've been wondering about for years."

She removed her arm and sat back in the swing. "Yes?"

"In the garden, as a child I remember wind chimes. I heard them again today. Why is that? And, how come Alex and Tim can hear them, too?"

Daisy's eyes widened and without answering she walked back to the yard. She knelt and touched the earth, running her fine-boned fingers into the soil like a caress. It echoed again, carried on the breeze as delicately as a dream, the musical peal of wind chimes.

Inhaling sharply, I stared at Daisy. "Is that you?"

She shook her head and caressed the earth again with a loving touch. Faint notes danced in the air a second time and faded away. "No, that is our mother. For you, the connection is far more tenuous and lost in time. Still, she is your ultimate mother."

"The earth? The earth makes the chimes?" I gasped. "How?"

"She," corrected Daisy. "If she can create the First Ones and all our cousins with Father Sky then naming and greeting her children is a small thing to do. I confess I love her name for me."

I smiled. "I do, too. It's amazing that she you named after wind chimes. How lovely."

Daisy shook her head at me again. "No child, I am far older than wind chimes, far older than mankind. I come from a world before this one of your God's creation. Wind chimes were inspired by my name, not the other way around."

"Wow." I tried to take it in. After a moment I asked, "So, when you appeared and when you left?"

"She was saying hello and good-bye," said Daisy, settling herself cross-legged on the ground. "Naturally, anyone can also hear her call. It's a common enough sound; most think nothing of it."

"Wait, one time, in the garden with Ian, I mean Innon, I thought I heard chimes. He heard them, too."

Daisy glanced around in the moonlight. "I might, possibly, have been in the vicinity," she admitted. "Just to be sure you were safe. I hovered in between worlds. And, naturally, the Fallen know my name."

"Are there others she named?"

"Of course, all the First Ones have names from Mother," said Daisy. "Perhaps someday, when this is over, you will be fortunate enough to hear a birdsong, or a brook babbling where you would swear there no bird or stream existed. Or perhaps you will hear a hawk's call or a flame's crackle though none are nearby. If so, know you are hearing one of my family being welcomed home. All The

Ones Who Came Before are so named."

"But they can't come yet?" I asked.

She shook her head. "No, not yet."

"When will they?"

"I don't know, dear one. No one does." Her fingers caressed the earth.

Despite my interest I yawned. The lateness of the hour had caught me. Daisy saw and smiled. "Go, sleep," she said.

"What about you?"

Still sitting near the roses, Daisy drew her knees to her chest and wrapped her arms around them in a girlish gesture. She smiled at the sky above. "I thought perhaps I would spend a little time with my father."

As I headed back to my waiting bed, I also glanced up. It might have been a trick of my tired eyes, but it seemed to me far more shooting stars lit the night sky than I remembered ever seeing.

Chapter Nine

Tim and Alex chose to regard the breakfast of bagels, shmears, and coffee set out on the sunny front porch as evidence Daisy had gone on a breakfast run earlier that morning. I, on the other hand, woke early and knew the dragon had not left her cottage. However, I did not feel the need to shatter the morning's calm with speculation as to the supernatural nature of bagels.

Alex stumbled out, looking only half awake. His auburn hair stood on end like a curly haystack on top of his head. I tried not to laugh. Alex had never been good at mornings, even when we were kids.

Tim, on the other hand, resembled me. His good morning held the cheer and vitality I remembered from the mornings of years past. I didn't dwell on the other memories that Tim in the morning inevitably brought to mind. I shut them off and instead enjoyed my coffee as Tim and Alex argued over the last onion bagel.

In time-honored fashion the two decided to Rochambeau for it, although that hardly seemed fair given Alex's bleary-eyed state. Sure enough, Tim's rock broke Alex's scissors.

Daisy shook her head and chuckled. "Very entertaining, but I fail to see the point."

"The point is, I win," Tim replied. "My bagel." He took a huge bite, smirking all the while.

Daisy tsk tsk'ed under her breath and said as if speaking to someone not very bright, "Yes, but there is another onion bagel in the box."

"No, I got the last one." Tim munched in contentment.

Alex dove for the box and with a triumphant cry, held a bagel aloft.

"No way," protested Tim, his expression chagrined.

The triumph in his voice triggered a memory in me. Another voice, one in my dreams, raised in cruel victory, crowed over my defeat. I blinked, trying to recall, to force the memory to fully coalesce. Fleeting snippets raced before my mind's eye: green eyes, full lips curled in a snarl, and a woman's voice. For an instant, I thought I had it then the image vanished, refusing to crystallize. I bit my lips. I couldn't force it. I returned to the great bagel caper unfolding on the porch.

Tim and Alex still argued over how another onion bagel had mysteriously appeared. Daisy's face remained a picture of innocence. She saw me watching and shrugged in a minute gesture. Stifling a laugh, I savored my poppy-seed bagel. I shuddered to think of the state of Tim and Alex's breath.

As we finished Turel appeared. His crossing between dimensions had grown so commonplace to me, I scarcely bothered to note the undulating waves in the reality. However, he startled Tim and Alex. To them the angel popped out of thin air.

"Good morning," Turel called to us as he sat on an empty chair next to Daisy. She nodded amiably in response.

"Where have you been?" Alex asked.

"Well, good morning to you, too," Turel said, as Daisy handed him a cup of coffee. I knew darn well each of the Starbuck's cups had been accounted for, yet, now Daisy had one more. As though she heard my thoughts, Daisy's eyes met mine and she gave me a slow wink of one golden eye.

"Sorry, Turel," Alex said. "Anxious to get going, I suppose."

"Where would we go?" asked Tim. "We have Daisy." He shrugged. "She and Turel can handle the bad guys. We go home, job done."

I shook my head, pacing the porch as I drank my coffee. "Bringing Daisy back just gets events moving, remember? Turel? Daisy? What's next?"

Tim bit his lip as he regarded the other four faces watching him. He slumped in the swing where he sat by Alex. "Right, right, I knew that. I just, well, ah, heck." He trailed off, light blue eyes gazing at the trees in the distance as he stroked Leia. "Ah, heck," he repeated.

Daisy gave him a sympathetic smile. Today she dressed all in green again, wearing another simple dress and sandals, her golden hair plaited in a smooth braid. Turel dressed the same way he had been every time I'd seen him: jeans, T-shirt, black leather jacket and black tennis shoes. The heat didn't seem to bother him. Only the T-shirt changed. Today's read, *Back off, man. I'm a scientist. – Venkman.*

"Tim, Alex." Daisy regarded them with affection as she spoke. "No one can blame you for wanting to be done or desiring direction as to what lies before us. In fact, Alex, I believe Turel has something to tell us this morning. Right, old friend?"

Turel grinned at us, his dark eyes shining. "Indeed. How'd you like to meet an oracle?"

"Where is she?" asked Daisy.

"How do you know she's a she?"

"They're always she's, Siobhan."

Alex and Tim sat straighter, eyes bright. I knew how they felt. The word oracle had opened a whole boatload of butterflies in my stomach.

Turel answered Daisy's question. "She's in Monte Rio, near here."

"How convenient," said Daisy.

"It is a nice coincidence," said the angel.

"There is no such thing as a coincidence," said Daisy, in the tone of someone revisiting an old argument.

Turel shrugged.

"What's an oracle?" asked Alex, eyes darting from dragon to angel and back again.

"It's time to hear the prophecy, right?" Tim surmised.

"Finally," I said.

Turel explained to my brother. "An oracle has visions of what may come, Alex."

"So, she sees the future?" Alex's brown eyes were wide.

"She sees the possible future," Daisy said.

"We should go," exclaimed Alex, leaping to his feet.

Daisy began clearing the remnants of our breakfast. "I'm staying here," she said.

"Why?" The word sounded more forlorn than I intended.

She smiled at me. "It's all right, Siobhan, dear. It's simply that we dragons have a way of influencing events around us. Depending on how strong this oracle's power is I could change her viewing by being present. It's bad enough you'll be towing a Fallen Angel in there with you."

Turel raised one eyebrow at her. "Right, bad enough."

"I don't understand," I said. "It's the prophecy you told me about years ago, right? You've both heard it?"

Turel and Daisy nodded.

"Well, why don't you tell us what it says? Why do we need to go see an oracle?"

Daisy shook her head. "It doesn't work like that, child."

"How does it work?" asked Tim.

"We, each of us, haven't heard the whole thing," explained Turel. "Oracles, or seers, respond to who is in front of them. When I heard the prophecy, I heard it as it relates to me. Likewise, Daisy heard her part in it. Some parts vary and some aspects of it do not seem to change."

I held up one hand to stop him. "Wait. What do you mean, do not seem to change? There isn't one prophecy?"

Alex sat again, his expression deflated, as Turel answered. "There is and there isn't, Siobhan. As an oracle examines the future, some points are fixed and others are in flux. There's a balance between destiny and free will. Different people will make different choices. Each choice will affect what comes. Each person touches the prophecy differently and so, colors the Oracle's reading with their future. Dragons are such an old and powerful force; Daisy's presence makes the reading more about her and less about you. And we really need to hear about your part."

"Why?" Tim asked, his fingers beating a restless rhythm on the swing.

Daisy smiled at me and spread her hands out. "Because no one's ever heard it. We've known she would come someday, and she would make the choice, but no one knows exactly how it will happen because she's never been to an oracle. Now is our chance to hear how Siobhan is supposed to carry out what she was born to do."

I bit my lip. "Somehow I thought prophecies were supposed to tell you what is going to happen for sure."

Turel smiled at me. "If it were already certain, we wouldn't need to live it. We'll be hearing what could happen."

Alex stood again. "So, she'll tell us how we can win?" he asked.

"Hopefully," said Turel.

* * *

Our drive to Monte Rio proved uneventful. A tense excitement filled the Jeep. We left Leia with Daisy. In the silence, I missed the German shepherd's comforting presence.

As we expected, it did not take long to arrive at Monte Rio. Alex passed under the large white and green sign that read, "Welcome to Monte Rio-Vacation Wonderland." I stifled a laugh, a case of the church giggles. Picturesque Monte Rio sits right on the Russian River, but Vacation Wonderland seemed, in my mind, to be stretching things.

Turel directed Alex to turn off the main road, and we headed away from the river, deeper into the redwood-covered hills. On a small, side street, scattered houses stood neglected and hidden among the trees. We stopped and parked at one home, even shabbier than its neighbors.

The small lavender house desperately needed a good coat of paint and an energetic gardener. What passed for the front yard displayed a chaotic collection of whimsical statues, signs with environmental slogans, and various potted, half-dead flowers made valiant efforts at survival.

Turel rapped on the door while we trailed awkwardly behind him. After a moment, a pale young man with light brown hair answered the knock. "Oh, hey, dude, it's you," the young man said, his nervous eyes flicking over each of our faces. "Like, come in. I'll let Missy know you're here." His prominent Adam's apple moved when he spoke.

He ushered us into the darkened living room. Beads dangled in the doorway opposite to us, which led to the rest of the small house. The young man went through them, calling, "Missy, the glow dude is back, babe."

The room he left us in smelled of sickly-sweet incense. I wrinkled my nose. The incense masked the stale, lingering smell of cigarettes, pot, and unwashed humanity. Posters for the band Phish, dream catchers, and God's Eyes' resplendent in their popsicle stick and brightly colored yarn glory concealed the walls. Throw rugs and bean bags covered the floor surrounding a battered wooden coffee table. The young man returned leading a woman, presumably Missy, by one skinny hand.

I'm not sure what I expected from an oracle, but Missy sure didn't fit the bill. Lank, pale hair fell just past her shoulders. Missy's locks couldn't be called blonde so as much as colorless, the pigment leached away. She wore a few random braids and a roach clip secured some ragged feathers on one side of her head. Her protruding gray eyes seemed too large for her thin, fined-boned features. She wore fraying cut-off jean shorts, exposing pale legs. Her knobby knees lent Missy the fleeting impression of a young colt. She seemed childlike, not more than a teenager. Viewing her, past the bracelets and the tie-dyed T-shirt that read, "Who Would Jesus Bomb?", I wondered how old she was.

As I studied her I saw the conflicting images now becoming familiar to me. Spirits hovered around the pale girl. A wizened crone with burning eyes fought a lurking shadow. Through the cloud of these eddying specters shone the light of Missy herself, a young soul fighting for control of her own body. I blinked, trying to use Daisy's advice and focus on the strongest presence, hoping the others would fade. However, all three images remained wrapped in a struggle so balanced none of the three had control.

"Hello," Missy said. She spoke to one side of me, as though to a little person only she could see perched on my shoulder. I involuntarily turned my head to check, but couldn't find anything.

Missy saw my gesture. "I don't do eye contact mostly," she commented to the wall behind me. "Easier that way." She giggled to herself.

The young man guided her to a bean bag. "Here, babe, sit here. Can I get you anything? Kombucha? Tab? What do you need?" He seemed tender, but worried.

Her misty gray eyes shifted from my general direction to his. "It's okay, Leo. I'm fine. Just sit with me, all right? I need to know you're here, beside me." Leo took a bean bag next to her, his anxious eyes never drifting from her drawn face.

Missy giggled again, a high-pitched, strange laugh. "Sit, friends, and I'll tell you what I see." She gave a vague wave to the bean bags surrounding the low table and waited, humming to herself.

Turel promptly took a bean bag, his movements elegant and sure. He raised one eyebrow at us as we hesitated. "You heard the lady," he urged.

I moved closer to Tim and Alex. When I took a spot around the table, they followed my example. As I peered around the room, I was struck by how wane and colorless Missy and Leo appeared, even with Missy's ever present spirit show enveloping her. By comparison, Turel, Alex and Tim radiated color, strength and vitality. I glanced at my own limbs and clothes and realized we glowed.

Missy met my eyes at last. "Tools of destiny, brightly shining, hear me." Her voice commanded, deeper and stronger than the wispy one she'd used a moment before. She blinked several times and shifted her gaze away from mine. I saw her shudder as the turmoil around her, a struggle only I saw, intensified. Leo stroked her back, his young face serious.

Missy hummed again. I thought I recognized the song. Her head tilted this way and that as she watched the three of us, ignoring Turel. She pulled her knees up and wrapped her arms around them, making herself into a ball on the bean bag. The oracle gave a high laugh and said in a little girl's sing-song voice,

"Hickory, dickory dock,
You just can't stop the clock.
You've lost but won,
The battle's begun.
Hickory, dickory dock."

She started as though surprised to hear herself speak. Missy hit her forehead again and again with the flat of one hand. "Silly, monkey. Stop it, stop it." She kept striking herself until Leo grabbed her arm, speaking softly to her.

For a moment she leaned against him, breathing in shallow gasps. She inhaled and drew herself up, sitting cross-legged on her bean bag. Her gray eyes flickered between the light gray and an intense silver color. "Tools of Destiny," she began.

"Wait, you mean, all of us? Not just Siobhan?" Alex interrupted.

Turel held up one hand and frowned at my brother. "Yes, to both questions," he said sternly. "Now, do not waste time. She cannot See for long. Do not squander her vision."

Tim swore under his breath and took out his phone, but otherwise the three of us remained quiet. Turel nodded in satisfaction and said to Missy. "Lady, please continue."

"Wait," said Tim apologetically, holding up his phone. "Can I record this, please?"

Missy acknowledged first the angel and Tim with a gracious dip of her head. Rich and full her changed voice continued, "Tools of Destiny, words I have for you and only for you." The seer paused, her eyes burning silver, so bright I wanted to look away from those blazing orbs, but she fixed each of us individually with her gaze. Tim flinched when her eyes met his. The oracle's words came surely and eloquent.

"Words of strength, but some of pain, this day I say to you,
Three golden trips mark the time for what you need to do.
For love, honor and faith the Guardian is there,
If everyone is gone, beg him stay, for love survives only if you dare.

Know what you've loved you will not keep,
Defender of Man has souls to reap.
Honor the Lord and answer her call,
Chooser of the Slain will be with you at the end of it all.

When the child who sees becomes the one who could,
That's the day evil defeats good.
Then lost sister and brother the blood shall wake
For Gracious Sight a blind leap she then must take.
In the Righteous' last breath it will be shown,
What once was Veiled shall become known.

With the Defender of Man, you'll find the door,
The path that is true you can't See anymore.
Beware the King with ancient eyes of grey,
But beware so much more his Lady, Queen of the Fey."

Missy's words echoed and faded away. The hairs on my arms stood on end. The prophecy's words conjured pictures in my head, the stuff of nightmares. Missy blinked and glanced around. "I have seen one thing more," she began, her rich voice fading. She shuddered and her shoulders drooped. She tilted her head to one side, grasping her knees in her arms again and with a finger conducted an invisible orchestra. She began humming. Her tune became manic as she got louder and louder. Missy giggled like a small child and tossed her hair back.

"Roses are red, violets are blue,
There's nowhere to hide,
Black god's coming for you."

Missy laughed again, shrill and high, like a gull's cry. I shivered as her gray eyes went black, the irises becoming indistinguishable from the pupils. The blue-black filled her body as she released her knees, leaning forward, one hand twisted like a talon. Missy's head contorted in an impossible angle, her face upside-down, murky eyes regarding us with open malevolence. Her voice rasped in a hoarse, wicked whisper,

"One, two,
There's no hope for you.
Three, four,
She'll open the door.
Five, six,
Two swords to fix.
Seven, eight,
It's your blood that's great.
Nine, ten,
Never dance again."

Missy's head snapped back as though a puppeteer controlled her limbs and her slender body convulsed. Leo and Turel both sprang forward. Missy's companion stroked her shoulders, trying to calm her. He whispered, "I love you."

Turel's healing golden light bathed all three of them, and his eyes were sad. After a moment she stilled. When she raised her head, her eyes shone misty gray once more, but not vacant. "It wants you," she whispered piteously, her gaze locked with mine.

Chapter Ten

"She used to be different," said Leo with a sad smile as he reclined on a bean bag. "Before these wacky visions, you'd never even think it could be the same girl. She's just nineteen." He bent his head and massaged his forehead with both hands. Without glancing up, he continued, "I'm wigging out, man."

It took Turel and Leo the better part of a half an hour to comfort Missy. The oracle collapsed, exhausted and terrified, crying in small sobs like a lost child. Leo insisted she rest. The pain on the young man's face added years to his features. Fortune shone on Missy in one respect; someone loved her very much.

Turel put a comforting hand on the young man's arm. His dark olive skin made a stark contrast against Leo's pallor. "It should not to be like this for her, my friend," the angel said.

Tim shook his head, his usual smile absent. "What do you mean, Turel?"

I leaned closer. We kept our voices low in consideration of the tortured young woman in the next room. Turel's handsome face was drawn. "You saw them?"

"Saw who?" I thought for a second and realized who Turel meant. "Oh, the old woman and the thing, wow. Yeah, I saw them. What on earth?"

"I'm missing something here," Alex looked back and forth at us while Leo and Tim waited. I bit my lip at the tears welling in Leo's eyes.

"In the usual development of an oracle," said Turel, "a young girl or woman will begin to display gifts, usually in a primitive way. Basic visions that aren't too far in the future."

"Like the twisted nursery rhymes?" asked Tim.

"She's always done those, ever since it started," said Leo, sitting straighter. "I used to think they were funny, sort of cute."

"The Missy part said that," I said. "The deeper, more confident voice came from the old lady and then the black-eyed, um-" I broke off, at a loss for a word that wouldn't be offensive to Leo.

"Exorcist nightmare," said Alex. My brother, as usual, did not share my scruples.

"Right." I frowned at him. "The exorcist nightmare part with the demented rhymes, well, that was the thing. They are fighting for control."

"Control of what?" asked Alex.

"Of Missy," I said.

"Why? What's the big deal?" asked Alex.

"Intelligence," said Turel. "Humanity and dragon-kind can only triumph through achieving a tight set of conditions which Missy has detailed for us. The other side has no seer. They can win in a variety of ways, one by denying Siobhan access to her Choice."

"Like the Universe balancing the scales," I mused. "We have more restrictions, but we have an oracle. They have more ways to win, but no one to tell them what to do."

"Unless the demon can take Missy," said Turel grimly. "Evil will know Siobhan's path. Then mankind will surely perish."

"So, who's the old woman Siobhan's seeing?" wondered Tim. "And, what is this thing? A demon?"

"Ugh, yes." I shuddered. "I hate to think about it. It gives me the creeps, like Chernobog did."

Turel nodded at me. "Exactly so, they share a similar evil nature, from a similar source."

"Can you see it?" Alex's voice rose as he spoke.

I leaned over and patted his hand. He gave me a half-smile in response.

Turel continued, "I cannot see as Siobhan does, no one observes as the Watcher sees, but I can sense certain presences and yes, when demonic elements are close by, I can see them, too, just as they can perceive me."

"And, the old woman?" Tim asked.

"She's another oracle, an older, wiser seer, come to help Missy," said Turel. "There are few oracles. Sometimes a whole lifetime goes by without one being born. Sometimes the only way to train an oracle is through a spirit guide, but Missy has been fighting hers."

"Yeah, man." Leo bobbed his head in agreement at the angel. "Dude, she was afraid she might be, like, losing her mind."

"No, loss of reason is not the problem here." Turel frowned. "Her instruction should have been completed already. Missy should be strong enough to handle her abilities alone by now. This resistance of the Oracle has given the creature an opening to use Missy. In time, if unchecked, it will devour her."

A shocked silence enveloped the room.

Tim repeated, "An oracle?"

Turel rubbed his beard, deep in thought. "The Oracle of Delphi, of course, that's the other woman, Missy's spirit guide."

"You're joking," I said. I learned about the Oracle of Delphi in my history classes. Kings and queens, priests and artists had gone to the oracle of ancient Greece for advice and counsel for centuries.

"No, it's true. I've known her for ages. I recognized her right off."

It struck me anew at that moment—Turel was not what he appeared. Just when I became accustomed to this smart, funny, sexy man, something like this reference to the mythical oracle of ancient Greece came along and reminded me he was not a man at all. He was an angel who had been alive for millennia and would live ages more. As I dealt with the sheer number of his probable age, the angel's eyes met mine and he beamed at me. His expression brought sunshine to the dim, incense filled room. Lifted up, I smiled back and decided of all the things I had to worry about, Turel's possible age didn't matter.

A soft cry emanated from the next room. Leo rose to his feet in a flash. He hurried to the bedroom where we heard the muffled sounds of two people speaking softly. In only a moment he returned, standing in the beaded doorway. "Missy wants to, like, see you." Leo beckoned to me.

"Why me?" I asked as I crossed the room, but Leo didn't answer. He stood to one side and held an arm out, indicating the bedroom door. My heart hammered in my chest. "Should we go?" I asked Turel. "The creature is there. It isn't safe. Shouldn't we leave? We have what we came for."

The angel's ebony brows drew together. "Siobhan," he chided, "she is a fellow soul in need. We cannot abandon her."

My cheeks burned. I bit my lip and joined Leo, my face still hot. Missy needed our help. I didn't like myself very much right then.

Turel followed me like a silent, dark shadow. Leo made a move as though he would have liked to prevent Turel from accompanying me, but Turel preempted any protest by cautioning, "If it takes control, I'll need to be there to stop it."

I didn't need to ask what "it" the angel referred to. I tried to control my trembling as I opened the door and stepped inside to see Missy.

A mattress lay on the floor in the middle of the room. Missy lay on her side under the covers. Drawn shades blocked the afternoon sun, but someone had switched on the small lamp next to her. Lacking chairs, Turel and I sat on the floor next to the mattress, our backs against the wall.

Missy stirred, again, not making direct eye contact. She pulled herself higher and used the pillows to prop herself the way a child would. This close to her I saw dark circles around her eyes like bruises on her fair skin. "Like, hey," she said in a vague way, "thanks, Turel." Her misty gray eyes moved in Turel's direction.

"You can look at me, Seer," he said. "It would be good for you to view me."

She shrank back at his words. "It gets angry when I do."

"Another reason why you should," Turel said to her. "You should open the blinds, too, let the sun shine on you, go outside."

Missy frowned. "But it hurts."

"Light only hurts the demon."

I watched the two of them, wondering why she wanted to see me, not sure what to say. My vision of them held me: Turel with his calm strength and the kindness in his dark eyes shining forth, Missy with her swirling aura of conflict. The ancient oracle became dominant and fixed her burning silver eyes on me.

Missy blinked and made eye contact with me for the barest of moments. "I need to speak to you, Watcher, alone."

Turel frowned and folded his arms. "I cannot leave her alone with the demon, Oracle. You spoke the prophecy, you know she is both needed and in danger."

Missy's eyes blazed and met Turel's. "Turiel, the child will be protected."

Turel's eyebrows rose in surprise. "Oracle, are you in control?"

Missy's shoulders shrugged and her mouth quirked in a smile too wise for a nineteen-year-old's face. "We are in accord for the moment, she and I. Perhaps it is not too late for her."

Turel hesitated. He said in a stern voice, "I have your word, Pythia?"

"Yes." The smile that did not fit grew wider. "You remembered. Thank you, Turiel. It is good to hear my name spoken after so many years."

Turel rose and gave a slight bow to the Seer. "You are more than the title you've carried. You are still a person." He paused and then continued, "Oracle, Watcher, I shall be right outside if you should need me, either of you." His worried eyes caught mine as he left, taking the sunshine from the room with him.

I turned to the seer. "How can I help?"

Missy shook her head. "She's busy. It's just me right now." She sat cross-legged, her palms resting on her angled lap. "Your eyes, they are so different, like, *really* green. Are you studying me? It's like you see everything. What do I look like to you? Are you an oracle, too?"

I blinked. "No, my vision doesn't work like yours. I See what is, exactly what is."

"I don't get it."

"Well, if you lie, I know it."

"Cool," she said. "What else?"

"I don't know, all sorts of things, I can see angels, demons, doors to and from other dimensions. At the age of five I found a hidden dragon." I realized I spoke with confidence. For the first time in my life, I told what I saw with pride, no fear of disbelief or censure. Not only that, I spoke to someone with abilities of their own. For a moment being the Watcher did not seem like such a bad thing. I smiled inside. No more doctors for me.

"And me," she pressed, "what about me?"

I shook my head. "I think you know what I see. I see you, I see the Oracle, and I see the monster. All three of you are fighting for control of this body and those magical eyes."

"Watcher," she said, "why are they in me? What do they want? How can I get rid of them?"

"Them?"

"The old woman and the monster," she said. "How can I make them leave?"

I explained to her what Turel told us about oracles, her training and spirit guides. Her gray gaze widened and she made eye contact with me. She pursed her lips and asked, "But, why the demon? How does that train me?"

"It doesn't," I said. "The way I understand it, this monster wants to use your Sight and consume you."

She shuddered. "It's, like, something that lived under my bed when I was little."

"It never could have found its way inside if you hadn't been wasting your energy trying to shut out the Oracle."

"So, she's, like, good?" Missy seemed doubtful.

"That's what I hear," I said. "She's a teacher, a friend."

"Great, some stranger, telling me what to do," said Missy. "Far out, not."

On impulse I leaned forward and grasped her slender hands in mine. They felt fragile, even birdlike. "I hear her name is Pythia."

Missy returned my squeeze and smiled the first real smile I'd seen on her face. To my surprise she spoke with strength, but completely Missy, no one else, "Pythia, you have something to say?"

Missy's eyes blazed and a rich chuckle rolled out of her lips. "Yes, young one, it's better to burn out than to fade away."

Missy's eyes burned in a mixture of blazing silver and misty gray. She laughed and I found myself laughing with the oracles, for I Saw both Missy and Pythia. After a moment, Missy collected herself, and from her posture and aura, Pythia took front and center. "Watcher," said the rich and distinctive tones of the Oracle of Delphi.

"Yes, Pythia."

The ghost of a smile crossed the seer's face at my use of her name. "I told you, I saw one more thing." I realized I held my breath as she paused. "Watcher, hear this last gift, I have for you." She hesitated again before her fiery silver eyes caught and held mine.

When the Guardian's passion shall surely wake,
Then the Black God's last prison chain will break.

"Young one, Watcher," she said to me, as a chill ran through my body. I knew of only one instance where someone had mentioned a final chain breaking, Chernobog. I'd do anything to keep that from happening. Even the thought of the demon's evil stench made my knees go weak, like I had to run away, like I *would* run away.

"Siobhan," she said urgently, though I did not recall anyone telling her my name. "This *must* come to pass." Her brilliant eyes widened and the light in them faded as she uttered these last words, "*Trust in me.*"

* * *

Our weary group reached Daisy's house as evening gathered and the stars appeared in the sky. We spent many hours at Missy's house and although I had finally heard the prophecy, I had more questions than ever. Had we heard it all at last? I questioned Turel on its meaning, but he shook his head and shrugged. "Watcher, I cannot see our way clear yet," he said. "Yet, I know I must soon, for we have but three days."

"Three days?" we said in shock.

Turel studied the group. "Didn't anyone else hear the words,

'*Three golden trips mark the time of what you need to do?*'

"Oh, Holy Mother," swore Daisy. "He's right. That has to mean we have only three days. In three days this comes to a head."

"Does today count as one of the three?" asked Alex.

Three days? I sagged against the post of Daisy's porch as everyone else talked at once. Tim, Alex, Daisy and Turel had their opinions, but no one knew anything for certain. The peace of the night air beckoned me. I glanced behind me as I moved away. They would not miss me. I needed some time with my thoughts, perhaps even commune with my ultimate grandfather.

On the edge of Daisy's meadow, past the cottage, ran a split rail fence. That's where I headed. I didn't see as many shooting stars as when Daisy contemplated Father Sky; enough sparkled that after a while I felt at peace with the universe.

"You okay, Siobhan?" Tim's hushed tones pierced the darkness behind me. I leaned against the fence in the warm night air as he joined me. Like the previous evening, the moon illuminated the sky. I could not count the stars. Daisy's house rested far away from the interfering glow of a city. Tim stood close enough for our shoulders to touch, his handsome face lit by the moon. His familiar presence soothed, a welcome relief after the stresses of the day.

"I'm fine," I answered, my voice also hushed.

"Humph," he said. "If I recall, fine does not equal good, as in a code for something completely *not* good like, 'you ate my last meatball' or 'I totally saw you check her out.' Fine is bad. It's a four lettered word starting with f."

A smile tugged at the corners of my mouth in spite of myself. "You have a good memory."

"Sometimes."

In the companionable silence, I put my head on my folded arms and exhaled deeply, trying to clear the chaos in my mind the prophecy had unleashed there. Tim's strong hands gently kneaded my tight shoulders. "That feels heavenly," I said.

"I'll bet. You're knotted up."

A weary chuckle escaped my lips. "Yeah, well, it's been one

of those days."

"Tell me about it. Looks like the next couple are going to be doozies, too."

"I know, I know."

Doubts, questions, and worries weighed me down, but I had to set them aside. I needed my sleep tonight so I could function at my best in the coming days. "I told you, I'm fine." I pulled away from him.

Tim, knowing me better than almost anyone, persisted. "And I told you, fine sucks. Come here, you dork."

"Doofus," I shot back without missing a beat, but I let him gather me into his embrace. My arms wrapped around his waist of their own volition. One of his hands stroked my hair, and I sighed, relaxing further into his arms.

"We'll figure it out. You'll see, it will be okay, and then we'll go home."

For a moment, I let my mind go blank, and I took comfort in holding another person, feeling someone else's heartbeat, and the reassuring weight of him against me. Something subtle changed, and I became very aware of Tim, every line of his body, every breath he drew, and my pulse quickened. His arm around me tightened, and the hand that caressed my hair moved, pressing the back of my neck. I felt, more than heard, the barest of whispers, "Sh'belle" before his mouth covered mine.

Tim and I stand at about the same height, a wonderful thing when we were lovers. Our forms fit together, by instinct finding the best angles. There may have been years apart, but our bodies remembered every nuance, every touch. My lips opened under his. At that moment, it did not seem possible to be close enough to him. Our kiss deepened, and I ran my hands under his shirt and over his back, reveling in the smooth skin and hard muscle I touched.

His hand slid down the curve of my spine and over my hip, pressing me more firmly against him. I gasped in pleasure. My breath exhaled in a kind of ragged sensual shudder. No thought mattered now. Worry fled, leaving just him, only him.

Tim trailed kisses across my jaw and down the most sensitive part of my neck using the slightest tip of his tongue to send shivers of delight through me. As he worked his way to soft skin above my breasts he whispered, "I always knew you'd come home to me."

"To you? What?" I disentangled myself from his arms.

"It's true, isn't it? Admit it, you and I belong together."

"Not this again," I muttered. "Tim, I can't do this same conversation again. Not now, not with so much at stake."

"You love me, Siobhan, I know you do," Tim protested, taking a step toward me. "And Alex said you'd gotten engaged once, so I know you got over your whole never getting married thing."

"That was different."

"How?" Tim's eyes widened.

I lowered my voice and took a deep breath. "I guess, I don't know, maybe I said yes because deep down I knew it would never happen." With a sinking sensation in the pit of my stomach, I realized the truth. I'd said yes to Chuck's proposal because on some level the relationship was doomed. I'd been safe. I'd been safe and heartbroken all at once. What a neat trick. Bitterness rose inside me.

"Wait, you didn't come home for me?"

"No, I didn't have a job, but I inherited a house. Where else would I live?"

"But, then Alex called and I thought…" Tim broke off as he studied my face.

"What?"

"I thought—"

"Timothy Macauley Collins, did you think I wanted to beg you back? Using my kitchen?"

He shrugged, still examining the ground by our feet. I put each of my hands on his cheeks, cupping his face so he would look at me. "I care about you, Tim. I always have and always will, but I'm not going to settle down and raise your fat babies."

"You love me, Siobhan." The set of his jaw hardened.

"Yes, I do," I admitted. "Why can't that be enough? Why can't we love each other and simply be? Why does it always need to come back to marriage?"

He grasped my two hands, his heart in his eyes. "It just does, Siobhan. Can't you see? I am a marrying kind of guy."

An old, familiar resentment boiled in my chest. The blood pounded in my temples. I exhaled. "But, I am not a marrying kind of girl. Never have been. I can't see that changing now."

"I don't believe you." Tim's voice rang with sincerity.

"That's the problem, Tim. That's always been the problem," I said, as all the worries and cares of the day settled back on my shoulders. "But right now, I'm going to bed." I broke away from him and didn't turn back. I ignored the sense of déjà vu that came over me.

Chapter Eleven

I woke filled with the dreadful certainty that I was not alone. Blinking, I tried to see around me. In the faint light, I discerned the shape of a man sitting in a chair by the window. I started to cry out when I realized a faint, growing luminosity filled the room. It came from me. I glowed with a silvery light. A slender illuminated cord came off me, traveling upward. Pulses of energy flowed along the cord away from my body, leaving me drained and weak. Movement seemed incredibly difficult, impossible. As my eyes followed the shining strand aloft, I saw in sick horror that some kind of creature hovered above me.

I couldn't figure out at first if this dreadful phantasm actually lived. Fragile, paper-like skin covered its skeletal frame. She? He? I couldn't say, but the thing's emaciation made it difficult to tell if skin actually covered those bones. The thing appeared all cheekbones, its features shrunken and shriveled. The being possessed wild, wispy hair so white it shone in the shimmering glow projected from my body. The strands floated in all directions around the apparition as did its robes, more rags than clothing. I was grateful for anything shrouding any part of the wraith-like figure.

I'll never, for all my days, be able to explain the dread radiating from its presence. The sensation came from the thing's eyes. They burned with an electric red, yet, this flame burned in a cold fire, devoid of any warmth or compassion. Though it wore a humanoid form, nothing remotely human emanated from it.

I drew in breath to scream for Daisy, Turel, anyone. More than anything I wanted to call for help, to be as loud as possible.

Instead, I whimpered. No other sound came. The thing turned its withered head to the man in the chair. "Abraxas, it speaks. Never do they talk."

. "That's because they usually don't wake up and even if they did, they couldn't see you," explained the man named Abraxas. "This one is special."

"Yes," it rasped. "I see it is. I like it, so delicious, my ducky." The thing's voice rasped as thin and emaciated as its form. The death rattle sound of those words conjured nightmares from the dark corners of my mind, places where nameless terrors lurked, and my fears scurried like beetles under a rock. The faint smell of death and decay clung to the air around us.

"What are you?" I managed to whisper. My voice sounded faint, a breath, nothing more.

The thing floating over me cackled, an insane, evil sound. "Now it speaks to me. I love its fear. See it? So pretty, wants to run and hide, but can barely move." It drifted an inch or two closer to me and I cringed, but couldn't look away; its hellish eyes consumed me. "Soon it will never move again. Never, ever move, little pig."

Abraxas snorted at the creature. "Why the pet names, Hag?"

The nightmare above me reached out with one bony finger as though to tap my face. Locked inside my head, I became a screaming, gibbering thing, beyond rational thought. It didn't touch me though; it moved the finger back and forth as though conducting an invisible orchestra, its blood-red eyes burning into me. "It is food for me. I am calling it food names it understands, so it will know, it will suffer. Going to eat you, pretty lamb, eat you up." It made a slithering noise, a slurping sound.

I strained again to scream, but only mustered a gasp. "Why? What are you?" Speech grew even more difficult. The draining left me a shadow of myself. So tired, so very tired.

Abraxas shifted in his chair and fumbled around in his pockets. The faint flick of a lighter registered and then came a small flame as he lit a cigar. As he puffed furiously I had my first glimpse of his face and shuddered. Abraxas wasn't human.

I'd lay odds he looked human to anyone else gazing upon him. However, to my eyes, even weakened, I saw the clever-faced demonic visage peering out from under the sharply dressed businessman exterior. It was as if he wore a people suit. He smiled at me with wickedly pointed teeth. Abraxas puffed on the cigar and remarked in a matter-of-fact voice, "You should save your strength. I have already answered your question."

"Yes," hissed the creature above me. "Save for me, all of you for me."

I made my lips move. "No, you didn't."

The sound came out so softly, I didn't know if I said it out loud, but Abraxas heard me anyway. His eyebrows flipped up in surprise. He leaned forward, exposing short, pointy horns on his head like a goat, or to more accurate, like a devil. He puffed his cigar. "Certainly, I answered you, she's a Hag."

"Hag," agreed the terrifying vision above me. "Riding you, taking you, soon all gone."

Abraxas shrugged. "She calls it riding, I say eating. She's draining your life force, your will to live."

"And fear, Abraxas, fear and hope. I take them all, yes, ducky."

Abraxas crossed and re-crossed his legs in an impatient gesture. "Get on with it. We need to finish before Turiel returns. I don't want to be meat for that tiger."

The Hag snarled at him, "No rush me."

"Oh fine, have it your way," Abraxas grumbled, glancing at his watch. He smiled a nasty grin. "Just think, Watcher, if you had left a broomstick by your bed, folklore says she'd have been forced to ride away on it, instead of riding your spirit. A broomstick, isn't that the craziest thing you've ever heard?" He chuckled, an evil sound, and shook his head. "You can't make this shit up, I tell you."

The Hag exhaled in a quivering, rattling way. The sound created images of broken body parts and decomposing flesh rolling through my mind as I shuddered again in pain and fear. She commanded Abraxas, saying, "We go now. No nasty angel and I take little lamb with me. I drain her slowly, play with her forever."

Her eyes burned like two pits of hellish fire as she examined me again. "So special, so delicious, little piggy."

"No, the Black God wants this finished before Gwyrdd can find a way back to this world. I didn't hire you for playtime," snapped Abraxas. "Finish and let's get out of here."

"No broomsticks," said the Hag. "Bad Abraxas."

He held up his hands. "Right, no broomsticks. Just hurry up."

"Poor ducky," said the Hag, gloating.

Somewhere in the back of my mind, I remembered in a drifting way a program I had once seen on television. It was a wildlife show, one of those safari ones. Some lions ambushed a zebra and began to eat the poor animal before it even died. I remember being shocked at the way the zebra lay there, waiting to die, waiting to lose enough blood to bring on oblivion. I was the zebra now. My body grew colder. It no longer seemed important enough or worth the effort to be terrified, although the Hag looked even more frightening now as she fed on me. The more of my life force she consumed, the brighter she burned luminescent, as I faded. As she devoured me, she became more substantial.

The faint odor of an open rotting grave became a ripe, overwhelming stench. If I could have gagged, I would have. All thoughts of escape, of curiosity, vanished as I waited for the end. The Hag smiled, showing rotten, yellow bits of teeth, her evil, red eyes danced. In her deathly voice she said, "Good chickie. Good. Never moves again. No, it doesn't want to. It belongs to me. Mine."

Something stirred in me at that moment. I didn't belong to her. I belonged to me. No one else got to decide who I was or who I belonged to. I spent my whole life hanging on to my sense of self. No one else, not even a supernatural Hag sucking out my life force, and killing me in my own bed got to take that away from me. If ten different psychiatrists and more prescriptions than I could count hadn't changed my mind, then I'd be damned if I'd let her decide for me.

There in the darkness, with my glimmer disappearing and a chill enveloping my limbs, I found a small spark inside of me, a stubborn iota of will. I searched my mind, seeking some way out. Then I did the only thing I had left, the only recourse still in my power. I prayed.

I didn't pray to God. At the time, I don't think it ever even crossed my mind to pray to Him. I didn't have the strength of Tim's quiet faith. Still, I knew who I needed. I prayed to Turel, only this time I called him Turiel. I prayed to him, partly in my heart, partly through lips like ice; lips gone numb. I prayed with fervor, hanging on to the spark even as I grew still colder, darker, and the Hag above me glowed in stolen radiance.

My breath slowed, and I fought for each inhalation. Each heartbeat echoed through the room. That, too, slowed. My world reduced to these things: breathing and my heartbeat. Still my frozen lips moved and my spark of will pushed my prayers out into the universe. With my vision blurred as Abraxas regarded his cigar from his chair. He tapped his foot, frowning at us.

The Hag tilted her head in a gesture that in her hideousness suggested a caricature of a human's movement. She seemed puzzled. "It is saying something, Abraxas. This I do not understand. What does my duck say?" She leaned closer and the stench of death and decay enveloped me. Still I prayed.

"What is it?" asked Abraxas, impatient.

The withered Hag tilted her head. "I do not remember the word for what it does. It is asking for help," she answered. "It does not know no help will come? What a strange lamb it is." She shrugged her now much more substantial shoulders, her hideous features twisting in concentration. "Ah, Abraxas," she continued in her gruesome voice, "I remember the word. My piggy prays."

Abraxas sprang to his feet in alarm. "She prays? To whom?"

CRACK!

A bolt of lightning exploding in the small room blinded my eyes. Turel appeared in its flash, his face drawn in a snarl, glorious wings extended. Sunlight, beautiful, sweet sunlight, filled my night shrouded bedroom. Turel took one look at me and the Hag over me. "She prays to me," he roared. His arm drew back in a graceful arc and a second bolt of lightning shot toward me.

The Hag's back arched when the bolt struck. The draining stopped and my heartbeat steadied as I took an unimpeded breath. The Hag dematerialized. Starting with her feet and working upward, she disintegrated. Bits of her scattered like ashes on the wind, twinkling for a brief second, and then disappearing. As she went, she fixed her repugnant, blood-red gaze on me one last time. "Bad ducky," she lamented. Then she disappeared.

Turel turned to Abraxas, but the chair stood empty. Through the open window the sound of rapid footfalls grew fainter. With a growl, Turel started toward the window, but stopped and examined me. The sunlight faded from the room, leaving the angel glowing golden in the dark. "Watcher?" he gasped and rushed to me. "Watcher, talk to me, say anything."

I wanted to answer him, I did, but all I could do was lie frozen on my bed and think about breathing. At that moment, my job consisted of clinging to life. I struggled to keep the oxygen flowing. Turel gathered me and held me close to him, searching my eyes. "Oh, merciful Heaven," he swore ardently, "Siobhan?" His voice broke on my name. "Gwyrdd," Turel called, "Gwyrdd. Come to me."

Everything around me glowed golden, wrapping us in amber light. I basked in the shimmery light which held us both. Yearned for sensation flooded my limbs in the sheltering warmth.

The light faded and Turel laid me back on the bed. He straightened, his expression focused. I heard the off-key resonance I remembered from the night at my house. Strange to think what had happened in only a couple of days. A melodic sound danced almost, but not quite, out of my range of hearing. He called another angel.

First Daisy, then Nefta stepped through dimensions into my bedroom. The returning warmth to my body brought on a delirium of pleasure and relief. Getting crowded in here, resisting the near-hysteric urge to giggle.

Nefta sized me up, taking in the situation. "Well? Out with it." Her words hit a brisk and businesslike beat.

"Hag," said Turel in a hard tone I had never heard him use before.

"How bad?" asked Daisy in a hushed voice.

"Bad, very bad."

I had a sudden, important thought, so overwhelming I needed to say it aloud. I tried to speak, but only the barest breath came forth. No one heard me. I whispered too soft even for an angel's incredible hearing. I focused every part of my being on moving my hand. My fingertips grazed across his jeans, enough to get his attention. "Yes, Watcher?" He sat with me, holding my hand in both of his.

"Alex, Tim," I whispered, forcing the words out.

Turel raised his head, his face stricken. "She's right. They didn't come running. I used a bolt, they should have heard."

Nefta moved at his first word. "On it." The blonde Valkyrie vanished before I could blink.

Daisy inspected the chair, her face set in a cold mask. She sniffed the air and turned toward Turel.

"He's getting away," Turel said in frustrated anger.

The woman who was a dragon held up one hand. "Not from me, dear one. Give me a moment. Let me know who I am following into the night."

Turel waited his impatience palpable. I concentrated on breathing. The world floated in and out of focus. Clinging to consciousness by my metaphorical fingernails, I listened to Turel and Daisy.

"Cigar," noted Daisy.

"Little weasel," Turel said, delivering the words like a curse.

"Abraxas will not be an issue," promised Daisy. She came to me and laid one gentle hand on my cheek. "Turel, she's like ice."

Turel shook his head; his chiseled features resembling a statue. He showed no more emotion, except for his clinched jaw and a certain grim set to his eyes. "You should have touched her when I first arrived. I can't imagine how she's still alive."

Daisy smiled at me. "Stubborn," she said, brushing my hair aside. I managed a small quirk of my mouth at her. "You can heal her?"

"I can. I will," he said. "Now, Abraxas? I must stay with the Watcher. I will not leave her again, not for anything."

"Agreed."

In a blink Daisy disappeared. The sound of immense wings filled the night air outside, fading into the distance. Turel stared out the window for a moment. I sensed more than heard the discordant music of another angel speaking to him and Turel's shoulders relaxed. The angel closed the window and came back to my bed.

He studied me before taking off his leather jacket and kicking off his shoes. Turel tucked his wings away. He pulled back the covers and slid in beside me still wearing his usual jeans and T-shirt. With no more effort than moving a cat, he lifted me across the bed, making room for himself, and slid me on to my side. Tucking the blankets around us both, he wrapped his arms around me. The soft aura of the angel's healing energy surrounded me, and I relaxed. Filling me up where earlier I had been drained.

"You are so cold. How can you bear it?" he asked.

"No, I feel warm," I said and though quiet, my words already came more easily.

"Only by comparison to what you were a short while ago. Your lips are blue and your skin is like ice."

"Believe me, this is better."

Turel squeezed me closer. "You'll need to help me, Watcher," Turel said.

Sleep closed in and I struggled to reply. "Sure."

"You need sleep, a deep, healing sleep. No dreams, and especially, no nightmares. I can ensure that for you, but I'll need to go into your mind. It won't be the same as with Gilbert, but it will be similar."

"You'll read my thoughts?" That had me more alert, even battling exhaustion.

"No, well, I mean, I'll try hard not to pry. Will you trust me?"

I smiled even though he wouldn't be able to see it. "Of course, Turel." My eyes hovered on the edge of closing. The covers enveloped me, warm and comfortable. Safe.

Turel placed one hand on the side of my head. "Sleep, Siobhan."

In my mind's eye, a simple wooden door appeared and Turel nudged me toward it. *Duh, way, way ahead of you, buddy.* Opening the door, I sank like a stone into unconsciousness, his deep chuckle in my ear.

Chapter Twelve

Someone spied on me again. This time green eyes, not red, terrorized me. Hate permeated my sleeping state. She'd always been watching me, all my life. I always had the dream. No, not a dream, my nightmare. A thought came. Details bubbled to my mind's surface, revealing an old fear, but then tumbled away, lost. I slumbered on.

Once again, I woke knowing I was not alone, but this time peace woke me, not terror.

I opened my eyes to late morning, maybe even midday. My limbs felt stiff, as though I had stayed in the same position too long. The odd prickle of being watched prompted me to roll on to my other side. A tingle of memory danced across my brain, but I couldn't recall my dream. Who spied on me?

Turel sat propped up by pillows regarding me. Today's T-shirt showed a Star Wars Storm Trooper's head and read, "Support Our Troops." "Great shirt," I said, propping myself up to lean on one arm, noting his somber and intent expression.

His shoulders sagged in relief and his smile blossomed. "Watcher, it's still you."

I frowned at him. "Hey, still me last night, too. What, do Hags have a body-snatcher clause in there somewhere?" Despite the horror of only a few hours ago energy and joy coursed through me. The euphoric feeling infused my entire being, body and mind.

He gave a soft laugh and shook his head. "Not everyone comes back after they've been so drained. You were close to death. Such a near thing, even with a night's Healing. I am very—", he paused and laughed again, "I am *extremely* happy to see you are one of the rare ones. Of course, we already knew that, yes? Bless you, Siobhan."

The worry faded and sunshine returned to his dark eyes. I loved his eyes both for their physical appearance and for the compassion and joy radiating from them. Now they considered mine. I blushed and didn't know how to respond.

For few seconds we stayed there, each watching the other. I found my voice. "I should get up, pull myself together, and find some food."

He got to his feet in a graceful motion. "I'll be right outside while you change and get cleaned up."

"Turel, it's okay, I don't need a bodyguard."

He crooked an eyebrow at me. "Oh, don't you?"

Feeling like an idiot I ducked my head. "Point taken, I'll be quick."

"I'll be right outside."

After the door closed I leaned against it, wondering what the new day held.

* * *

When I emerged twenty minutes later, I found everyone gathered in the living room of Daisy's home. I walked in, Turel at my shoulder like an angelic shadow, and saw Tim, Daisy, Nefta, and Alex focused on me with a collective air of expectation. I breathed a deep sigh of relief at seeing my loved ones there in one piece. My knees went weak in reaction. A great deal of everything I held dear in the world sat gathered in this room, and I gave a profound thank you to whatever God might be listening.

The tableau suggested a war council. Three deep-burgundy couches set in a U-shape in front of a large fireplace with a square coffee table in the middle of them. Opposite from the fireplace a huge picture window let in bright, summer sunshine. Tim and Daisy sat on couches, Alex sprawled on the third, wearing a foolish grin, his legs propped on the table. Nefta perched gracefully on an arm of the same sofa, composed, glancing now and then in a disapproving way at my handsome brother. Turel took a seat next to Tim. Tim watched every move I made, but I avoided meeting his eyes.

Hurrying to Alex, I threw my arms around my brother. "Thank God, you're okay." My deep sense of relief coupled with my amazing energy had me feeling like I could take on the world. Giving Alex another quick hug, I took a place next to Daisy.

Alex's smile widened. "Howdy, sis. How're things?"

Nefta's flawless brow creased in a frown. "Shhh, young Alex."

Alex gave an irreverent salute. "Rightie-O."

I examined Alex. Even by his casual standards, my brother's attitude verged on downright flippant. "What's with him? He's okay, right?" I indicated my goofy-faced sibling. "Tim? Daisy? What happened last night?"

Daisy put one arm around me, squeezing briefly. "He's fine, Siobhan. I'll explain in a moment. More importantly, how are you faring this morning?"

I ran a hand through my tangled curls, wishing I'd pulled them back. "I'm good, Daisy. Actually, I can honestly say I've never felt better, which is weird, right? After the Hag last night, shouldn't I be a mess today?"

Daisy waved a hand at Turel. "That would be due to Turel, dear one. He stayed with you all night, replacing the life energy you lost. So, too, did Nefta for your brother."

My eyes went first to Turel and then to Alex and Nefta. My heart rate accelerated. "Two Hags," I whispered, "there were two Hags?"

Nefta nodded curtly. "Even so, Watcher."

"Thank you," I began, but I couldn't find words big enough for the emotions running through me.

Nefta inclined her head and gestured to Turel. "And now, friend Watcher, we have Gifted you. You and your brother are part angel."

In confusion, I turned to Daisy. "It's true enough, child. You've received angel life force. Though still human, you'll never be what you once were," she said.

"Wait, you healed Gilbert, too. Does that mean he's part angel?" I asked.

"No," said Turel. "There is a big difference between simply

healing and receiving an angel's life force."

Panic flooded through me. "Tim, were you? I mean, did a third hag attack?"

Tim made a face, and said, "Nope, just the two. I, err, couldn't sleep, so I went for a walk. I got back and the place seemed deserted until Daisy found me and filled me in on the Hags."

"Freaky deeky," said Alex, staring out the window.

"That's one way to put it." I shuddered. "Don't ever call me ducky."

"Sorry, I didn't catch that?" asked Tim.

"Nothing," I muttered.

Daisy continued, "Alex did not experience as much danger as you, dear. First of all, he's bigger than you, so the draining went more slowly and, second, the Hag Nefta pulled off him was not nearly as old and powerful as the one Turel destroyed. Abraxas didn't take any chances. His mission was the Watcher drained and gone."

"I heard him say the Black God wanted me dead," I added in a soft voice.

"Who is Abraxas?" asked Alex. "Abraxas, that's a funny word, isn't it? Abraxas."

At the same time, I said, "Who's the Black God? That's in the prophecy, right?"

We mortals watched as the supernatural beings in the room exchanged glances. It reminded me of watching the adults decide if the kids were old enough to learn about a grown-up topic.

Tim shook his head at me. "No," he said. "Not the prophecy. One of Missy's rhymes, remember? *'Roses are red, violets are blue, there's nowhere to hide'…*"

"*Black God's coming for you,*" finished Alex with a laugh. I tried to ignore the chill on the back of my neck as I remembered another reference to the Black God from Missy/Pythia. "*Black God's last prison chain will break.*" I debated whether to say anything about those lines spoken to me alone.

With a start I realized Nefta glared at me. "Yes?" I looked around guiltily. I hadn't been listening.

"I said, how much do you remember?"

"Everything, I think." I shrugged. Even in the bright sunlight with the life force of an angel in me, I didn't want to reflect too closely on last night.

"What can you tell us? Did they know whose house this is? How did they find you? Did they know you were the Watcher?" asked Nefta, leaning forward. Her pose and intense gaze reminded me of a bird of prey.

Daisy started to say something, but I held up a hand. "No, it's okay. I remember." I took a breath, collecting my thoughts. "Let's see. They didn't mention you, Nefta, of course, you hadn't been with us in a couple of days, but they did know Turel was around. Abraxas seemed nervous. He didn't want Turel to catch him."

I waved one hand toward Turel and added, "He called you Turiel though." He nodded. I continued, "They didn't know Daisy returned. Abraxas said the Black God wanted me dead before Gwyrdd found her way back to this world."

"Excellent," said Nefta.

I sighed and said, "As to knowing I am the Watcher, oh yeah, that cat is way out of the bag."

Turel scratched his beard and said, "Which means every evil beastie in the dimension will be searching for you."

Tim's face blanched. "That means you guys can't leave her alone, not for anything. More could come back."

"Agreed," said Turel.

Nefta smiled at Tim. "Oh, they'll be back," she purred. "When I get done with you three humans, the 'beasties,' as you say, Turiel, will not like what they find here."

I didn't know if that sounded more ominous for the predicted beasties or the three frail humans. I wanted to appeal Alex for support, but he stared out the window at a hummingbird outside. Exhaling in a huff, I suppressed the urge to throttle my brother. Did he have to check out now?

I caught Turel's eye. His presence buoyed me. Squaring my shoulders, I asked Nefta and Daisy. "What do you mean when you get done with us?"

"Weapons training," explained Daisy.

Nefta's smile widened. Butterflies cavorted in my stomach. Alex continued to commune with birdies. I took a deep breath and tried to ignore him.

"Wait," broke in Tim. "Is anyone going to talk about the elephant in the room?"

The rest of us, except for Alex, stopped and stared at him. Nefta licked her lips and cocked her head to one side. "I'm intrigued. An elephant, you say?"

Tim smiled his crooked smile I knew so well. "Not an elephant, exactly. It's a human saying for the topic staring everyone in the face, yet no one is talking about it."

"Oh, really?" Nefta folded her arms in an expectant manner, and the rest of us regarded Tim in confusion.

"The prophecy?" Tim's voice rose. "Siobhan waited her whole life to hear it, even if she didn't know it. Now we've finally got it. This is huge. Alex and I have been on this ride with her the whole way. Well, until today. What is up with you, man?" He directed the last question at Alex with a jab to the shoulder. My brother ignored our friend.

Daisy waved a hand, dismissing Tim's question. "Don't worry, it's temporary. He'll be fine."

"Whatever," Tim said. "Fact is we should be figuring this thing out."

Daisy sighed and turned to Turel. The dark angel smiled. "What? He's not wrong. There is so little time."

"Not enough," said Daisy. "There's just not enough."

"There could never be enough," said Turel, "not for what we are trying to achieve. We must have faith. We push ahead."

Tim reached into his jeans' pocket. "I hope you don't mind, but I, uh, recorded Missy on my phone. Then, I jotted down some notes."

"Of course, you did." I smiled at Tim, meeting his eyes for the first time that morning. Somewhere deep inside, something that had been tense, without me even knowing, relaxed. He smiled back. We both glanced at my brother, who waved at us. Tim and

I rolled our eyes in unison. Shaking my head, I said to Daisy. "Okay, Yoda, guide us."

Tim frowned at me. "Why wouldn't she be Obi-Wan?"

"Yoda's older. Besides, he's green and so is she, um, usually."

Daisy said, "It always saddened me Alec Guinness didn't get the Oscar for his Obi-Wan role. He played the archetypal mage to perfection."

Nefta responded to Daisy with surprising passion. "I agree, Jason Robards performed well, but the Academy robbed Alec Guinness in seventy-eight."

Confused, I glanced at Turel. In an undertone he said, "Nefta adores the Oscars, always has. She throws a great party, too."

I shook my head. "Right, note to self, bring a nice hostess gift if Nefta invites me to her Oscar party. Meanwhile, prophecy, people? Focus."

"Quite right, my child," said Daisy. "Let's answer a couple of the excellent questions you and Tim have put forth. First, Abraxas was a low-level demon, no special powers, but clever, always has been. He's been hired by a lot of more powerful creatures to carry out their dirty wishes. One of his favorite tricks was dealing with Hags, parasitic creatures who feed off the life force of others as their victims sleep."

"Sounds like a great guy," said Tim.

Daisy winked at him. "Exactly. I believe the term is a peach? You asked about the Black God. Well, I hate to use the word god for him, though in truth that is the literal translation for his name. I wonder, can we change the language, make it mean something else?"

My dragon friend directed this last question to Nefta and Turel. With a start, I realized she was serious about changing the actual language. Turel made a "hurry up" gesture and she went on. "Right, sorry, where was I? Well, dear ones, Chernobog is Russian for black god."

"Really?" said Tim.

"No, it's true," said Nefta. "Chernobog is a senior-level demon, one of the most senior levels there are."

"Except for Lucifer," my brother said.

Turel and Nefta shook their heads, but Tim spoke quicker than them. "No, Alex, Lucifer isn't a demon. Lucifer is an angel."

Alex's shoulders slumped. "Doesn't seem right, somehow, angels being bad guys. It's backward. Oh, cool, a dragonfly."

I whispered to Daisy, "You're *sure* he's okay?" She patted my hand in a motherly fashion.

Tim smoothed out his piece of note paper. He smiled at the rest of us. "This is exciting, isn't it?" he said. "To think, Siobhan, here we are at last."

I smiled, too, and gestured to the paper. "What next?"

"Well." He hesitated. "So, we have just three days to see this through, right?"

"That's how I read it," agreed Turel.

Tim continued, "I guess the next bit would be to try and figure out who are the players, right, Daisy?"

"I see no reason to disagree." Daisy sat back.

Tim perused his notes. "So, we've got a *Defender of Man*, right? The way I see things, it must mean Turel. I mean who else could defend us?"

"Excuse me?" asked Nefta, folding her arms.

"Sorry." Tim held up his hands. "But, you're already mentioned. Doesn't Valkyrie mean 'Chooser of the Slain'?"

Turel wagged his index finger at her. "That would be you, old friend. You get *Chooser of the Slain* and I get *Defender of Man*."

Nefta frowned. "Yours sounds much more uplifting than mine."

I moved on. "So, who's the *Guardian*?"

"It might be me," said Daisy.

I thought of Pythia's stanza to me and shook my head. "I don't think so, Daisy."

"Maybe it's me," said Tim in a thoughtful voice.

Daisy frowned. "How did you come to that conclusion, dear?"

Tim reddened and didn't meet my eyes. "Alex and Siobhan spent every summer at their grandparents' house in Calistoga.

Siobhan was about the prettiest thing I'd ever seen, but she always got into trouble. Seemed like a full-time job trying to look out for her."

I fidgeted, wanting to be somewhere else, but confined myself to saying, "It's a gift."

Alex grinned. "Cuz' you *love* her," he teased Tim.

Tim ignored us and continued, "For as long as I can remember, I thought, well, it's my job to make sure she's okay. You know, to protect her."

Turel and Daisy glanced at me and nodded. It made sense. He'd always been there for me. So, the bit about Guardian's passion breaking the last chain, well, I could prevent that, no problem. Besides, I needed to put some space between Tim and me. No sense leading him down a dead-end road.

Armed with this bit of insight, I took it a step further. "And the *brother and sister* would be Alex and me, right?"

"Maybe." Daisy didn't seem sold on the idea. "Prophecies aren't always what they appear, Siobhan. One only knows what they mean once the events they foretell are through."

"What's the point?" Alex asked in a loud voice.

"They are still a guide, lamp posts in the dark," said Daisy. "No traveler should be lost."

Tim reviewed his notes, ticking items off with a pen and frowning as he did so. "I still don't see where Gracious Sight comes in here."

Daisy patted my hand. "That's our Siobhan," she said with a smile. "Her name means 'God is gracious.'"

Tim blinked. "I'd forgotten that," he admitted.

Turel's steady regard rested on me. "Such a lovely name," he said.

Tim continued. "This bit has me worried. *When the child who sees becomes the one who could, That's the day evil defeats good.*"

Daisy held out a hand to Tim, indicating his notes. "If I may, dear one?"

He handed them over saying, "That has to mean Siobhan, right? I mean, she's *the child who sees*. Or is it Missy?"

"Hardly a child now," I protested.

Nefta shook her head. "Oracles reveal the prophecies. They do not figure in their verses."

"Perhaps this part has already happened," Tim theorized. "Siobhan began to believe in her abilities and her vision the day Chernobog's servant, Gilbert, stole Daisy's gateway. Chernobog destroyed the statue, temporarily cutting off her return to this world. That day, evil won."

"But it's out of order," I said. "It's after the part about three days, *Defender of Man, Chooser of the Slain, hearing her call*, all of that."

"Don't pay too much attention to the order of the elements," said Daisy, her amber eyes narrowed in thought. "The oracles have never seen time the same as other beings do. To them it is not merely a linear phenomenon."

"So, we're *all* in the prophecy," I said. "Although, there isn't anything about Daisy, is there?"

"There are always companions," said Nefta. "And Gwrydd heard her role in days gone by ago."

This explained why Turel hadn't objected when Alex and Tim joined us to meet Daisy. They were supposed to come.

"I don't understand anything you're saying," Alex said in a happy, sing-song voice. "Nope, nope, I don't get it." We ignored him.

"That's not my main worry," said Turel.

Daisy wrinkled her nose. "The King and the Queen reference? Goodness knows the last thing we need is the Fey involved."

"We were foolish to hope otherwise," said Turel. "They have controlled the Veil's location for eons."

"Still," fretted Daisy, "it is vexing. One never knows what those two will do from one second to the next."

Nefta smiled, her eyes fierce. "I find the stakes to be more worthy of my involvement. To square off against the true immortals, the elementals, the King of Winter and the Queen of Summer, what better a contest could one ask for?"

Turel's expression sombered. "Every treasure has a dragon

guarding it. The Fey are the monsters guarding our treasure."

Daisy's brows bent. "I hardly think I qualify as a monster."

Turel held out his hands. "Of course not, dear lady. It is only a metaphor."

"Wait," I said. "The Fey? Who, what, are the Fey?"

"The Fey are what humankind call the Faeries," said Daisy.

My muscles tensed. "Faeries? Faeries are real?"

"Many things you think are imaginary are actually real. You need to adjust your world view," said Daisy.

"Faeries don't sound bad," said Tim.

"Ha. You display your ignorance," said Nefta. "Did you not hear my words? Faeries are the true immortals. They are elementals with unlimited power."

I swallowed. "Are they evil?" I asked.

"Not exactly evil," said Turel, "nor are they exactly good either."

"Capricious," added Daisy. "And very, very dangerous."

My stomach sank. "Great, more to worry about," I said and leaned over her shoulder, studying the notes she held. "Seems pretty clear there's a door, or a gateway, we'll need to find," I said.

"There is," said Nefta. "You heard Turel, the Veil."

Daisy elaborated, "We're searching for a gate called The Veil. It's been lost for millennia, but references to it keep coming up in each of our prophecy readings. That should tell us it will be reemerging in the next couple of days."

"The Veil leads to places even angels cannot travel to," said Nefta, "other dimensions, different universes."

"We just need to be there at the right time," said Turel. "Legend says if you can get past its guardians and know how to seek, inside the Veil you can find the path to the perfect future, Paradise on Earth."

Tim pointed to me. "Isn't that what we've got her for? That's what she does, right? Sees what others can't? Sounds like the perfect fit, yeah?"

"*What once was Veiled shall become known*," Daisy quoted, her eyes narrowed. "You might be right, Tim."

"Course I am," he said. "I've got this. Couple of days, we'll get this dialed and then it's off to home." He smiled at me on the last word, and I tried not to squirm. Turel studied Tim and me. The angel's poker face did not give me any clues on what his thoughts might be.

Daisy broke the silence. "Well, children, it's a start," she said. "The best bit is the other side doesn't know the timeline. They're working blind."

"Yes," I said, an awful thought going through my brain.

"What is it, Siobhan?" Daisy's expression froze. "What's going on behind those green eyes of yours, young one?"

"It's just…" I hesitated, then blurted, "Should we be more worried about Missy and Leo? What if Missy and Pythia don't win their fight for Missy's Vision? Won't the other side have their own oracle? She would tell them everything. Right, Turel? That's what you said yesterday?"

Turel, Nefta, and Daisy exchanged stares and, again, I got the feeling the adults communed without the kids.

"We have to do more to help them," I insisted. "We can't count on Pythia to protect Missy."

Nefta shook her perfect head. "Spread thin," she said. "We already have the prophecy. We should concentrate on the coming days."

"Wait," I said. "There's still a lot we're guessing at. What if she has more to tell us? Are you going to risk it?"

"She makes a good point," said Turel.

"And it's the right thing to do," said Daisy.

Nefta slowly nodded. "So be it. We'll have to help her, but the spread, it will be very thin."

"We'll be spread thin," Tim corrected gently.

She waved one hand. "Whatever. I do not like the odds."

"It is what it is," Turel said, dismissing her pessimism. "The Watcher is right."

Daisy's eyes shone like citrines. "We move ahead. It's all we can do."

I met Turel's gaze. "I'll make some calls," he promised.

I exhaled. Missy's importance could not be over stated. Somehow, I knew it.

"So, Daisy, pray tell, what happened with Abraxas?" Nefta asked. Her tone held a certain professional curiosity.

Daisy readjusted her sleek headband. "As it turned out, dear one, our friend demon had a deep-seated fear of heights."

Nefta chuckled and leaned forward. "And, whatever did you do?"

Daisy shrugged, directing a smile at the group as she patted my hand. "I have always believed one should confront their fears head on."

Turel and Nefta exchanged identical tight grins and Tim gave a low whistle. "What happened?" asked Alex.

"I gave Abraxas a flying lesson from two miles up," said Daisy.

"How did he do?" asked Tim.

"Does enthusiasm count, Tim?"

"Um, no. Why?"

"Well, he certainly made enough noise going down, my child. How about bouncing? Does bouncing count?" The corners of Daisy's mouth twitched.

"Afraid not," said Tim.

Daisy sighed. "I am sorry to say the would-be Great Abraxas proved a poor pupil indeed. Naturally, once he failed the class, I had to incinerate him. Demons of his ilk don't die easily, and I couldn't have him running off to tell his employers I have returned."

Alex, who clearly hadn't been following the discussion for some time, spread his arms out happily. "I love you, guys, I *really* love you."

Nefta massaged her forehead. "Oh, dear."

Alex blinked at the battle angel. He wore a lopsided, happy grin, making my usually striking brother resemble a puppy. "And Nefta, man, I love you, too, this much." Alex spread his arms wide.

Nefta's frown deepened. "I am not a man. Clearly, this body is female."

Alex gave her two thumbs up. "You bet it is," he said.

Turel hid a smile behind one hand as Tim snorted. "How long until he's normal again?" Tim asked Daisy. "At least, as normal as he gets anyhow."

"Hey, only I can say things like that about my brother," I said.

Daisy made a shooing motion with her hands. "Dear ones, take him outside. Let him move around and get some fresh air. He'll settle down in no time, you'll see."

Alex jumped up. "What a great idea. Watch these moves." He headed out the door, humming to himself. Tim and I followed.

We found my brother dancing in the front yard past the roses. At the sight of his delighted grin, I stifled a sigh. This might take longer than Daisy thought.

Alex did the *Running Man* while singing MC Hammer's *Can't Touch This*. He switched to *The Sprinkler* and sang *Ice, Ice Baby* as his own accompanying music. Footsteps sounded as Nefta and Turel joined us.

"Pray tell, what is he doing?" Nefta's voice rose on the words.

"Um, dancing," said Tim.

Alex switched to the *Cabbage Patch* and winked at me. He changed songs and decades by singing, *Whomp! (There It Is)*. His brown eyes sparkled and his deep red hair shone in the sun. Unlike his dancing, his singing left a great deal to be desired.

"Nefta…" Turel said, hesitating, and then he nudged the ice-blonde angel next to him. "What in Heaven's name did you do to him?"

Beside me, Tim chuckled softly. As Alex hit another sour note, I laughed as well.

"Please, Turel, I told you already, I only did as you did with yon' Watcher. I healed him overnight, giving to him my own life force." She frowned again at Alex. He remained oblivious to her censure.

"You're *sure*?" asked Turel.

I didn't blame him. Alex switched to what we as kids had called the *Pat Benatar Love Is a Battlefield Shimmie*. Tim and I doubled over in laughter.

"I think I know what I'm doing," Nefta said through gritted teeth.

Turel threw his head back and laughed. I tried to catch my breath, but another spasm of giggles erupted.

"Well," the Valkyrie conceded, "I suppose it's possible I gave him too much."

"You think?" said Tim.

Chapter Thirteen

The afternoon started innocuously enough as we waited for Alex's angel high to wear off. As he danced the worst away, I turned to Turel. "So, why did Alex get goofy and I feel empowered?"

Nefta gave a sniff of disdain.

"What did I say?" I asked, wondering how I had offended the lovely angel.

Turel put down his sandwich to answer me; he did love mortal foods. "Do not trouble yourself, Watcher." His eyes twinkled at me. "She's merely annoyed at her own mistake. Alex was not as gravely wounded as you were. She judged the situation by your condition and acted accordingly. In doing so, she gave too much of herself to your brother."

Turel picked up his BLT again and gestured in animation. "She's connected to him now, in a way, as I am to you, and it offends her dignity to see him behave so."

"Of course, it's her own flaming fault," broke in Daisy's melodious voice, tight with contained amusement. "Better too much, than not enough, I always say, my dears."

Nefta's shoulders stiffened at Daisy's comment, but the Valkyrie did not respond.

Turel saluted the dragon in disguise. Grabbing a handful of chips, he smiled at me. "Don't worry, you're exactly as one ought to be after a proper healing. I know what I'm doing."

"I heard that, Turiel," said Nefta, spinning around, her icy blue eyes flashing.

The fallen angel seemed oblivious as he munched on his

chips. His bright gaze caught mine, sparkling with silent laughter and he winked.

Nefta stood, putting her hands on her hips. Without addressing any one of us in particular, she said, "I'll make the practice field ready. You will join me."

Daisy and Turel's cackling filled the room once Nefta left. Alex, Tim and I exchanged confused glances. "What the duck?" murmured Alex.

"Please, no ducks," I pleaded, to which Tim and Alex exchanged more perplexed looks. It could have been an Abbott and Costello routine, but I didn't explain myself. Just this once, the less said, the better.

Given that we had just faced actual monsters in our beds, Nefta's orders commanding us to work on our defensive skills seemed practical, even prudent.

I drained my soda and rose to follow the Valkyrie. Turel moved with me, like a mirror. He took this guarding me thing seriously. Considering the last week, the idea of an angel at my back also seemed prudent.

"Right," said Tim. "C'mon, Alex. Let's go."

Daisy beamed like a mom waving her kids off to school. "I'll catch up with you in a speck, dear ones," she called as we left the house.

The battle angel stood in the meadow outside of Daisy's cottage. Trees lined the field, lending their dappled shade to part of the golden expanse. It appeared the local deer population had volunteered to serve as groundskeepers, eating the grass short. Three does turned tail and headed for the trees as we approached.

The scene went from idyllic to strange. Nefta removed a wide range of weapons from a pocket of reality. Tim cried out, "What the...?"

I hastened to reassure him. "Don't worry. It only looks like they're appearing out of nowhere. She's really bringing them from another dimension. It's like when Turel appears to us or how he hides his wings."

Tim frowned at me as Nefta extracted a mace. "Um, Siobhan?"

"Yes?"

"How exactly is your explanation any different from saying she's pulling them out of thin air?"

I shrugged. He had me there.

Alex cleared his throat and said, "I'll go you one better. How is she doing that?"

Tim gave a low whistle. Nefta hung the weapons in a neat display, one next to the other. This would have been fine, except the weapons weren't hanging on anything. They dangled in thin air.

"Come friends," Turel said in his deep voice. "Does it matter how she does it? Angel of the Lord, remember?"

"Right," said Alex, though he sounded doubtful as he eyed the crossbows, pikes, broadswords, daggers, throwing stars, battleaxes, and other nasty pieces of metal. I had no idea what most of their names were.

Nefta saw us watching her. She inclined her head. "These weapons are special."

"Because they have anti-gravity superpowers?" asked Alex.

Nefta's face froze, and reminded me again of a figurehead on the prow of a ship. She held up one white hand. "Enough, young Alex, be still."

To my surprise, my irrepressible brother did as she directed. I covered my gasp of surprise with a muted cough.

Nefta began again. "These weapons are special." She shot a hard stare at Alex. Then she continued, "Because they will help me and Turiel ascertain where your talents, if any, in battle may lie."

"How can they do that?" Tim frowned.

Turel positioned himself to one side, his arms folded, dark eyes intent.

Nefta embodied grace as she moved toward a collection of swords. "Watch and learn, Timothy. As you each handle the weapons, we'll see how you respond to each other."

Tim's lips moved, mutely echoing her words, "to each other." His eyebrows lifted, but he remained quiet.

Nefta glanced around as though expecting more questions.

Her features relaxed at our silence. "Excellent," she remarked. "Now, let's get to it."

As she moved toward the swords, something shimmered on her back. I concentrated on the elusive shape, expecting to see her exquisite silver wings folded back, but instead, the image of a broadsword snapped into my vision with stunning clarity. I gasped.

Turel pivoted to me. "Watcher, are you well?"

"Ye…yes," I stammered. "When did Nefta begin wearing a sword?"

Nefta froze and raised an eyebrow at Turel.

He shrugged. "She is the Watcher," he reminded the Valkyrie.

"Yes, and her abilities are growing," she said. In one fluid motion, she reached behind her and drew the concealed weapon strapped there. Unsheathed, it glowed in the sunshine.

Alex exhaled and Tim's eyebrows flew up. "Damn, I am getting tired of my heart jumping out of my chest," Tim said.

"I hear that," grumbled Alex.

"This is Durendala," Nefta said, introducing the blade as though presenting a queen to court. "I am her caretaker." The angel hefted the blade and did a few passes with flourish.

Though I knew nothing of weapons, I did know beauty when I saw it, and the sword exuded loveliness in its graceful lines and evident balance.

"She's not yours?" I said, shocked. The two fit together so well: the battle angel and the broadsword.

Nefta caressed the sword's hilt. She shook her head as she resheathed the blade. "No, I stand ready for the one who will bear her. I have loaned her to others in their labors through the ages, but she has not chosen any of these as her own. So, I have borne her away again after each completed task. She waits even now for her master or mistress."

"Why couldn't Siobhan see her?" asked Tim. "I mean, I thought dragons were the best at glamour, and Siobhan sees right through Daisy's."

"True," said Nefta, "but this is a bit different."

123

Turel stepped closer. "Durendala demands not to be seen," he explained. "Most creatures, even supernatural ones, respond to order or command. It appears as though Siobhan stopped listening to the sword."

"Stopped listening?" repeated Tim. "How?"

Turel shrugged. "She is the Watcher."

"Can you see her?" I asked Turel.

He shook his head. "Not when she's sheathed. I did not know Nefta carried her today although I have known she is Durendala's guardian."

Tim rubbed his jaw. "Can you hear her? When she's telling you not to see her, I mean?"

Again, the dark angel shook his head. "No, that is her power."

Alex blinked. "Okay, color me officially freaked out."

Nefta sighed. "All this is beside the point. Watcher, I give you full marks for spotting Durendala. She has been lost from the world's view for ages and with reason. Too many desired the sword and what she brings with her. She hides herself to good cause." Nefta dusted off her hands and moved again to the collection of swords still hanging in midair above the golden grass of the meadow. "Now, where were we?"

No one answered her. Nefta beckoned to Alex. "You, Dancing Boy, step forward, away from the others, to me."

He did so, apprehension written all over his face. The lovely angel grabbed a rapier and tossed it lightly to my brother. "Think fast," she commanded.

To my surprise, Alex caught it in midair and in a movement as natural as breathing went to an *en garde* stance. Nefta's eyebrows shot up. "Impressive," she murmured. "How does it *feel?*" She placed an emphasis on the last word.

Alex frowned at the sword. "Honestly?"

"Always."

"It feels kind of pansy-ass, if you know what I mean," he said.

She smiled in her fierce way. "Indeed I do."

She tossed Alex sword after sword. "Too bulky," he said rejecting one. "That the best you've got?" he remarked on another.

"As if," he said with a shrug when she gave him a six-foot-long great sword.

Nefta folded her arms and smoothed her hair back, though her braid remained immaculately plaited. The battle angel frowned and appealed to Turel. "Well?" she demanded. "What do you think?"

"I say, you give it a shot," said Turel, sitting cross-legged on the grass under a tree. Tim and I followed his example. It beat standing in the warm summer sun.

"Turiel, I think it is highly unlikely," she said.

"Then you have nothing to lose," he said. "Shall we make it interesting?"

Her face relaxed in a genuine smile. "Certainly."

"So," Turel said, gleeful. "You have to eat six saltines in a minute in front of the Heavenly Host and whistle *Yankee Doodle Dandy*. Okay, not the whole Host, just whomever I can round up."

"You got it, Turiel, and if I'm right, you admit to the entire Guard the flood of 963 was *your* fault."

"Done," he agreed.

Without any further hesitation, Nefta reached between dimensions and revealed s second sword. It looked so much like Durendala that I squinted to clear my vision. With my new appreciation for my other sight, I knew it was not the same sword. To my regular senses though, the two blades appeared identical.

"Hey, isn't that...?" started Tim.

I shook my head. "You might think, but no. Trust me, it's a different sword."

Turel nodded in approval at me, even as Nefta tossed the new sword to my brother. Alex caught it and a grin spread over his face. "Now, that's what I'm talking about," he said. "Wow." He looked happier than I had ever seen him, barring the Christmas morning when he got a drum set from Dad.

"Indeed," said Nefta. "Who would have thought it?"

"That makes me the winner," said Turel, gloating.

Nefta waved one hand at him. "Yes, yes, we'll deal with you

later. You'll admit it's a one in a billion shot. Durendel's not awake though. It's merely acquiescent. Alex?"

My brother stopped waving the sword around. "Yes, Nefta?"

The angel's voice quieted as she said, "Alex, this is Durendal, twin to Durendala."

"Durendal," repeated Tim, his blue eyes far away. "I thought I'd heard the name Durendala, but Durendal is even more familiar. Why is that?"

"Chason de Roland," quoted Turel musically in a perfect French accent.

"Huh?" my brother asked, clueless. I groaned and put my head in my hands.

"The Song of Roland," explained Tim.

"And again I make with the 'huh?'" repeated Alex.

"Sometimes, dude." Tim shook his sandy head. "Honestly, I remember helping you with this on your history final."

"Which I'm sure I promptly forgot once I handed said final to my teacher," said Alex. "Pretend I know nothing."

"Pretend?" Nefta asked, scoffing.

Tim smiled his agreement with her., "Roland was Charlemagne's nephew. Legend has it an angel gave the sword to Charlemagne. Hey, wait." He turned startled eyes toward Nefta.

She bowed. "At your service."

"Wow," I whispered, feeling as if someone had knocked the wind out of me.

Tim swallowed hard. "Nefta, we're talking about thirteen hundred years ago."

She shrugged. "Give or take. Continue, friend Tim."

"All righty." Tim's smile waned, but he took up the tale again. "So, Nefta gave the sword to Charlemagne who gave it to his nephew Roland who used it to hold off over a thousand Saracens single-handedly, so the story says?" Here Tim broke off to glance at Nefta.

She smiled. "There might have been—what is the term?—an assist, I believe you call it."

"Got it," said Tim. "Even with an assist, Roland held off an awful lot of soldiers that day with Durendal. Tales said described the sword as indestructible, and Roland feared it would be taken by the advancing army, so he hid the weapon under his body. I have to admit, that part never made any sense to me. Anyhow, the sword has been lost since then."

Turel remarked, "Probably because he didn't hide the sword under his body. He simply gave it back."

"To you," Alex finally spoke, staring at Nefta. "So is it choosing me, or am I a caretaker?"

Nefta shook her head. "The sword did not wake up, much like Durendala with me. They tolerate us, they allow us to wield them, and they will serve us well, but we are not their master. That role goes to another still to come."

The gist of what she said finally hit home for me. "Nefta, you're saying these are living swords?"

"Of course, what else would they be?" The Valkyrie glanced around at the three mortals as though viewing disappointing students who had failed to grasp two plus two equals four. "Moving along?" she said, pointing to Tim.

Tim approached Nefta and the magically floating arsenal. She tossed him a sword which he tried to grasp and cut his hand instead.

"Humph," she said, disappointed.

Next she handed him a mace, but she took it back after one glance at his face. "Perhaps not," she commented. Nefta repeated the process with several daggers, a pike, an arbalest, throwing stars, and a billhook.

Stumped, she peered at Turel. "What do you think?" she asked.

"I think he's a devout man," said the angel, scratching his beard in thought.

"Ah," she said, her expression clearing. She turned again to Tim. "You do not relish the idea of battle, of killing anyone, do you?"

"I'm not afraid," he said, rubbing his hands together.

"That's not what I asked," she said. "I asked if you could kill

127

anyone."

Tim dropped his gaze. "It reads, 'thou shalt not kill'," he quoted.

For the first time since we had met the flaxen-haired angel, her icy blue eyes softened. "I think I understand." She reached into nothingness again and brought out a quarterstaff. "You are a righteous man."

Tim shrugged, but did not respond. Instead, he accepted the proffered weapon. "I will fight," he promised.

"I know," Nefta said. "How does that feel?"

Tim tested its balance and twirled it, his face breaking into a bright smile. "It feels perfect."

"Excellent." Nefta folded her arms and regarded me. My insides rollercoastered. Was I going to throw up? "It's your time, Watcher," Nefta said, beckoning.

My leaden limbs weighed me down, but I went to her.

Alex smiled, "It's nothing. Wait for what is right to you."

"Believe me, Siobhan, you'll know," said Tim.

Nefta grabbed a sword and tossed it to me. Even though I knew what to expect, I still flinched, dodging the blade. It fell to the grass. My cheeks burned. "Unbelievable," said Nefta, her hands on her hips.

"Not the sword, I think," murmured Turel, his lips twitching.

I steeled myself as she handed me weapon after weapon. Each one felt cold, even hostile to me. As this progressed my repulsion grew. I could not wait to get them out of my hands and back to Nefta. Finally, Turel gently touched my shoulder. "If I may?" he asked Nefta.

She held out an arm to the floating weaponry in a welcoming gesture. "By all means, otherwise we might be here all day. Unless, you think she's deeply devout, too?"

"Not hardly," said Alex.

Turel smiled at my brother. "No, I agree with Alex. The problem lies elsewhere." He turned back to Nefta as he gestured to me with one hand. "My friend, what is the Watcher's overwhelming characteristic?"

Nefta cocked her head to one side. "Her eyes, certainly. What does that have to do with—Oh, I've gone senile with the advancing centuries."

"I'm glad you were the one to say it," said Turel, but Nefta ignored him.

Instead, she brought forward an overlooked weapon—a bow and a quiver of arrows. Wishing I could beam myself somewhere else, I extended my hands and braced for the oncoming cold. Nefta placed the bow in my right hand and the quiver in my left. She stepped back and waited.

To my surprise the bow warmed my hands. A sense of completeness filled me. Startled, my eyes met Nefta's crystalline blue ones.

"Yes," the Valkyrie said with a fierce hiss.

Nefta regarded each of us. "This is good," she said. "Though mortal, you three have skills. The weapons have vouched for you. You will be able to contribute in the days to come. Well done, my friends."

We basked in her approval. Nefta continued so I tempered my excitement and paid close attention. "Now, you must realize," she said, "no one can hope to walk into a battle situation with a weapon they picked up mere days, or hours before and expect to prevail, not against what we shall face. So, I have a gift to give each of you, the gift of my eons of battle lore. I shall give you the skills of a Valkyrie."

We exchanged glances.

She went on, "Not just any Valkyrie. You'll receive mine." An elemental, basic fierceness in the way she spoke caused me to view her with fresh eyes. It crossed my mind that I never, ever, wanted to meet Nefta on the plain of battle.

More imperious than a queen, she beckoned to my brother. Alex swallowed, hesitating for an instant, but moved to stand in front of her. Nefta smiled at him. "Kneel, and grasp Durendal in both hands."

Alex did as she directed. He resembled a young man about to be knighted. To my surprise Nefta presented a wooden stick about ten inches long and perhaps an inch in diameter. "Bite down," she directed.

My brother's expression shifted. "Wh-what?" he stammered. I thought compassion flickered on the pale angel's face, but only for a second. Then the emotion vanished. "Bite down," she commanded. "Now."

Alex did as she bid and grasped Durendal with both hands. Nefta placed a hand on either side of his head and said, not without sympathy, "You'll need to bite hard, now."

She and Alex glowed in the afternoon sunshine. It was not the gentle warmth of Turel's magic. Violent electricity sparked and surged. The power made my brother's body jerk and twitch. His face twisted in pain.

I started forward and Turel caught me by one arm. "All will be well, Watcher," he said, comforting me. "There is information in Nefta, information that will help him survive. Only she can teach him how to use Durendal. When she is done, his body will be made over, his muscles will simply know how to wield the sword."

With a shudder I focused on Alex. His gaze locked with Nefta's, his body went rigid, and the fine bones in his neck stood out as though he silently screamed behind the stick held between his teeth.

Seconds spread out before Nefta released him. Alex's tanned face blanched, his brown eyes and red hair made a stark contrast to his skin. His breath came in ragged gasps.

"Are you well?" Nefta asked, and to my surprise she seemed concerned.

Alex took a moment, chest heaving, and said, "Yeah, I think I'll live." His voice sounded deeper and more serious than usual. I resisted the urge to run and hug him. Wearily, my brother drew himself to his full height. It may have been a trick of the light in the bright sun, but as his red hair lit up in the afternoon's rays he seemed taller than ever. He passed the wooden stick back to Nefta and walked a few feet away to collapse on the grass. For a moment he lay gasping, but pulled himself to a sitting position.

Nefta nodded at Alex, her expression satisfied. She turned to me. "Watcher," she called, "Kneel and bite on this." Her pale hand held the same stick my brother had used only a moment ago.

Trembling, I told myself if Alex could handle it, I could, too. I walked forward, took the stick in my teeth and, clenching my bow and my quiver, I met Nefta's ice-cold blue scrutiny. She placed her hands on either side of my head. The afternoon sun dimmed as an Arctic chill took hold.

"Wait, Nefta." Turel's voice sounded urgent.

Nefta roused herself. "Turiel, what is this?"

"You are not connected to her, as you are to Alex," he whispered intensely. "We need her intact, undamaged. We may only have two days, perhaps three. Let me, since we are bound, as you and young Alex are. As you were gentle with him, let me be so for the Watcher. I do, after all, have some small skill with a bow."

Nefta and Turel's eyes locked, an angelic staring contest. A part of me wondered, could angels speak mind-to-mind? Another part of me speculated, if Nefta had been gentle with Alex, what exactly did hard entail?

Nefta and Turel broke off their commune. "So be it, Watcher," she said. "Turiel shall school you in archery." She glanced at Turel in amusement. "Some small skill indeed, old friend. She'll thank you later."

"I hope so," Turel said as he moved toward me.

I started to sink to my knees again as I had seen Alex do, but Turel stopped me, guiding me up. He shifted the quiver to my back as it would normally be worn and placed the bow in my hand. He cradled me close to him. One of his arms went around my back and held me to him, while the other hand wrapped around my hand on the bow. Nervous energy surged through me. "Peace, Watcher," he said.

Relaxing in his grasp, I studied him. His arm moved from cradling my back to softly grasp the side of my face. His warm eyes drew me in; I could not look away. Power held us, binding us together, and in that instant, everything stopped.

I became conscious of each beat of my heart and heard every

pulse of my blood through my veins. My eyes viewed events through Turel's. He sighted target after target. I learned how he aimed. Lessons flooded my mind: how draw back the bow, how far to pull, when to let loose. Through his eyes, I saw countless battles. Over the ages he experienced many victories and many losses. Each shot counted. Each arrow had a tale to tell, a million stories in a tapestry of war. My vision splintered. I shared his past, and he saw mine.

A beautiful, raven-haired woman with a generous smile, laughing children with fat cheeks and Turel's dark eyes dominated his memories. In the past existed a different Turel, a glowing, bright Turel. It did not seem possible the angel here today could be faded and hurt. Yet, compared to this past version, shining from times long gone, the Turel I knew was a shadow. The moment of intimate contact extended and continued until voices called our names.

With a jolt, I found myself in the meadow again, still in Turel's arms. Tim, Alex and Nefta shouted at us, bringing us home again. Stealing one more peek into the angel's dark eyes, I recognized anew all he had lost through the eons. His hand tightened on my face, for one instant his breath mingled with mine and swept me up in a blur of emotion. He released me and cupped my hands over my bow.

"Will you be able to use it now?" he asked.

"I think so."

"That's my girl," he said, laughing.

"Yes," I agreed.

Alex met my eyes with a cheerful smile, but Tim considered Turel as though seeing the angel for the first time. His jaw set, Tim avoided my eyes. "Okay, what do I need to do?" he asked Nefta.

Turel caught Nefta's elbow, saying softly, "Remember, gentle, there is no bond between the two of you."

Nefta shook Turel's hand off and smiled in her frosty way. "Grasp your staff in both hands, friend Tim, and kneel."

Tim did as she directed. Nefta nodded her approval at him and held the stick out to him. "You'll want to bite down, hard."

Tim's expression grew strained, but he did as she asked. Nefta put each of her hands on either side of his head and stared deeply into his wide eyes. Once they achieved rapport, Tim's body convulsed. He bit down on the stick between his teeth. His back arched and his eyes bulged as his body shook. Another moment passed. His breath came in ragged, desperate gasps behind the stick. Nefta's blue gaze remained unfaltering. Tim's hands tightened in a death grip.

I turned to Alex and Turel in alarm. Even as their eyes met mine, Tim's breathing faltered. "Nefta," Turel exclaimed. "You must stop." Nefta remained fixated on Tim. "Nefta," Turel screamed. "Nefta!"

Tim fell, his body jerking. For an instant his eyes remained locked with Nefta's and then they slowly rolled to the back of his head. As his contact with Nefta broke, she appeared to rejoin the here and now. "Oh, sweet Heaven," she prayed, beginning to glow, "hear my call."

"I hear," said a deep, booming voice. It carried the eldritch overtones of death.

A black robed angel with outstretched midnight feathered wings strode through the meadow. He carried a scythe. The Angel of Death walked among us.

"Asrael," Nefta said, breathless.

"You called, my love?"

Chapter Fourteen

"Siobhan," said Alex, reaching for my hand. "Am I seeing who I think I'm seeing?"

"The Angel of Death," I said. My eyes fixed on Tim's still form in growing dread. As disturbing as his convulsing movements had been, at least he moved. I twisted my head around as the newcomer, Asrael, Nefta had called him, strode toward Tim.

"No," I entreated, blocking his path, my arms outstretched on either side to prevent him from passing. "No, you can't have him."

Asrael stopped in midstride, his eyes meeting mine for the first time. Facing him, I wanted to crawl away in terror, but I held my ground. Tim would have stood his ground for me.

The angel's already bleak expression twisted into a mask of offended rage. "How dare you address me? You? What are you? How dare you seek to deny me anything?" He extended his scythe toward me. I felt like a fly about to be swatted. Asrael flicked the scythe at me.

The meadow vanished. A thick, white mist flickered with energy, like electric pulses, as it shrouded me. The fog condensed around me, becoming thicker and more solid as if made of strands, each one extending. Like insulation, it began as fine cobwebs and grew larger. The gossamer tendrils shifted into piercing wire. Each sliver of mist burned sharp and electric. As the fog tightened around me, the wires sliced into my clothing and my flesh in a network of fine, razor sharp cuts. The pain ripped at me, excruciating, but nothing compared to what came next.

The flickers of energy set my nerves on fire. The tendrils

seared, leaving me ablaze in their wake, inside and out. Retreat from the pain proved impossible. I whimpered. My hands went up in an attempt to protect my face and head, but movement made the fog cut deeper.

The mist changed color, shifting to crimson. At first I thought hazily through my agony this might be some fresh terror, but no, my blood colored my prison. I stopped moving, trying to avoid the cutting, but there was nowhere to hide, everything hurt. The sound of my involuntary whimpers filled my ears as I held myself as still as possible. In the vault of my mind I screamed and screamed as green eyes watched with glee. Green eyes?

Agony obliterated the image. I became a bleeding statue, a study in red and pain. Dimly, as if a world away, a roar echoed, a sound I had never heard before.

Then the thick mist, my prison of pain, cleared, burnt away. Air rushed past me, like a hot storm passing overhead. Next, Daisy in her dragon form flew above me, breathing flames as her mighty wings stirred the air around me. Even with the web gone, my relief in the afternoon sunshine seemed weak, unreal, for though my captivity had ended, its injuries remained. Nerves ablaze, each and every wound screamed agony through my body. Dropping to my knees, I took in my surroundings. Alex still gripped Durendal. He held the blade now as though he knew how to use it, but his face blanched white and terrified. Nefta's features twisted in anger though she held no weapon. An angel on fire bore a burning sword. Turel stood between me and Asrael.

"You think you can stand between her and me?" said Asrael in sepulchral tones of disbelief.

"Yes," Turel contended, the fire of his sword blazing brighter at his voice.

Asrael's face morphed into sheer derision. "How can you? You don't have that kind of power anymore."

Turel shifted his grip on the hilt of his sword. "You are asking the wrong questions, my friend."

Not able to bear weight on my knees, I sat back on my legs and struggled to remain conscious. The drama unfolding in front me helped keep the onslaught of pain from swallowing me whole. Nefta scanned the skies. I found a certain black humor in the fact that I saw Daisy, though the Valkyrie did not. Asrael watched Nefta and followed her example, his grim face showing a trace of anxiety for the first time as he glanced upward. He returned his attention to Turel. "What could you possibly mean, Turiel?"

Turel's dark eyes flicked to me. "You haven't even bothered to ask who burnt away your net," he said icily, raising one dark eyebrow.

At those words the sound reverberated again. "ROAR"

Daisy swept in, flying low, and landed next to Turel, almost crushing Asrael. Her wings blasted the warm summer air against my face once more, and I winced as my cuts stung anew. She must have been glamoured until now or else Asrael would have perceived her. Daisy snaked her head low against the ground, baring her magnificent teeth. She roared a third time, a noise so deep and thunderous it reverberated throughout my body. The ground echoed her call, shuddering in response.

"Back away, Reaper," the dragon said, then hissed. "Back away now." Her elegant verdant wings spread in protection before me, blocking my view of Asrael, and her wyvern tail whipped like an angry cat's.

"Gwyrdd." Asrael sounded stunned.

I did not hear the rest of Asrael's reply. Now that both Turel and Daisy stood between me and the Angel of Death, my shattered body could not hold on any longer. Despite my desperate worry for Tim, I collapsed, tumbling toward unconsciousness with a graceless thud.

* * *

I woke to the glow of Turel's healing as he knelt beside me, his hands extended, burning sword gone. To my surprise Nefta knelt on my other side. Her silver healing illuminated her pale hands in a glow even brighter than the summer sunshine. My cuts vanished before my awed eyes. The wounds closed with a powerful tingling, a sensation to the point of pain.

Their healing didn't repair my clothes. The bloodstained rips provided mute evidence of my ordeal.

I gave a deep, heartfelt sigh of relief as the two angels finished their work. The cessation of pain soothed my soul. "Thank you," I said to them in gratitude.

"Of course," murmured Turel, his dark eyes still shadowed with concern.

"The least that I could do, Watcher," said Nefta. Her usually impassive face flushed.

"Watcher, you say?" repeated Asrael, from behind the screen of Daisy's shining wings. "What Watcher?"

Daisy folded her wings neatly against her body. Alex ran to me, still clutching Durendal. As I sat up, I spied Tim's motionless form, forgotten, where he had fallen.

"This Watcher. The Watcher, you dunderheaded fool," said Daisy. The dragon dipped her jeweled head toward me as her amber eyes blazed at the black-winged angel.

Alex scrambled to my side. Dropping to his knees and discarding the sword, he scooped me into his arms, hugging me tightly. "Siobhan," he said, "there was so much blood. Are you okay?" My brother's voice thickened with unshed tears.

"Can't breathe," I said with a gasp.

"Sorry." Alex's grip loosened enough that the oxygen flowed again. Taking a deep breath, I leaned against his chest.

For a moment Asrael's lean, sculpted face reflected a view of conflicting emotions until he regained control and his features smoothed out in a grim mask once more.

"What about Tim? We're sitting here, and he's—" I stopped, afraid to even finish the thought.

"Peace, Watcher," said Nefta, her voice soft. "That's why Asrael came."

"No." I jerked up, shaking off Alex's hands. "He can't take Tim."

"Siobhan, wait," said Daisy, folding her wings and backing away from us.

My anxious brother wrapped his arms around me. Daisy bathed herself in her own flames, swirling and scorching so as to dress herself once more in a human's disguise. When the fires settled, the woman in green had joined us again. I still saw the enraged dragon burning in her brilliant, golden eyes.

"Well," said Turel to Asrael.

Asrael inclined his head at Turel. He bowed to Daisy. "Turiel, Lady Gwyrdd, if you will allow me a moment." He approached Tim's fallen form, extending his black scythe.

"Tim," I cried out. Alex and I jumped up and started toward the Angel of Death. I had no idea what we thought we could do to stop the black-winged being, but we needed to try. Gritting my teeth, I blocked my terror of Asrael and his powers from my mind.

"No, Siobhan," Turel said, grasping my arm. Likewise, Nefta gripped my brother.

"All will be well." Daisy's voice reassured, though her clenched jaw radiated fury.

Asrael stood by Tim, his scythe over our friend's body. Nefta released Alex with a stern frown at my brother and joined the Angel of Death, considering Tim. "Can anything be done?" She asked.

He closed his eyes for a moment and his head tilted back to the sky. The meadow quieted. No birdsong or hum of insects interrupted, even the breeze stilled, as if in mourning. Asrael sighed and opened his eyes. "It is not his day to die," he said, setting the scythe again Tim's chest with one lean hand. He lifted his other arm to the heavens. "Blessed be," he called to the sky.

"Blessed be," repeated Nefta, Turel, and Daisy. They bent their heads reverently.

CRACK!

A bolt of lightning struck the Reaper's scythe. Tim's lifeless body arched. Energy crackled across his still form. For one awful moment, everything froze. My heart leapt to my throat. Hot tears stung my eyes. Tim's head came forward and he sat bolt upright. His vibrant blue eyes opened then locked with Asrael's steely gray regard. "It is not my day to die," Tim repeated to Asrael in wonder.

Asrael withdrew his scythe. "No, not today, it seems," he agreed, taking a couple of steps back.

Alex and I rushed to hug Tim. Asrael and Nefta spoke in quiet tones behind us. "You were not gentle, my love," the reaper said to the battle angel.

"No," she agreed, "it is difficult for me, this being gentle."

"For me as well," he said.

I shut them out, focusing on Tim. Turel and Daisy hovered, their concern written on their faces. "Tim," I said, hugging him. "Are you all right?"

He shrugged, but held me tight. "Honestly, I'm fine. I'm not even sure what happened."

"You died, dude," Alex informed him, putting one hand on Tim's shoulder.

"Alex," I exclaimed, as Tim's features morphed into an expression of disbelief.

"What?" Alex demanded. "Are we keeping it a secret or something?"

I asked Daisy and Turel. "Did he? Die, I mean?"

Daisy pursed her lips. "In a manner of speaking," she said.

"Tim is a Tool of the Prophecy," explained Turel. "Nefta called on Asrael as one of the Angels of Death for help when she realized how far she had pushed Tim. Asrael asked for a, well, let's call it a ruling as to Tim's fate."

"Who did he ask?" I wondered out loud.

"His superior," said Daisy in the tone of one who wants to end the conversation, but I couldn't let it go.

"Who's his superior?" I asked.

"Death, of course," answered my irrepressible brother. Everyone stared at him. "What, didn't anyone else see *Bill & Ted's Bogus Journey*? It's a classic."

Tim ran one hand through his tousled hair. "So, wait, I thought you were Death?" he asked Asrael.

"Death can't be everywhere," said Asrael to Tim.

"Yeah, right, clearly he hasn't watched the nightly news," muttered Alex.

Turel and Daisy both turned to one side, lips twitching with suppressed mirth. I sighed. It seemed like anything Alex said that made me want to roll my eyes, they found hilarious.

Asrael continued, ignoring Alex, "Therefore, Death has angels who report to him. They help collect souls and lead the dead away from the plane of the living."

Alex frowned at Nefta. "Isn't that what you do?"

The Valkyrie waggled one hand in a "so-so" motion. "I serve the Heavenly Host. It's only in specific instances where I am called by Death," she said. "I lead the greatest heroes onward."

"So, you moonlight for Death? Collecting heroes?" asked my brother.

"One might call it such."

"From the battlefield?"

"Yes, Alex. Although, there are many kinds of battlefields in life," Nefta said. "Before volunteering to help you, I had little contact with living mortals. You are, how shall I say? I find you are different alive. Quite stimulating."

Alex frowned again, but remained silent. Tim studied me and said, "Um, Siobhan, how long was I gone, err, out? And what on earth happened to your clothes?"

The atmosphere of our little group, which had lightened with relief at Tim's recovery, darkened again as Daisy, Alex, and Turel's faces took on matching angry expressions. I bit my lip.

Although Daisy intimidated less in her current form, she didn't let that slow her down. "What. Were. You. Thinking?" She rounded on the black-winged Reaper, punctuating each word with a sharp jab to his chest with one hand as she spoke, despite the fact she was now several inches shorter than the Angel of Death.

Asrael drew himself to his full height. "You forget to whom you speak, Ancient One," he said. "Even one such as you must face Death. Have a care."

His response further inflamed Daisy. Her golden eyes blazed. Was I the only one who saw the enraged dragon staring savagely out of those amber orbs? Daisy took a deep breath and spoke in an icy, controlled voice, her speech falling into the measured cadences of bygone days. "I am one of Those Who Came Before. When I meet mine own end, it will not be the Death of this earth who visits me, and I will not be led to the next plane by one so feeble as thou. It would befit thee well to regard whom thine reproaches, and know that though your kind may not die in a normal span of time, you can be destroyed with ease." Her eyes narrowed as she continued, "Lest thee forget, child, I can return to my true form quicker than thought. Fear my wrath and run."

Nefta put a hand on the agitated dragon's shoulder. "Forgive him, First One," the battle angel said. "He means only to serve the best and truest way he knows."

Daisy nodded graciously at Nefta.

"No, she does not speak for me. I can make my own case," Asrael burst out.

Turel smiled a tight grin which seemed to be more about baring his teeth than any display of amusement. "Oh, I hoped you'd say something so short-sighted," the dark angel said.

"Turel," I said, "he brought Tim back to us."

"Only because his master commanded that it be done. Your gratitude should be reserved for Death, and for the Almighty, whom they serve," retorted Turel. His hands clenched and unclenched as though trying not to ball them into fists. "He tortured you, needlessly. We are far from done here."

"Aye, Turel has the crux of it," agreed Daisy. "That's your first reaction? A mortal says or does something you don't relish and your first instinct is torture? You drop a Net of Purgatory on them?"

"A what's-it?" asked Alex.

"It's what Asrael put around Siobhan," explained Daisy. "It begins as a thick mist, but solidifies around the victim, cutting more and more deeply into their flesh."

"If left unchecked, the net will slice its occupant into little pieces," added Turel. I shuddered at the memory of the pain, closing my eyes to control the rush of emotions welling inside of me.

Alex's face flushed and he railed at Nefta. "Why didn't you stop him?"

Nefta's usual cool superiority abandoned her. Her lovely

features registered shock at Alex's accusation. "Alex, I'm sorry, it happened so fast. I had no time. Then Turiel and Gwyrdd flew into action. It was done before I could think." She entreated my brother, "I'm sorry. Please, please forgive me." Asrael's bleak face drew into a deep frown as he watched their exchange.

Alex strode to her and grabbed her by the shoulders. "Not me, Nefta, you don't say you're sorry to me. You apologize to her, you beg forgiveness from her," he said, releasing her with an angry shove and pointing to me as he spoke. "You call yourself a battle angel with those reflexes? I expected better of you. I expected more."

He confronted Asrael. "I may be nothing to you right now, but I won't forgive this and I don't forget. If ever I can hurt you, I will."

Asrael raised one eyebrow. "A most unlikely scenario," he said. Alex ignored him and walked toward Daisy's house. Swear words spewed from him in a vociferous stream. Tim and I exchanged glances out of habit. Without saying a word, we both nodded in agreement. Tim ran to catch up with my brother.

"You've made an enemy today," Daisy pointed out.

"A mortal one," Asrael said.

"A Tool of Prophecy," Nefta said, contradicting him. Her lovely features shifted, twisting into an expression of sadness and regret. To my amazement she dropped to her knees. "Forgive me, Watcher. I should have acted more quickly. I should have saved you from torment. I failed my God today." The sincerity in her face lent her features a touching vulnerability as she stared at me.

Moved, I knelt with her. "Hey," I said, "don't beat yourself up. There, all better. I'll live." I held out my arm, the skin whole and unblemished.

"I am sorry, Siobhan." For the first time she addressed me by my name.

She rose to her feet once more and stared at the Angel of Death. "You say you love me," she said to him.

Asrael blanched. "You know I do," he said in an undertone. His eyes darted around the group and then he glared at the ground.

"You need to make this right," she commanded. "You attacked The Watcher. There is no excuse."

"She provoked me," he said, his grip tightening on his scythe.

"She sought to protect her fallen comrade. You could have explained, used words. Instead, you chose poorly and inappropriately." Nefta's tone held scorn and contempt. "It was stupid and cruel. Should you truly wish for me to ever hear your suit, you'll make this right."

Asrael's pale face blanched further. "But, Nefta," he began.

"Stop." She cut him off, holding one hand up. "This is not up for discussion. Make it right with The Watcher, or I will not know you, not for all of eternity." She glanced around, inclined her head at me, and stalked away.

With a curse Asrael followed her. Daisy eyed me. "You know, dear one," she said, "We really should get you a change of clothes. You are a mess."

I blinked in surprise. "Switch subjects much, Daisy?"

She gave a graceful shrug. "It occurred to me. That's all." Daisy smiled. "Asrael's day has certainly taken a turn for the worse."

"I can live with that. There's no way it's as bad as mine has been," I said, examining my clothes. My limbs trembled with remembered agony.

Turel stepped closer and put one arm around my waist, pressing me to him in a comforting gesture. "It's over," he murmured.

I searched for control, but a shiver still ran through me. "I'll never forget it though. It will always be in my head."

"Don't think about it, Siobhan," Turel said.

"So, that stuff with Nefta and Asrael, he's in love with her?" I asked them. The pair spoke in muted tones. I wondered what Nefta said to her would-be suitor.

"Yes, Asrael has pursued Nefta for centuries," said Daisy.

"Why isn't he Fallen? How is that different from what you did?" I asked Turel, who still wrapped a protective arm around me.

Turel grimaced. "I fell in love and married without permission,

143

during a specific mission from God. Asrael used proper channels and obtained permission to woo Nefta."

"Sounds awfully official. Does Nefta get a say?"

"Of course, she does. You saw how she speaks to him," Turel said. "No one tells Nefta how to feel."

Daisy chuckled. "I think she's been playing hard to get."

Turel pursed his lips, releasing me. "It occurs to me, ladies, perhaps there is a way to make Asrael useful. He certainly owes us, particularly Siobhan, a debt."

"What are you thinking?" I asked.

"As Nefta herself said, we are spread thin, with much to do and just days, hours even, to accomplish our tasks. The oracle needs protection and Asrael is ideally suited to provide such," Turel answered, brushing an errant lock of my unruly hair from my face. "I say we put him to work."

"I don't know. She and Leo are more of those pesky mere 'mortals,'" I answered. "You can see how fond of us he is."

"Oh, I think the Oracle is high enough up the spiritual food chain to appease Asrael's ego, especially with Pythia involved. They've met," said Daisy. "Turel is right. Mother knows, we could use the help."

"It's settled," said the dark-eyed angel. "Asrael is hired."

"Asrael is what?" came Nefta's voice as she and Asrael reappeared.

"Hired," confirmed Daisy. "We think he will be of great service to our cause if he protects the Oracle and helps her through her transition."

"How so?" Asrael asked.

To my surprise, Asrael nodded with grave dignity at Turel's explanation. "The Oracle is important to my Father's Cause, the Cause of Light. I would be honored to assist. It will clear my debt to The Watcher and restore my beloved's good opinion of me once more."

"And?" Nefta prompted.

Asrael frowned. "It appears, Watcher, I owe you an apology." He hesitated, and then said, "It is possible I acted in haste."

My eyebrows went up at this, though I bit my tongue. Nefta's expression froze in growing disapproval.

Asrael noticed and backtracked. "More than possible, that I acted rashly. Please forgive me," he said stiffly.

I didn't trust myself to answer. Alex wasn't the only one in our family who could behave impetuously. Instead, I nodded.

Asrael seemed content with my response. "Excellent, I can see for a meat sack, you at least have the semblance of an intellect. I am happy not to have ended your life after all." With that comment, he bowed and stepped through the dimensions, disappearing from view.

Nefta's flawless face flickered with what I could only call embarrassment at Asrael's rudeness. I had seen more emotion from the Valkyrie in the last half an hour than in any previous encounter.

Nefta exhaled. "Sometimes," she admitted, "Asrael is not particularly skilled with the living. I'll update him on the Oracle and her needs, shall I?" Without waiting for an answer to this understatement of the century, she, too, vanished.

Chapter Fifteen

"Widen your stance," advised Turel as I nocked an arrow and pulled the bow back for what had to be the thousandth time. My arms ached, but he continued coaching me, pushing me to do better. Though the knowledge from Turel resided in my head, and my hands seemed to know what to do, I didn't connect with the target. Again, I missed and heard Turel's sharp inhale of disappointment at my performance.

True to form, Turel handed me another arrow in silence, only lifting one eyebrow at me as he did so. "What?" I demanded.

"I didn't say a thing," he said, his eyes sparkling at me.

"Right, sure you didn't."

A couple hundred feet behind us Nefta and Alex practiced swordplay. In addition to the clanging and banging of swords and shields, using a broad sword involved a good deal of other noise. Apparently, it required a lot of cursing and yelling. At least, it did for my brother. Setting Durendal and Durendala aside, Nefta provided wooden practice swords and leather shields to work with. The noise distracted. To be fair, Nefta made little noise, with the exception of the occasional musical peal of laughter. The ruckus screamed pure Alex.

At the other end of the meadow, closest to Daisy's house, the dragon in a woman's form taught my ex-boyfriend the finer points of wielding a quarterstaff. Tim and Daisy proved much quieter than Alex and Nefta.

Thanks to Nefta and Turel's transfer of memories and their skills, we skipped the basics and went straight for the advanced lessons. However, something lacked for me. To see Alex and Tim using their weapons at such an expert level while I struggled compounded my frustration.

With a sigh, I took up another arrow and raised my bow. As I prepared for the inevitable miss sure to follow, Turel came closer to me. His hands lightly guided my stance to a better form. "How are you seeing the target?" he asked, his mouth by my ear.

"What do you mean?" I said, trying not to be distracted by his touch.

"Are you viewing it as Siobhan or are you using The Watcher's focus?"

Lowering the bow, I studied him as he spoke. "I guess...I'm just aiming. Poorly, I might add," I said.

A fleeting smile crossed his lips and touched his eyes. "Try really examining it. I want you to concentrate the way you do when you stabilize multiple images. Will you do this?"

Nodding, I returned my attention to the now-despised target. Raising my bow, I tried to do as he asked. To my disappointment, I missed for the one thousand and first time.

"Try again," he urged, taking a step back, giving me more space.

Breathing deep, I exhaled, bracing myself. I closed my eyes for an instant. When I opened them I tried to See the target, studying the path in the air leading to my far off quarry, and then attempting to see inside or even beyond the elusive bulls-eye. To my surprise the arrow sped straight and true, nailing the center.

"Excellent," whispered Turel.

With growing confidence, I reached for another arrow and concentrated on the flight to my objective. In my Watcher's sight, the air warped and twisted away from my trajectory, leaving a perfectly highlighted lifeline from my arrow tip to where I wanted it to fly. I released my grip and my second arrow split the first one neatly in two.

With a shriek of glee, I raised my bow above my head. Turel's grin spread across his face as he wrapped his arms around me. Though only a little taller than me, he picked me up with ease and gave me a quick spin.

"I did it."

"I know, I was right here the whole time," Turel said, his eyes alight as he contemplated me. The sunshine in him arrested my attention.

As the instant of contact drew out to a moment, connecting us, though neither of us moved. He stretched out a hand and placed it on my hair as he leaned to me. I bent my head, closing my eyes. I expected him to chastely kiss my forehead in benediction as he had previously. Instead, his hand shifted forward, his fingers on my neck and beneath my chin, tilting my face to meet his. Turel's kiss was tender. His lips on mine parted, his mustache and short beard surprisingly soft. As his movements changed and his tongue sensuously parted my mouth, I realized I had wanted this kiss since the first time his dark gaze touched mine. Turel's arms tightened, enfolding me. Far too soon he drew back. I opened my eyes to meet his once more, but his expression remained a mystery. Silently, he released me and handed me yet another arrow.

I ducked my head; my heart beat faster, still feeling the imprint of Turel's lips on mine. Glancing around, the swordplay continued without missing a beat and the rhythmic sounds of Tim and Daisy's quarterstaffs carried on uninterrupted. My mind went back to Tim and his kiss only the night before. Without meaning to, I found myself comparing what each embrace felt like. More importantly, how different the emotions each encounter brought to the surface were.

* * *

I convinced Turel to leave me alone to take a shower. My hair still damp, I walked down Daisy's hallway to the kitchen. Outside, Alex, Turel, and Tim cheerfully talked on the front porch. Nefta left to check on Missy and Asrael. It seemed impossible that today, Tim nearly died. I hesitated, struck by the blur of events in the last day.

I had almost died, too, twice. Images of the Hag floating above me and the Net of Purgatory closing in around me clouded my vision. Though I tried to focus on my good fortune to have survived these nightmares, the blackness and sudden despair of my mood threatened to overwhelm me. Evil red eyes filled my mind. Entering the kitchen, I shook my head in frustration and concentrated on the triumph of making it through the day in one piece.

"Hello, ducky," a raspy voice said behind me. I whirled around but saw no one. Heart pounding, I trembled. Taking a deep breath, I struggled to regain some semblance of calm. The gruesome whisper came again, this time from another direction. "I eat you, little lamb. Gobble you up." Panic stricken, I spun the other way. Still, nothing.

The voice must be in my head, I told myself. Turning this way and that, I moved to the corner of the kitchen, my back to the wall. My eyes roved the twilight shrouded room in growing terror. Despite the lengthening shadows there remained plenty of light. Nothing looked out of place in the neat, modern room. The only scary things here were the ones living in my head.

Flashes of blinding, vivid memory seared my mind's eye: the Hag above me, draining me, her voice whispering as she glowed with the life force she stole. I remembered the deep, thick fog of the Net of Purgatory tightening its inexorable bonds around me, slicing my flesh. The shocking sting of the Net's pulses of energy added an extra dimension of agony to the pain of my wounds.

Memories stripped my mind of its ability to reason. I became a tortured animal, filled only with fear and reaction to the past twenty-four hours and their terrors. I slid down the wall until I sat on the floor, cowering in the corner of Daisy's kitchen, shaking, all control gone. I buried my face in my hands, closing my eyes, wishing I could shut my head's internal movie projector off.

"Child? Siobhan?" Daisy's calm voice sounded beautiful. "What's wrong, dear one?"

With an inarticulate sob of relief, I raised my head and then hid my face again, for beyond Daisy's shoulder I thought I saw two red evil eyes stare unblinking into mine. I tightened my arms around my knees, rocking. Daisy knelt, her gentle hands raising my face to meet her amber eyes. "Holy Mother, child," she said, her face twisted in distress.

When I didn't answer she wrapped her arms around me and hugged me to her, crooning a wordless song. I leaned against her warmth, but still couldn't manage to loosen the serpent's grip terror had on my voice and mind. For a moment we stayed this way and then Daisy backed up far enough to study me. She frowned and her expression became vacant and faraway. I saw, as though watching a waking dream, the diaphanous reflection drawn in light of a dragon leaving Daisy's human disguise to float through the air toward the outdoors, joining the others. The red eyes were nowhere to be seen and the comforting solidity of Daisy's human form stayed, holding me close. I found solace in breathing in tandem with her.

A moment later the dragon phantasm returned. Its spirit melded again with its human body. Daisy blinked and focused on my face in compassion. Standing, she gently, but firmly, grasped my hands, guiding me to her. "Come to the table, Siobhan," she commanded. "Sit here."

Like a child, I did as directed, taking one of the four chairs around the square table. There waited two glasses of red wine, where none had been a moment before. I stared at them as Daisy flipped on the kitchen light and sat across the table from me. "Drink," she said. "Turel assures me this will be acceptable to you."

My trembling hands spilled some of the wine on the table, but Daisy did not remark on it. Instead, she watched me take a cautious sip. "Again," she directed.

After we repeated this process a few times, she smiled at me. "Good, dear one." The shaking calmed to imperceptible tremors. Turel had been right, the wine tasted lovely. It calmed me. I tried to smile back, and this time I succeeded. Daisy raised her glass in a toast. "To my stubborn girl, who doesn't quit." She paused and added, "Now, drink your wine, child."

"Yes, Daisy." Her smile widened when I spoke. My glass refilled on its own. I noted this occurrence, but it didn't surprise me. Life with Daisy held certain perks. Good wine magically filling your glass was one of them. The near death experiences though, I could do without. I let out a deep breath and took a sip as my heart rate steadied.

Daisy regarded her own wine glass with a puzzled frown. She held it to the light and swirled it experimentally. Curious, the dragon sniffed the wine. "I have often noticed mankind makes much of this beverage," she said. "One wonders what the fuss is about."

"You've never had wine?"

"Certainly, eons ago. No offense, dear one, it left much to be desired." Daisy wrinkled her nose at her glass. Her expression lightened. "Of course, you had just invented it. Perhaps you've improved on it in past the last several thousand years. This certainly smells different than I remember."

Looking hopeful, Daisy took a deep sip of wine then gargled with it. With a muffled exclamation she spat it back into her glass. She stuck out her tongue, opening and closing her mouth like a small child forced to eat Brussel sprouts. "Alas, no," she mourned. "It's still just spoiled grape juice."

"Well, I'm not drinking yours; you spit in your glass."

"I did no such thing," said Daisy, all innocence.

Swallowing, I grinned back at her. The wine helped.

"Now, child, tell me what troubles you."

Setting my glass on the table, I spread my hands out. "This, everything. I've almost died twice in the past, what? Eighteen hours? And that's with you and two angels doing all you can to keep me in one piece."

Daisy blinked in surprise, straightening in her chair. "It has been busy, hasn't it?"

"Uh, yeah."

The dragon disguised as a woman frowned in thought. "I can't promise tomorrow will be any different," she said. "In many ways, you've crossed into a different reality, Siobhan. You'll never judge the world the way you once did."

I relived the last week. Like snapshots spread on a table, I saw again magnificent angel wings, shining swords, Daisy's jeweled scales, and Chernobog's terrifying visage. Visions of Gilbert's angry, pale-blue eyes, Turel's warm dark ones, the scars on Ian's back, the inky black of Asrael's scythe, and much more passed through my mind.

Daisy continued, "You now have something beyond even faith. You have the power of knowledge. You know the legends are true. Dragons and demons do exist. You know the angels of the Bible are real. This sets you, your brother, and Tim apart from others of your race. And, of course, as Watcher you have always been one apart."

"Why me?" I wondered aloud one more time. A welter of emotions cascaded through me. Injustice, fear, self-pity, self-righteousness tumbled and mixed with wonder, joy, gratitude, and curiosity. Wonder at the amazing world revealed these past days. Joy at my present company and the affection I held for them. Gratitude pulsed through me, at the miracle of being alive, that we all still lived. Most of all, genuine curiosity filled me as to how I had fallen into this role Fate dictated for me.

Daisy's amber gaze was solemn. "You are involved in great events, a crucial time in our shared history. I have never known how the heroes appear on the world's stage, only when they're needed, they do, in fact, arrive."

"So, you're saying, I'm just lucky, eh?"

She shrugged. "Who would you rather have dealing with the situation? If you had the chance to hand your ability over to another and walk away from this, would you?"

I sat still, thinking, remembering. I shook my head. My hands trembled as I admitted, "No, I think…I think I want to see what happens next." Despite everything, some perverse spirit inside me would never let me walk away from this—even if I could.

"It's understandable to be frightened, even overwhelmed, Siobhan. The important thing is once the moment has passed, you get up and put one foot in front of the other, continuing along life's path. We all have mountains to climb," said Daisy.

A gentle hand rested on my shoulder and I looked into Turel's face. "What mountains?" he asked us in a concerned voice.

Daisy waved this aside. "It matters not, Turel. Siobhan experienced a natural reaction to her brushes with death."

Turel nodded, sitting to my right, between Daisy and me. "Of course," he said, "you're only human."

"Exactly," agreed the dragon, her golden braid shining in the glow of the kitchen light above us.

"Daisy," I said as a sudden thought occurred to me. "Why did you send your spirit outside? Why didn't you go talk to Turel or use some sort of mind speak like he can?"

"I couldn't leave you alone," she explained. "Well, in a fashion I did, but I reasoned at least having warm, living, breathing arms supporting you would be better than completely leaving you."

I pushed away the thought of those red eyes I'd seen in the kitchen. I prayed that the image had been a figment of my imagination.

"Besides," Daisy went on, "I did not want to have everyone in here. You were in no shape to deal with all four of us, even as well-meaning as we would have been. I assume Tim and Alex are busy?" She directed the last at Turel.

"They're having a beer, playing horse shoes," he said to her.

"No telepathy?" I asked again.

"Telepathy between my kind and angels is not one of my gifts," she said and waved a graceful hand toward Turel. "Sharing the minds of others, even other species, is one of his specialties. I could not yell, because that would have brought all three running, and I only needed to confer with Turel."

"So, you sent your spirit." I understood now.

"To use my spirit thus, it is a small thing for one such as me,"

"Such a lovely sight," I said, remembering the graceful form of light and air. "Of course, I was in no position to appreciate it at the time. Your spirit is a dragon."

"Naturally." Daisy shrugged. "What else would I be?"

"Touché." The world seemed a brighter place with me surrounded by Daisy and Turel, a glass of fine wine in my hand.

Turel picked up the second glass. As he lifted it toward his lips, I cautioned, "Wait. She spat in that one."

Turel frowned at Daisy. "Why ever would she do that? Lady Gwyrdd," he said with exaggerated formality, "is there some ancient custom amongst the First Ones I've perhaps missed?"

Daisy pointed to her glass as though identifying a criminal in a line-up. "That is spoiled grape juice."

"Well, technically, yes," acknowledged Turel. "I fail to see how that is relevant to you spitting in a perfectly good glass of wine. Err, you did get the one I recommended?"

"It is relevant, my angelic friend, because as it happens, I do not care for spoiled grape juice." Daisy rose with exquisite poise from her seat. "I should join Alex and Tim. As Siobhan so rightly pointed out, one cannot be too careful. Besides, it's dark now. I'm sure horseshoes is done. And, Turel, of course I got the one you recommended, look at the bottle."

I blinked. Daisy's glass disappeared, replaced by an open bottle of Clos Pegase cabernet and an empty glass for Turel. Noticing my wine glass had been filled for a third time, I called, "Daisy, are you trying to get me drunk?"

She paused as she opened the screen door to the front porch. "Perish the thought, dear." She tossed a backward glance over her shoulder as she spoke. "Although, if it helped Turel press his suit with you, would that be such a bad thing?" She pushed through the door even as her parting shot went home.

My face warmed with an intense blush.

Turel shook his head. "Dragons," he muttered. "Nothing gets by them."

"True." Daisy stuck her head back in the screen door. "Now, Turel, be a pet, while I stand guard. Find out what terrified Siobhan to the point of losing all reason." With that she left again.

Turel poured himself a glass of the wine. Without meeting my eyes, he said, "I very much enjoyed this wine at your house."

"You have a good memory," I said, trying not to think about his kiss that afternoon, and worrying whether he could read my thoughts on my face.

"For some things, with some people."

Silence covered the room as I sipped my wine and let my blush fade.

"Well?" he asked, putting one warm, olive-skinned hand on my pale one.

"Well, what?"

He delicately placed one hand under my chin. My breath caught and my stomach tightened with fluttering butterflies. "What brought on the panic attack?"

"I told Daisy," I said, reluctant to even think about the Hag or the Net. "I have almost died twice in the past day, even with an angel and a dragon to protect me."

"And..."

"Isn't that enough, Turel?"

"For most people, yes," he said, sitting back and stroking his beard with his free hand. "For you? I'm guessing no. I've seen you hold it together pretty well, for a mortal."

"'For a mortal.' Gosh, thanks."

"Still," the angel said, his jaw set. "The question stands. What scared you?"

Toying with my glass, I said, "Well, I kept having flashbacks. You know, of the Net cutting me and those energy bursts bring agony to a whole new theatre of pain kind of extravaganza."

"And?"

Darn him, I thought.

"Siobhan?" Turel pushed, his tone gentle, but insistent.

"No."

"Yes." His eyes bored into mine.

I contemplated my glass. My words came haltingly. "She returned. I could hear her... whisper... I'll never forget it. She called me..." My voice faded; I stared straight ahead. The Hag's wretched face swam before me. I remembered the hurt. Turel waited for me to continue, his eyes never leaving my face. "Those red eyes," I whispered. "I saw them here, behind Daisy. I could still see...wispy hair, so thin, evil eyes. She called me... she called me..."

Turel leaned closer, trying to catch each of my faint whispers. "What did she call you?"

My grip on his hand tightened. Her face filled my mind. It

155

was all I saw, all I could think about. "She called me…"

"I call it ducky, yes, I do." A deathly new whisper floated through the kitchen.

Turel leapt to his feet, white wings unfurled. In the doorway to the hall floated the barest specter of the Hag. Turel put himself between her and me. My breath caught at the sight of my ultimate nightmare. Her wicked, red eyes brightened as they saw me. Her form drew closer. "I call it piggy," she said with a rasp. "Like piggy, eat piggy."

Without hesitating, Turel hurled a lightning bolt at the creature, but this time the electricity simply sizzled over her, illuminating her emaciated form then disappearing. "Bad angel, no-taste-good-angel," she scolded, scooting closer to me. "Here, little lamb, come here to me."

"Turel," I pleaded. The Hag's image filled my head, as well as occupying my terrified eyes.

Turel drew his flaming sword and advanced on the thing. He delivered what should have been a mighty blow, but his sword passed through the Hag with no visible effect upon her.

"Some icky angel in my piggy." The Hag snarled the words as she drew closer. "Not so yummy now, but still yummy enough for me."

I backed away from the table, knocking over my chair as I moved. The hard surface of the wall cabinets stopped my retreat. My breath escaped in ragged sobs. I couldn't let her touch me. I'd die if she touched me.

"Here, piggy, piggy. Come to die, come to me, my tasty-tasty." The wheedling Hag made a slurping sound. I whimpered. Shivering, cold sweat drenched my body.

"Be silent!" Turel raged at the creature.

Her evil blood-red eyes flicked toward him. "Bad angel. Ducky brought me back, ducky did, yes." Her hellish gaze burned into my eyes again. "Good ducky wants to die. Yes, it does, yes."

The sibilant hissing sound of her voice reverberated in my ears, echoing through my brain. If Turel answered the thing, I had no idea what he said. Turel grabbed my arms and shook me in frustration. "That's it. You brought her back. You're feeding her, recreating her from your memories. You can stop this."

I didn't respond as the Hag edged nearer. Turel shook me again. "Siobhan." The creature's relentless approach continued. "Siobhan, think of something else. Think of anything, except that thing."

The grotesque apparition came closer still. She would have me. Turel saw her reaching for me. His face twisted in desperation. "Damn it," he growled. He extended his wings further, blocking the Hag from my view. His fierce grip on my arms tightened, to the point of pain. Roughly, he pulled me to him, bringing his lips to mine. In stark contrast to that afternoon, his kiss demanded, urgent.

In spite of myself, I kissed him back. As my body responded, the terror of the Hag's image faded, replaced by the overwhelming reality of his lean frame against me. My mind let the fear go, concentrating instead on Turel's warm touch. His hands relaxed, releasing their iron grip on my arms and slid softly, surely over my body. I shivered, but this time with the exquisite sensation of Turel's hand slipping under my shirt and running his fingertips lightly down the curve of my waist and around to the small of my back. I pressed closer to him. The respite from fear intoxicated as much as being in his arms.

"Bad ducky, nasty angel," hissed a fading whisper.

All went still.

My breath came quicker. Our kisses were gentler now, but more passionate. This idyll proved short-lived as running feet and shouts brought us back to the here and now with a jolt.

"Siobhan, are you okay?" Tim burst through the door, followed by Daisy and Alex. Silently, I cursed both the interruption and that Tim had seen Turel and me together.

"I'd say she's fine, Tim." Alex said with an infuriating smirk.

"Right, Alex," Tim said through gritted teeth. His face tensed, features drawn in lines of pain.

"What?" asked my brother. "You can see she's already received mouth-to-mouth."

"He was helping me," I mumbled.

"I'll bet. A jump start, right, sis?"

Daisy patted my brother's arm. "Yes, yes, be still, child. We find you endlessly amusing. Now, Siobhan, Turel, what happened? I heard Turel shouting, and I'd swear I heard a bolt."

"You did," confirmed Turel. His demeanor was far more composed than mine. He went on to explain about the Hag and how I'd inadvertently invited my worst fear back to this plane of existence. We gathered around the table once more, filling the four chairs, and Tim dragging over a stool from the counter. As Turel finished, Alex squeezed my hand. For once, my brother sat without words, but then, he'd had a Hag attack him, too. He knew something of what I faced, even though he hadn't been able to see his attacker.

"Can you break the bond this creature has formed?" Daisy asked Turel.

"Once it would have been no great thing. Now? With the power I have left? I shall take temporary steps tonight until we have the luxury of more time to fully deal with the problem," he answered.

"If it does return, dragon-fire should do the trick," said Daisy, studying me.

"But, Turel, tried to use his flaming sword," I protested. "It didn't work."

Daisy smiled; not a nice smile. "Believe me, dragon-fire is different. It's far more powerful. Dragon-fire is the fire of life. It is the flame of creation, or conversely, of annihilation. I can unmake this creature like that." She snapped her fingers. The dragon spoke to Alex and Tim, "I do not anticipate that Nefta will be back from the seer's this night. You two should try to get some sleep. I shall patrol."

"Wait, don't you need rest?" asked Tim, his face concerned.

Daisy smiled in affection at him. "You are a dear, Tim, but no, I'm fine. I can go months without sleep if I need to. You rest up. Remember, according to the prophecy we only have two days left."

Alex bid his goodnights, hugging me. Tim seemed inclined to linger, as though he had something to say to me. However, it quickly became clear Turel planned on staying, and Daisy kept chiding him, like a mother hen, to get to bed. Finally, frowning, he went.

Daisy chided Turel and me. "Not too late, you two. I did not joke about the sleep. Time waits for no one."

"Yes, Mom," I said.

"Bite your tongue, Siobhan," she retorted. "I am certainly not your mother." Regally, she swept out the front door.

Alone in the kitchen again, Turel and I regarded one another. If I brought the Hag back, then how would I ever be safe? As my fear and anxiety returned, I wished for Turel's sure embrace. My face flamed and I cursed my telltale blushes. Even more, I cursed my impulse to hide in his arms. Certainly, I was stronger than some damsel in distress, wasn't I? I hazarded a glance at him. His dark eyes became thoughtful.

"Yes?" I asked, unsure of what came next.

He pursed his lips. "We need to find a way to protect you from yourself, it seems," he said.

"I thought she was dead."

"She was," he said, shrugging. "You brought her back. Mankind's dreams created the creatures of nightmares in the first place, so it is hardly surprising she made her way back into existence through your fear."

"We create the monsters?"

"Well, not all of them, but some." As he spoke the angel moved to me. Leaning to me, he laid one gentle hand on my head. "If I may?"

"What are you going to do?"

"I'm going to block your fear of her. Then she won't have a way back."

I nodded. He smiled at my eagerness and closed his eyes. The sense of him became heightened as he moved through my mind, yet he touched so lightly it seemed the most natural thing to have him with me. He closed doors, pathways of thought; in a shorter time than I would have believed possible, he finished.

As our eyes met, he smiled. "Siobhan, don't scratch at it, please."

I frowned, not understanding.

"Think of what I've done as a kind of patch, a bandage. Don't worry at it, or try to dislodge it. It's not permanent. I need to think of the right way of excising the Hag from your mind. This is delicate work, not something to be rushed."

"Thank you." I sighed in relief. The memories remained, but in a detached kind of way, as though the experiences made up someone else's story, and I listened in on it.

"Come, Daisy's right. You need sleep."

As we paused by my bedroom door, I hesitated. Should I invite him in? Did he want to come in? I struggled with what to say next, how to break the silence.

"Turel?"

He leaned forward, his eyes searching my face. "Yes, Siobhan?"

"Do you think Daisy has a broomstick somewhere around here?" My attempt at a joke sounded forced, even to me.

His shoulders sagged as he said, "Good night, Siobhan. Don't worry, I'll be right here."

Chapter Sixteen

I did not sleep well that night—again. My brain refused to turn off. My restless thoughts bounced from the horrors of the last week: the Net, Chernobog, even the creature seeking to devour Missy's soul. When my mind rested on the Hag, I made myself think of something else. My thoughts went round and round regarding Turel: my growing feelings for him, my confusion about this change in our relationship, and my anxiety over Tim's reaction.

Each time I thought of Tim I jumped to a different topic, which led me to think of the prophecy. As I dissected every word I remembered from Tim's notes I became more and more worried, not only for those I loved who were involved, but for the world in general. I made myself change the mental channel again which brought me back full circle to the horrors of the last week.

Somewhere in the fog between asleep and awake I must have tumbled into slumber. Strange dreams found me. A woman with brilliant, green eyes mocked me. I knew her. I had always known her. All my life this nightmare waited to torture my nights. I was useless, helpless, and she knew it. What good could my sight do? Mocking laughter taunted me, slicing my confidence, piercing my courage. I wasted time...and the sands in the hourglass dwindled. I would fail. In my dream state I tried to save precious seconds and make sense of the nonsensical. Nothing was right. I should walk away before I let everyone down. And the sands in an hour glass still emptied.

Darkness still gowned the horizon with a hint of dawn's first light in her train when I woke. This time I clung to shreds of memory: the hate, her eyes, and my futility. Going to the window, I peered outside, wondering if Daisy still patrolled. She counted on me. They were counting on me. Everyone expected me to save the world. They believed in the Watcher, but I didn't feel like the Watcher right now. I rubbed my forehead. What did I think I could accomplish anyway? I didn't have any magic. So I could See stuff. What good would that be against demons? Fallen angels?

I hated my thoughts, my weakness. I was terrible company—even to me. Still in my short pajamas and the soft cotton tank top, I opened my door. Turel stayed where I'd left him hours ago, sitting in the shadows of the dim hallway opposite of my room. His eyebrows went up in surprise though he said nothing. I gave him a tired smile and sat next to him. The air between us teemed with unspoken questions, but I'd rather deal with this tension than my lonely self-doubt.

Without turning my head, I said, "You're an angel."

"What? Are you handing out compliments or is this species identification time?"

"You're an angel," I repeated with more emphasis. "Can this, can you and I, can this even happen?"

"Siobhan," he said. "Look at me." I met his dark eyes. "You forget, I'm an angel cast out of Heaven for marrying a mortal woman. It seems I have a bit of history in this area."

I stared at the hallway in front of me, remembering when he had given me his archery memories and everything else I had glimpsed from his past. The visions of his wife, his children, and the ages he'd spent alone filled my mind. A welter of powerful emotions exploded in my tired head. Finally, I blurted out, "Here's the thing. I'm not planning to get married."

Turel held up his hands in a reflexive action. "I wasn't asking."

"Ever."

"Still not asking."

"I know, Turel, I'm just saying."

"Saying what?" He sounded confused.

I blinked. My eyes felt like they had sand in them. A monster-sized yawn overcame me. Another one followed. My eyes blurred with fatigue.

"Did you sleep at all?"

I shrugged. "Nope, couldn't shut my brain off," I admitted, glancing at him.

"You aren't happy," he said, frowning.

"Whatever."

His eyebrows rose a bit at my tone. "Grumpy, even."

Running my hands again over my disheveled hair, I tried to focus. Failing, I rubbed my eyes in a futile attempt to clear the stinging sensation from them. "Just tired," I mumbled. A huge yawn underscored my comment.

He held out an arm to me. "Come here, sleepy."

"Stop naming dwarves," I said, yawning again.

He gathered me in his arms and carried me to the porch. A few stars still twinkled in the dawn-touched sky as Daisy's roses perfumed the air. He sat on the swing holding me and put his back against one corner, cradling me against his chest. Sometimes I forgot how strong he was.

I stiffened and started to get up, but his arms tightened around me and one hand stroked my hair. "Shh," he said and his lips brushed the top of my head. "Go to sleep, Watcher."

To my surprise, that is what I did.

* * *

I woke hours later, still in the swing with an afghan over me and a pillow under my head. Turel was gone, and someone held coffee under my nose. I opened my eyes. The despair of the night seemed far away in the bright morning sunshine. I inhaled. A new day dawned. If I could just put one foot in front of the other, maybe I would get through this.

Tim sat on the front step next to me, looking out for me as he had so many times in the past. My guardian. A rush of affection ran through me. He held a cup up. "Milk, two sugars," he said. "That's right, isn't it?"

"You remembered, thanks." I sat up and took a sip. It was hot and strong.

"I remember a lot," he said mildly, taking a sip from his own mug.

Milk, no sugars. I remembered his preference, too, though I did not say it out loud. I waited to see if Turel's name would come up.

Tim blew to cool his drink. "You okay?"

"Better, now that I've gotten some sleep. What time is it?" My muscles protested from sleeping on the swing, but still a million times improved from my condition earlier that morning.

"Just past nine." Tim's eyes were intent as he answered me. He ran a hand through his sandy hair. It was short enough to be a little spiky in the morning until he combed it. "Turel said you hadn't been able to sleep last night."

He stumbled on the angel's name. I winced, but decided to dive in anyway. "Tim."

He waved a hand, stopping me. "Don't, Siobhan. It's fine. I don't own you, and I can't stop you from making your own choices. I know better than to even try."

"So, this isn't going to be a huge scene?"

"No scenes, but I'm not giving up on you either."

"Tim," I started again, thinking of Missy's private words to me, "*When the Guardian's passion shall surely wake, then the Black God's last prison chain will break.*" Chernobog had been terrifying enough the night he smashed Daisy's statue in front of my house. He'd still been chained. If Tim's passion could set the demon free, who knew how powerful the thing would be? Even if I had wanted to rekindle things with Tim—and I didn't—, it was out of the question now. I wanted to explain. Maybe it would help take some of the hurt out of the situation for him.

He wouldn't let me even get started. "It's fine," he repeated in a tone meant to forestall anything I might want to add.

"But—"

"Siobhan, I said, it's fine."

We sat for a moment, drinking our coffee in a companionable silence. "I thought you said fine is never good." I nudged his side with my bare foot.

"That's what I said. Everything is fine." His smile took the barb from his words.

"Morning ," Daisy said as she walked up the path. Today her human form wore green pants and a green T-shirt. Daisy always wore green when she appeared in her human form. She was a green dragon, after all, and people would be bound to talk if a green-skinned lady walked the street.

She had an extra spring in her step. Tim noticed her demeanor as well. "What's got you so cheery?" he asked.

Her smile lit up as bright as the sunshine. "Good news, dear ones, Asrael and Turel have decided to force a resolution to the oracle's problem."

Tim frowned. "What problem?"

I tapped his shoulder. "She's fighting for her soul, remember?"

His face cleared and he flushed. "Right, yeah, that's a problem."

Daisy nodded. "Indeed it is, and it creates a dilemma for us as well."

"How so, Daisy?" Tim asked.

"We need Missy," she said.

Tim raised one eyebrow. "She has to tell us where The Veil is," I reminded him.

"Oh," Tim said. "I think I forgot about that part. What did Turel and Asrael do?"

"They're bending the rules, dear one."

"Seems like Turel does that a lot," observed Tim. He glanced at me. "I mean, what with getting Daisy back to this world and all."

Daisy pursed her lips. "Come, it will be far easier to show you than to explain." She beckoned us toward the front door. "Everyone get dressed. We're going to the oracle's. Oh, and someone ought to wake Alex."

"You want to?" I asked Tim hopefully.

"Not even a little bit," he said. "Wanna Rochambeau for it?"

I shook my head. "I know better. You always win. I'll save you the trouble and wake sleepy-head myself."

Tim's bright eyes twinkled as he gave me the thumbs up and

returned to his coffee. I braced myself. Waking my brother was a painful process. He was not a morning person.

* * *

As we pulled up to Missy's little lavender house. Turel waited for us, leaning against the dilapidated fence. I got out of the car and noted with a smile his T-shirt today pictured two goblets and read, "I spent the last few years building up an immunity to iocane powder." Our eyes met with a palpable sensation, like a physical caress.

Before I could greet him, the screen door flew open with a bang. Missy headed straight for me, her tie-dyed sundress billowing around her as she rushed over. "Siobhan," she exclaimed, surprising me with the fervor of her greeting. "Like, such a relief to find out you were going to be here today."

"Really?"

"Totally, no one can, like, lie to you," she said. "You'll be straight with me, right?" I noticed she made brief eye contact with me, an improvement since my last visit.

"Of course I will," I promised, putting one arm around her slim, pale shoulders and squeezing.

"Awesome," she said in relief. "Leo, hurry up, babe."

Her earnest boyfriend with his worried brown eyes appeared in the doorway. Asrael emerged like a grim silent shadow at Leo's shoulder. Leo waved with an anxious grin. "Hullo." His gaze followed Missy's every move.

Missy stayed at my side, nervous and plucking at her dress with slender white fingers that trembled. I saw why Leo worried. While the battle for Missy's soul wasn't as evident in my sight as it had been on my last meeting with her, the strain in her expression screamed the realities of her situation. Dark circles marred the skin under her eyes, standing out in stark contrast against the pallor of her complexion. "How are you holding up?" I asked.

She shrugged. "It's less scary now that I know Pythia is mostly on my side," she said.

"Mostly?" I repeated.

Missy rolled her eyes. "Well, she's awfully bossy. Everything has to be her way." Her smile faded. "The thing, that creature, it's so hungry, so strong. Pythia's been fighting it for me, so that's helped me, like, get my head back together, you know?"

"Makes sense," I said.

Missy took a deep breath and continued, "But she's getting tired, we both are, and it's, well, it keeps getting stronger." The seer's voice trailed off, as though even the effort to speak tired her. Fine beads of sweat appeared above her lip and on her forehead.

I squeezed her shoulders again, wishing I could will strength into her.

Asrael and Nefta trailed outside after Leo, making the small front yard crowded as the others also got out of the Jeep. A silence spread, broken only by the thump of Leia's tail.

Alex said, "I don't think we're going to fit in there." He nodded toward Missy and Leo's little home.

"Agreed, Alex. Luckily, we'll be meeting the others on the hill," said Turel.

"We will?" said Leo, his voice cracking. "Others?"

"Yes, young one, others. You see, we'll need some help to bring this about," Daisy said. "We'll be leaving right now."

"Uh, like, how?" Missy said, her expression doubtful. "Are we walking?"

Nefta shook her head. The blond Valkyrie's smooth profile had shifted to the serene calm I knew. The angel who rebuked Asrael with such passion and laughed with my brother during swordplay had vanished. "Walking is too slow," she explained. "Watcher, you're with Turel. Alex and the oracle are with me, Tim hold on to Daisy's hand and Leo is with Asrael. Are we clear?"

Alex elbowed Tim. "Dude, you think we're getting beamed aboard?"

Tim ignored him and frowned. "What about Leia?" he asked.

"Who's Leia?" responded Nefta.

"My dog," Tim said. Leia sat beside him, her intelligent dark eyes watching everyone, as if she followed the conversation along with the rest of us. Her tail thumped as Tim spoke.

Nefta blinked. "I had not realized what you named her," she

said. "I know little of dogs."

Tim's eyebrows flew up at the angel's obliviousness.

Turel stepped forward. "Not to worry, Tim. I'd be happy to take Leia." I knew enough of Turel's facial expressions now to see he held back a chuckle.

Tim's face lightened. "Thanks, Turel, appreciate it."

Asrael shrugged his shoulders. "If we could move along now?"

Daisy nodded, saying, "Quite right, Asrael, let's get this settled. Besides, they'll be waiting." Alex and I exchanged glances. Who?

Turel walked over to Leia and with the same ease I would pick up my purse he hefted the large German shepherd on to his shoulder. He used one hand to steady her, speaking in soothing tones under his breath to the dog. To be fair, she seemed relaxed, her tail wagging and hitting Turel in the face. Smiling, he batted the tail away and held out one hand to me. "Watcher, if you would care to come with me?"

I smiled back and slipped my hand in his. Turel trod through the air, taking me with him.

I'm not sure what I expected from the place between dimensions. If anything, I thought perhaps of cold and emptiness. Instead, I stepped into a rainbow, prisms of reflected light refracting, dancing everywhere around me. It was bright, warm, and filled with sound. Music I had never heard, or even imagined filled my ears. The notes consisted of part harpsichord, part a kind of birdsong, and the mingled voices of a choir. It contained all of these and yet none of them, carried through the air in a choir of hundreds, thousands of voices, perhaps more. It filled my heart and renewed my soul. I could have stayed there forever. Yet, I experienced this in a few heartbeats as I took a stride from one part of reality, through this rainbow world and then into my mundane reality once more.

As we emerged I inhaled and took in my surroundings. We journeyed much farther than Turel had implied. We had arrived on an open hilltop. In the distance I saw the ocean. We traveled close enough to the coast that the breeze held a salty tang to it.

We stood on a grass-covered table-top, a flat plateau with steep drop offs on all sides. Trees, mostly redwoods covered the knolls around us, town left behind. An instant after our crossing, the others arrived in rapid succession. Turel put Leia down. I'm not sure what she thought of the process, but she licked his hand and sat, leaning her body against his legs until Tim arrived.

"Come," Asrael said in his forbidding voice, "Amitiel and the others await."

I stifled a gasp. A group of a dozen angels waited a few yards from us. They had not been present when we first stepped through the air so they, too, must have just arrived.

"Um, wow," whispered Leo.

"You said it, dude," agreed my brother. "Hey, Daisy?"

"Yes, Alex," she said.

"How come I can see angels now, like Siobhan? Am I changing?"

She chuckled, a rich and friendly sound. "Dear one, we're always changing, so yes to that question, but it's no mystery why you can see the angels. They are simply not hiding their true natures, or attempting to hide their wings."

Alex frowned. "Come again?"

Tim walked forward and laid a hand on Alex's shoulder. "So, you could always see Turel, just not always his wings, right?"

Alex nodded.

"And you could see Ian, but not the scars Siobhan saw, remember?"

Alex nodded again, saying, "Okay, so anyone can see angels, if the angels let them, is that right? If the angels want to hide themselves or their wings, they do a glamour thingie like Daisy did and then only Siobhan can see them?"

"Exactly," said Turel.

"Darn," said Alex, "I kinda' hoped I could be like Siobhan, you know, all Watcher-y. Think what you'd see."

I shook my head. "It's not all pretty," I said. "Some of it is giving me real nightmares. Imagine if you had been able to see the Hag on you…" I trailed off.

Alex's cheerful face went solemn. "No doubt. Guess I'm glad that I don't see what you see," he said.

"Are we ready now?" Asrael asked.

One of the angels broke off from the group and approached us. "Well met, my friends. My name is Amitiel," she said with a smile, making a short bow toward Daisy.

Amitiel was a copper-skinned angel with brilliant violet-blue eyes. Her magnificent wings displayed shades of purple and lavender. She possessed an archetypal African-American beauty with her full lips and strong cheekbones. Amitiel wore her long black hair in braids and pulled the many braids back into one ponytail. The angel's straight teeth flashed white against her skin as she smiled in a wide and generous way.

Like Turel, there radiated a warmth and strength to her that made me trust her. Her style of dress resembled his—jeans, motorcycle boots and a faded green army jacket over her plain black tee. She stood untouched by the heat of the day. The distinctive Samurai handle of a katana stuck up between her wings, strapped to her back. Amitiel carried a bullwhip at her belt. She moved with the same spare, efficient grace which characterized Nefta's movements.

"Amitiel," said Daisy, moving forward to enfold the angel in a loving hug. "It is good to see you."

"And you, Gwrydd, it has been ages," Amitiel responded.

"Literally. I like this body, much easier to hug and no flames." The two laughed.

"Thank you for allowing me to attend this occasion," continued Daisy.

Amitiel's wide smile disappeared. "Well, you know, as an Observer I can have no official opinion. However, between you and me, I could smite Chernobog myself. He has caused us no end of trouble and vexation."

"I can relate," Daisy said in grim agreement. "Shall I introduce you?"

"Of course, we can catch up on current events later," the angel agreed. She called to her companions, "Observers, to your places." The angels spread out in a loose circle around us, each of them standing where the flat edge dropped off to the steep hillside. None of them spoke.

With a satisfied nod, Amitiel turned back to our group. Her expression became serious as she regarded each of us while Daisy made introductions. When she said my name, shyness threatened to overwhelm me. Amitiel's violet gaze considered me, her face intent. "Watcher," she said, giving me a deep bow. "We've waited an age for you."

Not knowing if I should bow, too, I inclined my head and said, "It's nice to meet you, too."

Her wide smile reappeared as she continued, "Although, I have to say, it has been hard losing one of my best comrades-in-arms to you." She pointed to Turel. "Things are not the same without your counsel, Turiel."

"Oh, dear, I'm sorry," I stammered.

Amitiel hastened to reassure me. "No, no, Watcher, it is as foretold. Please, I speak in jest. Turiel is where he needs to be. The time of the Veil approaches."

"And on that note," Daisy said, "allow me to introduce this age's oracle. Her name is Missy and she carries the soul of the renowned Pythia as her spirit guide."

Amitiel bowed again. From their places around the edges of the plateau, her companion Observers also bowed. "Well met, oracle," Amitiel said. "It is for you we gather today. We must rid you of this affliction ere you can complete your task. Without your Sight, your guidance, all will fall to chaos and our battle for this world lost."

Missy visibly swallowed. "Thank you." Her fervent whisper carried despite its softness.

The remainder of my companions stayed silent in the pause that followed, then as usual, Alex spoke, "Okay, what next?"

Asrael scowled at my brother, but answered him nonetheless, "Amitiel is an Angel of Truth. Among her many talents, she has a gift for forcing truths into view, where they can be dealt with."

Missy frowned in confusion. "So, like, what does that mean?"

Leo's arm went around the frail oracle.

Daisy echoed what she had said to us earlier, "It is easier to show you than to tell you. Amitiel, if you would be so kind?"

The angel gave Daisy a gracious nod and said, "Everyone, you'll need to do exactly what you are told. No more, no less, and above all else, no interruptions. Do not speak unless you are spoken to. Am I clear?"

She directed this last at Alex, who grumbled, "Don't know why she's glaring at me." Tim elbowed Alex in the stomach, and my brother grunted but took the hint.

Amitiel waited a moment, allowing her instructions to sink in, saying, "Now, I need everyone to form a large circle around the oracle. Please alternate mortals and immortals as you do so. Missy, stay where you are." Amitiel herself stayed close to Missy. The Angel of Truth's glorious violet eyes sparkled in lively interest.

We did as we were told. I waited between Turel and Daisy then Alex on Daisy's left and, finally, Nefta. Next stood Tim, adjacent to Asrael, and Leo completed the circle between Asrael and Turel. Leia stayed with Missy. The oracle seemed comforted by the dog's presence. Her fingers entwined in the thick fur behind the shepherd's ears, petting Leia in a restless way.

Amitiel gestured to the silent Observers in the outer circle around us. "Angels, now, please."

As one, the angels spread their wings and with powerful strokes rose in the air. I contained a gasp. I had never seen an angel fly. Their wings beat graceful and sure, moving with such power the warm summer air gusted with each motion, blowing and tousling our hair. When they climbed about fifty feet above us, they hovered with mighty strokes of their wings, extended their arms, and sang softly.

The song carried a melody without words. Even without knowing what they sang, I tossed in a sea of emotions. I wanted to cry and to laugh. My heart filled with the need to hug those I loved, to dance, even do cartwheels at the sheer joy of being alive and in this beautiful world. Awe and wonder covered my companions' faces as well. The blood coursed through my veins. I felt vital and free, consumed with longing for the path not taken, for what lay just beyond the next bend in the road.

As the angels sang their soft, joyful refrain, a silvery-blue light surrounded them. The light brightened and spread around them and over us until we were covered in a dazzling dome of glowing azure more brilliant than the clearest, bluest sky. My gaze went back to Missy. Amitiel also sang, but she carried a different tune, her hands on either side of the oracle's head.

Missy whimpered and trembled under the Angel of Truth's hands. I saw why—the spiritual battle I remembered from my first visit continued. I concentrated on the vision I had learned to know as my "Watcher's sight." Pythia and the creature grappled with one another, sometimes with the pale spirit of Missy herself. A bestial wrestling match ensued, brutal and devoid of any grace or beauty. I shuddered to think how Missy survived it when, to my Sight, the fight ripped her spirit to shreds.

As Amitiel's song grew in pace and volume, this struggle became more vivid. The spirit forms hovered on the barest edge of being made flesh. Missy's hurt and anguish became palpable, her whimpers more terrified and pain-filled. Just as I was about to break the circle and run to her, to try to help or protect her, Amitiel's song reached a crescendo. A pure bolt of violet light erupted from her hands, blinding us for an instant. When I could see again, blinking my dazed eyes, Amitiel retreated from Missy. Three Missys stood in place of the one.

Chapter Seventeen

The three Missys stared at us as we gaped in shock. Even the angels and Daisy seemed surprised. I scrutinized the three, but there appeared to be no difference. Each looked the same, down to the colorless, lank hair, the tie-dyed sundress, and frightened gray eyes. The smallest details identically replicated: slender, pale fingers, and her smudged, dirty, bare feet. Leia whined her uneasiness and moved away, going to lie in front of Tim. As she settled herself, she whined again, her dark eyes moving over the multiple seers.

Daisy murmured, "It's always different, isn't it, my friend?"

"Truly," said Amitiel in agreement, "though I believe I know what needs to come next." She paused for a moment as the three Missys regarded each other. They seemed astonished at this turn of events. One inspected her tie-dyed skirt in wonder and another touched a hesitant hand to her own hair, bewildered. "Oracles," continued Amitiel, "which of you is the true Missy?"

One raised her hand. "I am Missy."

The Angel of Truth scanned from her to me with piercing eyes and asked, "Watcher, can you vouch for her?"

Concentrating, I found I did know the Missys. With my Watcher's Sight, I observed each of them. The true Missy waited with her fragile spirit and gray seer's eyes. When I regarded the body containing Pythia, I Saw the old woman with silver eyes I remembered from the prophecy reading. Lastly, I shuddered to behold the oracle's form camouflaging the evil black shape of her enemy. "Yes, I can. That is the real Missy," I said with confidence. I frowned. "Wait, you're an Angel of Truth, can't you See them, too?"

Amitiel shook her head. "I bring the truth to the light of day. This is my gift. It is up to Missy to choose what to do with these truths and how to best proceed with her life. No one can do this for her. Turiel, if you could please hold the other two for me?"

"Certainly," the angel said. His expression focused, and his eyes narrowed. A gentle glow of golden light enveloped the other two Missys. They froze under his power. It rendered them immobilized statues, except for their breathing and the occasional blink of their eyes. Throughout, Turel's grasp on my hand never changed.

"Excellent, thank you, Turiel," said Amitiel.

Turel gave a controlled nod, his eyes not straying from the two his power held.

Amitiel addressed real Missy. "My child," the Angel of Truth said in her kind voice, "in a moment I will ask Turiel to release these two. Know while they themselves are Pythia and the Sonneillon, they have also connected with certain aspects, certain truths about your own being."

I started when Amitiel named the creature. The angel continued, "They could not have entered your psyche and begun this struggle for your soul if there had not been some commonality in you to serve as their doorway. The Oracle of Delphi, Pythia entered, as was appropriate for your spirit guide, due to your shared abilities. She was best suited to be your specific teacher from certain traits you both share. That is why you did not receive some other seer to tutor you."

Missy grimaced. "I don't know. I mean, she's, like, really uptight, you know? So many rules, she's always telling me what to do. What part of me is that?"

"Child, no one starts out old, or rigid. Pythia was once a young woman, even as you are today. Once she, too, needed a guide. Seek deeper than her rules and orders, you may find more of yourself in her than you could imagine," said the angel of truth.

Amitiel watched as Missy thought this through. "So wait—if Pythia came in that way," said Missy, "are you saying this Sonneillon did, too? That it has things in common with me? Like, all the bad mojo, the ugly bits of me?"

"Yes, something in you let the evil in your soul. Your stubbornness and fear to work with your tutor helped open the way for this demon," said Amitiel.

Missy sighed. "Major buzz kill," she said, her tone mournful.

All of us remained silent. Fleetingly, I speculated how Asrael liked holding hands with two meat sacks.

The Angel of Truth gave more instructions. "Hear my words, truly, O' Pythia and Sonneillon. For I shall tell thee both what must happen next." Amitiel's voice grew stern. "You shall each have an opportunity to plead your case with the oracle." She moved closer to the frozen false Missys, and laid a hand on each of them as she spoke, "You will not lie, you cannot tell an untruth, nor will you tell who you are until after her choice is made." Violet lights sprang forth from her hands, dancing sparkles intermingled with Turel's golden glow. A burst of twinkling, lilac flashes punctuated each of the angel's words.

"Choice?" squawked Leo.

Amitiel did not answer him. She went on speaking to the two. "You cannot leave. My Observers will not allow it." She nodded her head to the brilliant dome which still surrounded us and the angels aloft who guarded its border. "Once the choice is made, one of you shall join the oracle and fulfill her chosen life's path. The other will be banished forever." She removed her hands from them and the amethyst lights died away though Turel did not release the two.

"I have to choose?" Missy whispered.

Amitiel turned to her. The angel's answer remained compassionate, but firm. "Yes, it is your choices which led you to this point, this struggle. Now only your choice can end it. Everything always comes back to choice."

"What if I choose the wrong one?" Missy's hoarse whisper sounded terrified. "What if I choose the Sonneillon? What then?"

Amitiel's face became a mask. "One road leads mankind and their world to The Veil, the other to chaos and destruction.

Choose wisely," she advised. She directed Turel. "Release them, old friend. It begins."

The golden glow disappeared and Turel exhaled as he let them go. I worried about him. He'd been using an awful lot of power the last few days. How long he could keep up this pace? Turel must have felt my anxious eyes on him. He winked and squeezed my hand. Together we stared at the three Missys.

The two duplicates did not immediately speak. All eyes rested on the real Missy. Her face looked pinched, but she seemed resigned. "Well," she said to her other selves, "Like, what's it going to be?"

"We are destined for greatness," the first Missy, the Missy on the right said. "There is nothing we cannot achieve together with patience and understanding."

The Missy on the left frowned and said, "You have so much potential. You can do so much good in the world with your talent, if it is properly used."

The one on the right continued as though the second Missy had not spoken, "I came to you because I saw the fire in you. I knew right away with my help we could change everything."

"And I came because you needed me. My experiences will help shape you and let you make the choices you need to make in your life," said the twin on the left.

"We don't need to be shaped, or changed. We are already becoming what we are meant to be. Mankind will sing songs about us," her opposite asserted.

"Don't listen to that one. It's trying to distract you from your path," cautioned the second Missy.

"Ha," the one on the right scoffed. "That is the one you should ignore. We can nurture your power. We can become the oracle the world needs us to be."

The real Missy turned from one of her doppelgangers to the other, her movements jerky and frantic. Clearly, she had no idea which to choose. Both of them seemed to be saying about the same thing. From their words it was impossible to know who was who. Of course, I had the advantage of Seeing who actually spoke.

The seer looked to me in desperation. "Watcher, can you See who is who?"

Conscious of Amitiel's steady regard on me, I focused on Missy's frightened gray stare. "Yes, I know," I admitted.

"Watcher," Amitiel said in a warning tone.

"Can you help me?" pleaded Missy.

I glanced at Turel who shook his head in the most minute of censuring motions. "I don't think I'm allowed to," I said with regret. "I think the whole point is for you to make the choice yourself."

"It is even so," emphasized Amitiel.

Missy's frightened expression tore at my heart. I couldn't bear the idea of not helping her. "Amitiel," I said, choosing my words with caution, "would it be against your rules to give the oracle a small piece of advice that might make her decision easier?"

Amitiel's frown did not encourage me, so I added, "Not easier, wiser. And, I wouldn't be giving away who's who, just a little advice."

Amitiel gave a heavy sigh and folded her arms. I held my breath, and from her expression, Missy did the same thing. The lavender-winged angel waved one hand at me. "Fine, Watcher. Give your guidance, but I warn you, tread most carefully."

I exhaled in relief and studied Missy. She stared back at me like a kid hoping to hear Santa Claus is real. Inside, I said a prayer that what I would say to her might be enough. "Missy, I wanted to remind you how important it is that you listen to everything they are saying."

Missy frowned. I risked emphasizing, "Listen to how they speak of you." The young seer still frowned, but with Amitiel and the other Observers staring daggers at me, I didn't dare add anything else. The two other Missys gave me matching flat glares, but otherwise did not acknowledge me.

The first Missy continued to argue her case, "Think of the things we can do together, the heights we can achieve."

"I can help, it's all I've ever wanted, just to help you," the Missy on the left said.

"Yes, help, that's it," agreed the Missy on the right. "Think of all we can help."

"Oracle," said Amitiel, "this is enough. Your others have made their case. Now you must choose. With whom will you join your life's path and who shall you banish?"

Missy's hands twisted the fabric of her dress like a small child, worrying the material. My heart pounded in my throat. I wanted to scream the right choice at her, but I could not intervene again.

"Oracle," Amitiel urged, "choose now."

Missy grimaced and shut her eyes for a moment. I hoped she wasn't going to simply guess. She opened her eyes and held out her hands to the doppelganger on the left, the second Missy. "I choose you to set me on my life's path," she said in a far more grown up and authoritative voice than I had heard the young woman use before.

The real Missy and her chosen twin grasped hands. In a brief flash of lavender light, the duplicate vanished. In her place appeared an old woman with silver eyes. I recognized her at once as everyone in our circle breathed a collective sigh of relief. "I am Pythia," said the spirit. "How did you know it was me?"

Missy flashed a smile at me and said, "You said I and you. It kept saying we. It was never going to let me go, but you will."

Pythia smiled at Missy. "Yes, child, when my teaching is done, I will depart, and you will go forward, on your own." The spirit made a gesture as though to touch a lock of Missy's hair and then came another lavender flash. When the light cleared, Pythia had disappeared and Missy regarded us with eyes that shone silver and gray. The Oracle stood straight and proud.

"And now," said Amitiel, "it needs only to finish this." She walked to the remaining duplicate. The angel's wings extended and her hands glowed with pulsing lavender power.

The Sonneillon Missy's eyes shifted to black with malevolence, and its mouth opened impossibly wide in a hoarse, discordant scream of defiance at Amitiel even as it glowed with the amethyst light of the angel's power. The angry screech resembled the high cry of a gull, only louder and full of hatred. Cracks appeared over its face and body. These schisms opened further and further. The widening fissures revealed inky blackness underneath the lavender of Amitiel's control. The splintering continued to expand until the Missy façade became stretched, disappearing.

Seconds later the Angel of Truth's light bathed the Sonneillon, exposing its true form. Shaped like a man, but with its form was distorted with stretched, exaggerated limbs. The demon's face also elongated, with a sloping brow and an enormous wedge jaw. It reminded me of a macabre cartoon character. Something that had started out one way, then pulled and reshaped into something ugly and, judging by the bleakness of its deathly black eyes, something cruel. An inky darkness emanated from it, like a shadowy sickness. It made another horrible screaming sound and twisted its body, fighting Amitiel's control.

The most beautiful sound I'd ever heard broke through the Sonneillon's hate. The angels above us sang. Their inhumanly perfect voices melded and intertwined in impossibly complex harmonies. The other Observers flew down to us. Their glorious wings formed a second tight circle inside our own ring of joined hands. As lovely as the angels were, their palpable, immense power intimidated me. Their faces became stern. Their brows set in determination as the singing intensified. The rhythmic beat of their wings provided a steady counterpoint to the glorious harmonies.

The demon struck at the air with what served it as hands. The fingers were so misshapen they were more like claws. Its gaping ebony maw opened and closed in futile anger. The Sonneillon's mouth distended, displaying row upon row of wicked teeth, like those of a shark.

The Observers converged on the Sonneillon, opening a doorway between realities. Through the gap, I caught a glimpse of what lay beyond, but this time it was not the world of rainbows and music I passed through earlier today. Rather, an alien place of angry, licking flames met my stare. My mind shied away from speculating on what else lay there. As the Observers and the demon vanished, the beautiful singing died away. After a moment the azure dome faded, leaving behind a warm, California summer day. Letting go of one another's clasped hands we broke our circle. I basked in relief.

Amitiel watched the doorway between dimensions close once more. As the seam in realities healed as though it had never existed, she said in a satisfied tone, "And that, takes care of that."

She readjusted the bullwhip at her waist and turned to Missy, held in a tight embrace by a very relieved Leo. "Oracle," the angel said with a deep and respectful bow, "congratulations. You are now on your path once more."

Missy smiled, aglow with happiness, not faded or frail. Even her cheeks held a rosy hue. "Thank you, Amitiel." She tapped the side of her head. "It is much quieter, much more peaceful in here now with only me and Pythia."

"You will complete your training?" Asrael's deep voice broke in.

Missy inclined her head at the solemn Reaper. "Yes, I will. Pythia has much to teach me, and I am eager to learn."

"That is as it should be." The grim-faced Asrael seemed pleased.

"About damn time," Nefta muttered, though when I shot a glance at the Valkyrie her expression remained as serene as ever.

Amitiel swept into a low bow. "And, if I may say, well done."

"Thank you, again." Missy sounded regal in her graciousness. I wondered how much influence Pythia exerted on her young charge.

Amitiel spoke to the rest of us. "Watcher, Reaper, Those of the Prophecy, young Leo, Nefta," she addressed each of us one by one, "and of course, dear Turiel and Gwyrdd, I will not say good-bye for we shall meet again soon enough." With that she strode through dimensions, disappearing from view in a decisive blink of an eye.

"I think I would like to go home now," said Missy, once Amitiel left. "Can anyone assist Leo and me?"

"I will," said Asrael. The bleak Reaper regarded Nefta. "My love, has my debt been discharged to yon Watcher?"

"I don't know," the blond angel said in cool tones. "Why don't you ask her?"

Asrael's wings shifted, which I took to be as close as Asrael would come to admitting any embarrassment or discomfort in the situation. He took a couple of long strides to stand near me. "Watcher, has my service to the oracle discharged my debt to you?"

I glanced at Missy who gave me an impudent thumbs-up sign. I stifled a grin. Apparently, Pythia didn't always get her way. "Of course, Asrael." I tried to be gracious, even though part of me still wanted to kick the Reaper in the teeth. "And thank you for helping Missy and Leo."

The Angel of Death inclined his head at me. To my surprise, he spoke to Alex. "And you, mine would-be enemy, does this satisfy you?"

Alex shook his head. "Nope, not even a little bit," said my brother in derisive drawl, folding his arms and staring at the astonished Reaper.

Asrael blinked in surprise. In a militaristic quarter turn, he faced Missy and Leo. "Come, we go now." Asrael gave Nefta a short bow, his expression bleak.

Missy and I exchanged shrugs. She mouthed Uh-oh, and made a sour face at Asrael's back. She said, "You need to come for a Viewing tonight, at twilight."

"I'll be there," I said.

"Siobhan," she said, "like, I owe you one. You saved me, you know, in the circle today."

I shook my head. "You saved yourself."

"Only because you showed me the way." Missy darted to me and gave me a quick hug. Her eyes shone as she reached for Leo again. The look he gave her appeared canine in its devotion.

"Uh, like, bye," said Leo as he guided Missy by the hand, following the angry Reaper. The three disappeared between realities.

Nefta sighed and said to Alex, "Was that necessary?"

"Yep," my brother responded. Daisy echoed Nefta's sigh.

"Don't even bother," Tim said to the dragon. "I've tried for years." Daisy smiled ruefully at him.

"Perhaps I should rephrase that," Nefta said. "Was that wise?"

"You know what?" Alex asked the Valkyrie.

"What?"

"Your boyfriend can kiss my fuzzy, white ass."

Nefta did a double-take at Alex. "Why in Heaven's name would he want to do such a thing?" She sounded bewildered.

My tall brother grinned and put one hand on her shoulder. "It's just a saying."

"I see." The Valkyrie pondered it. "I must say the visual on this is, most, err, disturbing." She met my brother's frank, brown eyes and then smiled, giggled, and finally laughed out loud.

Alex joined in and I chuckled myself. I glanced up to see Turel watching me. "Your brother is good for her," he observed, nodding toward the laughing pair.

I didn't answer him. I was too taken aback by the sight of my younger brother's shining face as he gazed at Nefta.

Chapter Eighteen

"Wow, that was something to see this afternoon," said Tim, leaning against Alex's Jeep as we waited for the others to emerge from Daisy's house. He scratched behind Leia's ears.

I nodded, examining my old friend. His face was tired and the merry sparkle of his eyes was dimmer than I remembered. He caught me watching and said, "Don't."

"Don't what?"

"Don't worry about me, Siobhan. I can see it all over your face. I'm okay."

"Really?"

"Really. I'm good."

I frowned at him. "You realize, of course, I know you're lying." I didn't even have to try hard. Either my Seeing had improved, or he was a bad liar. Probably a little of both, I reflected. Honesty had always been a big part of Tim's makeup. Leia whined in what I chose to take as agreement.

He exhaled and rolled his eyes, the ghost of his usual smile crossing his face and briefly lighting his expression. "Humph. Somehow, I managed to forget that. Must have blocked it out."

"Must have," I agreed.

I waited and the silence stretched between us. His sapphire eyes flicked to mine. "Okay, I might be a little homesick. That's all."

"Homesick?"

Tim's mouth twisted and he sighed. "Yeah, I want to go home. I want my bed, my big chair, a beer in front of a Giants game, and my world without angels or demons in it. It wouldn't kill me to go a whole day without anything supernatural happening."

"That's funny. You've always been the religious one. I would have thought this would mean more to you than to me or Alex."

"You'd think," he agreed. "But this—it's intense."

I touched his hand. "You'll see. We finish this and we'll go home. It's going to be fine."

"Yeah, right, fine."

We were both subdued on the way to Missy's with Turel and Alex that evening. Once again, Daisy elected to stay behind, still concerned that her powerful presence might sway Missy's visions of the future. Nefta did not accompany us, but she had not given any reason.

Tim's somber mood stifled conversation on the short drive to Monte Rio. Only the soft sound of Leia's panting in the back broke the silence in the car. I found the German shepherd's presence comforting. The company of a dog in the midst of our current adventures served like a talisman of normalcy.

The setting sun painted the horizon in a fiery rainbow as we arrived at Missy's. Alex gestured with one hand as he pulled up to the little house. "And, we're back."

Tim flashed a quick grin to me as he got out. "Let's get this done."

"Agreed," said Turel in a businesslike tone.

Leo greeted us at the door as though we were beloved relatives coming to visit. He wore a broad smile. "Dudes, what's up?" he boomed. I blinked at this new, animated Leo.

Turel turned back to us as we followed Leo. He raised his eyebrows and smiled. "I think it is improved, yes?"

I smiled back as we trooped into the bean-bag-filled front room. The whole house felt different. Light poured through open window shades. The smells of cleaning products liberally applied lingered in the air. "Good day, Leo?"

"The grooviest, Siobhan. Like, Missy's cooking again." His expression glowed euphoric.

Sure enough, in addition to the aroma of housekeeping, savory smells filled the small home. Missy poked her head from around the corner. "I'm in the kitchen, you guys. Come on in."

Obediently the four of us joined her, followed by Leo who, still grinning, leaned in the doorway watching the seer. "Sit," Missy commanded from her place at the stove, waving a hand toward the beat-up table and four mismatched chairs. To my amusement her T-shirt read, "Hokey pokey, man, it's what it's all about." She and Turel should open a store.

Missy wiped her hands on her jeans and leaned over to give me a quick hug. I squeezed her back. She beamed, her cheeks were pink, and her eyes sparkled. Even her lank hair seemed brighter. It shone a light, flaxen color in the cheerful kitchen. "Thanks for coming, everyone." Her smile widened to match Leo's, and she made brief, shy eye contact with each of us as she spoke.

"What cha' making?" Alex sniffed.

"Enchiladas, they're Leo's favorite."

"They smell awesome," Tim said.

"Yeah, they do," agreed Leo, his grin huge.

Missy blew him a kiss.

Turel viewed the pair with an indulgent air.

Alex continued, "You'll have to come to my café. We do a chicken enchilada with salsa verde I'm really proud of."

"We're, like, vegetarian," Missy said.

"Oh. Oops."

Missy waved a hand at him. "No worries, Alex. Let me get this filling simmering, and I can do your Viewing."

"How do you know when to do one?" I asked. That question had been bugging me all afternoon.

She seasoned, stirred, and then covered the pan. "It's like an itch, or an expectation. I know something's coming. It's not something I can explain, you know? It just is. Probably sounds nuts to you, right?" Her oddly gray and silver eyes met mine.

I thought about her answer. I did know what she meant. "It makes sense to me. I mean, I can't tell you how I know someone is lying or what exactly is off about an angel hiding their wings, but I know it all the same."

We exchanged an understanding smile. Missy set her spoon

aside, shifting gears from cook to oracle in the blink of an eye as her demeanor changed. She straightened and held her head high, her shoulders back. "Friends, are you ready to hear?" Missy spoke with authority and a new assurance.

Turel nodded. "We are," he said.

Tim brought out his phone again to record her pronouncements. "If you don't mind?"

The oracle inclined her head at him. She walked to the middle of the crowded kitchen. Her bearing and seriousness were at odds with its cheerful, mundane comforts. Missy belonged in a magnificent temple or at the altar of a great church, rather than in this humble room. She bent her head for a moment, her arms at her sides with her palms facing forward and tilted upward. My heart beat faster, and I held my breath until she lifted her head once more. Missy's eyes brightened. She fixed her intense gaze upon each of us as she said in ringing tones,

"Hey, diddle, diddle,
There's no time to tiddle,
The Devil's Punch Bowl at first;
Not thru land or sea
The Veil will be,
Through the bridge take the path to the worst."

Her voice died away, leaving silence in its wake. Only the gentle simmering sound of the pot on the stove broke the quiet as her words hung in the air.

"Pythia doesn't like my style," Missy finished in normal tones. "But them's the breaks, you know? We've agreed to disagree."

Leo spoke to Tim, "Did you get it, man?"

Tim nodded. His blue eyes dimmed as he tucked his phone back into his pocket. "Another uplifting poem," he mused.

"Can't you tell us anything more?" asked Alex. "That's seems awfully vague."

Missy shook her head in regret and shrugged. "Sorry, there's nothing left. There's no telling when I'll have another vision."

"But…"

"Alex," said Turel, reaching one hand across the table to tap my brother's arm. "That isn't how these things work. Missy has given us what she can. Now it's on us to find our own way."

I frowned. The ghost of a memory wafted through my brain. Try as I might to pin it down, I could not make it stick. I glanced up to see Missy watching me, her eyes now silver, mute evidence of Pythia's presence. "Troubles, young Watcher?"

"Yes, Pythia, I know I've heard the name Devil's Punch Bowl, but I can't figure out where. It's driving me crazy." Everyone stared at me now. I shrugged, helpless. "Sorry, guys, it won't come."

"Do not attempt to force it," advised Missy's mentor. "In time, you will remember."

"Yeah, but that's just it," said a worried Alex. "We don't have time. The prophecy said it would happen tomorrow."

"I've watched prophecies unfold for these last three thousand years, young man. Believe me, your sister will remember. Everything continues at its apportioned pace, and we cannot hurry it along, nor slow it down. Cultivate patience, it will serve you well," advised Pythia.

Tim typed on his phone. Scratching the stubble on his chin, he said, "When you Google Devil's Punch Bowl, you get some park in Socal outside LA."

Pythia shook her head. "That cannot be right. The prophecy shall unfold near here. Of that I am certain."

"Well, you're the expert," said Tim, tucking his phone into a pocket. "Guess we'll figure it out somehow."

The oracle blinked. Her eyes morphed back to the combined gray and silver of Missy and her teacher. "Wow," said Tim, "I'm never going to get used to that."

"You'd be surprised what one can get used to," commented Turel. Standing, he beckoned to us to do likewise. "Oracle, we owe you our thanks. We will have much to think about and to plan this evening, I think."

"Far out, man," said Leo. "Always glad to help a friend."

Missy gave Turel a big hug. "We should, like, be thanking

you for everything you've done for us."

They walked us to the front door. I lingered, last to leave, giving Missy another hug as I said good-bye. "I'm glad you and Leo have your happy ending. At least your story ended all right."

She and Leo exchanged glances. "Siobhan, we don't get a happy ending if you guys don't win," Missy explained in her soft voice.

"What? Why not?" I asked. Inside I kicked myself. Of course they wouldn't have a happy ending. No one would.

"If your side loses, like, so does everyone." Leo echoed my thoughts. "But, the big baddies will come for Missy first," said Leo.

She nodded. "A seer is far too valuable, too rare to leave alone. They'll be coming for us."

"But, how would they know where to find the two of you? The Sonneillon is banished. Who would tell?" I asked, my heart sinking.

"Turiel found her. Others will, too," said Leo. His puppy dog eyes were huge in the fading light.

"Well, no one will ever hear of you from me," I promised.

"Siobhan, if you lose or are taken, you'll tell them. They'd torture it out of you. You won't be able to help yourself. Besides, Pythia says some of the Fallen Angels can simply rip the information from your mind." Missy spoke to me, but her worried eyes lingered on Leo. She tucked her hand into his.

"I guess," I swallowed, "we'll have to win."

I walked to the Jeep, trying to get the word torture out of my head. The thought of what else might be out there terrified me, yet I burned with shame at Missy's words. She was my friend, but she was right. Images of the Hag and Asrael's Net flickered through my brain—I could be broken. As I reached the Jeep, Turel stopped me at the door. With his sensitive hearing, he hadn't missed a thing. "You won't be alone. I'd die before I let anything hurt you again."

"Thanks." I mustered a smile for him.

In the car, Alex and Tim jabbered away in a jubilant mood.

We pulled into the road, waving to Missy and Leo. However, I remained quiet as I wrestled with my worries and fears.

"Yo, sis. What's up? Why the sad face?"

I met Alex's eyes in the rearview mirror. His face was wreathed with a happy and excited grin. I hated to burst his bubble, but I related what Missy and Leo shared with me. Tim and Alex, in the front seats, refused to allow their spirits to be dampened.

"No, you were right earlier, Siobhan," said Tim. "We've got the prophecy, the timeline, and now the location. The other side knows nothing. They don't even know we have Daisy. We're off to the races."

Alex chimed in, "Right. We go to the Veil, you do your Watcher gig, make a choice and, voilà."

"We go home," finished Tim in exuberance.

I glanced at Turel. He smiled, his dark eyes twinkling at me. "It certainly could be worse."

"But Leo and Missy?"

"Are two more reasons to succeed," the dark angel said. "I worry more for Leo than the oracle. His only use would be to make her more tractable." He paused and pursed his lips. "I believe what is bothering you lies not in our actual circumstances, Watcher. I think you are, for the first time, beginning to realize in some small part what is truly at stake." He enfolded one of my hands in both of his. The gesture made me feel better.

"You do get that we haven't exactly figured out where the Veil is yet, right guys?" I couldn't resist adding. "I mean, we still have to sift through Missy's mumbo-jumbo."

"And sift we shall, Siobhan. We'll sift and sift, and sift some more," said my brother. "First things first though. Smelling Missy's cooking has my stomach all woken up. I'm starved."

"I could eat," said Tim.

Turel raised his dark brows at me. "I could also eat," I admitted. Now that the subject had come up my stomach growled.

"Excellent," said Alex, pointing up the road. "Don's Dogs and More, anyone?"

Without waiting for an answer, he steered the Jeep off the

road and parked in the gravel alongside the casual restaurant with its welcoming wooden decks. The smells coming from inside made my mouth water.

"I'm in," said Tim, bounding from the Jeep.

"Me, too," added Turel.

"Me three." I followed them up the wooden steps.

Don's Dogs proved to be a homey hotdog and sandwich spot. The two resident dogs on the deck welcomed Leia with the customary sniffing of noses.

"Better get some for Daisy," I reminded Tim as he ordered.

"And some for Nefta, I bet she'd love their grilled sauerkraut."

"Nefta," said Turel, "will never eat a hotdog, Alex. Sauerkraut or no."

"Sure she will," my brother insisted.

Turel pursed his lips, but let it pass. He and I exchanged glances, and I shrugged. At least it would be entertaining.

Once we purchased enough food to feed a small army, we set off for Daisy's house. We drove no more than a few hundred yards when Alex said under his breath, "Huh, that's weird."

"What is?" asked Tim.

"It's probably nothing," my brother said. "But I keep seeing the same van over and over again. A déjà vu thing, I guess."

I watched behind us. Some distance back there followed, indeed, a nondescript gray van. "You sure it's the same one?" I said.

"Probably not," he said. "Just seems like every time I check my rear view mirror I see another gray van."

Turel frowned. "Pull over here and park. Quickly, Alex," he commanded as we went through a winding section of road.

Alex threw a startled glance back at the angel, but stopped at the parking lot of a convenience store. A few seconds later the van passed us and continued down the road.

"Onward?" asked Alex, glancing at Turel.

"Not yet, wait a moment."

We sat in the car, the Polish dogs and sandwiches smelling tantalizingly yummy in the enclosed space. My stomach protested the delay with vociferous intensity. Just as I thought to say something to Turel, or open one of the bags of take-out, the van returned, coming back down the road toward us. As it approached the store it slowed. I gasped. Gilbert drove the van.

Tim whistled. "Son-of-a-bitch."

"Even so," agreed Turel.

An anxious silence fell over us as the van paused. In the still light summer evening I spied Gilbert, the man who stole Daisy's statue, the man who brought Chernobog to my home. For one chilling second my eyes made contact with his faded blue ones across the parking lot, and then with a roar, the van accelerated and sped down the road.

"What do I do? Chase him?" asked Alex as he rev'ed the engine.

"No, let's get to Daisy's as quickly as possible," said Turel. "I'd feel better if we had her and Nefta with us."

"Because of Gilbert?" I asked.

"No, because of whoever else is here with him."

"Ian?" asked Tim.

"Or worse," said Turel. "Alex, trust your instincts more often. That was a good catch."

"How long do you think he's been following us?" I asked as we started back to Daisy's. Alex drove too fast, but for once I didn't complain.

"Long enough," Turel said, his jaw set in a grim line.

* * *

"And you are certain, it was this, Gilbert? This creature of Chernobog's you saw?" Daisy paced back and forth, gesticulating with a pulled pork sandwich.

"Hmm," I said with my mouth full of Polish dog.

"Positive," Turel confirmed. "Judging by the demon stench coming off that van."

"No chance this was the first time he followed you?" asked Nefta with a certain professional curiosity. An uneaten Polish dog sat in front of her. Every once in a while she would pick it up or smell it, as though uncertain how to proceed.

Alex shook his red head vigorously. "No way," he said. "I've been seeing this van for a while. I just couldn't believe it could be the same one."

"Well, it would explain how Abraxas knew where to find Siobhan, and set the Hag on her," Nefta observed in her cool voice. Her eyes rested on me with clinical interest. "I wondered."

"Then they'll know about Missy and Leo, too," I exclaimed.

"Naturally," said Nefta.

"Well, yes," said Turel, "they had to be gathering information from somewhere. And in this part of the dimension, all roads lead back to Chernobog."

Nefta folded her arms. "He said the last chain's about to break. Are we dealing with Chernobog, free on this dimension, at last?"

An unladylike growl came from Daisy's human throat. "If only," she hissed. Her amber eyes swept over us. Her scrutiny rested on Turel. The angel endured her examination stoically. "What about you, old friend?" asked Daisy. "You of all of us have a lot invested in that demon's imprisonment."

"If he is free, I stand ready. If he remains chained, I stand firm. There are gains for us should he be freed. Sometimes a loss is a win."

Nefta's eyes narrowed at Turel's reply. "I remember a phrase from the humans I always greatly enjoyed. I believe you say the game is afoot."

She and Daisy exchanged flinty glances. The gleam in Daisy's eyes startled me. I had seen her protective as a dragon, breathing flames and roaring, yes. This aspect was new. She resembled a general measuring her forces. Daisy took a step toward Turel and Nefta. "Find them, report, time grows nigh. I shall guard. I shall not sleep and they," she waved a hand at Alex, Tim and me, "shall be protected."

Nefta gave a short bow to us. "I shall not fail you," she promised. She fixed her gaze on Alex. There was no mistaking the pain in her expression. "You, human, Tool of Prophecy, I am loath to leave."

Alex drew Durendel. "And I hate to see you go," he replied,

his brown eyes glowing with emotion. His expression lightened and he continued, "We're kicking ass and taking names, baby doll."

Nefta winced, but she drew Durendala. The two crossed the twin swords silently, wide eyes locked on one another, not speaking, not touching. Nefta said, "I'm counting on it." The Valkyrie bowed low. "Gwyrdd, I shall seek them out."

Daisy returned Nefta's courtly gesture. "Angel of Battle, I thank thee. Move with haste. Find our enemies forthwith."

Nefta bowed low. "First One, so it shall be." Without glancing at my brother again, she straightened, nodded to our company, and marched through the dimensions.

Daisy gazed after her and said to Turel, "Nefta is still relatively young, would thou follow after her?"

Turel bowed and, upon straightening smiled at the dragon. "I am fond of her, too, Gwyrdd, though she likes it not."

To my surprise, he did not disappear through dimensions. Instead, he strode to me. "Siobhan Isabella Orsini?"

"Yes?"

"Stay. Out. Of. Trouble."

I tried not to tremble as I stared into those dark eyes. Eyes black as night, but filled with all the sunshine and kindness in the world. A million things flowed through my thoughts, but one overtook the rest. "Turel?"

"Yes, Siobhan?"

"I'll be here when you get back."

His smile bloomed, brighter than the sun. He was lovelier than anything I had ever seen. Despite the people watching, he gathered me close, and I found that I did not care who saw. Turel drew my face to his. We faced one another eye-to-eye. "And I, Watcher, will be back."

I could not help, nor would it have occurred to me to try, not leaning into his kiss. It felt as natural as breathing and just as essential. As the angel moved through dimensions to hunt down our stalkers, I faced the bald fact that nothing about this experience was temporary. I was and would forever be changed by

Turel and this war.

Tim twisted away from seeing Turel and me embrace. I caught Alex humming Aerosmith's *Angel* and gave him a hard look. He grinned, but stopped humming. Once they disappeared a chill silence ensued as the question, "What next?" hung in the air. Leia broke the pause with a couple of insistent barks.

Daisy grinned. "She's right, you know, there's work to be done."

Leia leaned against Tim's leg, tongue lolling. He took out his recording of Missy's latest Viewing and we got to work.

"Devil's Punch Bowl?" repeated Daisy. "That sounds like a spell or invocation, not a place."

"Oh, great," moaned Alex, "Um, Daisy, spells? Not my strong suit."

We had to nod in agreement. Spells? I didn't know what to say.

"What about the bit about not land or sea?" I asked. "If it's not land or sea, what's left? Air?"

"It's possible," admitted Daisy. "There's something we're missing."

"And what about '*the path to the worst*?" I asked, trying not to sound too worried. "That can't be good."

"Siobhan."

"Yes, Daisy?"

"You can't lose yourself in the details of the prophesies. Sometimes you simply need to let events unfold and *trust*."

I met her golden eyes, wondering if she could see the trembling inside of me.

"There's one thing I haven't been able to work out, Daisy," Tim leaned forward, still in his own world.

"Yes, dear one?"

"I get why the fallen angels prefer our world to hell. Who wouldn't? But, why do the dragons want to come back so badly? I mean, it seems like you have found another world you've been living in all this time, right?"

"You mean besides the fact that this is our *home*?" she

responded in arch tones.

Tim blinked. Alex cuffed him. "Yeah, dude, besides that," my brother needled.

"I understand about wanting to go home," said Tim, sheepishly.

Daisy patted his arm. "I know you do, Tim. It's not a matter of simply coming home for us though. We do have an alternate refuge, as you pointed out just now."

We leaned forward as she paused.

"Children, we have to come home if we, the dragons, are to continue."

The mortals in the room exchanged confused glances.

Daisy smiled. "Dragons can only nest here, with our Mother. If there is no access to Earth, then there will be no eggs and someday, no more dragons."

She patted my hand. "You three are very dear to me, but one day I would like to have children of my own. That can only happen here, upon our return home. There is nothing like having a family."

Alex popped a French fry into his mouth and said in a flippant voice, "Oh, I don't know about that. Our parents split when I was a baby. I can't even remember having the whole mom, dad, nuclear family thing. I've always had a bit here and a bit there and that seems to have been enough."

I knew what he meant. I had a few memories of the four of us together as a family: eating dinner, playing "Go Fish", camping, but mostly Mom and Dad fighting. Finally, just about the time I met Daisy, our dad left. Something stirred in my brain. It had to do with camping. "That's it," I marveled. All heads swiveled to me, questioning. "I knew I'd heard of the Devil's Punch Bowl."

"What gives?" Alex ate another fry.

"The Devil's Punch Bowl is the name of a place," I said as the memory came flooding back. "Mom and Dad took us camping at a state park, somewhere near there. It was just before Dad left, maybe Memorial Day Weekend? Right before I met Daisy. I remember a beach, the waves and…" My voice trailed off.

"Siobhan," prompted Tim.

"There's a bridge. I remember a beautiful bridge way high above me. It was so big."

"Dear one," said Daisy. "Where is this campground?"

"I don't know. I was only five, and Alex was a baby, but I do remember the waves crashing and lots of rocks and Daddy calling it 'The Devil's Punch Bowl'."

"Okay, let's try Google again." Tim pulled his iPhone out again. "This time with a bit more finesse. Adding 'northern California' to the search."

He typed as we watched, anxious and excited. "Well?" demanded Alex.

"What did Pythia say you should do? Something about patience?"

"Shut up, Tim. What's it say?"

Tim looked up from his phone with a broad grin and sparkling eyes. "Ready?"

"Yes." We said at once.

"Siobhan's right, it is a place. The Devil's Punch Bowl is a collapsed sea cave about fifty miles north of Fort Ross, south of Fort Bragg. It's part of the Russian Gulch State Park. And…" Tim paused for dramatic effect. "Would you like to see the bridge?"

He held out his phone and we hunched around him, gazing at the photo he had brought up on to his screen. The photo showed a graceful, white suspension bridge across a beach with a shallow river running to one side. Redwoods and the craggy Mendocino coast surrounded it. Beautiful, just the way I remembered.

"This says here the park is closed right now because of budget cut backs."

"Good," said Daisy.

"Why good?" asked my brother.

"Fewer civilians in harm's way should this get messy, young one, and if these Prophecies are any indication, it *will* get messy."

Missy's words echoed through my head. "*Through the bridge take the path to the worst.*"

Chapter Nineteen

Though late, Turel and Nefta had not returned. Daisy patrolled. Alex, Tim and I sat around the kitchen table. No one spoke. Alex cradled a glass of whiskey, Tim a beer, and I had a glass of red wine.

Leia, lying at Tim's feet, lifted her head, alert. Her whine gave us the warning we had. Nefta and Turel burst through the dimensions into the room. We leapt to our feet, and I found myself reaching for my bow as though I had used it all my life.

Both angels had been in a fight, and neither fared well. Turel's handsome face sported bruises with a welt above his right eye. Blood dripped from his left thigh, soaking his torn jeans. The edges of the ragged wound looked septic and infected. Worse still, his right arm between the hand and the elbow was so bloody with jagged cuts that the flesh appeared to be shredded.

Still, Turel's injuries paled compared to Nefta's. The entire left side of her platinum hair and face was burned to ruin. One cheek reduced to raw flesh and the skin blackened from her hairline to her jaw line. The battle angel's lovely hair lay singed and charred.

I sprang forward, controlling a shudder at how much pain those wounds must be causing the Valkyrie. She swayed on her feet, but as quick as I went, Alex moved faster. With more tenderness than I had ever seen from my brother, he gathered Nefta to him. For an instant I had the fleeting impression of a dove in his arms, although Nefta would have to be a dove of steel, the fragile and unbreakable were so interwoven in her. The battle angel leaned against him with her eyes closed, not speaking. She slipped in and out of consciousness. Alex's brown eyes grew huge as he turned to Turel.

"Sweet Jesus," said Tim, speaking for all of us. "What on earth happened to you two?"

"We found Innon," explained Turel, his dark eyes grim. "He was not alone. He had a covey of the Fallen with him. We fought our way out."

"Can't you heal her?" Alex's voice warped as tight as a wire, taut and twisted with unexpressed emotion as he held Nefta.

"I already have," Turel said. "Granted, we were on the run, but it was all I could do, wounded as I am."

We stared at him in shock. "Oh, shit." A small muscle in Alex's temple ticked.

A sense of revulsion crawled over my skin as I stared at Nefta's burns with a new appreciation for the destruction there. As someone who had experienced firsthand the potency of angelic healing, I imagined how much worse the initial burns must have been.

"How many is a covey?" I asked, trying not to stare at Nefta's burns. A frightening macabre fascination demanded one's attention.

"Thirteen."

"So, you took on fourteen including Innon?" Tim gave a low whistle.

"Plus their demon pets," Turel confirmed, his mouth twisting in a pain-filled grimace. I hurried to his side, hating to see him in pain, wishing I could help.

"I wish I could help her," said my brother in anguish, his voice echoing my thoughts.

"You already are."

We stared at Nefta, startled to hear her speak. Her eyes opened. Their azure gaze stood out with painful clarity against the burned and bloodied flesh of the left side her face. Her voice was soft, no more than a rasp.

"Nefta," Alex said. He only had eyes for the wounded angel. For a moment I felt like I trespassed on their intimacy.

"Alex," she said. Her blue eyes locked with my brother's as

though they were only the two in the world.

After a moment Turel cleared his throat, recalling them to the here and now.

Tim came forward. "You said he is already helping you. How?"

Alex carefully stepped away from Nefta, pulling a chair from the kitchen table out for her. As he released her, I saw the Valkyrie's fine features etch in new lines of pain. I felt more than heard her sharp inhalation of agony. "Alex," she gasped. This time the name was not a loving caress. It was a plea.

My brother's face turned stricken as he went back to her, but Tim caught her. He moved as carefully as if he held something infinitely precious and breakable. His expression solemn, Tim cradled Nefta as Alex reached for her. As soon as my brother's hands encircled her, taking her from Tim, Nefta's agonized eyes transformed with relief. "Ah," she sighed.

"He takes your pain away?" asked Turel, watching Nefta with compassion, but also curious.

She nodded. "When he touches me, the pain leaves."

Turel frowned, his expression thoughtful and then extended one blood stained hand to me. "Siobhan?"

Without hesitation I joined my hand with his. In that instant, our connection became palpable. I raised my eyes again to his and saw, to my relief, his expression lighten and the lines of pain and fatigue appear fainter. "Turel?"

"She's right, Siobhan," he said in wonder. "With your touch the pain is gone."

He released my hands and his expression tightened. His jaw clenched in renewed agony. "Turel, don't," I exclaimed, reaching for his good hand again.

Alex lifted Nefta in his arms with the greatest of care and, hefting her with ease, walked toward the living room and the semi-circle of couches waiting there. Settling himself against the cushions with the blonde angel across his chest, he said in a bleak voice, "Come on, guys, I'm sure there's an explanation for all this, like at the end of a Scooby-Doo episode. We might as well do it some place comfortable while Velma talks. I'm not letting go of

Nefta again for anything."

Without speaking, Turel raised my hand to his lips, imprinting a soft kiss. I squeezed his hand, glad to see the pain leave his face at my touch. We followed Alex to the couches, Tim behind us. We had become two couples: Alex and Nefta, myself and Turel. Only Tim watched alone. The contrast was not so stark when Daisy was with us. With her gone hunting, I speculated as to what might be going on in Tim's head, though I did not know how to help the situation.

As we settled on the couch adjacent from Alex and Nefta, Turel removed his hand from mine. I shot a startled glance at him. He patted my knee and said to my brother, "Alex, if you would give me your hand for a moment, I'd like to see something, please."

Alex grimaced. "Gee, Turel, you're a nice enough guy and all, but you aren't really my type."

They clasped hands for one moment. The silence in the room was only broken by Nefta's ragged breathing. Turel retracted his hand and sank back on to the couch beside me, entwining his hand into mine. I put my other hand over both of ours, as though I could keep him safe. "The connection does not exist between Alex and me," said Turel.

Tim brought our drinks from the kitchen table. He added another glass of wine for Turel and, after a moment's hesitation, he poured a glass of whiskey for Nefta, neat, the same way Alex took his. He walked over to them and said to Nefta, "If I may?"

She raised her eyebrows at him. "Yes?"

He lifted the glass to her lips and helped her take a sip. She sputtered a bit, but managed a large swallow. Her face, at least the undamaged portion, transformed to a mask of conflicting emotions. "It burns, but not in an unpleasant way," she said.

Alex watched the proceedings with a smile. "Oh, I get it, no food, no wine, but the whiskey you'll do."

Nefta regarded him without expression. "And this is relevant, because?"

"Perhaps because I find all things about you relevant."

"You are attempting to compliment me?"

"You got a problem with that?" he said, but his gentle hands on her belied the challenge in his words.

"No." She frowned and hesitated. "Alex, I accept your compliment. I…, I also find you relevant."

She glanced around as though surprised to find the three of us watching the two of them. Her undamaged skin colored, but she said, more dignified than ever, "I think, Tim, I would like to have more of that drink. Would you pour me another glass? I do still have one hand which can hold it."

Alex beamed and Tim went to fulfill her request. She balanced the glass in one hand, on her knee, as she leaned against my brother's chest. Struck by the fragility of this picture: the Valkyrie in the arms of my brother, the chef, and their shy smiles, despite her wounds, I found myself praying nothing would break this newfound happiness.

Tim's voice roused me from my thoughts as he sat again. "Turel, I'm fairly certain Alex outed you as the Velma of the group a few minutes ago. Can you explain what is happening here with you?"

Turel sighed, and to my surprise, released my hand and grabbed the whiskey bottle off the coffee table in front of us. He took a large swig and reached for my hand again. "Fair enough," he said.

Nefta stared at her glass. "Velma?" she repeated. "This Velma, I do not know. Wait, this is the material which attaches to itself? The small ones, they use it on their shoes, yes?"

Alex's mouth twitched. "Uh, no, Nefta, that would be Velcro."

For the first time since returning, Turel's smile shone. "I'm not sure I know how to follow that."

I leaned forward and picked up my wine glass, smiling back at him. "Start with what's happening with us? With Nefta and my brother?"

"In its simplest form, at its core, we are connected: Alex to Nefta and you to me. When we gave of ourselves after the Hags drained you both, you became more than human, but not angels."

He paused. "You remember Daisy said you would never be as you once were, right."

I nodded.

Turel continued, "If I had to guess, I would say under normal circumstances, a dose of angel life force would simply mean a longer life, perhaps better health for the two of you. However, we do not find ourselves in normal days. Now, that connection buoys Nefta and me. It allays our pain. You give back."

Tim's expression was grim. "But, will you be better by tomorrow? Before the Veil?"

Turel frowned and held his shredded arm and torn leg out. "With a lesser wound, yes, but now with these injuries? I cannot say."

I swallowed. A chill fell over the room.

"Still, we angels do heal swiftly. See, my leg is better and the pain subsides from my arm."

I squinted and couldn't argue his point. The poisoned, putrid edges of his horrible thigh wound were clean and, although bloody, no longer appeared septic. Likewise, his arm no longer looked shredded. Instead, I saw deep, ragged cuts.

Turel stretched one hand toward Nefta. "And mark this, friends, Nefta's burns are improved."

We examined Nefta. In the soft light emanating from the kitchen, Nefta did appear better. The skin that had been raw now oozed clear plasma. The areas which had been blackened now showed tender pink flesh. It hurt just to look at the naked, damaged areas, but the sight was better than the char.

"So," said Alex, "you're saying if I hold her all night, it will help keep her more comfortable?"

"Assuredly."

"Well, how about that," said Alex to no one in particular, a small smile playing about his lips.

I held back a chuckle. Tim rolled his eyes, but said to Turel, "So, what on earth happened? How did the bad guys get their mitts on you."

Nefta stirred in Alex's embrace. "I'm going to gut Innon like a fish."

Alex patted her arm. "Of course you are, baby doll. Would

you like me to hold him down for you?"

"Thank you," she said. "That would be most helpful."

"Of course," I couldn't resist adding. "He has it coming."

"Well put, Watcher," said Nefta.

Turel smiled at me and leaned into me in an affectionate gesture. It warmed me and made the butterflies in my stomach take flight. He regained his serious expression. "We had no problem finding Gilbert. We saw him meet with Innon. From what we overheard, it's apparent they have both been in the area for almost as long as we have. The thing that seems to have saved some part of our element of surprise is only Gilbert has been by this house and Daisy's human disguise has him fooled. Innon followed us to the oracle's, but Daisy never went there, so he did not realize Gwyrdd is back. Still, obviously Innon knew far too much about us and our activities. Nefta and I decided the best course would be to neutralize Innon and Gilbert."

"We planned to kill them both," Nefta said. Already she sat straighter and her voice sounded stronger.

I reflected that battle angels must be very hard to kill.

"I am not sure how we gave ourselves away, but when we entered to finish the deed, we were beset upon by Innon, the covey, and their demon minions. We fought a good fight, but they had Lahatiel with them."

"Lahatiel?" Tim repeated. "Who or what is that?"

"A Fallen," said Turel. "He's an archangel who went bad, very dangerous. Archangels are in a different class in terms of power compared to me and Nefta."

"His name means 'the flaming one of God' and he is aptly called," said Nefta, gesturing to the ruins of her beautiful face.

"And you." I touched Turel's knee. "What happened to you?"

"Demons," he said, grimacing. "I had to get Nefta out of there, Lahatiel lit her up like a Roman candle, and a half dozen of their hellhounds beset me, hence, my arm and thigh. Luckily, Lucifer's Fallen are arrogant and lazy. Had they given a true chase, it might not have gone so well."

"Tomorrow?" asked Tim. "How do we face them tomorrow?"

"What worries you, Tim?" asked Turel.

"Gee, I don't know. Death, my friends dying, demons loose in the world that I love? All of it? More? Isn't that enough?"

"It is, friend Tim, nor is there any shame in these fears. Know we each face our own fears. Even those on the other side have their nightmares. You, my friend, may be some demon or Fallen's nightmare, though you know it not," said Turel.

"Me?" Tim's face twisted in disbelief.

"Indeed, for many on the other side, a mortal man of faith and goodness is their one fear. The one thing they hope never to meet, and do not know how to defeat," explained Turel. "Faith can be a powerful weapon."

"Well," said Tim, his expression thoughtful, "that's something, isn't it?"

"Truly, it is."

In the short pause that followed we reflected, each of us, I suspected, on our own fears. Tim rose. "Tomorrow, that's it, right?"

"So they say," said Nefta.

Turel nodded. Tim crossed the room and, to my surprise, gave me a bear hug. He turned to Alex and Nefta and carefully hugged each of them. "Night, guys, get some rest, okay?" As he headed to his room, he did not address Turel.

After a moment, Alex rose, carrying Nefta. "Tim's right. It's bedtime for us."

"What is this us you are talking about?" said Nefta, her words sharp. Her expression shifted, becoming stiff and angry in the half light from the kitchen behind them.

"Well, um, you need healing, and, um, I'm sleepy, so…"

"Did you think to take me to bed so easily, Alex?"

"Not exactly, Nefta. Kind of… but just to sleep, I swear."

"Put. Me. Down."

Flushing, Alex did as she directed. Nefta walked away from him, but after only a couple of unsteady steps, she faltered. Alex sprang forward to catch her as she swayed. "Nefta, please, let me help," he begged.

She turned to him, her profile backlit and stunning in its

beauty. "One does not carry a Valkyrie to bed," she said.

"You're just being stubborn, I would never hurt you," Alex said.

"That goes without saying. I am a battle angel." Her sniff held pure disdain.

"Nefta, what can I say?" asked Alex.

"As I said, one does not carry a Valkyrie to bed." She paused, adding, "*Without asking.*"

"Oh," my brother said. "*Oh.*"

She waited and Turel and I exchanged glances as Alex processed this.

"Nefta?"

"Yes, Alex?"

"Could I please… I mean, may I, err, can I help you to bed?"

"Certainly, Alex."

Even these few moments of standing taxed the battle angel. Tiny beads of sweat spread over her face and neck, shimmering in the artificial light. As soon as my brother had her in his arms once more, her rigid shoulders sagged in relief.

"Night," called Alex, shutting off the kitchen light as he left. I smiled when Nefta laid her head on his broad shoulder as they went down the hallway, leaving Turel and me alone in the living room.

We sat together in the dark. My eyes adjusted to the night. I had rarely been alone with Turel. Not really, since there had always been a Hag, my brother, a dragon, or me passed out, in desperate need of healing.

Turel ran restless fingers over the stem of his wine glass. I waited. It was late and tomorrow promised to be a busy day, but I found myself reluctant to leave him and go to my room. Despite the fear and horror I experienced the past few days, the joy Turel's presence brought outshone the nightmares. Sitting there, with him, in the darkened living room with the soft breeze of a summer evening wafting through the air, it was impossible not to be happy.

"I find myself uncertain what to do next. What do you want me to say?" he asked, his deep voice soft, breaking the silence first. His face remained in the shadows. He held my hand, gently caressing my fingers with his.

I hesitated. Other than a few stolen sentences, we had not talked about this new relationship burgeoning between us. "I'm not sure what I am waiting for."

"It is difficult for me," he admitted. "As an angel, it is sometimes hard to know when one is eliciting true emotions and when a mortal might be, swept away, I believe the phrase is?"

"What? Because you are so irresistible?"

"No, I am not as vain as that, but the magic, the wings, the connection to God can be… a distraction. I have seen other angels fall in love with mortals and then, the emotions in return proved false. One realizes they are an illusion, an infatuation. The human object of their desire could not help but say yes. Later, regret sets in and the pain begins." His words sounded sad and resigned.

"But, Turel, that happens between ordinary people every day," I said. "We misunderstand one another's emotions all the time. All relationships have an element of risk. We choose to try anyway."

"True, but what I am trying to tell you, Siobhan…" he paused. Had I not known better I would have said he was nervous. "…Is there is an accepted rule amongst we Observers. We try to avoid falling in love, but should a relationship develop, we let the mortal dictate the terms and the pace. I cannot ask. I will not push you."

"I don't understand."

"I cannot ask," he repeated, his eyes wide. "I cannot risk influencing you. It would not be fair to you."

"Yet," I said, "you began this. You kissed me first."

"Yes, and I do not regret it. I would do it again. I simply mean at each new stage, before going any further, we must progress only according to your desires."

My eyes adjusted to the soft darkness of the night. Behind us a large picture window showed the porch and the roses beyond. The full moon rose and bathed everything in its silver glow. I considered Turel, everything about him. It was a luxury that during the day, with so many people around and my tangle of emotions so raw, I rarely had.

He sat next to me, close enough that his warmth spread over me. My right hand entwined with his uninjured left hand.

I marveled at the resiliency of angels. Turel's wounds stopped bleeding. The welt on his forehead closed and his leg seemed healed. Bruises lingered and his right side had to still be painful, but miles better than when he and Nefta arrived. Beyond the catalog of injuries and their status, I allowed my eyes to linger on his face.

I loved his hawk-like profile, his dark hair, and the distinctive Persian cheekbones. My gaze lingered on his short beard and mustache that did little to disguise the sensuality of his lips. The urge to run my fingers along his olive skin intoxicated me. I hesitated, trying to decipher from his words and actions over the last week what he wanted. A little voice inside of me took the reins and gave me a daring I would never have. What did I want?

Thought transformed to action as my other hand stroked his cheek. He turned at my touch, his dark eyes intent on me. I faltered for an instant; his presence overwhelmed me. "My desires?" I whispered. "*Whatever I desire?*"

He did not answer, but his breath quickened.

Before I lost my nerve, I leaned closer, to his neck. On the side, at the precise point where his pulse beat, I nuzzled a soft kiss. "And if I desire to do this?"

He did not move as I withdrew my hand from his grasp and slid both of mine carefully over his chest, mindful of his bruises. His warmth and the clean, hard lines of his body made rational thought difficult.

I pressed closer. We faced one another, my lips close to his. "Or this?" I whispered. I leaned in and for the first time, I kissed Turel, instead of being kissed by him.

His lips parted for mine, and his hands slid around my waist to draw me closer. He made a sound in his throat somewhere between a strangled growl and a groan as our embrace intensified. For a moment the sheer pleasure of his kiss overwhelmed all other thoughts.

I rose and backed away, my eyes never leaving his. "I should think about getting some sleep," I said. I sensed rather than saw him lean forward to listen to my words. This was what he had been waiting for the night before—an invitation. My heart seemed to be beating out of my chest as I continued, "Would you...," I cleared my throat, "...stay with me tonight?"

I'm not sure what I expected, but Turel did not answer me in words. He crossed the floor to me in a couple of sure strides. The dark angel swept me into his arms with such passion, such force that we pressed against the opposite wall of the small living room. I worried for his wounds, but he didn't seem to care.

He brought his hands to either side of my face and slid into the tangle of my disheveled curls as his mouth lingered surely and exquisitely again on mine. With a gasp, I broke the embrace. Turel looked stricken and froze, as though thinking I changed my mind. My heart racing, I held out one hand to him. "To bed?" I asked.

His warm smile pierced the night and he put my hand to his lips, his breath caressing the back. He turned my hand over and gave my palm a lingering kiss. Every nerve in my body extended to that caress as we went into my room and closed the door. As the latch clicked Turel's arms wrapped around me once more. This time, our kisses burned like fire, the heat and need growing for both of us. My skin set ablaze, each nerve ending alight and intensely sensitive, responding to his every touch. At last, we found the bed together.

Chapter Twenty

The knife sliced through Nefta's pale throat. Alex screamed in horror and despair. Her blood soaked him. "Siobhan. Help me. Save her!" he cried. I watched, helpless. The sands emptied. My brother fell to his knees, cradling the Valkyrie in his bloody arms. A triumphant shout filled my ears. "You are lost, my dear. Mankind shall fall," a voice purred. "I see your weakness. You wallow in self-doubt. Now my lord will never back you." The woman sounded close to me, at my shoulder.

I whirled around to find her. Instead I saw Turel chained. Demons sliced his flesh with their claws, slowly ripping his wings from his body. Crimson stained the pure white of the feathers. I sobbed at the agony etched across his face. "Your pain," the woman said, "I have always loved your pain. So sweet. Think how much worse it will be tomorrow when you let everyone down." The pleasure in her voice sounded aroused, full of sexual undertones. "I can't wait to see the sands empty."

I woke with a gasp as Daisy burst into my room, saving me from my nightmare. "Pretty things," she called, finding us asleep and disheveled amongst the sheets. In the soft light of dawn, I blushed even as I thanked God for the interruption to my nightmare. I wiped tears from my cheeks so Turel or Daisy wouldn't see.

Without waiting for a response from us, she continued, "The last chain's broken, Turel. Didn't you feel it?"

Turel sat up. He frowned with concentration and then he exhaled. "Yes, now I do. I was, hmm, busy earlier."

Daisy gave a thoroughly dragon-like snort. "Of course you were. That's how the chain broke."

210

"What happened?" A sinking sensation enveloped the pit of my stomach even as I asked the question.

"Chernobog is free, of course," Daisy said.

"Oh, no, no, no, no." I moaned, putting my head under my pillow. How could I have been so blind? Of course, Turel was the Guardian, not Tim. I had brought this on us by releasing the demon, although I couldn't understand exactly how it had happened. Fresh misery washed through me. I *would* fail them all. "This is all my fault," I said, drawing myself up again.

Turel and Daisy gaped at me. "Child, what are you talking about?" exclaimed Daisy.

"Missy, no, Pythia said this would happen," I said, "in a prophecy she gave to me alone."

I watched Turel and Daisy exchange a lengthy stare. She shrugged. "Meant to be?"

Turel turned to me. "Can you tell us what she said, love?"

Glowing inside at his endearment, I tried to keep my telltale face still, knowing how my expressions showed. I nodded, thinking for a moment, more to prepare myself for actually saying the words out loud than a lack of memory. I had spent many hours agonizing over each syllable of the short verse. Drawing a deep breath, I recounted, "*When the Guardian's passion shall surely wake, Then the Black God's last prison chain will break.*"

Turel exhaled, as though tension ran out of him. He glanced at Daisy. "Well, Gwyrdd?"

"Meant to be, old friend." She rubbed her hands together in glee. "I've wanted a crack at Chernobog for ages, simply ages. I'm going to rip him to shreds. I'll unmake him."

"Bloodthirsty much, Daisy?" I couldn't understand. She acted like this was a good thing. "Isn't his freedom a huge problem?"

"Well, yes… and no," Turel said.

"It's also an opportunity," said Daisy. "When he was imprisoned I, err, I mean, no one could get at him to finish him off. Now, well, now things are different."

"But… I let this happen." My insides twisted with self-loathing. "I thought Tim had to be the Guardian. I never would have..." I waved my hand over the bed. "...if I had known."

"Well, dear," Daisy spoke with delicacy, not meeting my eyes. "I hardly think you did this, how shall we say? Alone?" Her eyes drifted toward Turel as her mouth quirked in a smile. "I mean, it does take two? If memory serves."

I stole a glance at Turel. His broad smile reassured me.

"Siobhan," he said, "were you trying to run away from a prophecy?"

"Maybe a little? It sounded so dire."

"Take it from me, child," said Daisy, "the quickest way to make a prophecy happen is to try and prevent it. Works every time, just ask the Greeks."

"Did the seer tell you that this must happen?" continued Turel.

I thought for a moment. "I didn't believe her," I admitted. "She said it must happen, to trust her."

Turel nodded. "As I said last night, sometimes a defeat is actually a victory. You didn't let this happened, you were a Tool of Prophecy."

Daisy paced like a caged tiger back and forth at the foot of my bed. "This means we are one step closer."

"Closer to what?" I asked.

"This war has been on hold for eons, Siobhan."

"I remember."

"Your appearance on the scene, the reemergence of the Veil, the discovery of the Oracle here, these are elements that will bring us closer to a resolution, an end to this interminable conflict, and hopefully the chance to bring my brothers and sisters home. Chernobog was mentioned more than once by the oracle. Clearly, his presence is one of the conditions the prophecy has set which will allow Siobhan, the Watcher, to make her leap of faith. Remember? '*For Gracious Sight a blind leap she then must take.*' Perhaps events will begin moving forward again at last, and the dragons will return to protect this world."

Turel rubbed his beard. "There are still problems with Chernobog loose."

"Obviously, old friend," said Daisy. "Why do you think I

woke you lovebirds up? He'll be coming here first. You're the last of the four, aren't you?"

"Unless you count Lucifer."

"I don't."

"Yes, Gwrydd, he'll be coming for me," agreed Turel.

"Well, that won't do," said Daisy, "The oracle told you needed to be at the Watcher's side, correct?"

"Yes."

"Wait," I broke in, "you heard a prophecy about me?"

Turel continued speaking to Daisy. "Yes, I'm supposed to be by the Watcher. We can't have him anywhere near Siobhan. We need her at the Veil."

"I better get moving. My people's allies stand ready. It's time to send out the call. Then I shall hunt down Chernobog," said Daisy. "He'd never resist a challenge from me. We loath one another." She spoke the last words with obvious relish.

She walked to my side of the bed and hugged me, despite me being naked under the sheet. "I love you, my dearest, stubborn Siobhan. And I'll see you at noon today, in a few hours, in fact."

"Why noon?" I asked.

"The prophecy didn't say when we need to be at the Devil's Punch Bowl, just that today's the day. Noon is when a demon is the weakest. I like to stack my odds."

"Makes sense," I said.

She winked at me. "This isn't my first rodeo, Siobhan."

Daisy faced Turel. "Three hours, Turel. In three hours this house will disappear. It's connected to me. Once I hunt Chernobog down and come out in the open, we won't want anything connected to me around where the other side can sniff it out. Leave everything you do not need here. Should we prevail, I can summon everything again. Should we fail, well, such trifles as luggage will be unnecessary." She gave me another squeeze and blew Turel a kiss.

She contributed one last piece of advice. "Do not drive a mortal car. Use the Paths of Light, where Lucifer's Fallen and their demons cannot tread."

Turel nodded at Daisy. "We will do that, Gwyrdd." Satisfied, she walked across my bedroom, her back to us.

In one fluid motion, she launched herself at the window. I gasped as the wall disappeared. The flaming change from woman to dragon form occurred so smoothly, the two seemed to coexist together for an instant. Next the wall reformed and the outline of the dragon's wings was illuminated against the sky as she flew away.

I started to find Turel regarding me with intensity, rather than staring at the incredible sight of a dragon changing forms. "What?" I asked. My cheeks burned under his regard.

"Come here." He reached for me, drawing me into his arms, snuggling us entwined under the sheet once more. "You are an amazing woman, Siobhan Orsini."

As he caressed me, I realized his injuries had disappeared. His skin appeared as smooth and unmarred as though the horrible wounds of a few hours ago had never been. "Turel, you're healed."

"I know," he murmured as his lips traced sweet kisses down the sensitive skin of my neck. "Now, kiss me."

"Turel," I protested, which proved difficult as his hands traced my skin, and his mouth traveled to one ear, delicately nibbling the lobe. He set my heart racing again and destroyed my ability to focus. I tried again. "Daisy said we only have three hours. This is no time for…"

He stopped and propped himself up on one elbow, gazing at me. His voice resonated with emotion as he said, "This is exactly the time for me to make love with you. I've been alone for a long time, lonely and apart. It eats at the soul."

Yes, I knew loneliness.

"Now darling Siobhan, we have these few precious moments here together. Let me have this time, let me love you and feel you loving me back. I do not know what the next several hours hold for us, but I do know that we have this. We have now."

He bent his head to me in a passionate kiss. He was right. We had this moment. I kissed him ardently in return. After my latest nightmare, I didn't want to think about what the waiting hours held. I gasped as he bent his head down, his tongue encircling and flicking one nipple and then the other. I pulled him to me, hungry to have his lean body against mine, wanting the perfect sensation of we two, skin-on-skin.

As our bodies joined again, together as one, his dark eyes locked with mine, one of his hands caressing the side of my face, locking us both in an intimate moment of connection. This time as I climaxed I felt the light touch of his mind on my thoughts, extending and accentuating the pleasure to something I had never experienced or imagined. Nor did I look away when he came immediately afterward. With our minds joined even as our bodies, I knew his pleasure and joy, as if they were my own.

We lay motionless in a perfect moment, him still inside of me, both sweating and spent. When he smiled, I smiled back, happiness bubbling up within me. I found myself laughing, and his rich, deep chuckles joined mine. I tightened my arms, squeezing, never wanting this moment, this transcendent instant to end.

* * *

After we showered and woke the others, I joined Turel in the quiet kitchen to wait for Tim, Alex and Nefta. Without Daisy, the magical dragon breakfast fairy, to provide for us, it meant slim pickings. Scrounging what I could, I watched as Turel packed a few things into his backpack. I took pleasure out of just ogling him, seeing the smooth muscles ripple underneath today's T-shirt, which read, "Come to the nerd side, we have Pi." He had found another pair of jeans, yesterday's ripped and bloody pair discarded. His dark hair was still damp from his shower. I ran my fingers through the moist curls at the nape of his neck. He leaned close and gave me a quick kiss.

I said in a light tone, "So, you're all better, eh?"

"Better than ever."

His face glowed with health and vitality. I shook my head in disbelief. "I did that?"

"Well, not exactly."

"What do you mean by 'not exactly,' Turel?"

"You helped ease the pain, but Chernobog's release restored me."

"I don't understand."

Turel sat at the table and patted the chair next to him. I ignored his hand and sat down on his lap instead. "Since your leg is not injured…"

He raised eyebrows then hugged me. "You are the loveliest thing."

"You were saying?" I said, but his compliment sent my pulse racing.

"Right, Chernobog." He pursed his lips in thought. "Ages ago I and three other angels fought the demon lord you know as Chernobog."

"Demon lord?"

"Right, they have rank. Demons are not creatures of free will. They can only do what their superiors, or even a good magician, tell them to do. Chernobog is one of the most powerful and highest demon lords."

"Sounds pretty scary."

"Well, he is. You saw what even the tiniest sliver of his soul did to you, Alex, and Tim back at your house. Or that pathetic creature, Gilbert." Turel shook his head. "Poor little man. I'm afraid he never had a chance.

"Where was I? Ah, chaining Chernobog. So, having a demon lord of that magnitude, that strength, free on this dimensional plane wreaked havoc. This was before I Fell, you understand? I was an archangel in those days. Three other angels and I were charged with restraining and imprisoning the beast. The chains we used to accomplish this were chains of pure energy forged of our will, heart, and intellect. Each of us contributed three chains, but one gave a fourth forged of his passion."

"It always seems to come back to the number thirteen, doesn't it, Turel?"

He stroked my cheek as he answered me, "It's true. Certain numbers have power. We used thirteen chains to subdue Chernobog, four angels to call the corners and set the prison from the four directions. Hadriel set the guard to the east, Shamsiel to the South, and I set the western watch."

"Who took the north side?"

"Lucifer."

"*The* Lucifer?"

"Even so. Remember, Siobhan, he was and still is an angel, my brother." Turel fell silent for a moment. An emotion I couldn't name flickered across his features. He stirred and continued, "Over the ages, one by one, the chains have been broken. Lucifer cut his himself after he Fell. The chain which had been of my will broke when I fell in love with my wife and was expelled from Heaven's Grace. My heart's chain broke when she died. The chain of my intellect broke when I tried to circumvent an event foretold for me."

"Like I did?"

"Yes, I also tried to evade what had been prophesied."

"Can I ask? What did you try to avoid? Something horrible, like me releasing Chernobog?"

I wondered from his expression if I asked too personal a question. His dark eyes bored into my soul. "I tried to avoid meeting you, Siobhan."

"What? *Why?*"

"My prophecy foretold I would guard you and stand beside you at the Veil. This happened a few years ago when you were still in college. After learning this, well, I admit, I was curious. I sought you out. When I saw you, beautiful, sparkling, and full of life, those bewitching green eyes…" He paused, looking away for an instant and then studied my face again. "I knew I could love you, would be drawn to you. I couldn't… I wouldn't… I didn't want that pain again."

"Loving someone hurts you?"

"The pain of watching the one you love age and wither, while you go on, untouched for ages more. I watched my wife fade, my own children age and die as I continued on, alone. I fled, shut myself off from the pain."

"What about your grandchildren?" I asked.

"How many generations would you have me watch die?" he responded.

The silence stretched out. Turel shifted me off his lap and on to the chair next to him. Holding both my hands, he drew close and kissed me. First, my forehead and then a soft kiss, hardly more than a breath, on my lips. Drawing back, he smiled, but a sadness crept into his eyes. "Sometimes there is free will and sometimes there is destiny. One does not run from fate. I should have known better. In fact, I did know better, and so, another chain broke."

The silence stretched out and I asked, "So, who forged the last chain, the chain of passion?"

"I did."

"And, last night?"

"All that passion, contained for ages, all the power of what I once possessed, has been released again. You see me restored, at the height of my powers. That is what truly healed me, not you, although I thank you nonetheless."

I pondered this for a moment and then had a thought. "Of course," I said slyly, "as Daisy would say, you didn't, um, break passion's chain alone. It does require two... if memory serves."

He grinned like the sun coming out after the rain. He shook his head and laughed. "So, I guess you did do this."

"Did what?" asked Tim, entering the kitchen. The "thump-thump" of Leia's heavy tail against the cabinets accompanied him.

"Nothing." I smiled. "Have you seen Alex this morning?"

Tim nodded. "I checked in on them a few minutes ago. Nefta's better, but still pretty crispy. Alex is worried sick." Tim paused and shook his head. "Nefta doesn't seem to be concerned though. She keeps saying she'll be fine."

"Of course she does," muttered Turel. "Valkyries, such masochists. I better see what I can do."

"That would be good," agreed Tim.

We trooped down the hall to Alex's room, Leia following Tim. He knocked politely.

"Alex, can we come in? Turel thinks he can help," I called.

"I sure hope someone can," my brother's voice answered.

We burst in; Alex and Nefta were still in the same clothes they'd worn the night before. Nefta's burns appeared improved, but still raw and oozing. "Nefta," said Turel in an exasperated tone.

"Yes?"

"How are you feeling?"

She arched her right eyebrow, the not-charred one. "Fine."

"You don't look fine."

She shrugged. "Other than the fact that Alex insists I stay in this bed. How is the state of being horizontal at all helpful?"

"I can heal you."

Nefta shot him a withering glare. "Please, Turel, we tried last night. Focus on your own wounds. I am a Valkyrie, not some mortal."

Tim and I exchanged looks. "She says it like it's a bad thing," he said.

"The last chain broke last night, Nefta."

Her cool blue eyes flicked to me and then met Turel's. "Your wounds, they are gone?"

"Completely."

"You are restored, Turel?"

"I am as you once knew me."

She gave a short laugh. "Won't Asrael be annoyed?"

"I find I can contemplate that eventuality with great equanimity."

Nefta glanced at the humans in the room and said, by way of explanation, "Asrael and Turiel have never been close. Asrael enjoyed these ages of lording his greater strength over our friend there."

"I knew I didn't like that guy," remarked Alex.

Turel moved to where Nefta sat. "With your permission," he asked courteously.

"Yes, please," she said.

I expected Turel's steady golden glow. I'd seen him heal several times now and it had been the same in each case. This time though, when he laid his gentle hands on Nefta's smooth platinum hair there came a brilliant flash, filling the room with a brief stunning sunburst.

We blinked, our eyes dazzled. Nefta paced around the room,

stretching her limbs. Once again, she prowled with dangerous grace. Her flawless face shone with an ethereal beauty.

Alex watched her, a relieved smile of his face. "Better?"

"I am me, Alex."

"That's perfection, baby doll, let's rock and roll."

"What's next?" Tim asked.

"Get packed and head out," said Turel.

"And weapons," added Nefta. "Daisy has made some adjustments to yours."

As we headed out Tim exhaled heavily. "You, okay?" I turned back to him in concern as the others continued.

"Just relieved our side is back up to full strength is all, Siobhan."

I lightly punched his shoulder. "I told you, you should have let me go to the courthouse by myself."

"And I told you, you and Alex are more than clients to me."

"I love you, Tim."

"I know. I love you, too, Siobhan." His eyes sparkled as he grabbed me in a big bear hug. We squeezed tight and then let go. "We good?"

"Yes, we're good," I said with emphasis. We fist bumped and went into the kitchen, now lit with the morning sunshine.

"Not much time left until this house disappears," Turel said as we entered.

Nefta beckoned to Tim. "You and Turel, come with me. I have some items you can carry for me."

"Oh, we can, can we?" Tim laughed as they followed the imperious battle angel out the door, leaving my brother and me in the house.

"Only hours away now," I said. "How are you holding up, Alex?"

"Not bad, actually." His eyes drifted toward the door where Nefta had gone with the others.

"Missing home?"

"What, Siobhan?"

"I said, are you missing Calistoga? Your café?"

He fixed his brown eyes on me, for once serious. "You know what, sis? I think maybe I'm home already."

"You know this place won't be here in about thirty minutes."

"It's not this house."

"I'm not following, you, Alex."

He shuffled his feet and said, "Maybe Tim and I have had it wrong all these years. Maybe home isn't a place. Maybe…"

I nudged him with my shoulder. "Yes?"

"It just sounds so damn sentimental."

"Try me."

"Well, maybe home really is where the heart is."

I remembered my dream, but forced the gory images away. Instead, I focused on the memory of him and Nefta sitting together on the couch, their fragile happiness shining. "Yes, maybe you are right. Maybe the real trick is figuring out what the heart wants."

Turel beckoned from the doorway. "Hey, you two, let's get these in your hands."

We followed him on to the porch. Nefta handed me my bow and quiver. I frowned. "They don't look any different," I said.

"Daisy, used some of her, what is the word, Alex? Her 'mowed joe' on them," Nefta explained.

"Mo-jo, doll," my brother corrected.

"Thank you, Alex. Daisy used some of her mo-jo on them. Now, your quiver will never be empty of arrows," the Valkyrie said.

"Wow," I said, impressed. "That might come in handy."

"I would still advise retrieving your arrows whenever possible, Watcher."

"Why is that, Nefta?" I asked.

"It is never wise to leave pointed objects where your enemies can use them. Of course, sometimes it is not possible to take the necessary time."

"Good point," I said. "Thanks."

Next she handed me a cross bow. "For close quarters fighting," she said. "Cumbersome to reload, but a bolt well-placed in your enemy can be most effective."

"Gotcha'," I said.

"You are my Alex's sister," she replied, "as well as the Watcher. I would keep you whole."

Nefta continued, focusing on Tim. She tapped the tall quarterstaff he held. "This cannot be broken, not by anything."

Tim regarded his weapon, his broad smile creasing his face into the laugh lines I always loved about him. "I like it."

"And for Alex," She held up several throwing knives. "Daisy had these made for you. You will cover your person in blades."

"It would have never occurred to me to carry knives," he said.

Nefta shrugged. "My idea. I would be better comforted if you were armed to the teeth on the battlefield, especially if I am not by your side to smite your foes."

I blinked, my eyes automatically seeking Turel's. He blew a kiss at me, his warm eyes twinkling. Coming from Nefta, this seemed like quite a declaration of affection. Alex looked dazed and he wore a broad smile.

"Ready?" asked Turel, shouldering his familiar backpack. I didn't even need to concentrate anymore to see where he hid his wings. Now I could observe him, or any other angel, and See easily. Another way this week changed me… We walked down Daisy's path, past her roses. We went a little farther and something made me stop and glance behind.

The kaleidoscope of images I saw the first night I arrived at Daisy's cottage bombarded me, but this time they did not disturb me. I went with the flow, seeing one and then another incarnation of Daisy's home. Soon they vanished, and as my eyelids opened and closed once more, so were the cottage, the roses and the little walk to the dragon's house. Only the open meadow remained on a sunny, summer morning.

Gazing at the meadow, I said a silent prayer for all I loved and this beautiful world of ours. Who knows? Maybe we'll win.

Chapter Twenty-One

We stepped through the dimensions. Holding hands, we followed the Paths of Light, the angels' ways through worlds. Turel and the Observers used them despite being fallen since the Two Hundred still served the cause of Light. However, Lucifer's Fallen and their demons were forbidden access. Dragons, as I had seen, made their own passages through worlds, though they did not cross as often or with the ease of angels.

My whole body tingled in a mass of electrified nerve endings, wound too tight. After a second session spent with our weapons, testing our new skills, learning about the attributes and dangers of various angels, archangels and demons, my head swam with visions of death, killing and battles. My failure in my dream lurked just below the surface of my thoughts—always there.

We left Leia with Leo and Missy. Thinking of their stake in this day did not make for an easy heart. Despite everything, I reveled in the beauty of the Paths of Light. Their beauty soothed. As we passed through them again, my spirit felt buoyed, lifted up. Their unearthly music filled my soul, bringing to mind every happy moment, every peal of laughter. I remembered each source of joy in my life. The refracted rainbow-light gave me strength. In my mind I saw the faces of those I loved and who loved me in return. As we returned to our world once more, I exhaled a cleansing breath of release and peace, for the moment letting go of everything that had weighed me down.

Turel heard me and smiled. "The Paths of Light, Siobhan?"

"They are beautiful. I feel new and yet, more myself than I can remember being in a long time."

He brought my hand to his chest and wrapped his other hand on top of it. Bringing his face close to mine, he said, "Such is their power, and that is what we serve: Light."

His lips found mine. After a sweet, lingering moment, we parted. He released me, saying, "Now, we face what may come."

I squared my shoulders and concentrated on not throwing up.

We joined Tim, Nefta, and Alex, who studiously turned away, allowing Turel and me our moment of intimacy. "Well," I said, "here we are."

We stood on a cliff on the rocky Mendocino coast. The blue-green Pacific Ocean shimmered in the bright sunlight. The waves crashed below, spray sparkling like diamonds in the sunshine. Farther inland lay the deep green of redwoods, California bay and oak trees. The hills reflected a sun-kissed gold. It seemed an incongruous place for the impending violence to come.

I felt it before I heard it. A reverberating, awesome noise that sounded like it should be coming from the depths of the earth, and working its way outward. Instead, it filled the air around us, forceful sonic waves battering us.

"It begins," Turel said to Nefta. To my surprise he offered his hand to the battle angel.

She grasped it. "Yes," she said in a fierce hiss. She let go, took two strides, and with a graceful leap Nefta took to the sky, silver wings flashing as she vaulted toward the heavens.

"What was that?" asked Tim in an awed voice. I wondered if I looked as stunned as he and Alex did.

"Gwyrdd's Call. She is summoning her allies and announcing to the world that The Ones Who Came Before want to come home."

Turel contemplated us. "We need to see the lay of things. We'll be back." With that he, too, took off. It was the first time I had seen Turel fly, and I watched, awestruck by those beautiful white wings against the blue sky.

Alex elbowed me. "Hey, sis, that's your boyfriend. Kinda flighty, doncha' think?"

"So? *That's* your girlfriend."

Alex opened and then closed his mouth. A silly grin spread across his face. The two angels flew higher and higher until they became dots against the sun.

I scoured the coast and the hills inland, seeking sign of anyone, friend or foe. Automatically, as I had for days now, I concentrated on my Watcher's sight, searching for what might not be visible to anyone except me. After waiting, listening, straining, the hair on the back of my neck stood on end. We were not alone. "What do you see, Tim?" I asked in a quiet voice, staring at the spectacle converging in the sky above us and the landscape around us.

He glanced anxiously up the coast to the north. "It looks like a storm is coming, a big one, dark and wild."

Alex shook his head. "But it's the wrong direction for a storm, bro. They usually come from out at sea and blow inland."

I spoke, my words slow and neutral, "And out to sea what do you see, Alex?"

"Lightning crackling on the horizon, flashes of gold light, even bits of rainbows. What am I really seeing?"

Wordlessly, I stretched out one hand to Alex and the other to Tim, so they could see what I saw. I had no idea why this worked, only that it did. Around us a motley invisible crowd gathered. We found ourselves flanked by black bears, cougars, red and gray foxes, their growls and snarls mixing in a rough, raucous cacophony. Snorting, ferocious boars surrounded us, massive in girth and muscle. Coyotes let out their laughing, yipping call.

"Why can't I see the animals without you?" whispered Tim.

I concentrated. Frowning, I glimpsed a mist through my human sight. Next I used my Watcher's sight again to see what changed between the two views. Scattered throughout the clearing gathered several large shaggy creatures. Standing at least nine feet tall, these lumbering figures remained silent. One was grizzly brown, another darkest black, a third was whiter than Turel's wings, others in shades of caramel, red, and brown stood ready.

As I gaped at their sensitive, intelligent faces, recognition flooded me. "Big Foot, the Chupacabra, and the Yeti?" The three nodded at me while their remaining brothers and sisters, whom I could not name, remained silent, watching. Wookies floated through my mind. I suppressed the thought, promising myself I would share this observation with Tim later. The *Star Wars* nut in him would love it.

"The animals are being hidden," I explained to him. "The Guardians of the Forests are here: the Yeti, the Chupacabra, and Big Foot, plus five or six I don't have names for."

"Wow," said Tim.

"Dude," said Alex. "This is some serious shit."

Even as I watched more fantastical creatures joined the company. Silver and gold clad nymphs armed to the teeth with daggers and bows flitted amongst the company. Their massive trees marched with them over the rocky shore, roots up and branches morphed into formidable clubs.

A chariot drew into view, drawn by stags. A slender maiden with dark braids held the reins, a bow and quiver on her back. When I made eye contact, it hurt to see her. This was no human. Huntresses followed in her wake. I swallowed. "Guys, I think maybe Diana or Artemis just joined us."

My companions made no answer. Seeing their slack jaws, I made a conscious effort and closed my mouth.

Above the ocean I spied Daisy's other allies. Eagles, hawks, falcons, even swarms of wasps and hornets filled the air. Everyday creatures flew alongside those of myth and legend: phoenixes, gryphons, and others whom I could not put a name to. I even spotted a few angels. Since Observers were barred from taking sides, other than Turel, I surmised these must be volunteers like Nefta. The display around us was jaw-dropping in and of itself, but not what had my pulse racing and the pit of my stomach churning in fear. Relentless, spreading like a disease from the north, the Fallen and their demonic allies came. Their forms blackened the sky, the beauty of the angels chilling next to the twisted, nightmarish countenances of their servants. Not all of the demons flew, many more came overland, as did those Fallen who had cut off their wings. Their numbers appeared so great that it reminded me of an inky blackness covering the road, the trees, and the rocky bluffs over-looking the surf. As they advanced I thought of the Hag and though I could visualize her in my mind's eye, she no longer held any terror for me compared to the approaching onslaught.

"Dear God," said Tim reverently.

"Exactly," I said.

I glanced at my brother, wondering if his silence meant he had been overcome with the same terror I fought. Instead, his jaw set and his brown eyes fixed on the oncoming storm with fury and determination. "Will I be able to see them to kill them?" he asked, letting go of my hand. His fists flexed and un-flexed in an unconscious gesture.

From behind me Turel's deep voice answered, "Gwyrdd says she will break their illusions as the battle is joined."

"Good," said Alex sounding as fierce as Nefta.

In relief at his return, I embraced the angel. His lean strength in my arms refocused me. I took a deep breath and forced myself to put the debilitating fear aside. It would do me no good to run now. The demons or one or more of the Fallen would hunt me down and kill me. My only chance lay in fighting. More importantly, I remembered Missy and Leo. My mom was out there. So were my dad and his latest wife. Old friends, neighbors, classmates, whether they knew it or not—they needed us.

As I released Turel, his lips brushed my cheek in passing. I gripped my bow. A realization crystallized amidst my chaotic thoughts, shattering in its simplicity. My days of walking away were done. For the first time in my life, I had committed.

"Battles are chaos. My place is at the Watcher's side. I must protect her at all costs. We lose her and humanity will be doomed," Turel said. "Stay with her, and I will do my best for you."

Tim and Alex looked uneasy, but nodded, weapons ready.

Turel continued, "Siobhan, take no risks. Stay out of harm's way as much as you can. Stick close to me. Sooner or later we'll have to make a run at the Veil, there." He pointed toward the graceful bridge just inland. From where we gathered I could see the foot path.

"Why shouldn't we go now, ahead of all that?" Tim gestured to the black storm that now roiled even closer.

"The oracle said the 'Devil's Punch Bowl,'" Turel said. "Something is supposed to happen here, some event, some condition is supposed to be met before we can proceed."

"Can't we ignore the prophecy?" asked Alex.

"No."

"Why not?" my brother insisted.

Turel's eyes met mine then he said, "You could try. I've tried. Siobhan tried, too. It never works out. In this case the Veil will not be revealed until all the conditions are met. Without the Veil, we cannot win." His words sounded flat, final.

We waited, ranged on the rocks between the Devil's Punch Bowl and the trailhead. I thought again of the Hag. In my mind's eye I visualized her.

"Ducky should run," I heard the whisper in my mind. *"Ducky should run quick, quick."*

"Shush."

"Why little lamb no run?"

"It wouldn't do me any good. They'd simply run me down. Besides, I don't want to. This is my world. This is my fight." She crouched in the back of my head, lurking. Between Turel's intervention in my mind and the hellish army only moments away, I was free.

"Poor ducky, bad angels, bad demons," she mourned.

"Why don't you like demons? I thought you worked for one?" I asked.

"Greedy demons kill everything. No yummies for me...poor me."

I supposed that made sense for a creature that survived by sucking the will to live from other living things. What a ridiculous conversation to have. I forced myself to think about something else.

Daisy's army came closer. There were gryphons with the majestic heads and wings of a huge eagle and the massive hindquarters of a lion. Their fur and feathers shone in warm golds and browns. I saw gargoyles interspersed with the gryphons. I recognized them from the tops of older office buildings and churches, silent, motionless guardians. Life breathed into stone. Their ugly faces were endearing, even sweet. Their huge, earnest dark eyes contrasted with their leathery bat-like wings of stone gray.

Huge birds, blacker than storm clouds and larger than gryphons, soared overhead. Thunder and lightning trailed in their wake. "What are those?" I asked Nefta.

"Thunderbirds," she said tersely.

"Wow," I said.

"Indeed," she said.

Following the tempest of the thunderbirds came birds the size of condors with plumage of such brilliant graduated shades of red, orange, and fiery gold that their wing tips seemed on the verge of bursting into flame flew toward us. I questioned Nefta. "Are those phoenixes?"

"Naturally," she said.

Bright jewels caught my eye, dragons in miniature, the size of eagles, breathing fire. I gasped. "Baby dragons? I thought they were still banished?"

"Those are fire drakes," she said. "They are dragon-kind's smaller cousins."

"Beautiful," I said.

Nefta sniffed. "I find them annoying, worse than pigeons." She paused. "But, I admit, scrappy, mean—good in a fight."

"Are there any flying horses coming?" I asked.

"*Please.*"

"What did I say?"

"That's just a myth, Watcher."

"Oh, sorry." Chagrined, I glanced at Turel. He shrugged his shoulders and winked. I marveled at his composure, but reasoned that living about a zillion years must give a person some perspective.

I envied his calm as the Fallen and their legions of demons gathered along the coast. The millennia of hate and aggression filled the air as the two sides faced one another. I tried to rein in my fear. As terrifying as a nightmare is in the black of night, it is worse in the light of day. The twisted limbs, gaping maws, evil eyes, and wicked claws of the demons revealed themselves as more fearsome in the sunshine, not less. To see such creatures gathered by the thousands, when just one alone would have haunted my dreams, terrified me. The only thing that kept me from running away was the certainty that everyone I had ever cared about would suffer. I would not run.

An expectant calm settled over our allies. The assembled hordes ranged themselves on the inland side of the collapsed sea cave named The Devil's Punch Bowl. The howling and screaming of the demons' twisted, monstrous voices filled the air. My heart sank. Our footpath to The Veil was blocked. If we went, we'd have to fight our way through. When we went.

As though at some unseen signal, the awful noise stopped, cut off in mid howl, leaving the air heavily laden with expectation. The ground reverberated beneath our feet. The vibrations continued, growing into trembles and still becoming larger until the earth shook. I cried out, fighting to stay on my feet.

"Earthquake?" Tim asked.

Nefta shook her head. "Perhaps, but not natural. The timing is highly suspect, Tim."

The shaking grew so violent I lost my balance. Tim and Alex fought to keep on their feet, and the two angels took to the air above us.

"Get away from the bowl, everyone," Turel yelled.

Even as those words left his mouth, water shot straight in a shining column up and out of the Devil's Punch Bowl. Alex, Tim and I backed away, trying to put as much distance between us and the erupting water as possible. Something huge and dark twisted within the column. "Oh, my God, what is that?"

No one had time to respond to me; the answer exploded into the sky for all to see.

Chernobog was not the same as he had been mere days ago in front of my house. Now freed of his age-old bonds, he loomed colossal, blacker than night. He encompassed every evil thing I feared put together into a single monstrous form. The giant demon possessed wicked horns, the span of his wings rivaled a dragon's and his red eyes stared balefully at the assembled armies. "He's huge." My limbs shook.

"Of course," said Turel, landing at my side. "He's a demon lord, top of the food chain." He did not seem fazed by Chernobog, simply ready. Of course, they had already met.

Daisy, an immense vision of verdant beauty, dove toward Chernobog, roaring a challenge and breathing sheets of fire.

"Wow, she *really* doesn't like him," Alex muttered.

With a deadly whip of her mouth, she ripped a chuck out of one of Chernobog's shoulders. The wound oozed with a fetid, black ichor. First blood had been drawn and with that the battle began. Daisy's roar of triumph shook the air.

"*Gwyrdd*," howled Chernobog.

Her taunting laugh sparkled like the diamond spray of the ocean below her, heard by all present. "Yes, mine own enemy? What say you, worm?"

"I shall slay thee today, Gwyrdd."

"Ha. Today thou shalt be *unmade*."

Chernobog launched himself into the air at his ancient enemy. She stopped laughing and evaded him with ease. The two sides converged, the Fallen and their demons attacking Daisy's allies. A scream caught in my throat as the masses of evil started in our direction. I double checked the crossbow strapped to my thigh and then knocked an arrow and aimed, waiting for the first enemy to come in range.

"I am Cearneigh. Gwyrdd sent me," said a deep voice beside me. Turning, I found a gryphon next to me and two more behind him. "Watcher, if you would be so kind as to climb on board?"

"Wait. What?" I said.

Turel smiled in obvious relief, saying, "I can't fight, fly, and carry you all at once. Thank the nice gryphon and let's go."

I blinked, cleared my throat, and then said to the courteous beast, "Thank you so much."

Cearnaigh bent his head to his companions. "This is Aoife and Ronan to help your friend and your brother. And, if I may say, we should make haste, here they come."

The 'they' he referred to consisted of the howling mass of demons and Fallen, both on foot and flying toward us. We scrambled on to the gryphons' broad backs, perching where the eagles' head and wings met the sturdy lions' backs and legs. "Hold on to my shoulders," Cearnaigh called and took off with a surge, ahead of the first combatants. Peeking behind me, I said a quick prayer of thanks as Alex and Tim also made their escape via gryphon. Turel and Nefta flew alongside.

I worried that the winged demons or Fallen would catch us, but my fear was needless. As we took refuge behind our side's line, I saw Daisy's friends proved far better flyers than their adversaries. In mere moments, each side's strengths became apparent. The gryphons, thunderbirds, phoenixes, and even the gargoyles outdid the demons as far as speed, agility and intelligence. The thunderbirds, though fewer in number than the Fallen, possessed the elemental power of the storm. Each thunderbird equaled an army of one, endowed with the lightning to smite a foe and the thunder to terrify. They glamoured themselves during battle. While not as good as Daisy, unless you were a Watcher, you'd never see them coming until the storm engulfed you.

What Daisy's friends possessed in deadliness and intelligence the other side made up for in sheer numbers. Turel said once that millions of angels fell. Even more demons gathered in the host. Hell had not marshalled all its forces, but what they deployed overwhelmed nonetheless.

Turel was right; battle was chaos. Cearnaigh and the gryphons carrying Tim and Alex dove and climbed through the skies, evading all comers, keeping we three humans from the worst of the fight. I concentrated on staying astride my acrobatic steed as he did not come equipped with a saddle or reins. Turel stayed with us, wielding both his flaming sword and lightning bolts at any who approached. Now restored, he fought with a casual assurance. At full strength as he was now, few on the field of sky matched him. Silver-winged Nefta seemed to be everywhere. Teeth bared in a fierce smile, a battle axe in one hand and Durendala in the other, she created her own storm of joyful destruction.

I found myself unprepared for the swirling mass of life and death, the sheer noise of it as creatures, friend and foe, roared, howled and hissed curses upon one another. Exotic sights and unidentified smells assaulted my senses with a titanic struggle of good versus evil. Everything around me was foreign. Cearnaigh's spicy musk surrounded me in sharp contrast to the exotic perfumes of a phoenix passing close by, or the sulfuric stench a malevolent demon. Daisy left behind the smell of burnt flesh in her wake.

In the brief instant I spent scrying the battle forces, she and her fiendish opponent joined in a true struggle. Both Daisy and Chernobog used magic as well as physical weapons. The demon blotted out the sunshine of summer high noon with sweeping clouds of darkness, only to be burned clear with Daisy's flaming breath or cleansing spells.

Daisy concentrated her blows toward the devil's chest, aiming for the thing's heart. As I surveyed Chernobog I saw two vulnerable places. I blinked, not trusting my eyes at first. "Cearnaigh," I called over the din of the battle. "Is Gwyrdd aiming for Chernobog's heart?"

Cearnaigh grunted as he evaded a flying snake-like demon, a warped and twisted version of a dragon in evil miniature. "That is the general plan," he said. Out of the corner of my eye, I saw Alex lean away from his gryphon and slice the head off the snake demon. My brother seemed to be enjoying himself as much as Nefta. I'd kill him if he fell.

"Can you get Turel over here?" I asked. "I need to get some information to Daisy."

"Who?"

"Gwyrdd. Get me closer to Turel."

"I'll see what I can do."

Cearnaigh wasn't far from Turel to begin with, but with the chaos, the flying bodies zooming in and out of one another, getting within speaking distance presented a definite challenge. After a couple of tries, I finally thought, "*Turel, I need you.*"

He joined me so quickly I wanted to kick myself for not

trying it sooner. Cearnaigh fixed me with one eagle eye. "Nice," he said. "Next time, let's just do that. Shall we?"

"Yeah, sorry."

Turel hovered next to me, flaming sword in his hand. "I need to get a message to Daisy," I said.

"Is it important?"

"No, I want to talk about the weather. Of course, it's important."

Turel crooked one elegant eyebrow at me. "Yes?"

"Is it possible a demon could have two hearts? Or have divided its heart?"

The dark angel frowned and loosed a lightning bolt at a creature resembling a flying monkey from the *Wizard of Oz*, only with much larger fangs. "Yes, I can think of several ways it could be done. It would make the demon much harder to kill."

"I'll say," agreed Cearnaigh.

"I think that's what Chernobog has done."

"How do you know, Siobhan?"

"I can't explain it. Something about my Watcher's Sight, I think. I can See another's vulnerabilities, their weak spots."

"Handy," observed Cearnaigh as he dodged two harpies.

The wicked-looking birds had the bodies of vultures, but the heads of hags. I shuddered as they headed for Tim and the gryphon carrying him. To my surprise, Tim expertly turned this way and that as they flew, cracking the harpies over the head with his quarterstaff. Unconscious, the monstrous birds fell out of the sky to the rocks below. I grinned at Tim and he waved, both of us caught in the heady triumph of the moment. "Can you tell Daisy for me? She has to know this," I said to Turel, my worry returning full force.

"Of course, Watcher. Where are the two pieces?" he asked.

"Lower left stomach and right thigh."

Cearnaigh whistled in surprise.

Turel nodded at the gryphon. "Agreed, Gwyrdd's been going about this wrong. Nefta."

In an instant the Valkyrie joined us. "Yes, Turel?"

"Can you keep these beasts off me and Siobhan while I get a message to Gwyrdd?"

"Child's play."

"Hey," said Cearnaigh. "I'm not helpless."

Turel gave a half bow which looked odd in mid-flight. "Of course, I meant no offense. Simply being cautious."

"Humph," said Cearnaigh.

Turel's face went blank as he communicated with Daisy. I tried not to hold my breath as the seconds stretched out. Cearnaigh dipped and swerved, keeping us out of the worst of the fray. Nefta was as good as her word. She continued her rain of death on all who came within range of her battle axe and Durendala's razor edge.

Relief washed over me when Turel's face took on its usual alert expression. Daisy's renewed roars sounded as she redoubled her attack. "Sorry," said Turel, "it can be a challenge to get her attention when she's in a fight."

"Naturally," sniffed Nefta, "now, I go to Alex. It's his first battle. I want to share the joy."

"Valkyries," said Cearnaigh.

"You said it," I agreed. "So, Turel, she knows?"

"Yes," said Turel. "Damn it."

Chernobog finally managed to get his claws on Daisy. He wrapped his evil, black talons around the jeweled dragon, biting and mauling her flesh. Blood, as red as my own, streamed from Daisy's many wounds. The two massive beings wrestled and ripped at one another, half falling, half flying through the sky. Daisy outmaneuvered her opponent, ripping his thigh wide open. This time his diseased blood did not ooze from the wound, it spurted black in an evil stream. The dragon spat a huge chunk of demon flesh from her mouth as she ripped herself from Chernobog's grasp roaring in triumph and soaring free. Blood flowed from several of her wounds, but the injuries didn't seem to be slowing her down.

"Yes," Turel exulted. "One down." The dark angel veered off as one of the Fallen advanced upon him, her lovely face twisted in hate.

At that instant, Chernobog landed heavily next to the Devil's Punch Bowl. Though his leg was ripped to shreds and largely unusable, he remained full of battle lust. The action around me pulled my attention in different directions. I wanted to keep track of Turel and Daisy, while still maintaining my grip on Cearnaigh, and trying to locate Alex and Tim in the winged brawl around me. I had the sneaking suspicion I might throw up from the circles we flew, and a tiny portion of my brain wondered what my dignified mount would have to say when I did.

"*Little piggy must think now.*" The Hag's whisper in my head surprised me. I hadn't been thinking about her.

"*What?*"

"*Not good to be wondering, worrying. Battle here, battle now. Focus on bad things trying to kill ducky, otherwise…*"

"*Otherwise, what?*"

"*No more ducky, so sad. Bye-bye.*"

"*Why do you care?*"

"*No more ducky? Then no more me, poor me.*"

"*Shush.*" I tried something Turel had once done for me. I visualized a thick, wooden door in my mind and I shut it on the Hag. A hiss of indignation sounded as I locked the psychic door on her.

I focused on the battle raging around me. Being present helped my nausea. I flew with the gryphon, moving with his body, instead of simply being a passenger. After a few minutes, Cearnaigh remarked, "You fly better now."

"Thanks."

Before I could continue fresh roars erupted from Chernobog. The demon lord thrashed on his side, clutching a gaping wound in his abdomen. Daisy roared in victory, soaring above him. As she swooped over him, crowing her triumph, the evil claws of her fading opponent thrust out one more time. He sent a burst of malevolent blackness after Daisy, a kind of curse. I Saw it, black, malicious, a creation of the purest evil. He sank back, dying and she dove, breathing fire on him, unmaking him as she promised. Then his curse entangled my dragon.

It resembled a black, sick, sticky web to my other sight. It wrapped around Daisy, capturing her, freezing and seizing her lovely wings. Instantly, she turned her head, using her own fire to burn off the evil magic, but wherever she burned she left raw skin. The curse was incinerated, but left Daisy horribly damaged.

I screamed as she fell out of the sky. Every fiber of my being reverberated in shared terror for her. For a beat of my heart, it seemed the entire battle stopped to watch her fall. My world tilted on its axis. The green dragon hit the sea with a terrific splash. She disappeared beneath the surface. I screamed again.

"Gwyrdd," said the gryphon I rode. He sounded stunned.

Turel spoke in my mind. "*Peace, Siobhan, she's fine. The Nereids have her.*"

Breathing once more, I relayed this information to Cearnaigh. He repeated it to the other gryphons, and the word of Gwyrdd's safety spread. A ragged cheer went up on our side. I considered the place where Chernobog fell and a deep satisfaction stirred in me to see all that remained of the demon lord was a burnt scar on the rocks.

"*Cearnaigh?*"

"Yes, Watcher?"

"Who are the Nereids?"

He shot me an amused look over one feathered shoulder. "This really is new to you and your friends, isn't it?"

"That's one way of putting it."

"They're the daughters of Nereus, the Old Man of the Sea."

"Sea nymphs? You're kidding?"

"Yes, sea nymphs and no, I am not in jest."

"Wow."

Cearnaigh veered off, joined by Aoife and Ronan with Tim and Alex on their backs. Turel flew beside us. "What's up?" called Alex.

"I'm fairly certain the fall of Chernobog was what we had to have happen at the Devil's Punch Bowl. With him gone, his troops have shifted position. The path is clear now," said Turel. "We need to head to the Veil."

"Where is it?" asked Cearnaigh.

"Through that bridge, inland," said Turel.

"Could you be more specific?"

"We'll know more when it's time. You know how it is with prophecies."

"Truly," agreed Cearnaigh.

We raced toward the bridge. Ronan, carrying Alex, cried out in pain. A Fallen flew after us, throwing living ropes of flame. One had singed Ronan. The gryphon increased speed, carrying my brother out of the Fallen's range.

"Lahatiel," Nefta grated.

The arch Fallen was one of the most beautiful beings I had ever seen. He seemed to have stepped out of a Renaissance painting: golden hair, perfect features, and an ivory complexion. Even at this distance, his blue eyes enchanted the soul. Yet, hate distorted his beauty, changing his face to a fearful mask of dark passions. I thought of what he had done to Nefta, and fresh fear gripped me.

"How fast can you fly?" I asked my gryphon.

"Fast enough," said Cearnaigh grimly.

Turel whipped his head around to Nefta. "Don't let him take you again. Focus on your task. Get back up, now. I'll find a defensible spot."

Nefta gave a tight nod and disappeared.

Those of us remaining headed through the bridge, down the river canyon, and the chase was on.

Chapter Twenty-Two

The Veil beckoned—so close, and yet so far away. Either that or we were lost. We raced and fought our way through the air along the river to a small clearing at the base of a waterfall that crashed down from forty feet above us. On another day, it would have been an idyllic spot. Today it was hell, but at least it was a defensible hell.

Nefta did not return, but we had help. A squad of gargoyles joined the three gryphons in the sky above us. As our enemies followed us, they defended us from the air. Tim, Alex, and I fought on the ground. For the moment the focus remained on the struggle at the beach, but more enemies kept coming inland.

Turel and the fallen archangel Lahatiel fought above me. Fire battled fire as the Fallen threw coiled whips of writhing hellfire at Turel. The flames danced independent of Lahatiel and yet, still doing his bidding. My dark angel drew his burning sword and used it in such intricate moves it seemed as if his blade became a living blaze moving in a deadly ballet of its own.

I kept my back to the hillside, surrounded by boulders. This protected position left me largely out of sight. My hands flickered faster than I could have ever believed possible as I sighted and took out monster after monster. Each nightmare was more horrible than the last. Daisy's gift was a blessing, a quiver that never emptied. I carried an endless stream of projectiles matched with as many targets. With Turel's skills imprinted in my arms and hard wired to my brain, my Watcher's sight proved deadly.

Turel roared in pain and anger. I whipped my head around to see what had happened on the hillside above me. One of Lahatiel's whips of hellfire had found its mark, wrapped around Turel's neck, and burned him as it tightened. For the second time today, my world shuddered and tilted on its axis. This time, I did not scream. There was no time. I went cold, everything focused on my other Sight to seek any weak points. At first I despaired, though I could damage the vessel, an archangel like Lahatiel would heal so quickly the effect would be indiscernible. My other sight revealed where his soul tied to the human vessel. I prayed that my plan would work and Lahatiel's body and soul would be ripped asunder at the point of attachment..

I would have to leave my cover and venture further into the battle, leaving me exposed, even if only for an instant. In a cool, rational corner of my mind, I weighed the odds versus the instructions Daisy and Turel had given me to stay protected. I had no other choice if I wanted to save the one I loved.

Stepping forward, I remained cold, focused, and took aim, even as Lahatiel directed another whip of living flame at Turel. As my dark angel screamed once more, my bow loosed arrow after arrow. They needed to sink deep.

Lahatiel cried out, first in anger then in true pain as more arrows found their mark. I narrowed my eyes and concentrated on my target. Harried, the archangel's flames attacking Turel faltered, sputtered, and went out. Lahatiel fixed me with a hate-filled glower as he prepared to set his flames on me. This gave me the opening I needed. I shot three arrows in rapid succession through his left eye. I'll never forget the vision of his soul leaving his vessel. As it wafted upward, his physical body crumbled. The beautiful arch-Fallen, Lahatiel, would not be a problem this day.

I lowered my bow for an instant of satisfaction. Turel recovered and healed himself in the moment I took Lahatiel's focus off of him. He shot a grin my way, and I grinned back.

Those seconds of inattention proved costly. A blur of movement followed. Gilbert threw himself on top of me. "Bitch," he spat in savage hate. "My life has never been the same since the morning I woke up at your house. The things I've seen." He sobbed, a lonely, mad sound. "The things I've done for him."

I struggled against Chernobog's creature. Pity combined with disgust. The demon lord lay defeated. Though freed, Gilbert remained horribly damaged. His pale-blue eyes were bloodshot, his thinning hair disheveled. Spittle hung from his mouth. He clawed at me, ripping my shirt, and exposing tender flesh. One hand held a wicked knife. Acting out of instinct, I viciously raised one knee in a sudden and savage kick. He grunted in pain and his body lifted for an instant. In that second, I found the crossbow strapped to my leg and shot the first bolt. I hoped to hit him in his chest. In the frantic close quarters struggle, I shot him through the shoulder. He sustained a painful wound, but not a killing one.

As he moaned, rolling off of me, I scrambled to my feet. I raised the crossbow again. Tim appeared at my side, quarterstaff whirling. Gilbert struggled get up, his face twisted in madness. Tim took one end of his staff and masterfully jabbed it full in Gilbert's face. Bones crunched audibly and Gilbert lay back, his limbs twitching as life emptied from his body. Tim's face blanched, and his eyes saddened as he watched Gilbert die, but he squared his shoulders. This fight continued.

Tim and I nodded to one another and prepared to face the next opponent. We fought back-to-back in the middle of the melee, far from my agreed upon sheltered spot. Still, I could handle this. "Siobhan," said Tim through the din of the fight around us, "you were supposed to stay out of the way until we can get you to the Veil."

"I know, I know. Sorry, that plan didn't work out. I had to get Lahatiel off Turel."

"Great, now, can we get you someplace more protected?"

"Like where?"

He didn't answer, as two hellhounds, each the size of a small pony attacked him. He wielded his staff faster than I could follow. I dealt with the demons coming up the narrow path to join the fight in the small clearing. The gryphons wheeled and struck from above. Bodies piled up, blocking the trail, but more monsters crawled over their fallen brethren's corpses. Tim dispatched the dogs amid chaotic yelping.

"Siobhan," yelled Alex, cutting a path through the demons to us. He used Durendal like an extension of his body. "You aren't supposed to be out in the open."

"Yeah, Tim covered that," I snarled.

"Can you get back to the rocks?" Alex asked.

"What do you think?" The situation had become bleak.

The fighting around us intensified. We were surrounded. My arrows flew. My arms trembled with fatigue and my lungs burned. I thanked God for my Watcher's sight. The vulnerable spots on these horrific bodies were not always where one would expect. Without my Sight I would have shot the wrong body part. I didn't have the luxury of multiple tries.

Innon appeared, his perfect face twisted in passion. Whether hate or desire coursed through him I couldn't tell. "Watcher," he purred. "I told you, I found you first. You are mine. My prize, and I will dispatch you, as I promised."

He raised his sword to run me through. I managed to get an arrow off. It sunk into his thigh with a satisfying *thunk*. I tried to knock another arrow, yet I knew I wouldn't be in time. As his sword came down, I expected the pain. Instead, I heard a ringing clang. Tim's quarterstaff struck Innon's sword aside and Tim stepped into the breach between the fallen angel and me.

"Fool," hissed Innon to his one-time boss. "I'll be right back, Watcher."

Alex entered the fray. Innon produced a second sword from nowhere and the fight joined. Alex wielded Durendal like a master as Tim's quarterstaff whirled and rained blows too quick to see. I couldn't get a clean shot on Innon. The three spun and attacked in a deadly ritual. I contented myself with continuing to strike down the unending river of demons before they joined Innon, overwhelming my brother and my friend. Turel fought a short way from me, dispatching demons around us with his lightning bolts.

Tim made a small mistake. He miscalculated a blow, and one of Innon's swords penetrated the whirling wall of quarterstaff blows. Tim's wounded arm bled profusely. A few drops of his blood splattered on Alex's sword. Durendal became a blinding, shining ray of light. Within seconds the sword rang as though just struck in a smithy. The ringing became a song.

"Alex."

Nefta stepped through dimensions to my brother. She held Durendala unsheathed. The Valkyrie handed the sword to Alex. "I heard Durendal. Cross the blades, anoint Durendala with Tim's blood."

Confusion warred with self-preservation as I watched, still trying to keep the battle in focus. Why Tim's blood? What had Tim's blood done to Durendal and why did Nefta want Durendala to feel the blood, too?

Alex crossed the twin swords. A couple of drops of Tim's blood touched Durendala. She shone golden, ringing in her own song.

Meanwhile, Tim fought Innon alone. As skilled and strong as Tim was with his quarterstaff, he fought an immortal wielding two swords. Though still on his feet, Tim bled from multiple wounds. Alex straightened. He, too, seemed to glow with the brother and sister swords he held.

"They are yours; they have chosen you," called Nefta, drawing another sword from nowhere and growling in an unladylike way as another of the Fallen approached her. She struck a feline pose, her lips curled as she sprang at the other angel.

"Alex," I called, "help Tim." I sent another arrow into Innon's thigh, a third I planted into his back. I searched for where his soul was tethered to his physical body as I had with Lahatiel. Tim kept getting in the way.

My brother advanced, but even as he re-entered the fight Innon sliced Tim's other arm. When my old friend parried the next attack, Innon used his other sword to run Tim through, twisting the blade as he withdrew it. Tim's face froze, turning white, and he dropped to his knees. I screamed, grief slicing through me, a different kind of knife.

Alex sprang forward with a wordless shout of rage. He came at Innon with the twin blades glowing. The swords and my brother radiated fury. Alex danced, oh, how he danced. His swordplay went beyond anything from Nefta's muscle memory. This dance screamed Alex, with his lifelong grace and rhythm, yet with the skills of a warrior I had never met.

Innon retreated in the face of my brother's wrath, his eyes showing fear for the first time. Tim fell into the dirt. I ran to him, all the while shooting arrows at the oncoming hordes.

"Turiel," I entreated. I used his angelic name on purpose. I prayed. In a burst of gold, Turel appeared at Tim's side. The melee raged on around us, but Turel folded Tim and me into a golden shield, buying us precious moments.

The attacking demons outside pressed and pushed on Turel's shield. They threw knives, even swords at us but nothing penetrated it. I hated to think what it cost the angel to build this protected oasis, yet for now I only had eyes for Tim.

Turel closed his eyes and laid his hands on Tim's chest. I tried not to see the torn flesh and my friend's ragged, gaping wounds. Through the dirt and blood on his face Tim's blue eyes stood out in shocking lucidity.

Turel shook his head. Something inside me broke. With a wordless cry I fell on my knees beside Tim.

"Sh'belle," Tim rasped, reaching for my hand. "It hurts."

In the vaults of my mind I heard Turel's voice, "*He's dying, Siobhan. Help him. He needs to find his way. I cannot heal him. His soul has already taken flight.*"

With those words an onslaught of images hit me: Tim laughing at me, running through the woods with Alex and me as children, and taste of his skin. I remembered seeing him on Christmas visits and stealing cookies, our first kiss, my first kiss. There he was swimming on hot summer days, bringing me daisies, making love in the morning sun. I still felt the weight of his letterman's jacket. Every page of my childhood, my early womanhood, contained a picture, a memory of Tim.

These memories took no more than a few seconds. It's funny how the mind works at life's critical points. With a shock I came back to the here and now. I glanced at Turel. My heart broke and

I knew Turel understood that heartbreak.

"Siobhan," Tim said, his voice faint.

I stared into his blue eyes. "Yes, I'm here."

"It's okay for you to be happy."

"I don't understand."

His grip on my hand grew tighter, even as his voice became softer. "It's okay for you to be happy without me."

"Oh, Tim, stop. Don't do this, they can heal you, somehow," my voice broke on the words, ending in a sob. "Don't go," I whispered.

Tim spoke to Turel. "Take her home."

Turel gave a quick nod, his face drawn in lines of fatigue, holding the golden shield over us. His dark eyes were somber. "I shall, my friend."

The tears openly spilled from my eyes now, blurring my vision as I held Tim. "Don't worry. I'm going home, too," he said. His eyes lost their light, staring past me, and his grip on my hand slackened.

"Tim."

His eyes focused on mine again. One corner of his mouth quirked in the beginning of the smile I knew so well. "And you, Siobhan, will be late, again." His smile spread across his face, and then, my oldest friend, his head in my arms, drew one final breath.

As Tim exhaled for the last time, everything stopped. An impossibly slow rhythm beat. I should recognize the sound, but my mind remained stuck, unable to process anything. I could not get past the idea that Tim lay still at the end of it all. It was the end of us; Tim was gone.

"Watcher."

I stayed where I was, staring at the blood on my shirt, on Tim's face, on my hands.

"Watcher."

I frowned. The ghost of a smile lingered on Tim's face.

"Watcher, Siobhan."

Reluctantly, I raised my head, hearing another thud as I did so. Nefta appeared in front of me. Where Nefta had come from?

What was happening? As Tim exhaled, his breath emanated in a silver mist, lit from within. All around us the air sparkled and glowed. Startled, my eyes went back to the body I held.

"Stand, Watcher," commanded Nefta.

I did as she directed, gently letting Tim's head down as I did so. Gazing around, the rest of the world had paused. Life stopped for everyone, except for the few of us with Tim as he died. Now Turel stood by my side, next to him Alex mourned, tears streaming down his face. The beautiful Angel of Truth, Amitiel, appeared from nowhere, regarding me with compassion in her violet eyes. The golden shield vanished.

The glaring sounds of battle were absent. Around us everything else froze. The combatants froze in place as they had been in mid-swing, mid-stroke. To my immense gratification, Innon's body lay split in two, the beautiful Fallen's form cast aside and forgotten.

I blinked, staring around me. "How?"

Amitiel gestured toward Tim's body. "Such is the power of 'the last breath of The Righteous'. It buys us this instant outside the flow of time and, also, the revelation about to come. This unveiling was foretold and great truths are to be revealed, so I must be present."

"Tim?" I whispered. "He's *The Righteous* from the prophecy?"

"Of course, surely you knew him as a righteous man throughout the years you've known him."

"Well, sort of." I met Alex's eyes.

"Tim wasn't righteous," my brother said, frowning, "He drank and cursed. He had sex. How can he be The Righteous?"

Turel smiled at us. "You are tougher on humanity than God is. These small matters, they do not change who Tim is."

Amitiel nodded. "A righteous person keeps faith and above all else love in his heart. This person keeps trying, remains true to his principles, and always champions the side of light. A person who is patient, kind, and without judgment. Your friend lived these things. He was not perfect, but that is not for mortal man. Perfection is for God."

Turel wrapped one arm around me, saying, "Goodness is

something humanity can aspire to, and Tim did so. To all who knew him, he was a good man, a man of faith, in short, a righteous man. More than that, he became the Righteous foretold of by the Oracle."

New tears sprang fresh in my eyes. Through my blurred vision, I saw the sparkling mist slowly drift in the air toward the waterfall as Amitiel continued speaking, "We have only this precious time before his breath fades and his heart stops beating."

Another dull thud sounded around us. Tim's fading heartbeats echoed, as his body wound down like a slowing clock. Nefta watched, listening, her whole body attuned. The Valkyrie waited there for the end. "*Chooser of the Slain will be with you at the end of it all.*" Nefta had come for Tim.

"Look," said Turel, pointing to the waterfall, frozen, like the embattled beings around us. The sparkles flitted here and there surrounding us as the faint mist of Tim's last breath wafted through the air.

"Shh," said Nefta, speaking at last. "It ends."

The dull beats of Tim's heart faded and fell silent. A ghostly silver apparition of Tim floated up, out of his own body. "Alex," I whispered, "sheath one of your swords and give me your hand."

He did and gasped as he, too, saw Tim's spirit standing there.

Nefta beckoned to the shade. "Come, it is time to go." She opened a gateway to another world. While we were becoming accustomed to these doors between dimensions, this time it was profoundly different. Tim held a hand up to us in farewell, but did not speak. Turning, he walked with Nefta and together, they disappeared into a place where we could not follow.

Amitiel smiled sadly and said to Turel, "It was all in the names, was it not, my friend?"

He frowned. "What was his given name?"

"Timothy Macauley."

Turel glanced at me and I nodded. Tears burned my eyes and choked my throat.

"Oh, I should have foreseen this," lamented Turel.

"I don't get it," Alex said.

"The name Timothy means 'one who honors God' and Macauley means 'righteous,'" explained Amitiel in her gentle voice. She pointed to the waterfall. "Onward, my friends. Soon we will lose what Timothy's sacrifice dearly bought us."

The faint, twinkling mist of Tim's last breath draped itself across the waterfall. As it faded, runes appeared in the sunlit air, etched in silver light. The light spread and grew, illuminating more details until I saw that we faced a beautiful doorway. Elegant runes, a script I could not read, covered it. The words glowed with an ethereal beauty.

"*In the Righteous' last breath it will be shown, what once was veiled shall become known.*" Alex quoted beside me in an awed voice, his face still wet with tears.

"It's time," Amitiel commanded. "The time has come for *Gracious Sight* and *Defender of Man* to enter the Veil together."

"Okay. Good luck, sis, Turel. I'll defend your way back."

I shook my head as my eyes met Turel's and my brain unraveled what Amitiel had said about names. "Turel is the *Guardian*. He isn't *The Defender of Man*, Alex."

"Who is?"

"*You* are, Alex."

Their gleam pierced me, as though she saw inside my soul. Did I know her? How? Her eyes were the exact shade as my own. When I tried concentrating on her my world spun. Doubling over, I clutched Alex's arm. It reminded me of seeing Daisy's cottage for the first time, only far worse. If the dragon's house had been a kaleidoscope, now I gazed into a maelstrom only to be blown away.

I straightened, fighting for control of my vision. As the world balanced again for me, I asked, "Where are we?" To my relief my voice remained steady.

The queen raised one elegant eyebrow. "Beyond the Veil, of course. You're in the Hollow Hills."

"The Hollow Hills?" repeated Alex. "I've never heard of it."

"I should imagine, my young Defender of Man, there is much you have never heard of." Oona walked into the darkness of the tunnel with an orb of light leading her. "Come, and do not lag behind. The Cave contains many things, but none that you would want to meet."

Alex and I exchanged glances and followed her. Tim died to bring us here. The only way lay forward, into the black.

Fear of the dark is one of humanity's great unifiers. We all have experienced that crawling sensation on the back of our neck as the hairs stand up when we know on the most basic level that something watches us. It is the unnamed fear in the corner of the room, behind the door, lurking in the shadows as we walk at night. Following Oona through the Cave became an exercise in terror—numb, blind, helpless terror. We couldn't see what lived there, but we sensed them around us, pressing in on the queen's bobbing light.

Growls and hissing, wordless threats and sliding noises, like scales over stone tormented us. Chewing, cracking sounds filled the air. The snap beneath our feet echoed like breaking bones.

At last we emerged into a forest glen. Twilight reigned in paradise. Two elaborate thrones stood side by side under slender birch trees. In front of these mighty seats, there burned a fire pit. Bright-colored flowers abounded in the clearing, perfuming the air with their fragrances. To one side, a small, joyful spring bubbled water into a clear pool. Lights like Oona's orb of all shades lit the glade. It took me a moment to realize that these lights lived. In each a tiny pixy flitted from blossom to blossom.

Beautiful young people, men and women, played musical instruments, talking and singing, some danced. Birdsong joined the symphony as the harmonies mixed and mingled. The scene exuded life, youth, and the promise of sweet immortality. The air reminded me of summer evenings long past. Those times when I walked into the night thinking anything might be possible and I would live forever.

"Finn, darling, I have brought them," said Oona. "Mortals, this is my lord, King Finvarra."

One figure came forward and the music ceased, even the birds silenced, as all eyes turned toward us. There strode a being as close to perfection as I had ever seen, even angels paled compared to his physical beauty. Where his queen wore a diaphanous gown to display her loveliness, the King wore black leather so tight it also left nothing to the imagination. As it had with Oona, my vision swam and swirled when I gazed at him, but I stared anyway. I had never met a being older or more complex.

His hair and beard shone deep black. His clear eyes resembled the sky after a storm, the most amazing shade of gray. Like his queen's King Finvarra's skin was the purest ivory. He was stunning, but a sense of danger walked with him. He wasn't human. He didn't exude angel or a demon either. I didn't know what he was. I remembered Daisy's description of the Fey, elemental beings of great power. Whatever that meant.

"So, the Watcher has come at last," he said as Oona glided to take her place at his side. "Perhaps Earth will be entertaining again."

"It better," said Oona with a petulant twist to her full lips. "The last hundred millennia have been a yawn."

"This next bit promises to be interesting," said Finvarra striding toward the pair of thrones. "Whenever you are ready to begin, my pet."

Oona examined her nails for a moment then flipped one hand in an absent motion.

I sensed no sound, no feeling of motion or traveling, but I blinked and in the millisecond flicker of my eyelid's movement the scene changed. Alex and I stood in front of a wooden, ornate rectangular table. The king and queen sat across from us. The glade, the fire pit, the beautiful dancers, and pixies disappeared. A huge chamber replaced them, lit in the center above the massive piece of furniture, but dark elsewhere. The darkness obscured the details of the room surrounding us. From the rustling and sibilant whispers in the shadows, we had an audience.

"Siobhan," said Alex, his tone amazed.

I followed his gaze to the tabletop. A map with figures on it covered the surface; set up like a general's miniatures. Each precise detail exquisitely replicated. "That's amazing," I said in a low voice. Panic built inside me. I knew this place. I had been here, a thousand times.

Wicked laughter broke out in the dark chambers around us. "You think so, my dear?" asked the king with a sardonic smile. "You like my toy?"

"It's beautiful," I said, feeling small, vulnerable. Not here. I can't be the Watcher here. "It's so intricate." More laughter ensued. The glint of many eyes shone in reflected light. Not here. This is where I fail, where I always fail.

"Indeed, well, we have time. Perhaps I should show you and your brave brother here how exact my map is. My dear?" said the king. I struggled with my terror, my personal hell.

Did we have time?

Oona swirled one finger over the map in an idle gesture. By some trick of the light the air swirled in a tiny dust devil, a miniature twister. She smiled like a little girl about to do a trick and blew a gust of air to me, her rosebud mouth puckered in a pantomime of a kiss.

Before I could respond, the air swirled around me. I had the sensation of being lifted and then of falling. My surroundings blurred in a cloud of noise and color. When my vision cleared,

I found myself in the center of a tornado, blown and buffeted. I collided with the debris the whirlwind carried with it. My head reeled and I tasted blood on my lip. An instant later the cyclone threw me clear, rolling, bouncing on the ground, aching as though every bone in my body shattered.

Weak. Small. I was nothing. Certainly not the Watcher. Recognition surged as I examined my surroundings. This was my dream. Again.

In agony I raised my head. Gazing around, I lay in what had once been a street in some suburban neighborhood. Destruction tumbled around me. People's dreams, their homes and belongings discarded. All of it reduced to the confetti of chaos.

I laid my head back on the street, my body screaming with pain. Contemplating the stormy skies above me I thought of Turel, of Tim, and wondered what had gone wrong with the prophecy. Why were we in my nightmare? As I regarded the black clouds overhead, I used my Watcher's sight. In the sky I perceived the faces of Oona, Finvarra and, last, my brother's worried features regarding me. I was in the map, or on earth. I wasn't sure which or if they were the same. "Oh, holy fuck," I moaned. "What now?"

"Come see," said Finvarra's deep voice and an instant later I returned to the place called the Hollow Hills. My hell.

I groaned and laid still.

Alex kneeled next to me. "Um, Siobhan?"

"What?"

"I think you need to stand. You're pretty banged up, and I think it's making the crowd a little..."

"A little what?" I asked.

"Hungry." Alex's features drew into deep worry lines. "I can't fight us out of here."

"Very true, Defender of Man, how astute you are." I could not see the King, but I heard his amusement.

"She's bleeding. Oh, pretty, she's bruised and bloody," Oona's voice crooned, sexual in her pleasure at my wounds. I remembered that tone. She loved it when I failed. And I always failed here.

"Get up," urged Alex. He helped me upright. I leaned on him, one arm braced against the table, my eyes transfixed by Oona's tornado on the map, which still raged, wreaking who knows how much havoc in its wake. I winced at the thought of the shattered houses.

"Fear not, Alex. I can make her stand on her own," said Finvarra. "She requires proper motivation. Take a moment, Watcher. Observe what my queen can do." He nodded to his lady who simpered and leaned over the map, waving a slender finger at the assembled figures.

"Eeny, meeny, miny, moe." With a delighted giggle Oona plucked a figurine off the map. In a graceful motion she tossed it several feet away from the table. As it flew, the little statue grew in size, becoming a middle aged man as his feet hit the ground. His brown eyes widened and one pale hand rubbed his balding head in a nervous gesture as he gazed around the room in confusion.

I blinked, tearing my eyes from the map in disbelief. My head rang and I struggled to focus. "Why are you doing this?" I whispered. "Why?"

Finvarra leaned back in his throne, his eyes on me. "Alex, be a good man and release your sister." A ring of steel to his words made it clear this was not a request.

Alex stepped back from me.

"Stand, Siobhan," the King commanded.

I sagged against the table and started to fall to the floor. That's always how the dream went.

"Tsk, tsk, Watcher. I expected better." Finvarra snapped his fingers, gray eyes gone cold. Quicker than thought, a black shape sprang from the shadows at the man, then another, and still another. "You're better than this."

The man's tortured screams were brief and soon eclipsed by the sounds of tearing flesh and cracking bones. Sounds I couldn't block out made my stomach cramp. As I collapsed on my hands and knees I saw between the thick wooden legs of the table mangled pieces of what had once been a person being dragged into the dark. Blood pooled on the parquet floor.

"Another, I think, pet?" asked Finvarra, his tone sounded charming and indulgent.

"Yes, please," said Oona with relish. "I pick… this one."

At those words, I reached for the edge of the table, hoisting myself up. I shut the pain out and got a foot under me.

"Hurry, Siobhan," said Alex, his voice strained. "Hurry."

"Too slow, Watcher. Too slow by half," mocked the Queen.

This time a woman screamed. Standing, I clung to the smooth edge of the map. I saw fresh blood rivulets coursing the floor. I glimpsed blond hair, a pink shirt, and blood, everywhere there ran blood. Somewhere behind me came more chewing and swallowing sounds.

My stomach lurched, tears started in my eyes, and I clamped down on my body's visceral reaction to the casual cruelty. "What is this? Who the hell are you people?" Alex cried. I shook my head in disbelief. Nothing in the prophecy warned us of this, but I should have known. She hated me. She had always hated me.

"Why do you hate me?" I asked, voicing my thoughts, the question I'd always wondered in my nightmare.

"Well, my pet?" asked the King. "Will you tell her?"

"Stupid, spoiled brat." She sniffed. "Let her wonder."

He shook one finger at her. "Now, now. Bad form. I shall explain to her." He crossed his legs. "Siobhan, what strikes you most about my stunning bride?"

"Her eyes," I said. "They're like mine."

"Indeed, they are exactly like yours," he agreed. "Where do you think your wonderful Watcher's sight comes from, young one?"

I shrugged. Beside me, Alex stood perfectly still, his gaze darting about the darkened room. "I don't know."

"There is a finite amount of magic in this universe," the King continued. "When a gift is bestowed upon one, it is taken from another. The Watcher's sight is borrowed from my lovely Queen."

"She isn't worthy," snarled Oona.

"Will she ever get it back?" I asked.

The two immortals laughed. Oona's laugh held a particularly

nasty ring. "Certainly, I shall," she said. "Just as soon as you die. Which should be any time now."

"But," I said, "this isn't fair. I didn't take your power. I never wanted it." Time. The word resonated in my thoughts. It was important. Why? Fear slowed my brain.

She shrugged. "I care not for fair. It's mine, and I want it back."

I struggled with the perverse injustice of it. A power I never sought and now I would die for it? And all of humanity with me? Dull anger stirred inside of me.

"But the prophecy?" I said. "Why isn't the prophecy working?"

The King and Queen did not answer right away. After a moment Finvarra chuckled once more, and Oona joined him, her laughter like bells, musical and youthful. Around us the laughter from the darkness joined theirs. My blood pressure increased, and my head pounded with the pulse of my anger and pain.

I took an involuntary step back from the table, swaying, staring at her in horror. "I, I don't understand," I said, my voice quavering with emotion as my rage built. "We found the Veil, our friend died to open it. We're here, just as the prophecy said we would be. What, what…"

"What fresh hell is this?" finished Finvarra, raising one dark eyebrow at me, his expression intent. "Please, Siobhan. Come now, did you think it would be so easy? Cross the Veil, fulfill the hero's quest, and have the answer handed to you?"

"It wasn't easy!" I yelled. "You sick son of bitch!" I screamed. "You killed them! You'll kill us all!"

"Me?" Finvarra sculpted face wore an expression of innocence. "We did see blood spilled today. However, I did not draw a drop of it. As for mankind, I will not harm them. Not I."

Through the sounds of the hidden audience and Oona's laughter a memory hit me of Missy's high tortured voice saying in evil tones, "She'll open the door." Perhaps that hadn't been a taunt by the Sonneillon at me, maybe it had been a warning for the other side. Maybe the prophecy unfolding this way meant I hadn't fulfilled all its conditions yet.

"King Finvarra, I demand to see the doorway." I straightened.

This wasn't a dream. It was real. It could be different this time.

All went silent except for the sound of Alex's breathing next to me. He was on alert, eyes wide.

The King held up one finger at me, as though making note of something. He shrugged then using one hand, Finvarra reached through the dimensions and plucked an ancient hour glass from somewhere unseen. It floated in the air next to him. Grains already slipped through the glass. I gasped. The sands of time and they drained.

"When you crossed through the Veil you were granted safe passage in my kingdom for as long as the sands still run," said Finvarra.

"But, the sands are more than half gone," said Alex.

"Alas, that is not my problem," the King replied. "Perhaps your sister should not have gotten distracted by side issues."

"I'll kill you." As I said the words I meant them, thinking of the wasted time, the tornado's destruction, and those killed.

Oona's perfect features contorted in rapt concentration. "Do it, do it, do it," she murmured to me. "Feed your anger, and die for my amusement. I love your failure. The stench of agony is so sweet. Do it. Do it."

Her words goaded me. My blood responded to the rhythm of her call. I wanted to sink my teeth into Finvarra's flesh, to drive my nails into his face, to punish him. I needed to rend, to destroy. Without meaning to, I drifted closer to the table. I pushed away Alex's restraining hands, approaching the King. I found my strength again, pushing aside my pain and fear.

"Siobhan, focus, they are doing this to you on purpose," said Alex in an urgent voice, reaching out again to stop me. "Siobhan."

Taunts in languages I did not speak filled the room, from tongues that were not human, hurled at me through the darkness, but I remembered the sounds. I'd heard the same at the battle for the Veil. An audience of demons gathered around Alex and me.

"Siobhan, the sands, remember the sands." Alex pointed to the crystal. It might have been my imagination, but it seemed as though the sands fell faster now, like in my dream.

I drew a deep breath, clearing anger's fog from my mind, and said again, "King Finvarra, I demand to see the doorway."

The room became quiet again and the King held up two fingers at me. "Take a moment to think of the Veil as the treasure," said Finvarra. "What treasure of legend did not have a terrifying dragon guarding it? Of course, for you, a dragon is hardly appropriate given your associations with that race."

Spitting and cursing, fearsome noises came from inhuman throats. I glanced at Alex. He blanched, but remained steady, ready to spring into action. The sands continued to fall, gaining speed. My heartbeat increased, keeping pace with the grains.

"So, we are your dragon," Finvarra continued, his features strangely gentle. "You need to get through us to make your Choice."

"We're almost out of time," I said, trying to keep the fear from my voice. "Let's get on with this."

"You've made her stronger, Oberon," said a voice, eldritch yet familiar. A shadow passed over us, briefly blocking the light. I glimpsed great wings. "Our agreement may be null and void."

"Stay out of this, Morning Star," said Finvarra in a snarl. "I am not subject to that name in this cycle. You were given leave to watch, not to interfere."

"I? Given leave?"

"My kingdom, my rules," said Finvarra. "I walked here before Time. Oona and I shall be here at the end of all things. Do not attempt to dictate to me."

"I am merely reminding you of the terms stated in our agreement."

"You and your contracts," muttered Finvarra, looking more human in his exasperation.

"Rule of three," said the unseen voice from the shadows.

The sound tugged at my senses. Why did I know it? My thoughts ran together in fearful agony, what would happen to us when the sands no longer fell? Through the tumult in my head the memory of my nightmare crystallized as if a spell broke. I still wasted time. I said for the third time, "King Finvarra, I demand to see the doorway."

"Siobhan, we're running out of time," said Alex even as I spoke. "We need to get the heck out of Dodge."

"Shhh, dear Alex," said Finvarra, holding up three fingers. "Your sister has made an interesting request. One I am bound to grant."

"About damn time," Alex muttered, glancing at the glass.

"Rule of three," said Oona inclining her head to me, green eyes narrowed as she eyed me.

The King walked around the map table and offered me his arm. "If you will allow me?"

With another peek at the emptying glass, I took his arm. At a wave of his free hand one end of the chamber opened into a great hall. Alex, Finvarra, and I stood in a hall with doors on either side. The passageway stretched as far as I could see with countless thresholds.

"Make your choice, Watcher." The gray-eyed king's hand gestured forward.

Alex groaned. "How can this be a dead end?" he asked.

"Alex, it's not a dead end."

"What are you talking about?"

"Can't you see the doors?"

"No, must be a Watcher deal."

I left Finvarra and held out my hand to help Alex see. He grasped it for a second, frowning. "Still nothing."

"What?"

"I got nothing. It's a hallway with a solid wall at the end of it."

"That's impossible. I'm staring at countless doors. Each one has an oval window in it."

"I think you're up, Siobhan. You'd better hurry."

I nodded. This must be what I was supposed to do, and I wouldn't be getting any help from anyone else. My stomach twisted at the number of doors and the falling sand. Each grain was precious to me now. "So little time," I said.

My words sparked the laughter and jeering again, evil sounds. I started forward, trying to concentrate, to focus in spite of the horror filling my ears. The sight of the sand slipping away filled my mind, driving me to panic.

"I will not be ignored, nor our bargain forgotten," said the voice as I entered the hall. A shadow passed through the light once more and I shuddered.

"Yes, fair enough, you shall have your third." Glancing back, I saw Finvarra regarding the board. He flicked a glance toward Alex and called to me, "This one I think."

A third figure flew through into the air, gathering size and flesh as it traveled. An instant later, we both gasped; Alex in anguish and me in shock. Nefta stood by the table, her sword unsheathed as the first dark shape sprang at her.

"Nefta." Alex sprang forward.

"Don't interfere, Defender of Man," said the king, "Or I'll release them all."

Alex drew back, his face twisted in pain, but the encounter went differently this time. This was no hapless human, but an armed Valkyrie at her full strength. As the hungry demons leapt, Nefta parried with neat, professional movements.

At first I could not understand why Finvarra conjured Nefta, but as the number of attackers grew and I saw my brother's face while Nefta fought on, weighed down, outnumbered, bleeding, and sinking beneath the weight of black grotesque shapes I understood. If Nefta died, it would destroy Alex and distract me. I needed to be here to make a choice. Alex had to be here to ensure I completed my task. I realized something even more important. I wasted time still.

Wrenching my eyes from the horrific scene unfolding, I ran through the hallway, peering through the windows of each door. I whimpered under my breath, soft sounds of fear and urgency. So many doors and time running out. How would I ever find the right one? How would I know which to choose?

The voice that had urged Finvarra to select another victim spoke again, "Much better, she's lost. You are lost, Watcher, lost and out of time." It gave a mighty shout of exultation. "And when you fail to Choose, chaos reigns, and with it, I triumph. Your world is mine."

I kept running, searching for some clue, some sign in the oval windows. Did I see futures or possibilities? Each view assaulted me with images of our world. Some displayed disasters, war, and famine. Others contained sunshine, prosperity, and joy. There was no way to see how to choose which track was the right one.

The demons' taunts, Oona's laughter, and Nefta's curses filled my head, driving away rational thought. Worse, the unseen voice continued to exult. Glancing back, I glimpsed Nefta, now slowly losing the fight. Faster, I needed to be faster. Tears sprang to the corners of my eyes. I would fail. We would die and my failure doomed the world. My strides faltered.

"Come on, Siobhan, you can do this," my brother called, his voice breaking. "You've always seen. You've always known. This is why. This moment is why you are the Watcher."

His words became a lifeline for me, and I blinked the tears away. I had to listen to him, trust that Nefta would prevail, and believe in her and myself. My slowing steps sped again as I raced the endless hallway. I came to a door whose window swirled with a thick mist. Here and there I caught glimpses in the mist, but I could not see any clear images. A wild excitement ran through me, as though I was poised at a cliff, about to jump, hoping I could fly.

"This is it," I said, out of breath. In agonizing slow motion, the last grain fell in the hour glass even as I drew a huge breath and yelled, my hand on the door handle, "This is it."

"This is your choice?" King Finvarra appeared in the hall next to me with Alex at his side. The king's gray eyes were solemn instead of cruel.

I nodded and quoted, "*The path that is true you can't see anymore.*"

"Open the door, Watcher, if you dare." Finvarra stood aside.

At his words the chamber, the map, the thrones, Oona and Nefta vanished. As I twisted the handle an enraged voice screamed and great wings flapped.

Alex and I walked through the door. As we passed the King he called, "Siobhan." I turned back as he spoke, "It is a world of free will. You have chosen wisely, Watcher." The King bowed to me, his courteous motion a graceful echo from an age long gone. "*Au revoir.* I shall see you again."

"See me again?" I echoed, but the door closed. A chime sounded, then many bells rang again from far away. We remerged on the coast, near what remained of the Devil's Punch Bowl. Twilight glowed. No sign of the battle we waged remained. As our feet hit the earth, Turel materialized. He scooped me up in a fierce embrace. "Siobhan, Alex, thank God."

Alex frowned. "Where is everyone? Where's the battle?"

Turel released me. "It ended three days ago. I've been patrolling the area between here and the waterfall, hoping you'd be back."

"Three days?"

"That can't be right," I said. "It only seemed like an hour or so."

Turel nodded. "That is one of the dangers of the land you visited. They call it Underhill. Time runs different there for the Faery Court."

"The Faery Court?" Alex repeated. "That's who Finvarra and Oona were?"

"You and Siobhan may know them better as Oberon and Titania."

"Wait, you knew about them? Why didn't you warn us?" Alex asked.

Turel frowned. "We did."

I patted Alex on the shoulder. "You weren't exactly yourself that morning. After the Hags, remember?"

"Oh, right. That." My brother flushed.

"I need to alert the others," said Turel.

Alex and I exchanged weary looks as Turel bent on one knee and brought his fist to his forehead, bending his head downward. Once again a pulse of light sped outward away from him, a visible sonar wave calling other angels. In an instant, they began arriving. Nefta came first, leading Daisy in her human form by the hand, then Amitiel the lavender-winged Angel of Truth and finally others of the Observers.

I wallowed in a wonderful moment of celebration as Nefta

and Alex embraced. "I shall rip apart those faeries," said Nefta.

"Later, doll," said my brother, kissing her passionately.

Daisy hugged me. Soon Turel's arms wrapped me close again. Everyone seemed to be hugging and talking at once in a relieved babble. Thinking of Tim, I wished more than anything he could be here celebrating, too. I never did get to talk to him about the Wookies.

One by one each happy reunion fell silent. Only Alex still spoke. His hand gestures were exaggerated and his voice boomed as he reenacted our experiences Underhill. At last became apparent even to him that his words echoed unnaturally in the silence. Alex stopped. "What? What's going on?"

I couldn't speak. Instead, I pointed.

The sky teemed in vibrant rainbow hues: golds, silvers, indigos, every shade of blue and green, sparkling pinks, oranges, and reds cavorting above the waves. The setting sun flashed off thousands of jeweled hides, blinding us with their beauty. Sparkling wings and tails filled the air as far as the eye could see.

Daisy ran at the cliff and leapt off the edge. Her wordless cry of yearning and delight morphed into a fierce dragon scream of elation as she reclaimed her true form. Calls answered her, some low and deep, others high and bell-like rebounded back on us, carried over the waves in a mighty roar. The green dragon flew to a joyful reunion of her own.

Sounds that were completely out of place filled our ears. Bells sounded, hawks shrieked, brooks babbled, flames crackled, lions roared, larks warbled, steam hissed, bubbles percolated as Mother Earth welcomed her first children back to her sheltering sphere.

The dragons had come home at last.

Afterword

I stood where it started, under the apricot tree in the garden behind my house. No little, green dragon statue lay beneath the tree. Chernobog destroyed it. Daisy didn't live here anymore, though I would see her again. I hoped often. Other things changed, too. We buried Tim a week after the Veil in the St. Helena cemetery. Thanks to some adept dragon glamouring and a few magical assists, everyone believed his horrific injuries to be sustained in a car crash. We marked his passing with an intimate, heartfelt funeral. It still hurt to even think his name.

I owned a dog now. Leia lived with me. I did offer her to Tim's father, Thad, but the old man shook his white head in sadness. "She's yours. She stays with you. It would make Tim happy, knowing his two favorite girls are taking care of one another."

With Turel and Alex's help, we finished the remodel, though without the happy bickering and joking of its first days. Without anything being said in our little group, an unspoken agreement developed to get it done and move on. The four of us spent most days together these past weeks: Nefta, Alex, me, and Turel, but not for much longer.

Nefta and Alex were leaving. Apparently, the role of the Defender of Man did not end at the Veil. Nefta and Alex needed to hit the road. As I understood things, they would be defending the defenseless, righting wrongs, and helping with the war effort. My once-goofy brother had changed forever. A superhero stood in his place.

My choice at the Veil did not end the War between the dragons and Lucifer's Fallen. It only changed the terms, and to some extent it changed the players. As Turel and Daisy explained it, when I chose a future of free will, I eliminated many of the demons. Demons were not creatures of free will, differing from humans, dragons, and even the Fallen. By taking the path of free will, I exiled the demons. Only the lords could participate. Chernobog was dead; the other lords had not revealed themselves. Without the demons, the war would be on a different scale. Daisy flew with the dragons even now, planning the next stage. I prayed the world and humanity would not be destroyed in the process.

Footsteps crunched on the gravel. I turned to see Turel coming toward me. I felt unsure and confused by him in these weeks since the battle for The Veil. A silence between us had grown out of Tim's death, cutting me off from him. Now that the prophecy had come to pass, I still did not know where his heart lay. He stayed with me here in my grandparents' house and shared my bed, but our lovemaking held a bittersweet edge. I feared each time might be our last, yet, I also feared to ask him his plans. Pythia's words haunted me: "Know what you've loved, you will not keep." Had she meant Tim? Turel? Both of them?

Somehow, I thought triumphing at the Veil would leave me happier, but Nefta and Alex were leaving, Tim had died, and Daisy no longer abided in my garden. What of my dark angel? Looking into Turel's somber eyes now, I knew the moment I dreaded above all others had arrived.

"I thought I would find you here," he said.

"Yes, me and my memories."

"Of Daisy? Or Tim?" The expression in his eyes mystified me.

I shrugged, not knowing how to put my sadness or my fears into words.

He hesitated and held out his hand. "We should talk."

I clasped his hand as he led me up the path to my back deck and the table we sat around when this began. Images of raspberries, Alex saying, 'Prove it,' glasses of red wine, and Tim's brilliant smile hung in the air around Turel and me as we each took a chair.

"I want you to know what this time here with you has meant to me," he began. My heart froze. A sick pit roiled in my stomach as I bowed my head. Tears rolled silently down my face. He was leaving. All other thought and feeling meant nothing in the shadow of that reality. I'll never know what he said next, because I stopped listening. I couldn't hear another word.

Turel's hands over my trembling ones roused me. Through blurred eyes I watched first one, then a second tear splash on to his olive skin.

"Siobhan?" He leaned closer.

"You're leaving."

"I think it's for the best." He wiped my tears away and placed one hand under my chin, forcing me to look at him.

The pain cut me.

"The prophecy is played out. You don't have to be a pawn of fate, Siobhan. You are free to make your own choices. Remember, free will? You could love another human, have a family. You could build a life for yourself."

"What about Alex? Nefta is staying with him," I said, desperate to stop this.

"Alex chose to continue down the path destiny put before him. As the Defender of Man, he is worthy of this role and of Nefta. It will not be an easy life, and he will likely die younger than he should, but such is the risk when one loves a battle angel."

"What of me? I'm still the Watcher. I can't stop what I see, who I am. Aren't I worthy of you?"

He looked stunned. "Of course, you are. I want to spare you the pain of a life of danger like Nefta and Alex will have. I want to give you a chance at the life you want. I will be called away sooner or later. If I leave now, there will be no reason for supernatural visitors. You'll be out of this War."

"Will I? I made the Choice that cost the Fallen their greatest allies. Will they let that go?" I pointed out. "What about Oona? You think she's going to leave me in peace?"

He frowned. "You are right. You'll need protection."

"I don't want protection. I want to be with you, to go with you."

"You…you want to go with me?" Turel's expression shifted

to incredulous. "You and Tim, you talked of going home many times. I thought this was what you wanted, your grandparents' house and your life back. I may not always be able to stay. I have duties and obligations that will not allow it. You deserve to be happy. How can I ask you to leave everything you love for a dangerous existence with a disgraced angel?"

My tears stopped, a sliver of hope blossoming in my heart. He glanced away from me, his face etched in new lines of pain. "You have been so sad since Tim's death, and… I promised him I'd bring you home." His voice trailed off.

I stared at him. "Turel, Tim wanted this, coming home to Calistoga. For years, Alex dreamed of the café, until he met Nefta." I gestured to the house behind us. "I have beautiful memories of this place and I love it, but I've never really known where I belonged."

"You haven't?"

"No." My heart pounded so hard, I wondered if he heard it. In my head I replayed my conversation with Alex weeks earlier.

"What are you thinking, Siobhan?"

"I remembered something Alex said to me before the Veil. He said, 'Home is where the heart is.' And I said…"

"Yes?"

"I said, 'Maybe the trick is figuring out what the heart wants.' "

Turel and I stared into one another's eyes for a moment. I remembered the only other line of Pythia's prophecy I had yet to explain. "*If everyone is gone, beg him stay, for love survives only if you dare.*"

A familiarity fell over this tableau. Turel watched me. His entire body tensed. Only this time, I didn't need to ask myself what I wanted. Once my sense of déjà vu crystallized, I acted.

I placed my hands on either side of his face, feeling his beard and smooth skin under my fingers. "My heart, all of me wants you, just you. Not only for now, forever. Wherever you are, that's home to me, and any place you are not *will* never be my home. You want me to use free will? Then, I *choose* you. I love *you*, Turel."

At last I dared to tell him what had been in my heart for weeks. The relief of speaking these emotions out loud overwhelmed me. As soon as the words left my mouth, the angel rose silently, drawing me up with him and brought his lips to mine. He kissed me fiercely enough to bruise my lips. It didn't matter. I kissed him back just as hard. Turel said hoarsely, "And, I love you. Dear God, Siobhan, how I love you."

For a moment there no words mattered. At last he lifted his lips from mine and his dark eyes shone. "My place is at your side."

"And mine is at yours, wherever that may be."

Hand-in-hand we went into the house. It finally felt like home.

About Erika Gardner

Erika is a sixth generation San Franciscan of Irish descent. She attended the University of California at Davis and completed degrees in Medieval History and Biological Sciences. A lifelong lover of books and a scribbler of many tales from a young age (her first story was completed at age five) she turned to writing full-time in 2011.

Erika resides in Northern California with her incredibly hot husband, their three amazing kids, and their chocolate Labrador named Selkie. To reach Erika regarding her books, wine recommendations, or to debate which Iron Maiden album is the best (clearly, it's Brave New World), you can find her online at www.erikagardner.com.

Find Erika Online

Website
www.erikagardner.com

Facebook
www.facebook.com/pages/Erika-Gardner-Writer-and-
Storyteller/423796817705288

Twitter
twitter.com/Erika_Gardner

Blog
www.bbbgals.wordpress.com

Tirgearr Publishing
www.tirgearrpublishing.com/authors/Gardner_Erika

Made in the USA
Charleston, SC
22 November 2016